UNDONE

The Woodstone Falls Series
Book 2

ANNA JERR

Copyright © 2025 by Anna Jerr

All rights reserved.

No part of this book may be reproduced in any form or by any electronic or mechanical means, including information storage and retrieval systems, without written permission from the author, except for the use of brief quotations in a book review.

Cover Design by Books and Moods

Developmental and Copy/Line Editing by Maddi at EJL Editing

Sensitivity Reading by Kiarah Shannon

For those who were dealt a losing hand full of heartbreak and betrayal, yet still found the courage to reshuffle and choose to love again.

This one's for you.

Author's Note

When I set out to write the Woodstone Falls series, my goal was always to create a world that felt inclusive and real—a place where people of different races, neurodiversity's, and sexual orientations exist naturally, just as they do in real life.

From the very beginning, before *Unbearable* had a single word written, I knew Noah was biracial. Her identity wasn't an afterthought; it was an essential part of who she is. As a white woman, I understand the responsibility of portraying her character with care and authenticity. I never want to contribute to a narrative where only white characters take center stage, but I also recognize that writing outside of my lived experience requires thoughtfulness, research, and guidance.

This book wouldn't be what it is without my sensitivity reader, Kiarah, who helped me navigate the nuances of Noah's experiences as a biracial woman, both black and white. Her insight was invaluable, and I am deeply grateful for her time, patience, and honesty throughout this process.

Noah is such an amazing character. She is strong,

endlessly resilient, and faces the heavy challenges in her life with grace—because that's just who she is.

While I can never understand what it's like to live Noah's experience, my hope is that this story offers a glimpse into her world with authenticity and heart. Writing diverse characters is not just about telling their stories; it's about honoring their truth. I am grateful for the opportunity to share Noah's journey with you, and I hope she resonates with readers in the same way she's touched me.

Thank you for reading, and for joining me on this journey.

Content Warnings

While this story is a work of fiction, it addresses some heavy subject matters that you should be aware of before diving in. Some material in this novel may not be suitable for all.

You can find a list of trigger warnings after the acknowledgements section. These are not meant to be spoilers, but rather a precaution in case you find certain content upsetting.

Please skip this page if you do not wish to see these warnings.

ONE

Dorian - September

TAKE ME HOME, COUNTRY ROADS - LANA DEL REY

LIFE IN WOODSTONE FALLS WAS IN ITS FULL SWING, A BLUR OF activity; taking care of Gracie, family dinners, running the clinic and caring for all kinds of animals.

Cows, sheep, dogs, cats—I'd even treated a damn chinchilla recently.

And today was no different. My calloused hands gripped the leather steering wheel as the truck rumbled over the familiar back roads. The tires hummed against the asphalt as I steered toward the farm right outside of town.

One of the mares was having trouble with her leg, and the owners called in a panic, knowing I'd be going to Seattle in the morning for a veterinary networking conference. I made sure to let all my clients know, posted it on the clinic door a month ago, and gave everyone the contact information for the closest emergency vet.

But Mary Whitmore called me earlier, asking if there was any way I could run out before leaving town, and I agreed. I'd been out to their place more times than I could count, usually for routine checkups.

Being the only vet in town meant that life never slowed down as much as I might have wanted, but the busyness of it all kept me grounded.

Despite the demands of my job, I always made time for Gracie and my family. It was something my dad instilled in me from an early age, and that lesson stuck with me as I became a father. It's why I couldn't imagine leaving Woodstone Falls, even for a better-paying job in the city. As much as I'd been tempted, the pull of family and familiarity always won out.

Gracie was surrounded by her barrage of uncles, her aunt, my dad, and others who weren't related by blood but were just as willing to step up for her as needed.

I forced my grip to loosen as I pulled up to the farm, dust kicking up behind my tires. As soon as I stepped out of the truck, Ed and Mary Whitmore rushed toward me, their faces lined with worry.

"Dr. James, she's limping pretty badly." His shoulders tensed as he cleared his throat. "We don't know what happened. She was fine yesterday, but this morning…"

His words faltered as he looked to me for reassurance. I nodded once, keeping calm for their sake. Ed and Mary weren't just any clients—they owned The Pine Ridge Lodge, one of the oldest and most beloved spots in Woodstone Falls.

Growing up, it was where my family celebrated everything from birthdays to graduations. The crackling fireplace, hearty meals, and stories shared over dinner made the place feel like home, and the Whitmores were always at the center of that.

"Show me," I said.

They led me toward the pasture, walking into the open field. The grass was thick, gently swaying with the breeze. A few chickens clucked nearby, scratching at the dirt by the coop, while a dog lay sprawled lazily by the barn, its coat a stark white against the deep green of the grass.

Up ahead, the mare stood by the fence, her chestnut coat gleaming. She lifted her head as I approached, ears flicking toward me with a soft snort, but she kept her weight off her back left leg, the limp subtle but there. I moved closer and watched her eyes carefully.

Mary wrung her hands nervously. "Do you think it's serious?"

I crouched down to examine the leg, running my hands along the tendons, trying to get an idea of what I was working with.

"Could be a sprain. Might be more. Need to take a closer look." I kept my tone even, not feeding into their panic, but not offering false comfort either.

Ed exhaled sharply. "We'll do whatever it takes. She's our best mare."

I glanced up at them. "We'll get her sorted." I straightened up and gave the mare a gentle pat.

"Let's get her back to the barn. I'll check her out." Without another word, I motioned for them to lead the horse inside.

They nodded, moving swiftly, as I grabbed my kit from the truck. The whole time, I stayed focused on the task at hand, keeping my words short.

I wasn't known as the small talk kind of guy around town. I was to the point. I wanted to get in, do the job, and get out, everyone the happier.

I followed Ed and Mary into the barn, the familiar scent of hay and horses filling the air. The mare's limp was more pronounced on the hard-packed dirt of the barn floor. I didn't say anything as I watched her, already running through the possibilities in my head.

Once we tied her up, I crouched down again, carefully

lifting her leg. She shifted, and I kept a firm grip, murmuring under my breath to keep her calm.

"Easy," I said.

Mary stood off to the side, frantically lacing her fingers as Ed hovered behind me.

My focus was on the mare. As I examined the leg closely, I checked for swelling along the tendons and joints. It wasn't great, but I'd seen much worse.

"Looks like a sprain," I said, keeping my tone neutral, letting the words land with little emphasis. "Nothing too serious, but she's going to need rest. No riding for a while. I'll wrap it and give you something for the inflammation. It's straightforward—no need for an X-ray."

Mary sighed in relief, and Ed nodded, his tension easing. "We can manage that. How long until she's back to normal?"

"Depends on how she heals," I replied, reaching over to grab a roll of bandages. "A couple weeks at least, maybe more. I'll stop by when I'm back next week to check her progress."

Ed opened his mouth, ready to ask more, but he closed it again and nodded instead. "We appreciate it. I know you'd probably rather be with Gracie before you leave town, so… thank you."

I glanced to him, giving him a curt nod.

I wrapped the mare's leg with firm, steady hands, careful not to meet their gazes for too long. The less talking, the better. They didn't need me to soothe them with words —they needed action.

Results.

That's what I was good at.

Once the wrap was secure, I took a step back, my fingers tracing the edges of the bandage to make sure it held. I wiped my hands on my worn jeans, the grit of dirt rough against my palms. My gaze flicked to the mare one last time as she shifted cautiously on her injured leg.

"She'll be fine as long as you follow the plan. Call me if anything changes."

Ed gave me a grateful nod, glancing over at his wife. "We will."

I grabbed my supplies and turned to leave, giving the mare one last pat on the neck. "I'll see myself out."

Mary called out as I walked toward the barn door, "Thank you. Really."

I lifted a hand in acknowledgment but didn't look back. There was no need for more conversation.

The heavy door creaked as I pushed it open, stepping out into the fading late afternoon light. As I made my way back to the truck, the exhaustion of the day settled in. I tossed my kit onto the passenger seat and climbed into the driver's side.

I turned the key in the ignition and pulled away, the ranch fading behind me as the sun cast long shadows across the fields. My mind wandered back to Gracie as the road stretched out in front of me. No matter how long the day was, how many calls I made, it always circled back to her.

I always couldn't wait to get home.

My mood lifted the moment I turned down the driveway and saw her little pink bike propped against the porch steps.

I parked in the driveway and killed the engine.

Stepping inside, I found Gracie in the corner, hunched over a coloring book, her tongue poking out in concentration. Markers were scattered in all directions, her strokes fast and messy, completely absorbed in her world.

My dad sat with his reading glasses resting low on his nose, and his ever-present mustache twitching. Gracie glanced up first, her eyes lighting up the second she saw me.

"Daddy!" she squealed, jumping to her feet and running toward me.

I barely had time to drop my kit before she barreled into me, wrapping her small arms around my waist. The force of it almost knocked me off balance as my hands came down to ruffle her hair. The wild, wavy strands tangled in my fingers.

She always reminded me of the photos of my mom when she was young—the same golden waves, bright and untamed. My own dark hair was a stark contrast to theirs, as if they belonged to a world filled with light that I couldn't quite touch.

"Hey, G," I murmured.

I set her down and crouched to her level. Her face was smudged with marker, a few freckles dotted across her nose.

"Were you good for Papa?"

She nodded enthusiastically. "Yep! We had pizza, and Grandpa let me have *two* sodas!" She held up two fingers, her grin showing the gap where her front teeth were missing.

My dad shrugged from his chair, a half smirk on his face. "Don't look at me. She talked me into it."

"You know she's six, right?" I muttered, shaking my head, though I couldn't help but smile. "Last I checked, I left you in charge."

"She can be convincing. She's got your mother in her like that," he chuckled.

It had been two decades since my mother passed—long

enough for the details to blur. I was just a boy, and as time went on, my memories splintered into fragments. I couldn't piece together a single moment clearly, but damn, I never forgot how much she loved us. I shot my dad a quick smile, noticing the same wave of nostalgia washing over his face.

"Two sodas, huh? You're not gonna sleep for a week," I said, nudging her gently in the ribs.

Gracie giggled again, and I couldn't help but pull her into a hug, breathing in the scent of bubblegum shampoo and scented markers.

There was something about being home with her that made everything seem right in the world.

"I made you something!" She wriggled free from my grip and rushed back to the pile of papers on the floor.

"See, look! It's a horse, like the ones you fix!" She held up a drawing, the horse's legs a tad short and its mane a rainbow of colors. It wasn't exactly anatomically correct, but it was very impressive for a six-year-old.

"It's perfect," I said. "You're getting good at this." Her smile grew.

"Can we put it on the fridge?"

"Of course. Where else would it go?" I stood, taking the drawing and heading to the kitchen, where I stuck it to the fridge with a magnet shaped like a cow.

I turned back right in time to see her racing to grab another stack of markers.

"Daddy, can we do one together? I'll draw the horse, and you can draw the barn!"

I glanced at the clock. It was getting late, and she was wired from all the sugar, but I found myself nodding anyway.

"Alright. One picture, then you're off to bed."

Gracie cheered, scrambling to get everything set up.

My dad pushed himself up from the chair and crossed the room. "She's got you wrapped around her finger."

"Yeah." I glanced at her with a smile, shrugging without even bothering to hide it.

I'm pretty sure the day Gracie was born, my heart grew three sizes. As much as I tried to keep my life compartmentalized, to hold back parts of myself from the rest of the world, with her, I was completely open. Not many people could do that, but there were a few who managed to sneak in and leave their mark.

"Definitely wrapped around her finger." My dad chuckled. "I'm heading out. I'll see you both later."

"Thanks, Dad," I said. "Appreciate your help."

Gracie scrambled to her feet and ran over to him. "Night, Papa!" she called, throwing her arms around him in a tight hug before scampering off.

He gave me a nod and slipped out the door. I sat down on the floor next to her, legs crossed and picked up a marker.

As we drew, she chatted away about her day—her friends, some new game she'd learned.

I listened, mostly content to hear her little voice fill the house. I wanted to imprint it to my memory and lock it away before she became sick of me in a few years.

She might have been growing up too fast, but those little moments slowed everything down and gave me something solid to hold on to.

Eventually, her marker strokes grew lazier. Her eyelids drooped as she let out a big yawn, even though she tried to fight it.

"Daddy, do you think... do you think I'll be as good at drawing as you are at fixing animals one day?"

I smiled, leaning over to tuck a loose curl behind her ear. "You'll be even better."

She nodded sleepily, leaning against me. "Okay," she whispered.

I scooped her up in one smooth motion, cradling her against me as she tucked her head into my neck. She was out in seconds, her little arms draped around my shoulders.

Carrying her up to bed, a familiar pang tugged at my chest. After tucking her in and brushing a kiss on her forehead, I stood in the doorway for a minute, watching her sleep. My heart squeezed with the deep, protective instinct that always rose when I was with her.

Heading downstairs, I picked up the scattered markers and papers, pausing for a moment as I glanced at the drawing she made of the horse. I smiled to myself, then turned off the lights and settled into the quiet.

By the time I set off for Seattle, the sky was a dull, gloomy gray, though the rain held off. I'd decided to drive this time instead of flying. Flying would've been quicker, sure, but driving gave me more freedom—an easy way to make my own schedule. And, with the insane hotel prices in Seattle, especially with all the conferences and events going on, Dotty's offer to crash at her apartment made sense.

At first, I didn't think much of it when I accepted, but then Dotty casually mentioned her roommate, and I realized I hadn't even considered that detail.

A weekend with a stranger in the same space wasn't exactly ideal, but it wasn't the end of the world either.

I'd heard bits about Noah over the years. Dotty always spoke highly of her—how easy she was to be around, and how she threw herself into teaching.

So, one weekend with a stranger who, from what I'd

heard, seemed like a decent enough person would be fine. Besides, I was here for a reason—work, business, nothing more. I could handle the small discomfort of shared space.

I'd keep my head down, do what I came to do, and get out without causing any waves.

It'd be fine.

TWO

Noah - September

EXILE (FEAT. BON IVERS) - TAYLOR SWIFT

It was official. My life was a mess.

After a week of broken-down buses and too many takeout dinners, my life without Dotty was a slow unraveling of chaos. Not to mention how oddly distant—and frankly, off—my boyfriend, John, was lately.

My best friend had only been in Woodstone Falls for a few weeks, yet it felt like my world imploded without her.

Okay, that might be a *little* dramatic.

Dotty and I couldn't have been more different, but somehow, it worked. She had a way of commanding attention just by walking into a room, while I was content to stay in the background, quietly observing. While her blonde hair cascaded in loose waves, mine tumbled in curls that framed my brown skin. She towered nearly six inches above me, while I barely reached five feet. Despite all our differences, we fit together in a way that simply made sense.

Those contrasts weren't a wedge between us. They made us closer—the yin to my yang, the sugar to my spice.

And now there was a big piece of me that missed the

easy friendship that Dotty and I had. There was something about having someone to confide in, especially now. With Dotty's physical absence and John's emotional one, I felt trapped in a pit of emptiness.

Adding to the upheaval, I wouldn't be able to visit her next week as planned, since John needed me for a work event.

The only reason he was taking me was to play the part of the rich, handsome career man, with the doting teacher on his arm as his charity case.

And I hated feeling like this—questioning every interaction, wondering if I was being unfair or if my instincts were screaming at me for a reason. His distance was more deliberate lately, like a wall I wasn't allowed to climb.

I stared at the sagging leaves of Dotty's last surviving plant on the windowsill.

"It's okay, sweet baby. You've got this. You can survive anything," I said, though I knew this one was as far gone as the rest.

But as I said it, the words felt more of a reassurance meant for myself.

Talking to someone, or I guess *something*, was nice, though.

Lately, my main interactions were with the mailman and sporadic lunches with fellow teachers. Occasionally Dotty when I could catch her at a good time. Most of my conversations lately were with my six-and seven-year-old students. And as much as I loved my job, I was desperately in need of real adult interactions.

A knock interrupted my thoughts, and I hurried to the door.

Shit, that's right. Dotty's brother is coming for the weekend.

"Coming!" I called out, hastily clearing away last night's takeout.

Another knock, louder this time, just before I opened the door.

And there he stood—a man unknowingly competing in my mind for the title of the most attractive person I'd ever laid eyes on.

Over a foot taller than me, with broad shoulders and the kind of physique that made a worn T-shirt look like it was tailored just for him.

His dark, wavy hair fell over his forehead, effortlessly tousled. A shadow of stubble dusted his strong jawline, softening the sharp, chiseled angles of his face and giving him a rugged, almost mesmerizing appeal. And then there was his mouth—the curve of a smile tugging at his lips, sending my stomach into a flutter I *really* didn't want to acknowledge.

His calm yet intense demeanor made me simply forget how to speak.

Snap out of it. You have a boyfriend.

He eyed the apartment number at the row of doors marking each unit.

His eyes, a rich deep brown, absorbed everything as they locked onto me, like he was reading me without saying a word.

I managed a hesitant greeting. "Um… hi." It was as if every thought escaped my brain, leaving nothing but complete emptiness.

"Noah, right?" He peered down the hall. "Apartment thirteen?" he asked.

"Yup, that's me," I replied.

He arched a brow and cleared his throat. "You okay?" he asked, leaning against the doorframe, his gaze briefly dropping down my face.

A flush of warmth spread across my cheeks. "Uh, yeah. Sorry, long day. You must be Dotty's brother?"

"Yes, ma'am. Dorian James. Pleasure to meet you." He extended a hand, and as I took it, the warmth of his touch sent a jolt through me.

"Yes, it's nice to meet you," I smiled, trying to focus, but it was hard with him standing there, so… present.

"Well…" He let out a rich chuckle. "Can I come in?" he asked politely, and a heat crept up my neck.

"Yes, yes… sorry." I stepped aside. He nodded in thanks and walked through the threshold.

I suddenly became self-conscious of the small apartment I shared with his sister. It wasn't the most extravagant place in Seattle, but it was ours. Soft light spilled from various lamps, casting a gentle glow on the worn wooden floors. I walked toward the kitchen to the right. It was small, complete with that stupid, slowly dying herb garden on the windowsill.

Dorian cleared his throat, glancing around the space, and he seemed even more imposing up close with a confidence that made me both nervous and strangely drawn to him.

"The conference I'm attending ends Sunday, so I will be out of your hair by Monday morning at the latest."

I tried to remember a single thing Dotty told me about her brothers. He didn't give off sports vibes, so I doubt this was the brother in the NFL. That left the detective or…

Wait, what did the other one do?

"Are you the cop?" The words spilled out, and I immediately regretted every single one.

Dorian laughed softly, the sound easing the tension.

"Wrong brother. I'm the vet."

"Right," I said, trying to shake off my embarrassment. "So, you like puppies then?"

Another wonderful fucking question, Noah. Not weird at all.

He chuckled again, and the sound vibrated my spine, sending flutters through me.

"Sure, I do. Though, my daughter might disagree. She's still mad I won't let her get one."

Okay, so he's the one with the daughter.

"Gracie, right?" While Dotty mentioned her brothers occasionally, she bragged about Gracie constantly and how much she loved her niece.

Dorian's smile was a little lopsided, tugging at his right cheek and revealing a dimple. "Yeah, Gracie. She's a spitfire."

"I've heard a few stories that would definitely back that up." I paused for a moment and moved to lean against the kitchen island, letting the cool granite cool my forearms.

"You can stay as long as you need. I'll be around most of the time, but my boyfriend's taking me out tomorrow, so you'll be on your own then."

"Well, thanks for letting me crash here."

I gave him a small smile. "No worries. Feel free to help yourself to anything."

"Thanks, Noah. I'll get out of your way." He pointed down the hall. "Dotty's room is..." His tone trailed off in a question.

"First door on the left. Second door is the bathroom. My room is on the right," I said.

He nodded and walked across the living room, his steps purposeful as he approached the sofa and wooden coffee table, stacked with magazines and my laptop. He paused in front of a photo on the wall, one of Dotty and me from our freshman year of college.

His eyes met mine. "Thank you."

I scrunched my nose in confusion, tilting my head.

He peered back at the picture. "For being there for her.

She needed someone then," he said, his eyes not meeting mine again.

"I did too." I smiled as images of our friendship crept through my mind.

He glanced back to me and that damned dimple slowly made its appearance. He nodded and then pointed to the room. "I'm going to get settled in."

"Yeah, of course."

He made his way to Dotty's room, closing the door behind him with a small click.

I shook my head, still trying to make sense of that exchange. Rounding the couch, I sank into the cushions, pulling my phone from my pocket. A new notification lit up the screen, and I saw John responded to my text.

JOHN

Hopping on a red-eye home now. See you tomorrow.

A knot formed in my stomach as I stared at his message. John and I met during our senior year at a private boarding school. He'd been there since elementary, while I was transferred from a public school to the city's most prestigious institution. My mom hoped it would steer me toward becoming a lawyer, like her, instead of a teacher, which was my true aspiration.

Despite my skepticism about changing schools at fifteen, it did lead me to meet John.

From the first day, I was drawn to him. It wasn't just the effortless way he commanded attention; it was something deeper. John didn't see people through the lens of status or image. He was genuinely interested in everyone, asking questions and listening as if the details of a person's life truly mattered.

Even as a teenager, he was charming and confident,

though a bit arrogant at times. I liked how he listened when I spoke, how he remembered the small things. He wasn't trying to impress me or win me over—he simply appreciated who I was, not what I could offer him. That's what drew me in. The attention he gave me was unlike anyone else's—it was real. For the first time, I didn't feel like another face in the crowd. I felt seen.

Growing up, I sometimes felt torn between two worlds. My mom, a strong woman of color, instilled pride in my heritage and constantly reminded me of my worth. But my biological father, from whom I inherited some of my lighter features, was never a part of my life. That mix of identities often left me uncertain of where I belonged.

But with John, none of that mattered. He never seemed to care about any of it. He never treated me like I was a puzzle to be figured out, or like I didn't belong. After a few months of friendship, he surprised me by asking me to prom. It wasn't just about the gesture. It was the fact that he saw me, and in that moment, he saw all of me—my complexities, my insecurities, and the parts of me I hadn't always been sure about.

And of course, I said yes—who could refuse *the* John Cunningham?

We faced our share of challenges over the years—dating on and off through separate colleges and our careers. But when John moved back to Seattle a little over a year ago, everything changed. My dad helped John secure a position at the same tech company where he worked in the city, and we finally decided to commit to a relationship.

I hoped a new chapter would bring stability. I loved seeing how much my father and John respected each other. After he took him under his wing, their bond grew even stronger, both professionally and personally. It seemed like everything was falling into place.

Our relationship hadn't been perfect. Our demanding schedules often left little room for us—his filled with constant travel and long hours, mine consumed by the grind of being an overworked, underpaid public school teacher. Yet, somehow, we made it work.

Lately, though, it felt different—like we weren't even in the same universe anymore. He'd go an entire day with only a text or two when he was out of town. When he came back, he was distant, short with me, unwilling to talk about anything, and insisted he made every plan, unwilling to compromise on the smallest of details.

I tried to attribute it to his heightened work stress, which is why I'd let it go and was eagerly anticipating our date. I hoped it would give us a chance to reconnect and enjoy some quality time together.

Needing a distraction from my thoughts, I decided to grade a stack of homework, answer a few emails from parents, and sort through other school-related tasks. But when that was done, I still couldn't escape my mind. I turned on the TV and settled in to start a new show, hoping it would help me unwind.

The light of the screen filled the living room. As the first few minutes played, the sound of Dorian emerging from the room drew my attention. He walked out in gray sweatpants, and I resisted the urge to give him a once-over, focusing instead on the unfolding scenes of the dystopian drama.

I'm taken. I don't need to be eyeing my best friend's brother.

"Oh, is this that new show based on the post-apocalyptic video game?" he asked.

"Yup," I said, attempting to sound casual.

He moved into the kitchen to fill his water bottle, the faded dark green T-shirt hinting at the strength beneath. The dim light highlighted the sharp angles of his face, giving him a strong, masculine look that was striking yet unmistakably reminiscent of Dotty.

"Mind if I join you?" he asked, nodding toward the couch.

"Sure." My voice cracked, but he either didn't notice or chose to ignore it.

He sat on the other end of the couch, leaving a cushion between us.

Oh, thank God.

"Have you played the game before?" he asked, as he leaned back, making himself comfortable.

"No, but the show has been all over social media lately, so I thought I'd give it a try."

"I've been meaning to watch this but haven't found the time," he said, adjusting the pillows. He rested his head along the back of the couch, exposing the strong column of his throat.

"You used to play?" I asked.

The muscles in his face softened as he gave me a wide smirk. "Yeah. Trent and I did growing up." His brown gaze drifted to the pictures against the wall. "We would play for hours while Dotty would read."

"That must have been nice, having siblings and friends to grow up with."

"Yeah..." His voice trailed off as he seemed to delve deeper into his thoughts. "I guess I never really thought about it, but it was nice to have them around." He glanced over at me, his smirk turning into something more genuine. "Do you have any siblings?" he asked. I managed a weak smile in return, appreciating the sentiment.

"Nope, only child." I shrugged, trying not to focus on how intently his eyes seemed to study me.

"Really?" He tilted his head, a small smile playing on his lips.

I wasn't ready to go into my family dynamics with him, so I instead nodded. We turned back to the show, the storyline captivating me immediately. We ended up watching a few episodes in a row, drawn into the unfolding story until the late hours of the night. The air was filled with a comfortable silence, only broken by our occasional comments about what was playing out on screen.

Eventually, fatigue began to catch up with me, my eyelids growing heavier as the credits rolled for the third time.

"I think that's the last one I can handle for tonight," I said, standing from the couch.

"I was thinking the same thing."

He stood too, but the coffee table took up most of the space, forcing us closer. In an instant, he was only inches away, towering over me. I immediately pushed back, but his presence still loomed over me, bringing a strange awareness to the space between us.

"Sorry. Guess being a little sleepy throws off my balance," he added, a playful edge to his tone.

"No worries." I waved him off and walked into the kitchen and grabbed a glass to fill with water.

"How about tomorrow night? We could watch another one?" he suggested.

I paused for a second, then moved to grab my keys from the counter. "I won't be around. Date night."

"Right."

I separated a spare key from the ring and held it out to him. Our gazes met, and the space between us suddenly became charged as he reached to grab the key. "Just in case I'm not here."

For a moment, his expression shifted—something unreadable glimmered in his eyes before he masked it with a soft smile.

My heart skipped, and I immediately cursed myself.

What the hell is wrong with me? Why am I even feeling like this?

But the way Dorian looked at me… it was different.

"Thanks, Noah," he said softly.

The silence hung between us, heavier now, as I turned to head to my room.

After slipping into my matching pajamas and finishing my skincare routine, I slipped on a bonnet before plugging in my phone. Scrolling through my notifications, I let out a sigh.

DOTTY

How's it going?

I sent a quick reply, a frown pulling at my lips as I thought about how much I missed her.

ME

My life's a mess without you, but I'm good.

DOTTY

How are things going with Dorian?

ME

Good, he's actually pretty nice. We talked for a bit and then watched some tv.

DOTTY

Wait, my brother? Talked to you? Tall, dark hair, lopsided smile Dorian? Are you sure you have the right guy?

ME

I sure hope so. That sounds like him though lol.

DOTTY

Interesting. He's usually pretty quiet and short around people he doesn't know well.

ME

Well, we practically know each other via you so... How are you?

DOTTY

I'm good. I miss you.

ME

I miss you more. I'm going to bed though. Talk tomorrow?

DOTTY

Yes, please.

The thoughts running through my mind finally quieted as I rested my head on the pillow. Giving me at least a few hours of sleep.

THREE

Noah - September

HIGH ROAD -KOE WETZEL

By the time I woke up, Dorian was already gone, leaving the apartment unusually quiet. With no one around, I decided to spend the day in relaxation mode—in my pajamas with my favorite movies on repeat, and an endless supply of popcorn.

By late afternoon, I figured it was time to get ready for my date with John, even though I didn't know what the plan was. I sighed as I swiped a layer of gloss over my lips, studying my reflection in the mirror.

John enjoyed planning our dates, and I usually didn't mind since I knew he liked being in control. As long as it meant spending time together, I went along with it.

This time, though, concern crept in. He hadn't responded to any of my texts all day. While it wasn't unusual for him to work weekends, especially lately, the complete silence felt wrong.

Is he seeing another woman? Is he going to break up with me tonight? What the hell is going on with him?

A knock pulled me from my thoughts. I rushed to the

door, thinking it might be John, but when I opened it, Dorian stood there.

He cleared his throat, his gaze dropping to his phone. "Hey, sorry. I realized I left the key here and didn't have your number. Glad you hadn't left yet."

I stepped back, holding the door open. "Not yet."

As he walked past me, I reached out and took the phone from his hand without thinking.

His head turned, his brows lifting in surprise. "What are you doing?"

I glanced up briefly, my fingers already tapping at his screen. "Giving you my number, in case you forget the key again tomorrow."

For a second, he said nothing. Then he took his phone back and sat on the bench in the entryway, slipping off his shoes as my own phone chimed.

JOHN

Sorry, busy day. Be there in 10.

I set it on the counter with a sigh.

"Everything okay?" Dorian asked.

"Yeah, I'm good. John's on his way, so I'm gonna get dressed."

Dorian nodded slowly before walking over to the couch.

I stepped into my room, pulling on a simple black dress and heels. I didn't usually spend much time on my appearance, especially knowing I'd typically be covered in glue, markers, and whatever else the day at work threw at me. But I wanted tonight to be different, so I put in a little extra effort.

As I walked into the living room, Dorian was opening the door for John. John's gaze swept over him, sizing him up briefly before meeting my eyes.

"Who the fuck is this, Noah?" he asked, his voice stern as he stood in a pristine suit, his blonde hair perfectly styled.

Dorian's body went rigid, his jaw tightening as his eyes flicked toward John.

"I told you. Dotty's brother is in town, and she offered her room up. John, Dorian. Dorian"—I pointed—"John," I said, grabbing my purse.

Dorian extended his hand to John, but there was a pause as he hesitated, weighing the gesture, before finally taking it. The handshake was tight, almost too forceful. It seemed like some sort of damn pissing contest between the two of them, as if they had shared property.

"Nice to meet you," John said, but his tone didn't match his words.

"Likewise," Dorian said, his gaze hardening. There was no trace of the easygoing smile from yesterday—only the edge of a silent challenge in his eyes.

John's gaze swept over my outfit. "Didn't mean to make you go through all that trouble," he said, his voice flat. "I was thinking we'd keep it low-key tonight. I'm wiped from the week and just want to go home and crash."

I sucked in a breath. "Okay, that's fine. I'll go change and grab a bag for tonight," I said, trying to keep my voice steady.

John ran a hand through his short hair. "I can drop you back here later. I've got an early morning tomorrow and need to catch up at work."

I forced a smile. "You know, why don't we walk down the street for some pizza, eat there, and call it a night?" I suggested.

"I'm not feeling pizza. Tacos?"

I bit back a sigh. "Yeah, sure. That works," I replied.

We made our way to the taco stand, the fall evening air

filled with the sounds of laughter and the sizzle of food cooking. Despite the lively atmosphere, John remained unusually quiet, or maybe it wasn't so unusual anymore. We ordered and found a spot to sit and eat, but the conversation was minimal, mostly filled with brief comments about the food or weather.

I continued to try to get him to open up, but his responses remained short. His mind seemed elsewhere, and I could sense a barrier between us that didn't use to exist before. The silence only grew as the night went on.

After we finished eating, he reluctantly agreed to walk me back to my apartment and hang out for a bit before heading home. It was a small concession, but at least it was something.

I set my purse down after walking in the door and sat to take off my shoes, John following behind me.

"How was your work trip?" I asked, hoping that if I brought up work, he might open up.

"Fine," John replied, his tone flat.

"Just fine?"

He glanced at me. "It'd be better if you came with me," he said, as if the answer was that simple.

Without fail, John always asked me to go with him, even though he knew of my responsibilities. My students counted on me. Hell, *I* counted on me to make rent.

"I can't just leave whenever I want, John. I have a job." My words came out sharper than I intended, cutting through despite my best efforts to give him the benefit of the doubt.

"Yeah, but you could quit then come with me all the time. I could convince your dad it's for the best and probably even get your mom off your back."

But I didn't want to quit my job. Teaching wasn't just

something I did, it was who I was, but no matter how many times I explained that to him, he never understood.

I still remembered my fourth-grade teacher, who saw something in me when no one else did. She'd stayed late after class one day to help me with a project I was struggling with, and in that hour, something shifted. I knew I wanted to be that for other kids, to see their potential and help them find their voice. Being a part of a child's life at such an integral time was fulfilling. So, staying home and playing John's housewife wasn't something I was willing to do.

"I'm not doing that. Teaching isn't just a job to me. These kids rely on me, and I really try to make a difference. I don't want to give that up."

"I know. I just wish you would."

I didn't bother responding, opting to sit in silence instead.

"Well, I'm going to head out. Doesn't seem like you want to be around me," John said.

He leaned over for a goodnight kiss, but I turned my head at the last second, offering him my cheek instead. His lips barely brushed my skin before he pulled back, his scoff cutting through the tense silence like a knife.

"What the hell is your problem?" he muttered, clenching his jaw.

I opened my mouth to respond, but nothing came out, as if everything unspoken was crashing down.

Dorian cleared his throat, breaking through the tension. "You okay, Noah?" He studied me as he moved into the room. His posture was careful, waiting to see if he needed to intervene.

"She's fine," John snapped, standing up with his hands clenched at his sides. He threw Dorian a piercing stare.

Dorian didn't flinch, locking eyes with John. "I think she can speak for herself," he said, taking a step closer.

John shook his head, muttering under his breath. Without waiting for an answer, he stormed out, the door slamming behind him.

Frozen, I stood facing the door, my eyes fixed on where John had walked out. A heavy knot settled in my stomach.

I brushed my face, where his kiss barely landed, and I wondered how it had come to this, from something that once felt so familiar.

Dorian's eyes roamed over me before he slowly retreated to the couch. There was something about the way he watched me.

"You okay?" he asked. The tone of his voice carried a deep seriousness I hadn't heard yet. I plopped down next to him, letting a long sigh escape.

"I'm fine…" I said, glancing over at him.

He tilted his head, studying me in that way that almost made me feel too exposed. "Your boyfriend's kind of a dick."

The directness of his words hit hard, and I shifted uncomfortably. "John's just under a lot of stress at work lately." The words felt hollow, even as I said them.

It pissed me off that I was in a position that I had to defend my boyfriend for being an asshole.

Because John *was* being a fucking asshole.

"He's not usually like this," I said, my words betraying the truth I wasn't ready to admit.

Dorian raised an eyebrow. I kept my focus on a spot on the coffee table, not meeting his eyes. "I'd hope he doesn't act like that all the time. You deserve better."

I exhaled, forcing a weak smile. "I can handle it, but… thanks." My tone was softer now, less defensive.

"Fair enough," he said with a nod. His back rested

against the couch, his arms folding at his stomach. Then his lips quirked into a teasing smile. "Want to watch an episode?"

I blinked at the sudden shift, surprised at how easily he let it go.

"Okay…"

And just like that, the tension dissolved, replaced by an unfamiliar ease he somehow brought out in me. We ended up watching several episodes, trading commentary about the plot and characters like nothing happened. By the time the clock ticked into the early hours of the morning, the moment with John felt like a distant memory, leaving only the comfort of Dorian's company as we said goodnight.

FOUR

Dorian - September

DOWN BAD - TAYLOR SWIFT

I THOUGHT THE LONG STRETCH OF ROAD MIGHT HELP CLEAR MY mind. But as I left the city behind, the lights fading in the rearview mirror, I couldn't get Noah out of my head.

Seattle had been a whirlwind—meetings, lectures, networking—everything I expected.

But what I hadn't expected was *her*.

The moment I met her, I knew she was different. There was something about her that drew me in without her even trying. She carried herself with a calmness that made everything feel a little more settled simply by being near her.

I tried to focus on the road, the miles of asphalt disappearing beneath my tires, but every mile brought another thought of Noah.

Fuck, even that name was pretty.

My mind replayed her standing in the doorway of her apartment, her hand resting on the frame as she took me in for the first time. Her dark curls framed her face, catching the light in a way that was almost surreal. The warm glow behind her outlined her petite frame, and her skin was luminous, like she'd stepped right out of a fucking paint-

30

ing. There was something captivating in her gaze that held me in place much longer than it should have.

And it wasn't just that she was beautiful, though she undeniably was. It was more than that. It was the way she stirred things in me that I'd worked so hard to bury, things I hadn't felt in years.

Dotty mentioned her best friend in passing over the years, but nothing could've prepared me for the way my chest constricted when I saw her.

I knew I had no business staring at her the way I did— at the way her lips curved, and how her curls bounced when she spoke. Her golden-brown eyes held a thousand stories I wanted to hear.

I couldn't shake the thought that she belonged there— not just in the apartment but in my orbit.

I stood there like an idiot, trying to gather my thoughts and play it cool, but failed miserably. And she stood there just as stunned, like she saw a ghost, probably because I was still fucking staring right back.

I tried to remind myself that it wasn't appropriate to stare at a stranger's mouth, *especially* when the stranger was your sister's best friend.

Even if her lips were a shade of mauve that complemented her tawny skin so perfectly.

She was so pretty.

So fucking pretty.

And she was tiny, but despite her small frame, she had curves in all the right places. Even her damn little scar above her eyebrow added to her appeal. She looked like I could pick her up and throw her around with my hand around her thro—

Nope, nope, nope.

I gripped the steering wheel tighter, shaking my head as if to physically dislodge the thought. This was insane. I'd spent one weekend near her, and yet here I was, replaying every glance, every second.

For fuck's sake, I needed to get a grip. If Dotty knew what was running through my head, she'd murder me and feed me to the damn wolves.

This wasn't me. I didn't let people get under my skin. My life was straightforward—take care of Gracie, run the clinic, keep my family close.

That was enough.

Even if Noah held a presence about her that just made me feel... at peace.

But I pushed it all down and turned on the radio, hoping some music might drown out my thoughts. Classic rock filled the car, a comforting presence dulling the noise in my head as I made my way home.

There, I was known as the no-nonsense vet, the guy who didn't have time for idle chatter or romantic entanglements. Since Hallie's passing, everyone knew that my world only revolved around Gracie.

As it should.

She deserved all of me, not just pieces.

But Noah... She was like a riddle I couldn't solve, a question that lingered. And now, after meeting her, I couldn't help but wonder if there was even more beneath the surface.

Fuck, you're thinking about her again, dumbass.

I ran a hand down my face, internally scolding myself again as the highway stretched out ahead, lined with trees that blurred into one another. I let the music fill the truck, my thoughts *now* drifting back to her asshole boyfriend, who took her for granted.

There was something about John that set off alarm bells —an instinct that nagged at me, telling me he wasn't what he seemed. Too polished. Too perfect. I'd seen it before—the way men like him could talk their way in or out of anything, their smiles hiding whatever was brewing beneath. I'd seen the way he dismissed her, acting as if her opinions didn't matter, belittling her career, and not giving a shit about her.

It *infuriated* me.

But what the hell could I do? She wasn't mine to protect. Even if I wanted to deck the guy in the face.

The clouds began to break as I crossed the state line. Rays of sunlight peeked through the puffs in the sky, and the sight was a welcome change.

I thought about Gracie, waiting at home with her usual enthusiasm—her laughter was the best part of my day. I couldn't let myself get swept away by feelings for someone.

After hours of nothing but the sound of the radio, my small southern Oregon town came into view, its streets lined with familiar shops with the heavy scent of pine in the air. As I pulled onto Main Street, a few locals were setting up for the market, waving gleefully as I passed by.

It was good to be back.

But as I parked the car in front of my house, I knew that something had shifted inside me. Noah made an impression, but despite my resolve, I couldn't deny how much I liked it.

I liked *her*.

And that was fucking scary.

She might have been in Seattle, miles away, but she'd unknowingly forced a way into my thoughts. And I only hoped the distance would be enough to eventually push her out of my mind.

For the love of God, please let the distance be enough to get her out of my head.

FIVE

Noah - November

GASOLINE - HALSEY

MY HEADPHONES BLARED AS I ATTACKED THE KITCHEN FLOOR with a mop, scrubbing away weeks of grime I'd let build up while Dotty was gone. Not only did she apparently keep my life together, but she also kept our house clean.

I needed a distraction, something to drown out the anger radiating through me. You'd think that my *boyfriend* would know better than to completely ignore me, especially on Thanksgiving.

Yet here I was, still holding out for a man who couldn't even be bothered to send a text. For three days now. Over the last few months, our relationship had only deteriorated. I knew we were on the rocks, but I wasn't even a priority anymore. I was something he picked up and put down whenever it suited him. With every ignored message, every brushed-off plan, I couldn't help but wonder what it would feel like to be in a relationship where I wasn't constantly questioning my worth. One where I wasn't a backup plan or someone's second choice but truly seen and valued for who I was.

Instead, I was being ghosted.

34

I wasn't just angry—I was exhausted.

Exhausted by the constant push and pull. The way John needed to control every decision we made and then turned cold the moment things didn't go his way. My mind wandered over the cracks that started to form in our relationship.

Was this how it was supposed to feel? Was I imagining the distance between us? Or had it always been there, buried beneath the excuses I used to accept?

I shook the thought away. People were supposed to be together because they cared about each other… but I didn't think we did anymore.

All relationships go through rough patches. Maybe this is ours.

But the nagging voice in the back of my mind wouldn't quiet.

The truth was, John never truly saw me for who I was. He saw what he wanted to see—the potential to mold someone who fit neatly into the polished image he constructed for himself.

And I let him.

I let his smooth charm and sharp ambition overshadow the rifts that had formed early on in our relationship. His arrogance, the same confidence that had skyrocketed him to success in his career, became a cage for us, even if I wouldn't admit it until now.

It suffocated any room for me to grow. Every decision, every plan, every little nitpick, even down to something as simple as choosing tacos over pizza.

My voice had always been secondary, my preferences an afterthought, if they were even considered at all. I'd convinced myself it wasn't a big deal, but now, those moments were heavy.

I stopped and closed my eyes.

I wasn't sure how much longer I could keep pretending that this was enough, that *I* was enough for him, or that he was enough for me.

The angsty Ellie Miles album was on repeat as I continued scrubbing and scrubbing at every bit of dirt and dust in the entire apartment, trying to calm my thoughts.

But it wasn't working.

Suddenly, a thud, followed by two more in quick succession, boomed from the front door. It was loud. So loud, in fact, that I heard it even through my headphones, making me jump.

Quickly, I crossed the room, ditching my headphones on the countertop in the process. I wiped my sweat-covered brow as I crossed the small living space, taking heaving breaths as I opened the door.

I assumed I'd see my soon-to-be *ex*-boyfriend. What I did *not* expect to see was two federal agents.

The middle-aged man with salt-and-pepper hair flashed his badge that read *Agent Roberts*. The tense lines in his face were void of any emotion. By his side stood a short brunette woman who appeared to be in her late thirties, her gentle smile contrasting with the man's cold demeanor.

She also flashed her badge, her eyes warm as she spoke. "I'm Agent Garcia, and this is Agent Roberts."

"Noah Reid?" The way Agent Roberts's tone was clipped and direct made it clear this wasn't a social visit.

"Um… yes," I replied, my hands playing with the edge of my sleeve.

My mind raced, running through every possible reason the FBI might want something from me. But I couldn't come up with a single answer.

The woman, Agent Garcia, gave me a reassuring nod before she added, "Can we come in?"

I blinked, feeling thrown off-balance, but I stepped aside without thinking. "Uh… sure?"

Agent Roberts stepped into the apartment first, his sharp gaze sweeping over the space, taking in every detail. His movements were calculated, deliberate. He didn't even look at me as he strode toward the kitchen bar stools. He gestured to one of the chairs.

"Take a seat," he said, leaving no room for argument.

I hesitated for a split second before obeying, perching on the stool. The leather was cold against my skin, sending an involuntary shiver up my spine. I clasped my hands tightly in my lap, my heart thudding in my chest.

"What's going on?" I asked, the words tight, my grip on calm slipping.

Agent Garcia stepped forward, her tone softer but no less direct. "We are here to ask you about John Cunningham."

John? Why did they want to know about John?

"Um… John? He's my boyfriend," I said. "I haven't heard from him in three days." My stomach twisted as the reality of my own words sank in. I swallowed hard. "He's not… dead, is he?"

Agent Garcia's expression didn't change, but her response was quick, steady. "We don't have a reason to believe that, no."

"So… what's going on then?" I asked, shifting on the barstool, my fingers gripping the edge.

"What can you tell us about him?" she asked. Her prior warmth was gone. It was the kind of voice that demanded honesty without a hint of aggression. Agent Garcia's pen hovered over her notepad.

I swallowed hard, my fingers twisting together in my lap. "Well… He usually texts me at least once a day. Even when he's busy, he keeps me updated." My voice wavered further, threatening to crack completely. I felt a wave of confusion building, the knot in my stomach tightening as I forced myself to meet their unrelenting gazes.

I reached into my pocket, retrieving my phone with unsteady hands. Pulling up our text conversation, I turned the screen toward them, the faint glow illuminating the tension etched on their faces.

JOHN

I may not be home for Thanksgiving.

ME

Okay... why not?

Can you at least let me know what is going on?

Are you really going to ignore me? What the hell is going on?

You need to call me. This is insane. You're an adult John you can't just ignore your girlfriend.

"When was the last time you saw him?" Agent Roberts asked, his tone measured.

"Monday when he left town," I answered. "What exactly are you accusing him of?" I leaned forward despite the chill crawling up my spine.

Agent Roberts' eyes narrowed, but then Agent Garcia stepped in. "We're gathering information right now. His recent activities raised some... red flags, and we need to confirm a few things."

"What kind of red flags? I've known John for half my life. He's never..." My voice faltered. "I don't understand."

Garcia's expression didn't waver. "Sometimes, people hide things from the people closest to them."

The next hour was a nonstop interrogation, their questions coming at me like a rapid-fire barrage. *What's John like? How did we meet? Has he been acting strange lately? What's his schedule like?* By the time they were done, the only thing they hadn't asked was what side of the bed he slept on.

They handed me their business cards, their expressions cold as they reminded me to reach out if I heard from John.

My mind was already miles away. As the door shut behind them, I collapsed onto the couch, the reality of everything sinking in like a weight I couldn't shake.

What the hell?

My boyfriend—the man I'd trusted for years—was being investigated by the FBI. *The FBI.*

Questions piled up, each one heavier than the last, with no answers in sight. Where was he? What had he done?

I was a public-school teacher, not someone who got tangled up with people on a federal watchlist. I'd known John for half of my life—or at least, I'd thought I had. Clearly, I only knew the parts of himself he wanted me to see. The realization hit me like a punch to the gut.

My heart pounded in my chest, fast and erratic. Without thinking, I grabbed my phone, tapped on Dotty's name, and hit call. I needed her before I completely unraveled.

Nothing.

This was fine. Everything was fine.

John could be mixed up in the wrong thing.

Maybe drugs.

Maybe he was just embezzling money?

What the fuck, Noah? He's just embezzling money? As if that made it any better?

I called Dotty again, to no avail.

As my thoughts entirely started to spiral—Dotty finally answered on the third try.

As her voice came through the line, my chest was tight, my breathing uneven, and my head a complete mess.

"Noah? Are you okay?" she asked.

"No. Not at all. I don't know what to do. The FBI came." My words came out fast and sporadic. "They were asking me questions, and I'm so confused and scared. Apparently, John's mixed up in something. They wanted to know where he's been, but I haven't spoken to him in days. I don't know what to do." Tears slipped down my cheeks. "Dotty… What do I do?"

"Okay. What do you need? What can I do?" she asked. Her urgency was palpable through the phone.

It hit me—today was her first big holiday in Woodstone in ten years. I didn't want to taint her day. And with that realization, a wave of guilt washed over me.

"Shit, it's Thanksgiving. I can't ask you to come back. I just… I needed to talk to you. I'm freaking out here."

"I'll be there as soon as I can. I'll book the next flight. We'll figure this out," she assured me.

We hung up, and I spent the next fifteen minutes obsessively Googling what it takes to get the FBI to investigate you. Every search result confirmed what I already knew.

This was bad.

Like *really* bad.

What if he's already in jail? What if he's hurt? What if he is actually dead?

I thought of all the little things I'd brushed off over the years. His cryptic work trips, the times he'd disappear for hours with barely an explanation, the locked drawer in his desk I never dared to question.

The thoughts spiraled, crashing over me in never-ending waves, each one more terrifying than the last, until it felt like my head was going to explode. My heartbeat pounded in my ears, the world around me blurring as the fear took hold. Every possibility led to another, worse than the one before, until all I could feel was dread tightening its grip on me.

My phone buzzed again, jolting me from my thoughts, and I answered. "Hey," I said, fighting to keep my tone even.

"Dorian booked me a flight that leaves in less than two hours. I should be there before nine. I'll take a taxi to the apartment," she said. Her words were steady, carefully measured, but I caught the faintest hitch at the end, like she was barely holding something back.

"No, I'll come pick you up," I insisted.

"Okay, but what exactly happened?" she asked. Her voice was quieter now, like she was afraid of the answer.

"I don't even know... But it's bad. John is being investigated. He left for his work trip the other day, and I haven't heard from him since. This morning, the FBI showed up to question me."

"What did they ask you?"

"If I knew where he's been. I don't even know what he's being investigated for. They wouldn't tell me anything," I said, frustration mixing with the helplessness I couldn't shake.

"I'll talk to Colt," she said quickly. "He might not have much sway, but it's worth a shot."

"Thanks, Dotty." The words caught in my throat, but I forced them out. "I hate that you're coming back under these circumstances, but... I'm really glad you'll be here."

"Me too," she said on a deep sigh. "I'll send you my flight details once I finish packing. See you soon. Love you."

"Love you, too," I said before the line died with a beep.

The stillness around me hit harder than before. I dropped the phone onto the table, staring blankly at it, willing my thoughts to make sense of everything.

But they *didn't* make sense.

SIX

Noah - November

WHERE'S MY LOVE - SYML

MY THUMB HOVERED OVER MY MOTHER'S CONTACT, DREADING the call I couldn't avoid. Our relationship was complicated, and she and my stepdad knew John almost as well as I did, making it even harder to face.

I had to give her credit—she handled single parenthood until I was ten, balancing it with a full-time job like it was second nature. Then she married my stepdad, who came into our lives after a messy divorce that left him with almost nothing. His ex-wife had taken most of his assets and even tried to get more after he remarried until she finally stopped coming around.

But it never made him bitter. From the start, he was kind and generous in a way that made it easy to love him.

Although my dad looked nothing like me and wasn't my blood, he was my father in every sense of the word. He showed me what it means to have a man show up for you, even when he wasn't biologically obligated.

I clicked call and waited, trepidation settling in my stomach.

"Hi, sweetie. It's been a while since I've heard from you. Happy Thanksgiving," she answered.

My parents lived just outside Seattle, but weeks ago, I told my mom I'd be staying home this year to spend the day with John.

"Hi, Mom. Is Dad there?" I asked, sinking deeper into the couch, curling my legs up beneath me.

"Rick, honey!" she called out. "It's Noah. I'm going to put you on speaker."

I exhaled slowly, the phone feeling like a lead weight in my hand. After a beat, I heard the soft shuffle of footsteps, followed by the calm, familiar tone of my dad's voice.

"Hi, Noah. How are you?" I shifted on the couch, resting my forehead against the back cushion, bringing my knees to my chest.

"Hi, Dad," I choked back the lump in my throat. "I'm… uh, not great."

"What is going on?" he asked.

I continued, my words muffled by the couch cushions. "Something's wrong… with John."

"What do you mean?" my mom asked. "Is he hurt?"

"I… I don't think so," I stammered.

John had always been a master at blending in, his charm and effortless wit winning everyone over—especially my parents. When we first met, his relationship with his mother was strained, and he'd never known his father. His mom, a nurse, worked long hours, and the few times they were together—usually during summer breaks or when he wasn't off at boarding school—she was distant, preoccupied, often too tired to connect.

He rarely spoke of her, and when he did, his tone would shift, revealing a vulnerability he usually kept hidden. The few times I'd been around his mother, I'd watch her correct him, belittle him, and make him feel small. But once John became a permanent fixture in my life, he quickly forged a relationship with my parents that filled the gaps left by his own. He became the son they'd never had, a bond that only grew stronger with time.

"What happened?" my dad asked, his tone soft.

"The… the FBI came to question me about him," I admitted. The pounding of my heart echoed through my ears and made it hard to hear their responses.

"What could they possibly want with John?" my mom's tone pitched higher, disbelief coloring every word.

"Good question," I said. "They wouldn't tell me anything, just kept asking where he is."

"And where is he?" my dad pressed.

"I don't know. I haven't heard from him." A heavy sensation pressed down on me. "At first, I thought maybe he was busy. But then two FBI agents showed up at my door, and now… I don't know what the hell to think."

"Language, Noah," my mom scolded.

I scoffed internally. "Mom, I think I get a pass here."

"Strange how?" my dad questioned.

"He's… distant. Always traveling, always glued to his phone when he's home. He's constantly making excuses to leave. It's like he's somewhere else, even when he's with me." The silence on the line stretched, heavy and suffocating.

"I'll look into it. I know he's been traveling a lot for work lately. He was supposed to be on a business trip these past few days. I assigned him to a major client, so he's been keeping busy."

"I'm sure it's simply a misunderstanding," my mom said, though there was a faint hesitation in her voice.

"Yeah… maybe it's nothing," I muttered, the words

feeling empty. I gripped the edge of the couch. "Dad, can you let me know if you hear from him?"

"Of course, sweetie," my dad said, his voice as steady as ever.

I swallowed hard, gripping my phone like it might slip from my grasp. "Thanks," I whispered before we said goodbye.

I shifted on the uncomfortable airport bench, my eyes glued to the stream of passengers trickling out of the secure area. Dotty hadn't texted me since she sent her flight details before leaving Woodstone, and that wasn't like her. Normally, she'd update me every step of the way—complaining about cramped seats or swooning over adorable babies.

But her flight had landed twenty minutes ago.

Maybe she was stuck waiting to deplane. Still, my stomach churned as I scanned the crowd for her.

Thirty minutes passed.

Then forty-five.

By the time an hour ticked by, panic had taken hold. Each text I sent went unanswered, the little delivered mark mocking me from the screen. When I called, it went straight to voicemail, the dull beep echoing in my ears as a cold sweat trickled down my spine.

I fumbled with my phone, my hands trembling as I dialed Dorian. My heart pounded louder with every ring.

"Pick up, pick up," I muttered.

He answered immediately. "Hey, Noah. What's up?" Confusion laced his voice.

"Dorian..." A wave of dread surged through me as I

forced the words out. "I don't know what to do. She's not here."

"What do you mean she's not there?" His words came out tense.

"She texted me her flight details. It landed over an hour ago. I was waiting for her, but she hasn't shown up. Her calls go straight to voicemail." I inhaled quickly. "I don't know what to do, Dorian. I'm ready to get in my car and drive to Woodstone." In the background, muffled voices and the quick pace of footsteps echoed, amplifying the worry. "Am I overreacting?"

"I don't think you're overreacting," he said. "Let's figure this out first. Go home, and don't open the door for anyone except Dotty. I'll check with the airline, find out if she boarded. I'll let you know as soon as I hear."

"Okay… Thank you." My voice cracked.

"It will be okay," he said, as though he was trying to reassure the both of us.

An hour later, we confirmed the worst. Dotty hadn't gotten on the plane. I was in my car, speeding toward Woodstone, the fear clawing at me with every mile.

My mind spun with questions.

Where is she? Is she okay? Why wouldn't she get on the plane?

My grip on the steering wheel was so tight my fingers ached. Anxiety threatened to overwhelm me with every passing minute, and the space around me felt suffocating.

Dotty was missing. My *best friend* was missing. And no matter how hard I tried, I couldn't stop the fear.

I glanced at the empty seat beside me, a cruel reminder

of her absence, and the ache deepened. She should've been there complaining about overpriced airline snacks, or how many movies we could go through over the long weekend.

Instead, there was nothing. No texts. No calls.

Just a void that screamed louder than anything else.

SEVEN

Noah - November

TRAIN WRECK - JAMES ARTHUR

THE HOSPITAL DOORS SLID OPEN WITH A MECHANICAL HISS, and I hurried inside, my pulse thrumming in my ears. The sterile smell of antiseptic and the hum of activity pressed in around me, but I couldn't focus on any of it. My eyes darted frantically across the lobby, searching for someone—anyone—who could tell me where to go.

At the reception desk, I stumbled over my words. "I'm looking for my friend, Dotty James. She's here for Trent… …Trenton Akers. He's in the ICU."

The nurse nodded, her face calm and practiced. "ICU is on the third floor. She might be in the waiting area there."

I didn't even thank her before bolting toward the elevators, my breath catching in my chest. The numbers above the doors ticked up agonizingly slowly, but the moment they opened, I rushed out, scanning the hallway.

And then I saw her. Dotty. Sitting in the waiting room, hunched over with her face in her hands.

Alive.

Dorian had already told me she was okay—physically, at least—when he called to give me the rundown of what happened. But hearing it and seeing it were two different things.

It turned out her longtime stalker was the very person responsible for her mother's hit-and-run nearly two decades ago. The truth was both horrifying and unbelievable, leaving her shaken to the core.

Seeing her in person, even with her flushed cheeks streaked with drying tears, sent a wave of relief crashing through me. The way she was staring blankly at the wall told me that, while she was alive, she was far from okay.

I slid into the chair beside her in the waiting room and could sense the worry radiating off her.

She'd held onto so much for so long, and now that the truth was out, I could see it taking its toll, especially with the way things ended. With her boyfriend, Trent, shot and fighting for his life.

Every second stretched as we waited, the minutes turning to hours.

"Have you eaten?" I asked, desperate to do something, anything, to ease her pain, ignoring my own in that moment. I moved my head to lightly rest against her shoulder and nudged her gently until her head lay against mine. Her blonde hair tumbled over my face, a faint reminder of her presence, fragile yet here.

"I'm not sure I can," she admitted, her gaze fixed on the wall in front of us.

"Coffee then?" I raised a brow. "Since I know you are too stubborn to sleep." She grabbed my hand and squeezed, a silent confirmation that she appreciated the effort.

"Sure…" she said. "That'd be nice."

"You got it," I said, and as she lifted her head, I stood.

I walked down the long hallway, memorizing the bright white speckled tiles along the way. I heard low cursing and banging as I rounded the corner and found Dorian's head resting against the vending machine glass. He raised his hand and pounded again on it.

"Could anything else. Fucking. Go. Wrong?" he shouted, punctuating each word with a bang of his fist. Until the bag of chips finally fell to the bottom.

I paused for a moment, watching him, before I gently cleared my throat to make my presence known.

Dorian peered over at me, quickly trying to mask his emotions, but his bloodshot eyes and puffy face gave him away. Slowly, he bent down, pressing the small door to the vending machine open to grab the chips.

"You okay?" I asked, as I took cautious steps toward him.

He squeezed his eyes shut, dragging a hand down his face before exhaling sharply. "Yeah... I'm fine," he muttered, though the tension in his jaw told me otherwise.

"Dorian..." I started, my voice trailing off.

His shoulders sagged, as if the world was pressing down on him. "What do you want, Noah?" he snipped, and the tone in his voice stung more than I cared to admit.

I don't have time for this.

I walked past him toward the machine and fumbled with my spare change.

"Nothing. I'm getting your sister a coffee."

There was a long exhale from behind me, followed by his voice—softer now. "Fuck, I snapped at you. I'm sorry."

"It's okay," I curtly replied, pushing the coins in and listening to the jingle as they dropped. I grabbed a cup, putting it in place before I pressed the button.

"No, it's not. You didn't deserve that," he said. Though I couldn't see his face, his voice dripped with guilt.

I turned then, catching his gaze. "You're right. I didn't." I said, as the coffee started sputtering.

He shook his head, squeezing his eyes shut again, and pinched the space between his brows. "It's just… I'm on edge. My best friend, basically my brother, is in there with a bullet in his chest he got protecting my sister. I can't wrap my head around it, but that doesn't mean I should've snapped at you. I'm just… scared."

"Me too," I murmured as I fed more change into the machine for a second cup.

He sighed. "I don't know what the hell I'm supposed to do right now. Every time I try to think it through… my heads' fucked right now."

I took the coffees from under the spout, and, turning around, I spotted a small seating area nearby. I glanced at him and gestured to the chairs.

"Let's sit," I said, handing him his cup.

He gave a small, tired nod before turning and heading toward the chairs. I followed, setting the other cup down, and sat across from him. I didn't rush him to speak, letting the silence stretch out as I waited.

"When you called me…" He let out a long exhale. "I knew something was wrong. I kept trying to tell myself it was nothing," he said, staring down at his hands, fingers twitching restlessly. His jaw clenched, then he released another breath, more tense than the last. "But I knew."

"I did, too."

"I need to be there for her, for Trent, but I can't sit in that damn waiting room, wondering when the next piece of bad news will hit."

I instinctively reached over to grab his hand, and his fingers curled around mine. "No one expects you to have it all together right now. It's okay to feel like this, to be lost in it all. You're allowed to be angry, to be confused, and to not know how to process it."

He stared at me, his gaze drifting over me before he

pulled back, letting his head fall against the back of the chair. "I'm her brother, her twin," he muttered, barely audible. "I should've been there to protect her. I'm supposed to have her back, but I let her down. I let all of this happen."

I frowned, shaking my head. "You can't blame yourself for some guy stalking your sister, or for Trent getting shot. This is not on you, Dorian."

His gaze snapped to mine at the sound of his name. His throat bobbed before he pressed a hand to his forehead.

There was a weariness etched into his features, and something in the rawness of it all made him almost beautiful.

"But it somehow feels like it's my fault." He sighed. "I sound fucking crazy."

The words escaped me before I could stop them. "Crazy? I don't think you are crazy. If anyone's crazy, that's me. I mean, I've been dating a guy that's being investigated by the FBI for God knows what."

The words left my mouth without thinking, a blur of frustration and truth. But the second they were out, regret washed over me. Now wasn't the time to unravel my mess.

"Sorry," I said quickly, my voice softer now. "I'm not trying to make this about me. I just… I get it. Sometimes it feels like everything is spiraling out of control, and yet somehow, *you* are the one holding the strings."

Dorian shrugged. "Nah, don't worry about it," he said with a dry chuckle, his voice quiet but appreciative of the shift in focus. "Do you know what happened?"

"With John?" He nodded and I continued. "I was questioned for hours, but all I really know is that I'm in the dark."

His gaze fell to the floor, lips pressed into a tight line as his fingers drummed restlessly on his knee. A sudden unease settled in my stomach.

"What is it?" I asked, leaning forward, my brows knitting together.

He didn't answer. Instead, his hands fidgeted, his focus glued to the floor, evading mine.

Finally, he spoke, but his voice was taut. "I don't think I'm supposed to say anything."

"What do you mean?"

The last twenty-four hours were a blur, and I was trying to keep my head on straight. But now, his silence only fueled the growing fear that there was still more to come.

Dorian opened his mouth, then closed it again, his jaw working back and forth. A flush crept up his neck and spread to his cheeks, his eyes darting to anything but mine.

He shifted in his seat. When he finally met my gaze, it was only for a fleeting second before he looked away again.

"What aren't you supposed to say?"

He still didn't answer right away. Instead, he stood and paced, his footsteps fast and uneven.

I stood, following his movements.

My mind was a tangled mess of thoughts, each one conflicting with the next, pulling me in opposite directions. I couldn't grasp on to anything solid.

His teeth clenched, muscles twitching before he exhaled slowly. "I… I'm not sure this is the right time…"

"Dorian, what's happening?" I pressed.

He stopped, his shoulders stiffening as he turned to face me. His gaze locked onto mine as he gave me a small nod. "Do you know about the Marketplace Murderer?"

I could feel the blood rushing to my head. "The what?"

"The guy on the news," he said quietly. "The one killing women across the country."

I frowned, trying to piece it together. "What does that have to do with anything?"

"They think…" he hesitated before taking a deep,

steady breath. "They think John's the Marketplace Murderer."

Suddenly, the world around me went still.

My mind spun with the image of John—a murderer? The disbelief sat heavy on my chest, cold and foreign.

My brain couldn't even begin to comprehend it. In all the possibilities I came up with, this wasn't even on the list.

"What? No. That's—no, that's not possible," I muttered, more to myself than to him. His gaze kept me still, even as my world seemed to tilt.

"It is, unfortunately," he said.

I refused to process the words, pushing them away like they didn't belong in the same space as the reality I knew. I wanted to argue, to dismiss it, but the truth in his eyes held me there, my hands trembling.

"You're lying," I said, though my voice faltered.

He was quiet, apologetic even, when he answered. "I wish I was."

"No," I said, shaking my head forcefully. "No, you're wrong. He's… he's not…" My hands clenched into fists at my sides, nails digging into my palms.

"I don't have the details," he added. "But I know that's why they questioned you. They think he's involved. I'm not supposed to tell you, but you deserve to know the truth."

Things with John had been rough for a while. I knew that. But this? This wasn't what I'd expected.

It wasn't that I thought he was perfect. Far from it.

Our relationship had always been a delicate balance—comfortable enough to enjoy our independence but still seeking each other's company when we needed it.

I convinced myself that was enough.

I believed he was a good person.

But now? I wasn't sure.

I knew his flaws—his temper, his distance. The times he zoned out.

He'd said everything was fine. Work was just taking over. I'd believed him.

But now… my stomach twisted.

Moments rushed back. Things I'd thought little of.

The way his moods shifted after work trips. Calm to restless.

Like wearing his shoes inside—a strict rule he followed religiously, except after those trips, when he'd casually leave them on as if it didn't matter anymore. As if he was… letting go.

And I'd let it go too, assuming he was decompressing.

But then—his temper. Snapping over nothing. A casual word. A small mistake.

And it always came back to one thing.

Me not traveling with him enough.

I'd gone when I could. Summer breaks, holidays. But he pushed and pushed and pushed.

Why? Why did it matter so much? Was he trying to keep me close? Distract me from whatever darkness was inside him?

"I can't… how is this possible?" The words seething out, too hot, too fast. I didn't want to believe it, but the frustration welled up, burning through me.

"I'm sorry," he said, his voice strained. "I can't let you stand here comforting me when there's something you deserve to know—something no one's told you," he said, but it barely registered over the pulse filling my ears.

"No," I repeated, as if saying it loud enough could push the nightmare away. I was supposed to be focused on Dotty, not caught up in the disaster of my own life. "This doesn't make sense. This… this is wrong," I seethed.

He didn't back away, though. He stayed right there, his

gaze resolute, letting me work through the mess of emotions tumbling out. I glared at him, even though I knew he wasn't the one I was angry at.

"How the fuck is this possible?" I bit out. "No. *No.* There's no way. How? How the fuck is this actually my life?"

His hands landed on my shoulders, steadying me as I fought to breathe. I felt his touch pulling me into the present moment. But my mind was reeling. I wanted to pull away, to push him off, as if distance could erase what he'd said, but my body didn't move. Instead, I leaned in.

Dorian's eyes narrowed, but he didn't say anything. He simply stood there, letting me fume. "I wish I had the answers…"

"What the hell even is the answer to this? You're telling me my boyfriend has been killing people? Fucking murdering them and pretending like nothing happened?" I let out a frustrated sigh. "I don't expect you to have all the answers. You have your own shit going on right now. But I can't… I can't do this. I can't deal with this right now."

It was suddenly *all* too much.

The overwhelming rollercoaster of emotions slammed into me, sudden and all-consuming.

My heart pounded erratically, each beat a painful blow. The dizziness creeped in. I blinked, trying to clear the fog that was obscuring my vision.

The need to move suddenly overwhelmed me, some desperate attempt to work out the havoc inside me. The stark white hospital walls seemed to close in, each step making it even harder to breathe.

I paced, my mind fixating on one thing. Moving.

Moving.

I had to move.

I had to get out of my head. *I had to.*

He's a murderer?

Someone I let in so close to me. Someone who could have hurt me, but instead was hurting other women?

Dorian's voice barely reached me, though I knew he was close.

It didn't matter. I kept walking, my feet carrying me mindlessly up and down the narrow corridor. Back and forth.

Suddenly, I stopped—frozen in place.

I tried to breathe, but my throat tightened. The world around me blurred at the edges, and the room spun. I reached out, gripping the back of the chair to catch myself. His voice still tried to cut through the haze, as Dorian's hand brushed against my back.

But I struggled to focus, my mind a tangled mess of disbelief and terror. Thoughts raced through my mind, colliding and fragmenting.

Everything around me was muffled, distant, as though I were underwater, unable to make out the sharp details of the moment. I reached for clarity, but it slipped out of my grasp.

The image of John, his effortless charm, his smooth gaze, everything I knew about him now replaced by a sinister shadow I couldn't reconcile.

The man who knew the most intimate details about me, who'd been by my side through all the messy, angsty years of adolescence—a murderer? Someone who could take lives for pleasure, then come home and act like it was just another day?

"Noah!" Dorian pierced through the fog, sharp and clear, pulling me back to the moment.

His hands were at the nape of my neck, instantly centering me in a way nothing else could. His touch was now the only thing keeping me from floating further into the panic.

My knees buckled, but he caught me.

"Easy," he murmured, his tone calm, a stark contrast to the disarray in my head as he slowly lowered us both to the ground.

I was deeply tangled in John's web of lies and deceptions without even knowing it.

Each breath came shallow and strained, as if unseen hands were slowly choking the air from my lungs—but Dorian was there, cutting through it all.

My body moved on instinct as he pulled me closer—his warmth anchoring me, feeling the rise and fall of his chest.

"Noah, look at me." His thumbs brushed against my cheeks, drawing small circles over my skin. "You're safe," he murmured. There was a storm in his brown irises.

An invisible vise gripped me, squeezing with every thought that threatened to unravel me.

"I… I can't…" I whispered.

"Just breathe. Noah, I need you to breathe. Breathe with me."

His words soothed the loud heartbeat in my ears. I pulled back and looked into his eyes. The calmness of them was comforting.

"Let's breathe in. Are you ready?" He stared directly into me, completely calm.

I managed a shallow nod. He guided me, counting out the breaths, as he exaggerated each one for my benefit. "In, two, three, four." I mirrored his motions. "That's it. Good job."

He was slowly bringing me back from the brink of hysteria, each exhale a thread weaving me back into the present.

After a few minutes of ragged breaths, the tightness

slowly began to ease, and the room stopped spinning. He stayed by my side, breathing with me until I started to regain my composure. His patience was unwavering, his presence a quiet strength I hadn't realized I needed.

And I drew on it. I selfishly took everything this man, who was fighting his own battles, was giving me.

His arms still held me close on the cold hospital floor, as his steady breathing gradually silenced my thoughts.

"I got you," he said, both a promise and a reassurance.

His voice was a lifeline. I took another deep breath, this time feeling more stable, more in control. The darkness of panic continued to recede, replaced by a cautious calm.

Even after my breathing evened out, I didn't pull away. His arms were the only thing keeping me steady, and for the first time in longer than I cared to admit, I felt safe.

I couldn't explain why, but I did. It was something about him that made everything else fade.

And in that moment of weakness, I allowed myself to stay in the arms of a stranger that, for some reason, was exactly where I needed to be.

Our noses nearly touched, his gaze searching mine. There were so many emotions running across his face—concern, fear, empathy, and more.

After several minutes, I shifted, creating a small distance between us. Dorian let me go, but not before his hand lingered on my arm. A second too long, waiting for some confirmation I was ready, that I was okay.

"Thanks," I whispered, breaking the silence, pulling away as I stood.

"Anytime."

He offered his hand, his fingers brushing mine as he helped me up.

"I'm… sorry. That's just a lot to process. I didn't mean to lose it on you. You have enough going on today."

"It's okay, really."

"This was not the day I had in mind when I woke up," I said with a small, self-deprecating smile.

"Yeah, me either," he replied with a weak smile of his own.

A long silence stretched between us, both of us standing there, unsure of how to move forward.

EIGHT

Noah - February

SOMEONE TO STAY - VANCOUVER SLEEP CLINIC

THIS YEAR, VALENTINE'S DAY LANDED ON A FRIDAY, allowing me to send the kids home to their parents to handle the aftermath of their sugar highs over the weekend. My day was filled with the joyful chaos of card exchanges and laughter. Excitement buzzed through the classroom, leaving colorful paper hearts and glitter scattered across every surface.

For a few fleeting hours, my students warmed my heart, softening the sharp edges of loneliness.

Valentine's Day wasn't just an overhyped excuse to celebrate love—it was a glaring reminder of what I didn't have and what I wasn't sure I'd ever truly had. It was just me, alone.

But even *alone* didn't feel like the right word.

Single.

Was I single?

Being single implied a breakup, some kind of conversation—an argument, or at least closure.

I had nothing.

The FBI questioning me months ago left me anxious and

angry, but Dorian's revelation of John's true identity felt like my world had been obliterated.

Since then, the news broke. Everyone knew John was a murderer. More victims were linked to him—each death disturbingly similar.

They were all warped versions of Sleeping Beauty—painfully pretty and perfectly posed.

And that's what gnawed at me whenever I was alone with my thoughts.

Was I an exception? A placeholder? Or just the biggest fool in his elaborate, deadly lie?

The FBI offered no answers, only curt acknowledgments and a vague promise that they were working on it. But I wasn't sure what was worse—knowing the truth or being left to fill in the gaps with my imagination. And on days like today, when love seemed to exist in every corner of space, those gaps seemed especially wide.

A lump formed in my throat, and tears stung my eyes, but I blinked them back furiously.

I wouldn't cry. Not here. Not in the only space that brought me joy.

Instead, I let out a breath, straightened a stack of glitter-covered papers, and told myself that Monday would come soon enough.

I shook my head and stepped out of the classroom, my footsteps echoing faintly in the empty hallway. Pushing open the front doors, I was met by the cool drizzle of a typical Seattle afternoon.

Memories of John played on a relentless loop in my mind. Despite months of therapy, a part of me still felt irreparably broken.

My mother loved him as her own; my dad became the only father figure he'd known, guiding him in his career and helping John get a job at his company.

The rain fell in heavy drops as I walked through the overcast streets, the fading light of the February afternoon guiding me toward my apartment.

My apartment—not mine and Dotty's anymore.

She moved out, and I couldn't blame her—she'd found her happily ever after, but I now had to face this new reality on my own. She'd invited me more than once to join her in Woodstone Falls. But I couldn't.

I needed to prove, even if it was only to myself, that I wasn't running away.

As I walked, a faint whimper caught my attention from an alley to my right. I hesitated, but curiosity and concern nudged me closer. The small cries grew louder, fragile and desperate against the sound of the rain. I moved carefully toward the sound.

Then I saw it—a dog, crumpled on the cold, wet ground. Its wide, frightened eyes locked onto mine, pleading silently for help. Something in that gaze twisted deep in my chest, a reflection of the loneliness I'd been carrying.

Abandoned. Vulnerable. Lost in a world that clearly turned its back on him. The same ache in my heart, the weight of betrayal and solitude—it was all there, reflected in his limp body.

But here, at least, I could do something. I couldn't fix my broken pieces, but I could help him.

He was a small Shiba, his wet fur matted with mud. A patchwork of browns and black marked his coat while his eyes were a deep brown. He tried to stand but refused to put weight on one of his legs, clearly injured.

"Hey there, buddy," I murmured, reaching out a tentative hand. He flinched slightly but didn't pull away. "It's okay. I'm here to help you." I knelt beside him.

I pulled out my phone, the chill biting at my stiff fingers.

Should I look up an emergency vet? Call animal control?

The rain poured harder, each drop striking the screen that blurred the display. My fingers fumbled uselessly, the moisture making every swipe a struggle.

What the hell am I supposed to do?

My breath hitched as I stared at the glowing mess, the answer nowhere in sight.

I stopped, forcing myself to take a deep breath. Panicking wouldn't help me or this dog.

Then suddenly, I remembered—Dorian was a vet.

Of course he was.

I'd even blurted out some awkward comment about him liking puppies…

Now is not the time to revisit that particular train wreck of a memory.

Dorian could help, at least tell me what to do. I felt an immediate rush of relief and dread all at once.

I tapped his name, holding the phone to my ear, hoping he'd answer quickly. I continued to pet the dog's side, my breaths more even now.

He answered on the second ring, his voice a low timbre. "Hello?"

"Dorian, I need your help," I said, keeping one hand on the dog's side, feeling the faint rise and fall of his breath.

"What's wrong?"

"I found a dog in an alley near my apartment. He's hurt and… I'm… I'm not sure what to do."

"Is he bleeding?" he asked, his tone immediately shifting to one of focused concern.

"I don't think so," I replied, peering through the gloom to better assess the dog's condition. "But his paw looks broken, and he's really dirty and scared."

"Are you close to your apartment?"

"Yeah, just a few blocks away," I replied.

"Okay," he replied. "I know a vet nearby. Send me your location."

I tapped at my phone, quickly sending off my cross streets. "Okay, just sent it."

"Got it. Let me get ahold of her."

"Yeah, of course. Thanks," I said, and then the line went dead.

A few minutes later, he called me back to let me know someone was on the way. He then guided me through each step, carefully explaining how to keep the dog comfortable and what to do until she arrived.

I followed his instructions. His patience was a tangible force, grounding me in the moment.

For a few seconds, the noise in my head quieted as I focused. A silence stretched between us, and I found myself absently rubbing the dog's side.

Finally, Dorian's voice broke through the silence. "Noah?"

"Yeah?"

He paused, and I could hear the slight shift, like he was carefully choosing his next words. "Are you sure he's a boy?" He chuckled, giving me something to focus on.

I blinked, momentarily caught off guard by the question. I looked down at the dog, his head resting on my knee, and gently examined him. "I guess I just assumed," I said, the tension slowly unwinding as I focused on the task at hand. "But definitely a boy. Poor guy's had a rough day."

"You're doing great. Sarah should be there soon."

"Thanks," I replied, a sigh of relief slipping out. "Honestly, I don't know what I would've done without you."

"You can always call me," he said. A beat of silence passed before he added, "How have you been?"

"I'm fine," I said, giving him the default answer everyone had received from me lately.

"I've been think—" There was a sudden silence on the other end. Then he said, "Worried about you."

"I'm good, really," I said, the lie slipping off my tongue a little too quickly. "Thanks for checking in, though. It means a lot."

There was another pause, but this one felt different. "Well… I'm glad you're doing okay," Dorian said, his tone quieter, like he was giving me space but still reaching out.

My heart gave an unexpected flutter, something about his voice doing things I wasn't ready for.

Nope, not again.

"Yeah," I replied, my voice a little softer than usual. "Me too."

I focused on keeping the dog calm, continuing to murmur softly to it. The rain fell steadily around us. I was soaked, but I hardly noticed as I kept my attention on the dog, my heart aching for the pain he was in.

The patter of rain was broken by the sudden flash of headlights cutting through the mist. They shimmered on the wet pavement as the car slowed to a stop nearby, the tires swishing through the water.

"Looks like she's here now. I'll let you go. Thank you," I said.

"I'll check in later. Let me know how it goes," he replied.

Sarah, the vet, stepped out with an umbrella and a smile, her presence comforting. Together, we gently lifted the dog into her car, careful not to jostle his injured paw.

"Let's get you both out of this weather," Sarah said kindly, nodding for me to join her.

We drove to her clinic, where she quickly took the dog

inside for a thorough examination, and I felt a sense of relief knowing the dog was in capable hands.

After a few hours, a vet bill I hadn't anticipated, and a stop at the pet store for supplies, I found myself back at my apartment with an unexpected new companion. He wasn't registered to anyone. I posted to a few local lost and found pet pages, but Sarah said it was rare that a dog in this condition was lost, most likely abandoned.

But at least now, he was cleaned up and bandaged, curled up next to me on the couch. Luckily, nothing too serious seemed to be wrong—just a sprained ankle and some scrapes.

I quickly typed out a message to Dorian to update him. His reply came almost instantly, making me smile, despite the exhaustion tugging at me.

ME

He is doing well now, and I apparently have a new pet, assuming no one claims him.

DORIAN

Glad to hear it went well. Think of a name yet?

ME

No, any suggestions?

I paused, taking a quick picture, his floppy ear all askew, and hit send.

DORIAN

He looks like a Stewart to me.

ME

Stewart is an awful name.

I couldn't help but laugh at the suggestion. It felt good to smile again outside my classroom.

DORIAN

Fair enough. What about Walker? It's a strong name.

ME

You really think he looks like a Walker?

DORIAN

Absolutely. Got that kind of serious vibe, you know?

He stretched out on his side, chewing at the edge of the blanket.

ME

Hmm, I don't know. I think he's got a bit more mischief in him than serious.

DORIAN

Mischief, huh? Could be a sign you two are a perfect match.

I smiled at that. Maybe he was right. The dog might be exactly what I needed in my life right now.

ME

Ha, funny. *eye roll*

DORIAN

I'll let you decide, but my vote's on Walker.

He now nestled against my leg, his head resting lightly on my knee. He looked so peaceful, and it seemed like we were starting to build some rapport. I reached down and gently scratched behind his ear, earning a soft, contented sigh from him.

"What do you think, buddy? How does Walker sound?"

He lifted his head slightly at the sound of my voice, his ears perking up as if he understood. He gave a content whine, then nuzzled closer to my side, his tail giving a small thump against the couch. It wasn't exactly a verbal answer, but it was close enough.

ME

Yeah, I think Walker it is.

The thought of Walker, all alone just a few hours ago, now curling up beside me, brought a strange feeling of peace.

It was a connection, simple and uncomplicated. Something that didn't carry the weight of my past or the noise in my head. I hadn't realized how much I needed it—how much I needed him—until I wasn't alone anymore.

NINE

Dorian - April

___

DAZED & CONFUSED - RUEL

THE USUAL CLATTER OF THE CLINIC ECHOED AROUND ME. DOGS barking, and a low murmur of voices in the waiting room. I thumbed through the pile of papers, most of it routine— vaccine schedules, intake forms, lab reports.

Everything was as it should be. Normal. Boring, even.

But even as I tried to focus on the task at hand, there was only one thing I could think about.

Noah.

My mind had been consumed with her lately, whether I wanted it to be or not. Awake or asleep, she was there. I dreamed of her, what her laugh would sound like when I was lucky enough to hear it, the way her skin would feel under my fingertips. The way she'd taste if I ever got close enough.

She hovered in the back of my mind, refusing to be ignored. It had been months since I'd last seen her. But no amount of time seemed to lessen the grip she had on my thoughts.

The sharp buzz of my phone against the countertop

jolted me out of my thoughts. My heart stuttered, hope flaring even though I knew better.

I flipped the phone over, the name on the screen immediately dousing that second of hope.

Dotty.

I released a tortured sigh as I registered the name and flipped my phone back over.

It wasn't that I didn't want to talk to Dotty—I did. But when it was Noah, it was different. I wanted to know how she was doing, what she was up to.

My mind was playing a constant battle of tug-of-war, moving between confusion and intrigue.

I tried focusing on the clinic, on what I knew, and not on the things I had no business thinking about.

But I wanted more.

Fuck, I wanted her.

I hated myself for it, but I couldn't stop. Everything I touched seemed to turn to ash, and I didn't know if I could live with myself if I brought her down with my fire.

I ran a hand over my face, gritting my teeth, as a faint squeak sounded against the linoleum floor, and Jennifer, one of the vet techs, stood in the doorway.

"Are you alright?" she asked.

My hands braced against the counter as my eyes drifted to the phone resting beside me. "Yeah… yeah, I'm good," I lied. Pushing off the counter, I let out a sigh and laced my hands behind my head.

She didn't look convinced. "Let me handle the next intake while you take a breather," she offered.

My arms dropped from behind my head and swung to my sides. "Thanks, I'll take five real quick."

She nodded in response before heading out to the waiting room. I took that as my cue and made my way to one of the doors leading to the back of the clinic.

The cold air hit my skin, and the overcast sky mirrored the storm brewing in my head. I walked over to the fence and leaned against it. The cold metal pressed into my side. My breathing slowed, but my thoughts didn't.

They never did.

What was it about her? Why couldn't I let it go?

Why had my life, which I'd been perfectly content living alone before, suddenly changed the moment I walked through her apartment door months ago?

It didn't help that she was going through so much already, and I didn't want to add insult to injury. The woman found out her boyfriend was a serial killer—there is no way you can go through that sort of thing on your own.

I surely wouldn't want to.

Maybe that's what drew me to her—knowing she deserved so much more than what life had handed her lately. We barely knew each other. We'd barely spoken, and yet…

The way she looked at me when I comforted her in the hospital. The way she called me for help when she found Walker. And even the way she said she was fine when I knew that was a lie.

There was a vulnerability in every exchange we had, something that let me see deeper than what she showed to everyone else. And damn, it sucked me in.

My intentions weren't exactly pure. I wanted her. I almost *needed* her.

After a few minutes, the door creaked open behind me, and Jennifer's voice carried over. "Ready when you are."

I glanced back and caught the concern in her eyes before she retreated inside.

The cool drizzle began to mist my face as I turned toward the clinic.

When I stepped back inside, Jennifer gave me a

rundown on the dog that needed basic vaccines and a checkup.

"The owner's in room two."

"Got it. Thanks."

I stayed for a moment, letting out a sigh. I glanced at where my phone sat on the counter, the screen dark and still.

I had to focus. There was work to do.

I shook off the lingering thoughts, pushing them to the back of my mind, and moved toward the exam room.

TEN

Noah - June

FOLLOW THE SUN - XAVIER RUDD

"What do you mean I'm being let go? I'm being fired?" I asked, my words trembling despite my effort to hold it together.

The school principal, a woman in her fifties, sat across from me. Her graying hair was pulled back into a neat bun, and her eyes, usually bright with encouragement and kindness, were now filled with genuine regret as she looked at me.

"I'm really sorry, Noah. The budget cuts for the next school year have been harsh, and we had to make some tough decisions. With so many veteran teachers, it's difficult. If it were up to me, you'd be staying, but the final decision isn't mine to make."

She slid a few papers across the desk toward me. "I'd be happy to offer you a letter of recommendation, wherever you decide to go next," she said, giving me a weak smile. "Take this as an opportunity for a fresh start."

While I knew her intentions were good, her words only reminded me of how others had been treating me for the last several months. John had been all over the news for months, and now that his identity was revealed, it was well-known that I'd been dating someone who turned out to be a serial killer.

I nodded, swallowing the lump in my throat. "Thank you."

"You know how to contact me if you need anything, professional or otherwise. I'm so sorry, Noah. You truly are one of the best."

We exchanged a few more words, her hand briefly squeezing mine in comfort before I turned to leave. The door clicked shut behind me, and the quiet settled in again.

On my last day, I began packing up my classroom, the finality of it sinking in as it marked the end of this chapter of my life. The once vibrant walls, now almost bare, seemed to close in as I sorted through my belongings. Every book, every flyer, felt heavier than it should, each one a reminder of dreams that now were impossibly far away.

Needing a distraction, I grabbed my phone and called for reinforcements.

"Hey, stranger!" Dotty's voice rang through the phone, light and full of energy.

"Hi," I muttered.

There was a beat of silence, then her tone shifted, instantly sharp with concern. "What's wrong?"

Dotty was the first person I called after the meeting last week, and hearing the change in her voice now made it sting all over again.

I hesitated. "Today's my last day."

"Ugh, I hate that," Dotty blurted, her frustration clear. "I still can't believe they'd do that to you."

"Me too," I admitted.

A heavy sigh came through the phone. "I'm so sorry, Noah." Her voice was soothing, always offering comfort even from miles away. "Have you thought about what you want to do next?"

I shut my eyes for a moment, trying to shake off the knot that formed in my stomach. "No, not really," I mumbled.

The uncertainty of my future was too big of a decision for me to make on a whim, and I wasn't ready to think about it. But time was running out, and I had no other option but to start figuring out my next steps.

There was a long pause before Dotty spoke again. "Ya know… you could always move to Woodstone." She hesitated. "Trent and I moved into the cabin, so his house is empty now."

I missed Dotty in my day-to-day life. Her company always helped keep the loneliness at bay, but I had only ever known city life.

There, I could blend in, losing myself in the crowd, but I feared a small town would offer no such refuge.

"I don't know, Dotty… What would I even do there?"

"Funny you mention it," Dotty said, a hint of excitement in her tone. "One of the teachers just retired, and they need someone to replace her in the fall."

I took a deep breath, letting the possibilities run through my mind. Maybe it was time to try something different.

"You know what? I'll apply."

"Wait, really?"

"Yeah. I will."

Dotty squealed, and the sound of her excitement made me smile despite everything. "Oh, shut up," I muttered, though I couldn't hide the laugh that followed.

"I would have convinced Mrs. Williams to retire six

months ago, if I knew that's all it'd take to get you to move here," she joked.

"Sometimes I forget how much I miss you, and then you always seem to remind me." The words echoed in the bare room as I watched the way my rings twisted around my fingers. "I'm… just feeling heavy today. I think a change of pace might be what I need."

Dotty continued to be my rock, showing her support in a million ways. After catching up for a while, we ended the call, and I let out a sigh, still processing everything.

Just as I started to gather my thoughts, my mother's name flashed on the screen. I froze, staring at it for a moment, suddenly aware of the conversation I'd been avoiding. My chest tightened at the thought of explaining everything, knowing how she'd react.

With a sigh, I answered, setting the phone on speaker as I reached for the faded decorations on the bulletin board. I hesitated, pulling down a tacked-up flyer from last year's school play.

"Hey, Mom."

"Hey, sweetheart!" Her voice was bright. "How are you doing?" she asked.

"Um… Is Dad there?" I asked, moving over toward my desk and staring at the blank whiteboard. Somehow, its emptiness made the moment feel even heavier.

"Yeah, I'm here," my dad said, his deep voice steady as always. "What's going on, kiddo?"

What's going on?

Oh, just my life in shambles—a murderous ex on the loose and now the added joy of telling the woman who'd been less than thrilled about my decision to teach that my career derailed, and I'd lost my job.

My mom was vocal about her doubts when I chose this path.

You're so smart, Noah. Don't you want to aim higher? she'd said when I told her I wanted to change my major to education. It wasn't out of malice, but her disappointment lingered in the air like a specter. Even after years of proving myself, I still was trying to convince her I'd made the right choice.

I took a breath, forcing myself to push past the knot forming in my stomach. I swallowed, gripping the edge of the desk.

"Actually, there's something I need to tell you guys," I said, hearing the shakiness in my voice. I cleared my throat, glancing at the mess of boxes scattered across the room. "I was… let go."

"What? You lost your job?" Her voice rose in surprise, but there was no immediate anger, only disbelief. "I mean… I always worried teaching might not be the best idea, but I didn't think it would end like this. What happened?"

"Budget cuts," I defended, rubbing my forehead, trying to stave off the headache that had been building over the last week. "The school had to make tough decisions, and I guess being a younger teacher means I'm first on the chopping block."

"That's absurd," my dad cut in. "You've worked your butt off."

"I know, but it's not personal. It's just how things work," I said, even though it felt deeply personal.

I hadn't realized how much I'd tied my identity to this job, the kids, the classroom. The loss was harsh. There was a brief silence before my mom spoke again.

"So… what are your next steps?" she asked. I let out a sigh, staring out the window at the empty playground, overwhelmed by being asked this twice in one day. "I could talk to my colleagues and try to get you into law school. It's never too late." Her voice carried the same matter-of-fact tone I'd heard so many times before.

"I don't know yet, but I'm not changing careers."

"You know," my dad chimed in after a moment, "you could always come back home for a while. Be with family."

I smiled at his suggestion, while my gaze traced a crack on the wall, letting the thought sit for a beat. Sure, my apartment felt quiet without Dotty, but at least Walker was there to keep me company. Going back home would mean more questions, more of my parents' well-meaning but incessant probing.

"Thanks, but I don't think that's what I need," I said. "Dotty mentioned a job opening in Woodstone Falls."

"Woodstone Falls?" my dad repeated. "That's... a big change from the city. Are you considering it?"

"I think so," I admitted, my fingers trailing over the desk as I paced. "I just feel like I need a fresh start."

The faint hum of the line filled the silence. Then my mom spoke again. "We understand. It can be a lot. Have you heard anything about John?"

The mention of his name brought a tightness to my throat. "No," I said, my fingers stilling. "Have you, Dad?"

The silence that followed was heavier than any words they might have said. Then my dad finally replied. "No, nothing."

John had gone completely MIA, but I guess being on America's Most Wanted list would do that.

"I'm sure it'll all work out, whatever you decide to do."

"I know. Thanks, Dad." I blinked back the wetness starting to form in my eyes. "I gotta go. Need to pack up the rest of my classroom," I said, trying to sound more certain than I was. "Love you guys."

"Love you too, sweetheart. Take care of yourself," my dad said.

I gathered the last of my supplies, carefully placing them in a cardboard box. Each item held a memory—the mug from my first year of teaching, the framed photos of each of my classes over the last several years, the books I read aloud to eager young faces.

As I closed the box, I took a moment to look around. The room felt both familiar and distant, like a chapter of my life I was reluctantly closing.

ELEVEN

Noah - July

HOME - PHILLIP PHILLIPS

WITH A TRUCKLOAD OF BOXES, THE CUTEST, FLUFFIEST passenger prince you ever did see, and an unusual amount of caffeine coursing through my veins, I finally arrived as Woodstone Falls' newest resident.

I'd accepted the teaching position at Woodstone Elementary, set to start when the new school year kicked off. The long drive was grueling, but the thought of a fresh start was exciting.

The small town unfolded before me like a scene from a storybook as I drove in. Tree-lined streets wound through the heart of the town, their leafy branches creating a natural canopy that dappled the sidewalks with sunlight. Quaint, well-kept homes with front porches adorned with rocking chairs and hanging flower baskets added to the charm.

The early summer air carried the faint scent of freshly cut grass. A gentle breeze rustled the leaves, creating a soothing symphony of whispers. In the distance, the sound of a nearby creek added to the serene ambiance.

As I pulled up, I saw Dotty waiting eagerly in the driveway, practically bouncing on her toes with excitement. The moment I stepped out, she threw her arms around me.

I hugged her back, but she held on tightly.

"Dotty, I love you, and I missed you too, but I've been stuck in that moving truck forever."

"Sorry," she said with one last squeeze before letting go, her grin never fading. "You're officially a Woodstonian! Or… Woodstoner? I have no idea. But you're here!"

Trent strolled up behind her, wrapping an arm around her shoulders, giving her a soft kiss to the temple. "Let the girl breathe, sunshine," he teased, giving me a friendly nod.

Dotty rolled her eyes playfully and turned back to me. "How was the drive?"

"Not bad," I said, taking in the rolling hills in the distance, dotted with weathered barns and grazing cattle.

Trent's old house, my new home, was a charming single-story home with a wide wrap-around porch, perfect for lazy afternoons. Its white clapboard siding looked freshly painted, and the deep blue shutters added a pop of color against the backdrop of lush greenery.

It was perfect.

Colt's SUV pulled into the driveway. As soon as the vehicle halted, Sawyer swung open the passenger door and stepped out.

He made his way toward me with a smirk on his face. "Hey, Noah!"

Colt tipped his chin in a subtle, welcoming nod.

Just as I thought Dorian might have stayed behind, the back door swung open. He stepped out, and a rush of electricity shot through me, like my pulse tripped over itself. I took a breath, trying to shake it off, but the reaction still whirled beneath my skin.

Goddamn it.

Over the last several months, I tried to convince myself that his effect on me was purely situational.

I tried to dismiss the way his gaze made my heart race as mere residual anxiety after the whole ordeal with John, not because I liked him.

I definitely *didn't* like the man who texted me weekly to check in on my dog, or the one who helped me through a panic attack.

But as Dorian stood there, in his worn jeans, cowboy boots, and glasses that only seemed to add to the effect on me, I knew I was wrong.

So unfortunately, wrong.

"Officially a Woodstonian. Welcome," Dorian said, crossing his arms loosely over his muscular chest. His gaze briefly met mine, and my stomach fluttered.

I forced a smile, trying to keep my composure, but it was harder than I wanted it to be.

Damn it, why did he have to look so good? Why did everything about him seem to affect me so easily?

"I knew it was Woodstonian!" Dotty chuckled.

"Thanks. It's good to be here," I replied.

"It's good to have you here," Dorian said, his gaze briefly flicking to my lips before meeting my eyes.

I swallowed, the brief moment stretching out like a current just beneath the surface that I didn't know how to navigate.

Dotty clapped her hands together, her excitement bubbling over. "Okay, let's get everything unloaded!"

Sawyer grabbed the back of the moving truck, pulling it open with a dramatic flourish. "I call dibs on the light ones."

Colt rolled his eyes as he strode past him. "Says the professional athlete."

"I'm here for moral support," Sawyer shot back with a grin, already lifting a small box as proof.

Dorian said nothing, stepping forward to grab a heavier crate, his movements efficient. I caught his eye for a brief second, and the corner of his mouth lifted ever so slightly. My heart gave a traitorous lurch.

Dotty tugged me inside, chattering on about all the ways we'd make it cozy, making me feel at home. But my attention kept flickering back to the group unloading the truck—particularly to Dorian, whose presence somehow demanded my focus.

I did my best to ignore him as he unloaded box after box, his muscular arms flexing with each lift, his shirt pulling tight across his broad shoulders.

Honestly, those arms should not have been the center of my attention, but somehow, they were. Every time he moved, the muscles in his back shifted under his shirt, and I had to look away.

It wasn't just his strength that was getting to me. The way he grunted when he lifted something heavy, the sweat gathering at the nape of his neck, dripping down to his shirt collar—it all seemed so... effortlessly masculine. It wasn't until I caught myself staring a little too long at the way his jeans hugged his hips as he bent over that I forced myself to focus on something else. Anything else.

Because the last thing I needed was to get caught watching him like that.

A couple hours later, the truck was unloaded, and Dotty joined the others to fix the sagging gutter on the side of the house.

I stepped inside the house, walking through the living room, which was now a mess of open boxes and crumpled packing paper. I sank into a kitchen chair, sorting through the contents, carefully unpacking the items.

Then I heard footsteps behind me. I turned, finding Dorian in the doorway, arms crossed, eyes studying me.

Walker trotted over to him, tail wagging furiously as he sniffed at him with excitement. Dorian dropped to one knee to meet him at eye level, his hand outstretched. Walker leaned into him, letting out a happy whine.

"I'm glad you decided to keep him." He paused, then smiled—a small, effortless gesture that pulled at something inside me. His dimple flashed for a brief second.

"Well, no one claimed him… unless you count me."

"I *definitely* count you." Dorian's smile deepened as he scratched behind Walker's ears. "It's nice to finally meet you, buddy."

He straightened up, glancing around the room, his eyes briefly skimming over the mess.

"Need a hand?" he asked.

I paused mid-motion and looked up at him. "I've got it covered." I swallowed, then gave a half-smile.

He glanced at the box I was now neglecting, then back at me.

His lips pulled up at the corners. "You sure?"

"Yeah, you've helped enough today."

He gave a slow nod, not quite satisfied, but he didn't push it. I bent down to open the next box, but the edge of the cardboard caught my finger, and I let out a hiss, pulling my hand away instinctively.

"Shit," I muttered, inspecting the small cut.

Before I could even think of grabbing something to clean it, Dorian was there, stepping closer. His hand reached out, taking my wrist with surprising care. I froze for a moment, caught off guard by the sudden closeness.

"That's gonna need a bandage," he said, his voice low as his thumb brushed over my skin. His touch was gentle, sending a shiver up my spine.

"It's fine," I said, trying to pull my wrist back, but he didn't let go. "Just a paper cut."

Dorian looked down at my hand and then back to me, his expression tender. "Better safe than sorry," he said, his fingers still holding my wrist lightly. "Let me grab something for it. I think Trent left a first aid kit in the bathroom." Without waiting for a response, he stepped away, disappearing into the other room.

I glanced down at my finger, the tiny red line staring back at me. I was thankful for the sting, a sharp distraction that pulled my focus from being in his proximity.

He returned a moment later, and moved without a word, taking a Band-Aid from the small kit in his hand. I opened my mouth to tell him I could handle it, but before I could get the words out, his fingers were already at my wrist again.

He unwrapped the bandage with careful, precise movements before gently taking my hand in his. I could feel the heat of his skin as he placed the bandage over the cut, his touch tender and steady.

"Really, I'm fine," I said softly, trying to pull my hand back, but he still didn't let go, didn't respond, just smoothed the bandage into place.

He looked up at me from where he knelt beside me. His eyes were as captivating as the rest of him—deep, rich brown, holding something more beneath the surface.

Dotty's voice cut through the silence as the door creaked open. "How's it go—"

I jerked back, my hand instinctively pulling away from his, heat rushing to my cheeks as Dotty's eyes flashed between us.

Dorian stood, his expression shifting to neutral as he cleared his throat.

"Minor injury handled," he said with a forced smile toward his sister. "I'll let you get back to it."

"Everything okay?" Dotty asked.

I flashed Dotty a quick smile. "Yeah, just a paper cut," I said a little too quickly.

Dotty's gaze flicked between Dorian and me, a crease forming between her brows. She didn't press, though, and turned toward the door as Dorian stepped out.

"Have a good night," he called, the door clicking softly behind him.

I stood there, taking in the scattered boxes around me. The room, a mess just hours ago, was starting to come together.

As the evening stretched on, I found myself grateful for Dotty's company. We fell into a rhythm, chatting like no time had passed at all. She didn't need to stay, but she did, diving into the mess with me without complaint, making jokes to keep things light as we unpacked and sorted. Her laughter cut through the quiet, and I realized how much I'd missed this—her presence, her voice, her ability to make everything feel normal again.

Dotty suggested taking me to her cabin for dinner, but I waved it off, urging her to spend time with Trent instead. After a full day of unpacking, I was craving some alone time.

Crouching down to give Walker a scratch behind the ears, I whispered, "I think I like our new home, buddy."

His ears perked up, and he nudged his head into my hand, as if he agreed.

TWELVE

Dorian - July

FADED - ALAN WALKER

With the summer days stretching longer, my workdays seemed to follow suit, the hours slipping away as I juggled the constant demands of the clinic. Woodstone Falls might be small, but the need for a local vet was not. Between the ranches, the farms, and the families with pets, there was always something that needed my attention, whether it was a sick calf, a dog in need of vaccinations, or the countless checkups that seemed to line up without pause.

I was starting to wonder if it was time to bring on more staff. The clinic was growing, and my schedule was tighter than ever. I found myself squeezing in moments with Gracie wherever I could, sometimes stealing a few extra minutes in the morning before work or tucking her into bed at night. But at the end of the day, no matter how stretched I felt, she was always my priority.

Becoming a father was not part of my plan at twenty-three. Becoming a single father sure as hell wasn't.

But when Hallie passed away giving birth to Gracie, everything changed. I was completely unprepared for the magnitude of responsibility that suddenly rested on my shoulders. And yet, there I was. The sole person responsible for a tiny human, navigating a life I never imagined. There wasn't a manual for this. No one tells you how to hold everything together when you're grieving.

But Gracie and I, we figured it out. Slowly, at first, but we did.

We grew up together, in a way. I had to face the hard realities of parenting much sooner than I ever expected, but there was something raw and fulfilling about it. Life wasn't always glamorous. It was often messy, tiring, and overwhelming, but it was ours.

Hallie's death taught me a lot—lessons no one could ever prepare you for.

How to balance life with a newborn, how to survive on little sleep, and even how to explain to a five-year-old that the Tooth Fairy doesn't adjust for inflation.

But it was the little things, the everyday moments, that kept me going.

I had family, I had a community that had supported me from the beginning, but at the end of the day, Gracie depended on me. Only me. And I would carry that responsibility without hesitation, no matter the cost, because she was mine, and I was hers.

So, I kept my world small. Between my daughter, my family, and my work, there wasn't room for much else, and that felt safer.

Easier.

The cool air hit me as I stepped outside after a long day at the clinic. My phone buzzed in my pocket, Trent's name lighting up the screen.

TRENT

Hey, you got a minute to swing by the
cabin after work?

ME

Sure. What's up?

TRENT

Just get over here, jackass.

ME

Fine.

As I walked up to the cabin, curiosity nudged its way to the forefront of my mind. Dotty had done more than just fix the place up—she'd infused it with a piece of herself. The cabin still had its old bones, the same weathered wood and wrap-around porch I remembered, but now it felt… different. Alive, in a way I hadn't expected.

The white porch swing, still hanging there, unchanged, like it had been in place for years. The scent of pine filled the air, and for a brief moment, I let it take me back. Back to summers that never seemed to end, when everything was a little simpler.

I spotted Colt's SUV parked in the driveway and made my way inside. The cabin had a familiar coziness, with exposed wooden beams stretching across the ceiling. The walls were lined with family photos—some old, some faded—each one capturing moments of our childhood, holidays, and those long-forgotten summers.

Colt and Trent were seated at the dining table.

"Where's Dotty?" I asked, glancing around, half expecting her to jump out from some corner.

"I bribed her to go spend the afternoon at the bookstore," Trent replied with a grin.

"Why?" I raised an eyebrow, intrigued.

He scoffed. "Sit down, asshole, and let me tell you." Trent grabbed his phone from his pocket and dialed

Sawyer. His expression shifted to something more serious, but I could see the spark of excitement in his eyes.

"Hey. What's going on?" Sawyer answered, his tone familiar and relaxed.

"Hey, got you on speaker with Dorian and Colt," Trent said. He paused for a second before exhaling slowly. "I already talked to your dad and got his blessing, but—"

Sawyer cut him off. "Oh shit, you finally asking her?"

Trent laughed, low and satisfied. "Yeah, I am."

It wasn't exactly a surprise. I'd seen how deeply Trent cared for my sister. But hearing him say it still hit me harder than I expected. I wasn't bitter, not by any means. I was glad it was him—my best friend, someone I trusted implicitly. And I was happy Dotty found her own version of a happy ending, one that was crafted just for her.

But it made me aware of how much my own life had settled into a routine. Comfortable, maybe, but a little too predictable.

Sawyer's voice broke through the quiet, bringing me back to the moment. "Well, I've always thought of you as a brother, man. It'll be good to make it official."

"What he said," Colt added. His voice was easy, but his gaze was serious. He tilted his head toward Trent, his lips twitching slightly in a half-smile.

I looked at my best friend, nodded. "You're the only man I'd ever trust with her," I said, and meant every word.

We spent some time talking about Trent's proposal plans, tossing around ideas and laughing at how Dotty might react. But eventually, Sawyer had to hop off the call, leaving the three of us.

Trent leaned back in his chair, tipping it onto its rear legs. "Feels good to have people in here," he said, gesturing around the cabin.

"Yeah, right," Colt muttered, cracking his knuckles. "Makes you forget the shit we've got to deal with."

Trent's eyes narrowed. "What the hell's that supposed to mean?"

Colt leaned forward, elbows on the table, eyes focused on his hands. "Talked to Lilah. Got an update on John."

The words dropped into the room like a stone, sending ripples through everything. I stood up before I realized it and paced toward the window.

"And?" I prompted, the tension already thickening.

Colt rubbed the back of his neck, avoiding our gaze. "Lilah's got a contact at the FBI. Found out how they connected him to the murders."

"Go on," Trent's voice was tight.

Colt looked at us, his jaw set. He straightened, his voice low. "He killed his mom."

"What?" Trent's voice cracked, his palms hitting the table with a loud bang.

Colt nodded. His lips pressed into a thin line. "Yeah. She didn't fit his usual victim type because of her age, but he did it the same way. Same signatures. He apparently was a little messier than usual too, and that's what tipped them off."

My mind struggled to keep up with the horror of it. "Why would he do that?" The question left my mouth before I could stop it.

Colt's eyes were hard, distant. "She sent him to boarding school when he was a kid. Spent more time focusing on her career than being his mother. They think it was personal, not just another kill."

"That's… fucked up," I muttered, shaking my head.

Colt's gaze met mine. "And it gets worse. His patterns are changing. The newest victims all have a butterfly carved on their foot. No clue what it means yet."

"What the hell?" I asked.

Colt's voice was grim. "He carves them into the skin. On the foot, below the pinky toe."

Trent swore under his breath.

I took a step back, my mind reeling. I couldn't wrap my head around it, couldn't make sense of it.

"Why?" I asked.

Colt's posture stiffened, eyes fixed on the door, as if the place itself were suffocating him. "I don't know. He's changing it up. Sending some kind of message."

Trent scrubbed a hand over his face. "This is insane."

"None of it makes sense," Colt muttered. His eyes moved to the door again, his jaw tight. "I know there's more, but that's what I've got. He's gearing up for something. Like he's got an endgame."

I paced the room, fists clenched so tightly my nails dug into my palms. The thought of Noah tangled in this mess, blindsided by John's lies, cut through me.

She deserved better than a man who treated her like an afterthought when they were together, who deceived her while pretending to care.

"We can't let him get anywhere near Noah."

Colt's gaze snapped to mine. "We won't."

Trent sighed, rubbing his neck. "And now what?"

"Now," Colt said, his voice hardening, "We keep it quiet. Lilah's already in too deep. If this leaks, it'll come back on her."

Colt's phone dinged, and he shoved his chair back with a harsh scrape and stood, walking toward the door. "I mean it," he said, his tone final. "This stays between us. If this gets out and falls on Lilah, I'll kick both your asses. She's got enough going on."

I nodded; my words lost under everything that had been said.

"You got it," Trent said.

"I need to head out. Happy for you though, brother," he said to Trent.

The door clicked shut behind him, and the room fell into silence.

I stared at the empty space where Colt had stood, adrenaline still surging through me, now mixed with a darker feeling in my gut.

Turning away from the window, I faced Trent. He stood still, hands resting on the table, jaw clenched.

"You good?" I asked.

Trent let out a sharp exhale. "Yeah, it's just… not my favorite thing to hear. That my girlfriend's best friend's ex is a murderer on the loose."

"Well, Dotty's your soon-to-be fiancée, if she says yes," I added, a smirk tugging at the corner of my mouth.

Trent chuckled, but it was tight. "Very true."

I grabbed my jacket off the chair and shrugged it on.

"Well, I need to head out and get G to bed," I said, heading for the door. "But, hey—good luck with the proposal, man. This other shit will work itself out," I said, trying to convince myself as much as him.

Trent smiled, a little relieved. "Thanks. I appreciate it."

I nodded, stepping out the door, and I walked into the quiet of the evening, my mind still racing.

THIRTEEN

Noah - July

LITTLE BIT BETTER - CALEB HEARN AND ROSIE

WALKER SAT AT MY FEET, HIS EYES FOLLOWING ME IN THE mirror. He lifted his head with a small whine, the kind he made when he knew I was about to head out. It was as if he understood that the quiet evening we'd shared was about to end, and he wasn't too thrilled about it. I fidgeted with my hair, trying to coax it into a low bun that wouldn't unravel halfway through the evening.

Tonight was my first dinner with the James family. Dotty's stories about the unshakable commitment to Sunday dinners, no matter how crazy the week got, left me feeling both honored and a little nervous about being included. A family so dedicated to spending time together? That was a bit odd to me—nothing like my family's dynamic.

My mother was a force to be reckoned with. A top lawyer in Washington State, she commanded respect and had an unyielding drive for success. But her high expectations were relentless. While I admired her strength and determination, it often felt like I was constantly falling short, unable to measure up to the bar she set. Her approval seemed out of reach, and that was a tough pill to swallow at times. And my father was the glue that kept our family together, always stepping in to mediate our conflicts and smooth over the tension.

That's why I was looking forward to tonight—hoping for a glimpse of what it might feel like to be part of a family that truly enjoys each other's company.

Dotty insisted I come tonight even though I hesitated; I couldn't bring myself to refuse. After months of being apart from my best friend, it was the least I could do.

As I walked up to the front door of the ranch house, I took a breath, trying to push past the nerves. I could hear faint laughter from inside. Before I could reach for the doorbell, Dotty swung it open, greeting me with a wide smile.

"Noah! Come in, come in!" she said, pulling me into a hug. I sighed in relief.

Stepping inside, the ranch house felt how Dotty always made me feel—comfortable, accepted, and at peace.

She led me toward the dining room, and my eyes immediately landed on a little girl with blonde hair and bright, curious eyes, chatting with Colt. Dotty noticed my gaze and flashed me a grin.

"You've met everyone else, but that's Gracie," she said. "She's going into first grade, so she'll be in your class."

"Oh, I didn't know that."

"Don't worry. She'll love you," Dotty reassured me.

As I approached, Gracie looked up, beaming at me. "Hi! I'm Gracie. My Aunt Dotty told me that you are her best friend, so that means we will be best friends too," she said with a confident nod.

I smiled, crouching down to her level. "Hi, Gracie. I'm Noah—or I guess Miss Reid, since it looks like you are going to be in my class."

"Really? That's awesome!" Gracie exclaimed, bouncing

slightly on her feet. "Do you think I can call you Noah, though?"

"How about if we aren't at school, you can call me Noah." I smiled at her.

"Yay! I love school. My favorite book is about a unicorn that travels through time, and I'm really good at drawing them!"

"That sounds amazing!" I replied. "I'd love to see one of your drawings sometime."

"Maybe I can draw us as animals!" She eyed me, squinting. "I think we'd definitely be unicorns," she giggled, clearly thrilled with her idea.

"I'd be honored to be a unicorn with you," I said, charmed by her enthusiasm and creativity.

"Do you like any other animals?" I asked.

"Oh, yes! I love elephants and horses. They're so smart and very beautiful," she said, her eyes wide with excitement. "Do you have a favorite animal?"

"I think I'd have to say dogs," I replied. "They're smart and love a good cuddle. My dog, Walker, is a silly guy and always cheers me up." I pulled out my phone and showed her a photo of Walker curled up next to me.

"He's so cute!" Gracie said, turning to her dad across the room. "Daddy, can I meet Walker sometime?"

Dorian looked away from his conversation with Colt and Trent and chuckled. "I'm sure we could arrange that, as long as it's okay with Miss Reid," he said, and I glared at him.

I looked at Gracie, ignoring Dorian's intense stare. "I'd be happy to introduce you to Walker. Your dad was the one who helped when I found him."

"My daddy is a vet and helps animals!" Gracie said proudly.

"He did?" Dotty asked, her confusion evident as she chimed in from across the room.

I didn't usually keep things from her, but with her new life in Woodstone, her job, and happy bliss with Trent, I didn't want to overwhelm her with every little detail of my life. I guess that was one of the things I left out.

I winced. "Yeah, I called Dorian, and he helped me get in touch with a vet in Seattle."

Dorian glanced at me. "Noah did a great job and got him the help he needed quickly," he said, attempting to ease the awkwardness of the moment.

Dotty offered a faint smile, her expression saying more than her words.

I went back to my conversation with Gracie, her excitement impossible to ignore. She began telling me all about her favorite movies and songs, her bright eyes and animated gestures making it clear she was full of energy.

As we chatted, I couldn't help but notice Dorian watching us from across the room. His thoughtful expression, combined with his dark, slightly curly hair and sharp jawline, made him stand out. He was tall, only a few inches shorter than Trent, but his broad shoulders gave him a lumberjack-like appearance.

Damn it, why couldn't I have moved to a small town where people were just… friendly, and not full of rugged, five o'clock-shadowed men who rescued animals for a living?

I tried to keep my focus on Gracie, but I could still feel his gaze.

Dinner with the James family surpassed everything Dotty described and then some. It was in the way they truly saw each other, how they leaned into their relationships without hesitation. It was the kind of connection I wasn't used to. It wasn't perfect, but it was real. Sitting at their table tonight, I'd felt a rare sense of peace, like maybe I could fit into a picture like that one day.

Just for tonight, that small sense of belonging gave me a glimmer of hope.

I was ready to step into the cool night air and head back to Walker when footsteps sounded behind me. Dorian filled the space, those brown eyes of his zeroing in on me. For a moment, I forgot to breathe. There was something about the way he looked at me—like he could see right through me.

"Did you have a good time?" he asked.

"Yeah, it was really nice. Gracie's a character."

"She really seems to like you," Dorian said, his dark eyes catching mine again briefly before moving away.

"She's great. Super smart too," I replied.

He shifted his weight, hesitating for a beat before speaking again. "Yeah, she's… creative, curious, amazing…" He trailed off for a moment, like he was deciding how to continue. Then, as if it was hard to say, he added, "But she's been struggling a little with reading. Nothing too serious, but enough that I think she could use some help. I was wondering if you'd maybe tutor her this summer. Just to give her a bit of a boost."

"Of course," I said, meeting his eyes with a reassuring smile. "I'd love to help."

His posture relaxed, a small smile tugging at the corner of his mouth. "She really likes you. I try to help her, but… well, she only tolerates me for so long before she starts digging her heels in. Stubborn little thing."

"I wonder where she gets that from?" I smirked.

He let out a low laugh, his gaze holding mine. "Careful, Miss Reid. You're starting to sound like you've figured me out."

"I swear to God, Dorian," I said, pinching the bridge of my nose. "If you call me Miss Reid again…"

"You'll what?" He leaned in closer with that teasing glint of his.

I crossed my arms, trying to look serious, but I could feel my cheeks warm. My brain kind of froze, and all that came out was, "You'll find out." I blinked.

Fantastic comeback, Noah. Very witty of you.

Dorian smirked, stepping a fraction closer. "I'm dying to know." His tone was light, but there was an edge to it that made my heart stutter.

I swallowed, trying to steady myself.

Is he… flirting with me?

"Miss Reid sounds so formal coming from you." I gestured to his plaid button-up and worn jeans. "You damn lumberjack," I said. "I mean, look at you."

He gave a low chuckle, his eyes narrowing. "You know, I'm starting to think you like *damn lumberjacks.*"

"Funny." I let out a laugh that was clearly forced.

"Ah, I've been waiting to hear that laugh," he replied, his voice dropping to a smooth, almost predatory tone. "But I think I'll have to keep working at it until I get the real thing."

"I have definitely laughed in front of you before." *Haven't I?*

"Nope. I've been waiting." His eyes gleamed with a challenge in them.

"You have not been waiting for that." I rolled my eyes, unable to help the exasperated sigh that slipped out.

Dorian's lips curved into a grin that sent a rush of heat to my face. "Shit, do that again. I liked it."

"Do what again?" I raised an eyebrow.

"Roll your eyes," he said, leaning a fraction closer. The teasing glint in his gaze only deepened.

I couldn't help the laugh that escaped me, then internally scolded myself for it.

"Worth the wait."

I scoffed. "I'm going to leave now. *Goodbye*, Dorian."

I turned around to grab my sandals, but before I could take another step, his hand reached out, halting me. I turned to find him closer than I expected, his gaze softer now, searching mine.

"Thanks for coming," he said.

He pulled me into a hug, his arms wrapping around me hesitantly, like he wasn't sure if I'd pull away, but the embrace lasted just long enough to make my chest tighten.

I wanted to leave, to move, but instead I stayed there content in the safety of his arms.

FOURTEEN

Dorian - July

YOU SHOULD PROBABLY LEAVE - CHRIS STAPLETON

I took a deep breath, both to calm myself and to soak in the sweet, subtle scent of her, letting it fill my lungs. It wrapped around me, settling in my chest like a familiar warmth. I inhaled deeper, as if breathing her in might somehow ease the ache of needing her.

The feeling of her beneath my fingertips, so soft, so delicate, was almost too much to bear. My hand brushed over her arm, and the touch was electrifying, as though every inch of contact sent a current through my veins. She was fragile in a way, like something precious I wasn't sure I could keep safe. Before I could stop myself, I pulled back just enough to press my forehead to hers.

Her eyes fluttered shut, the lightest tremor passing through her, and I couldn't help but hold on tighter. There was no space between us, no gap to hide the way my heart raced, the way the tension wrapped around us tighter than I could've ever anticipated.

I knew I shouldn't have let myself touch her.

The pull toward her was undeniable. It was magnetic, a force that felt like it was tearing me apart from the inside out. Every second we spent near each other, every brush of her skin, only made it harder to stay in control.

Her lips parted as I brushed my nose against hers, moving slowly as if the space between us was as much about restraint as it was about desire.

I should stop. I should step back.

But with her this close, breathing the same air, I didn't want to. I wanted to stay here, feeling the way she melted into me, just for a little longer.

When her eyes finally opened, she caught me staring.

"Dorian," she said, her voice firm, but the way she looked at me told a different story. There was something more there.

Damn, my name sounds good coming out of her mouth. Too good.

"Yes?" I replied, my lips nearly brushing hers.

"We can't do this."

She's right. We can't.

"Can't what?" I played dumb, letting my lips hover above the corner of her mouth, aching for just one kiss.

One would be enough.

Right?

She repeated herself. "We can't do this."

But her resolve wavered as my nose brushed against hers again, tracing along the curve of her cheek before drifting to the delicate line of her jaw. Our actions betraying her words.

The anticipation between us growing with every second. The gasp she let out, the way her eyes softened when I moved closer—it was all I needed to know.

She wanted this too. She *felt* this too.

"We're not doing anything," I whispered, my lips grazing her pretty, brown skin as I spoke what we both knew was a lie.

I could go back to my life and get this damn girl who plagued my thoughts out of my head once and for all. With just one kiss.

Just one.

I wanted to close the gap between us, let myself fall into her completely, but I knew now wasn't the time.

Not when she was tangled in the wreckage of a relationship I could never fully understand. I couldn't let my own feelings blur the line between what she needed and what I wanted.

Colt's voice broke through the heavy silence, and Noah quickly turned away, her face an expertly crafted mask of composure.

"Sorry to interrupt. I'm heading out," he said.

He bent down to grab his shoes but then stopped mid-motion. I sensed his shift in energy before I saw it—his usual stoic expression melted away, replaced with something unreadable. His eyes locked onto Noah's foot, and for a second, I didn't understand what was happening.

"Dorian," Colt said, his tone alarmed. "Look."

"What?" I asked. The expression in his eyes wasn't one I'd seen from him often. It was serious, urgent. Then the recognition dawned, and I followed his gaze to her foot.

The tattoo.

Her tattoo.

For a brief moment, I kept my face impassive, but the shock from seeing a damn butterfly tattooed on her foot nearly burned me alive.

I didn't want to believe it. But I knew what it meant.

Her startled laugh didn't fool me. I could sense the defensive edge in her voice. "What? Why?" she asked, trying to brush it off, but the tension between us thickened. "Do you have some kind of foot fetish I should know about?"

"Noah, please." Colt's voice softened in a way that caught me off guard. It wasn't like him to sound so vulnerable, especially not about something so serious.

She shook her head, trying to laugh it off. "Is this some kind of joke?" she asked. "It's just a tattoo."

I stepped forward. I didn't want to touch her in a way that would push her, but I needed to know. I knelt in front of her, my eyes on the tattoo as my hand hovered near her foot.

For a beat, I hesitated, meeting her gaze with a silent question. Her eyes were wide, but then she nodded.

I grabbed her sandal, slipping it off gently, my thumb brushing against her skin as I did, needing to offer some sense of reassurance.

The butterfly tattoo burned into my mind as I stared at it.

"It's not just a tattoo," I muttered under my breath, my voice barely audible, more to myself than anyone else.

"Fuck," Colt said, his voice dropping into something darker. He was no longer the unaffected professional I knew—there was worry there, too much of it.

"Can someone tell me what the hell is going on?" Noah demanded, her tone growing more desperate.

I pulled my hand back, feeling her skin slipping from my fingertips.

Colt's jaw clenched tightly. "It's identical to the mark on John's most recent victims."

"What? What mark?" Noah's voice cracked, the panic creeping in.

"He's carving a butterfly, just like this, into the victims' feet," Colt said, his voice filled with the grim weight of truth.

This wasn't a coincidence.

I could see it in her eyes before she said anything. All

the doubt, all the confusion she'd carried with her over the last several months, crumbling into one hard, undeniable truth.

My first instinct was to close the distance between us, to find some way to ease the pain that had so clearly broken her down. I wanted to tell her it'd be okay, but that was a lie, and we both knew it.

"No," Noah whispered, shaking her head in disbelief, her breath catching in her throat. "No, this can't be…" Her lips parting slightly as if to speak, but nothing came.

I hated seeing her like this.

I hated the way this situation robbed her of her strength, the way it pulled her into something she never asked for. I wanted to tell her that I'd make sure nothing else happened to her. That I wouldn't let her face this alone.

But I couldn't.

She stepped toward the bench by the door, and then lowered herself slowly, almost mechanically. Her hands pressed flat against her thighs.

"How could he do this?" she whispered.

I exchanged a glance with Colt, and in that split second, we didn't need to communicate the urgency. We both knew. We had to get to the bottom of this.

This wasn't just about John killing women anymore, nor just about Noah being left to grapple with the wreckage of his betrayal.

It was worse. He was dragging her into the darkness he'd created.

She deserved more than to be left floundering in the mess he'd made. She deserved the truth, to understand if she'd unknowingly been woven into the twisted reasoning he used to justify his crimes.

But a darker thought gnawed at me—what if they

couldn't uncover the truth? And worse, what would it mean for Noah if we did?

Her head dropped into her hands. Her fingers threaded through her hair before pressing hard against her temples. She stayed like that for a moment, her breathing uneven, the sound cutting through the silence.

She lifted her head, her eyes sharp as they locked onto Colt, avoiding me. "I don't understand. I've known him for half my life. Dated him off and on for years. He basically calls my parents Mom and Dad." Her tone grew sharper, the edge unmistakable as she gestured at Colt. "He was there when I got this damn butterfly. Why is he doing this to me?" Her voice rose, full of anger and disbelief, her composure fraying at the seams.

I moved closer. Gently, I took her hand, offering her something solid to hold on to, even if I knew it wasn't my place. I wanted to be there for her, though I couldn't shake the guilt that maybe I shouldn't be.

Her gaze finally met mine, and the storm in her eyes hit me hard—the sadness, the fear, the hollow ache of betrayal. I was looking at the shards of a life shattered by someone she'd trusted.

Noah had this way of slipping past every defense I'd ever built, making me feel like I couldn't stay away. Like I needed to be near her. To shield her from everything closing in.

But I couldn't let myself get pulled in. Not by her, not by anyone. And yet, it terrified me how easily she unraveled me in ways no one else ever had.

She shook her head slowly, drawing in a long, uneven breath. Her shoulders rose and fell as she exhaled, her voice softer this time. "Shit, I'm sorry, Colt. This isn't your fault..."

"No need to apologize. Anyone would be upset by

this." He ran a hand across his long hair that was pulled back, glancing out the window before returning his gaze to her.

"What can I do to help?" she asked.

"Do you think you could handle being questioned again?"

Before she could respond, I cut in, my voice sharp. "Absolutely fucking not."

The idea of Noah getting dragged deeper into this mess made my blood run cold. She was already too close to the nightmare, and I would do anything to keep her away from it.

"I'll do it if it helps," Noah said, her voice calm, but her clenched jaw and the tautness in her shoulders showed how much it cost her to speak with such assurance.

"You don't need to get involved in this," I insisted, my grip tightening on her hand, unwilling to let go.

Her gaze locked with mine, sharp and resolute. "I'm already involved, Dorian," she said, the words carrying a quiet strength as she fought to hold herself together. The tears were close to falling, but she blinked them away.

Colt cleared his throat, pulling our focus back to him. "From what I know, they haven't connected you to this yet, but..." His gaze moved to her tattoo. "This ties you to it."

Noah shivered, her eyes widening as disbelief and fear flashed across her face. "I'll do it," she whispered.

Colt stood a little straighter, his jaw set. "I'll make the call."

"I still can't believe I was so close to him and had no idea. He was out there killing people, and I had no clue. And now he's bringing me into it?"

"We'll make sure you're safe," Colt reassured her, already pulling out his phone. "I'll get things in motion."

He gave a nod to both of us and moved into the other room.

"You don't have to face this alone," I said.

Noah's composure broke. Without thinking, I pulled her up into my arms, feeling the tremors rip through her small frame. She barely reached my chest, her body shaking as her emotions finally spilled out.

And damn, I didn't want to let go. I didn't want to move away from her, not when all I wanted was to keep her safe, to protect her.

After a few moments, she moved back to look up at me. Her eyes were red-rimmed and swollen, but still, she was the most beautiful thing I'd ever seen.

"Sorry," she muttered, forcing a laugh. Her smile was there, but it didn't quite reach her eyes. "I guess I have a habit of falling apart in front of you."

"You're allowed to fall apart with me. Actually, I prefer it if it means you end up in my arms."

Her eyes widened, as if I'd caught her off guard.

Her dark hair, once perfectly styled, now had a few loose curls that framed her face. She looked younger this way, more vulnerable.

I instinctively reached up, tucking a loose strand of hair behind her ear. My fingers grazed her skin, and I noticed the slight catch in her inhale, the way her eyes softened at my touch.

"I'm fine, really. Just a little overwhelmed," she said, trying to sound composed. "I need to go home and process."

"Okay. I'm here if you want to talk."

"Thanks. Goodnight, Dorian."

And just like that, she was through the door.

"Goodnight, Noah," I called after her.

She stopped and turned, offering a small smile that didn't quite meet her eyes.

Fuck.

I turned to head back into the kitchen but stopped short when I saw Dotty glaring at me. The moment she spotted me, she stormed over, her finger jabbing into my chest like she was trying to burn a hole through me.

"Are you fucking kidding me, Dorian?" she snapped, her voice seething with fire.

I straightened, trying to keep cool, but the knot in my stomach told me I was in for it.

"What?" I asked.

"What? *What?*" She let out a sharp sigh, disbelief thick in her voice. "How about you hitting on my best friend? You know, the one who's still reeling after her ex turned out to be a fucking serial killer?"

"I'm well aware of her situation."

"You're one to talk, though, Dot. Considering you're dating your brother's best friend," Trent chimed in with a laugh, clearly enjoying the show.

Dotty didn't even glance at him. Her eyes were locked on me. She swatted at his chest without breaking her focus, silencing him.

"She's healing, Dorian!" Dotty shouted, low and protective. "She doesn't need you showing up and fucking with her head. This is enough already. She doesn't need anything else to throw her off."

I couldn't help the bitter laugh that slipped out. "What, so I'm just an asshole then?" I shot back, but as soon as the words left my mouth, I realized she was right. She always was.

"Yes, in this situation, you are," Dotty snapped, her eyes narrowing. "I haven't seen you with a woman since… well, in a long time. So don't act like you want anything more than a quick fuck. Go find your hookup somewhere else."

Her words landed, but not for the reason I expected. Not for the reason they should have.

Of course, I was attracted to Noah—anyone with eyes could see how perfect she was.

But the way Dotty threw out those accusations, like it was all about a quick hookup, hit deeper than I wanted to admit.

She had a point, though. I wasn't ready to give anyone more than that.

Dotty turned on her heel, her footsteps heavy with anger as she stormed off into the other room, leaving a heavy silence behind. I stayed rooted to the spot.

Trent cleared his throat, awkwardly rubbing the back of his neck. "That went well," he said.

"Sure did," I muttered, glancing toward the door where Dotty had disappeared. "It was overdue. Haven't pissed her off like that since she moved back."

Trent's expression softened, his earlier humor fading. "Look, I don't know what your intentions are, man. But Noah's important to Dotty, so she's important to me. Whatever's going on, if you fuck with my girl, I'm going to fuck you up." He smiled, but the underlying threat was clear.

"Everyone wants to kick my ass lately, damn," I said, trying to deflect. I patted him on the back, and he nodded, walking off, leaving me alone with my thoughts.

I couldn't shake the feeling that Dotty was right. Noah was healing, fragile in ways that made me want to protect her—even if it meant protecting her from myself. But the truth was, I wasn't the kind of guy who could offer her what she needed right now.

I ran a hand through my hair, exhaling sharply as I walked back toward the door Noah had walked out of.

It wasn't supposed to feel this way.

It couldn't.

And yet, the more I tried to push it aside, the harder it was to ignore the truth: that I was already in too deep.

FIFTEEN

Noah - August

FALSE CONFIDENCE - NOAH KAHAN

Dotty let out a long sigh, her fingers idly tracing the rim of her coffee cup as her gaze wandered out the window of Woodstone Perks, the local café.

"Honestly, I never thought planning a wedding could be this stressful. We're keeping it so simple, and somehow it still feels so crazy."

I smiled, watching the steam rise from my own cup. "Isn't that the point of weddings? Chaos with cake at the end?"

"Yeah." She smiled, her gaze still fixed on her coffee, the rich brown swirling lazily. "It will be at the wedding venue in town, with the mountains as our backdrop through these huge windows." She paused, her eyes lighting up.

I couldn't help but smile imagining it—a simple, intimate celebration. Nothing over the top, just something that felt like home. Their whole relationship had been that way, even the proposal.

It happened one quiet evening at the cabin, when he simply took her hand, pulled out the ring, and asked her if she was ready for forever. No theatrics, no speeches, at least none that were overheard, just the kind of honest simplicity that made sense for them.

Their love was timeless. Classic. Beautiful.

"That sounds perfect," I said.

"I'm so excited," she agreed, a soft laugh escaping her. "And I have the best maid of honor that ever lived."

I smiled at my best friend, who would drop everything to be there for me.

"Enough about me," Dotty said. "Gracie's out of summer camp, so your first tutoring session with her is coming up. Are you ready to see Dorian all the time?" I could tell by the way she asked that she was giving me space but not letting me off the hook. She knew we couldn't keep avoiding talking about her brother forever.

It had been weeks since that moment—I could still feel the heat of Dorian's breath lingering on my skin, like a whisper of something almost tangible.

It was on an endless loop—a silent reminder of what nearly happened.

Dotty hadn't said anything outright, but the tension between us had been building for weeks, hanging just below the surface.

"I was wondering when you'd ask…"

Dotty let the silence stretch, her gaze fixed on me. "Well?" she prompted, a single eyebrow arching.

I hesitated for a moment, then said, "There's nothing to talk about. It wasn't—"

"Bull," she interrupted. "It was almost something, from what Colt said." She leaned back and crossed her arms.

"I'm not exactly in a position to jump into anything right now, so you have nothing to worry about." I swallowed, looking down at my hand.

"Dorian… he doesn't get attached, and with everything going on with John now bringing you into everything," she said, looking down at our feet. "I just worry about you."

I thought back to the day I got the tattoo—an impulsive decision during one of those on-again, off-again phases with John in our early adulthood. I was looking for something to symbolize my independence, a way to assert my freedom from the expectations that weighed me down for so long from my parents. John, ever the charmer, was right there, urging me on.

The hopeless romantic inside me longed for a life that felt stable—one where love wasn't something to fear, but to hold on to. I imagined building a future with someone who understood me. But then there was my history with John. After everything he put me through, the idea of a love like that seemed like a distant, impossible dream.

"Where'd you go?" Dotty's voice brought me back to the present.

"Sorry, just lost in thought."

"Did… something happen between you and Dorian?"

"No, nothing happened," I said, my voice steady. "That day at the hospital… After everything went down, we were both barely holding it together." I paused, gathering my thoughts. "He needed someone, and so did I. We were both there for each other. I think that kind of... bonded us in a way. But we aren't anything more than friends."

Dotty shook her head slowly. "I'm sorry I wasn't there for you then," she murmured.

"Stop it," I chuckled, squeezing her hand. "You had a lot going on. You don't need to apologize."

Dotty let out a shaky laugh, a small sob slipping through. "Yeah, but you found out your boyfriend was a murderer on the same day mine was shot."

I smiled, though it was laced with sadness, and raised my coffee cup. "What a day for us both, huh?"

She met my gaze, her eyes full of both sorrow and understanding. "Let's not do it again," she said as she clicked her cup to mine.

As I pushed open the heavy door to Woodstone Elementary, a strange combination of comfort and anxiety curled in my stomach. The school was mostly quiet, with only the distant hum of a vacuum cleaner.

It was still summer break, and the hallways were nearly empty. I had gotten word that I could come by early to start preparing for the new school year and set up my classroom.

The floor beneath my feet gleamed from a fresh waxing, and I smiled imagining the students who would soon be filling these halls in the coming weeks.

I walked down the corridor, my thoughts drifting to how I'd arrange the desks and what kind of reading space I could create.

I rounded the corner and almost bumped into a woman hurrying past, her arms full of folders. She had a controlled mayhem about her. Her dark, shoulder-length hair was pulled back into a practical ponytail, with a few stray wisps escaping. She looked up, assessed me, and then quickly adjusted into a polite smile.

"Sorry about that," I said, stepping back to give her space.

"No problem," she replied, her voice clipped but not unfriendly. "You're the new first-grade teacher, right? I'm Miss Lane—Lana Lane. Fourth grade."

"Noah—Miss Reid," I said, trying to keep my tone light and professional. "I just moved here from Seattle."

She let out a short, amused laugh. "Big city girl, huh?"

She raised a brow with a hint of playful curiosity. "Well, welcome. Sorry I'm a bit scattered. Getting ready for a new school year always feels like a sprint, you know?"

"No worries at all," I replied.

She studied me for a moment, hesitating. "You're Dotty James's friend, right? I heard a rumor."

"Yeah, she finally convinced me to make the move," I chuckled, feeling a bit self-conscious. "You know her?"

"Not well," she said, her tone relaxing into something casual. "I dated her brother forever ago."

My curiosity piqued. "Oh, which one?" I asked.

"Colt. Ages ago, though," she added, her lips curling into a faint smile.

Interesting.

"They are solid people," she continued.

"They're a great family," I said. "They've made me feel really welcome here."

"Well, since you're new here, a lot of the teachers get together once a month on Fridays at Outlaw's, if you ever want to join."

"Okay," I replied. "I'll think about it."

She smiled. "I need to get back to my classroom, but it was nice to meet you, Noah."

"You too," I said, nodding. She gave me a brief but genuine smile before walking past.

As she walked away, I felt more settled. I turned the key in the lock and stepped into my new classroom, ready to make it my own. The blank walls and empty desks awaited my touch, and for the first time since entering the building, I was hopeful for the future.

SIXTEEN

Noah - August

CONTROL - HALSEY

Sitting at my kitchen table, the house was quiet, broken only by Walker's soft snores at my feet. I'd done everything I could to keep myself in check this morning, knowing it was just the calm before the storm.

Colt and Dorian were in the living room, keeping their distance but close enough that I could sense them—especially Dorian. He was impossible to ignore, no matter how much I wanted to avoid the man and the feelings he brought out in me.

The sound of footsteps broke through the stillness, and Dorian appeared in the doorway.

"You ready?"

I didn't answer immediately, just stared at the cup of tea sitting in front of me.

I wasn't, not really—not to be questioned again and to relive it all.

I gripped the edge of the table, trying to steady myself, my fingers pressing into the wood.

Dorian sat down in the seat next to me. His knee

brushed mine, sending a ripple of awareness at his proximity, making my head spin.

"You don't have to do this, Noah."

I sighed. "I know… But I need to."

If I didn't, I wouldn't be able to sleep at night—questioning whether I'd done enough, if there was something else I could do to help bring justice to his victims or reclaim some semblance of my own peace.

He studied me for a moment before nodding. Then he leaned in, his hand resting on my thigh.

"If it's too much, do this." I couldn't think—only feel the pressure of his fingers, the slow rhythm of his taps—once, twice, three times.

"Okay…" I replied.

I exhaled as the tension eased—not entirely, but enough. His hand stayed there for a moment longer, solid and unmoving, before pulling back.

I finally nodded. "I'm ready."

I still didn't feel ready, but I wasn't sure I ever would be thinking about all the ways my life had changed lately.

There was now this shadow that haunted every second, every decision I made. Dorian didn't say anything for a long moment, letting the silence sit.

But then reality crashed back in, with the knock at the door shattering the fragile quiet. I pulled my leg away, but Dorian's hand lingered in the air for a moment before he stood.

The absence of his touch left a void, a stark reminder of how much I'd been leaning on him without realizing it. Our eyes met, and his gaze threatened to crumble the walls I put up after John.

Colt appeared in the doorway, his features pulled tight with worry. "They're here."

I nodded, swallowing hard and trying to control my breathing.

"You've got this," Dorian said, his tone leaving no room for doubt.

I stood, my legs unsteady beneath me, and trailed Colt to the front door. When he opened it, Lilah stood on the porch with two FBI agents behind her—the same ones I'd spoken to right after John disappeared.

I'd first met Lilah months ago, after Trent was shot. The details of that day blurred together now, but I remembered her steady presence in the chaos.

Standing on the porch, her copper hair framed her face. Her sharp features showed a glimmer of empathy breaking through the professional mask she wore.

"Noah," she said, her tone measured in a way that hinted at both care and caution.

"Hi," I replied. I swallowed, trying to clear the sudden dryness in my throat. Walker padded over, sniffing at the agents before offering a few snuffles and a wag of his tail. He retreated to his bed in the corner, curling up with a heavy sigh.

The man, whose hair was even more gray since the last time I saw him, stepped forward.

"Agent Roberts," he reminded me, offering a small nod, his voice measured, carrying a note of authority.

Next to him, the brunette woman spoke. "Agent Garcia," she said as a reminder, her tone softer yet still professional.

"Thank you for your time," Agent Roberts said.

Lilah stepped forward, her movements deliberate. "The FBI is leading this case," she explained, "but I wanted to be here since this is my jurisdiction."

She entered the room, the agents trailing behind her. I

sank onto the couch but forced myself to sit straighter, my hands restless against my lap.

Dorian sat beside me, his presence anchoring me with the support I needed. Colt stood behind the couch, his shoulders squared and his stance rigid, prepared for whatever this moment might bring.

The agents positioned themselves in the seats across from me, while Lilah stood off to the side of them.

Agent Garcia placed a thick file on the coffee table. The pages made a crisp sound as she flipped through them, her dark eyes darting briefly to mine, sharp and calculating.

"We're hoping you can help us clarify a few things," Agent Garcia said, stopping on a page and glancing up. "Colt mentioned you have a tattoo near your pinky toe. Is that correct?"

"Yes," I answered, keeping my gaze fixed on my hands. "I've had it for years. John was with me when I got it."

I slipped off my shoe and extended my leg slightly to show them. Agent Garcia leaned in, studying it closely without a word.

"Can you tell us about it?" she asked.

I hesitated, the memory lingering uncomfortably in the back of my mind. "There's not much to say. I was young and wanted to do something reckless after deciding not to follow the path my parents wanted me to," I said evenly, avoiding the sharper details. "John helped pick it out."

"He chose the design?" Agent Roberts pressed, his pen hovering over his notepad.

"Yeah," I muttered. "There were a few options, but he was the one who decided on the butterfly."

The words were bitter in my mouth, the association now tainted. I couldn't stop thinking about the same butterfly etched into the skin of another victim.

Agent Roberts flipped through the notepad, then spoke.

"The women he's been linked to all have... similarities. They're independent and high achieving, wealthy. Several were nurses, mothers, or similar caretakers in some way. We believe this may tie back to his childhood."

"His mom was a nurse... He wasn't exactly fond of her. But why is he pulling me into this now?" I asked.

"That's what we need to figure out."

"And in addition to that," Garcia said, leaning back slightly. "The last two victims displayed other details. We're hoping you might recognize something, anything, that could give us some insight."

I hesitated, unsure where this was going. "Okay..."

Roberts glanced at Garcia before continuing. "The first victim... she had earrings. Four total—two on each ear."

Garcia added, "The second victim had a few fingernails painted, only on one hand."

Confusion washed over me, my brow furrowing. "I don't—what does that mean?"

"Everything else matches the prior victims," Roberts explained, his tone careful. "The victim profile, the positioning—those remain consistent. These new details are deviations from the original pattern."

They both watched me intently.

"Does any of this mean something to you?" Garcia asked.

I shook my head, then stilled. "I'm not sure. I don't think so."

Garcia hesitated, then leaned forward. "Would you be okay if we showed you photos? Only the details we're describing. Nothing else."

The room seemed to press inward, and my pulse quickened.

I turned slightly, my gaze moving to Dorian. His finger brushed against mine. But it wasn't demanding, just a quiet reassurance. A silent question—*Is this too much?*

I focused on it, on the quiet strength it offered, forcing myself to stay in the present instead of spiraling into the nightmare of what John had done.

The need to know burned inside me. It wasn't only for myself—it was for everyone who'd been affected by all of this. I glanced at Dorian, noticing the subtle change in his expression, the way his lips turned down. I took a deep breath, meeting the agents' eyes and nodded.

"These are from the first victim," Roberts said, his voice more cautious this time as he slid the photographs across the table.

The first image showed the left side of a head, a small stud and silver hoop glinting in the light. The next photo captured the other side—another hoop and a simple stud.

I instinctively reached up through my hair, fingers grazing my own ears. Two earrings in each, just like the photo. My chest was heavy as I tried to push back the thought forming in my mind.

Garcia exchanged a sharp glance with Roberts but said nothing as he pulled out the next one.

It was a photo of a lifeless hand, fingers pale except for the deep emerald polish painted neatly onto three nails. My stomach twisted.

"That's..." My words faltered, and I cleared my throat. "That's my favorite color. It's called Evergreen." My gaze dropped to my own nails, painted in the same shade. I looked at Garcia. "I don't understand. Why would he— why would they—"

"We don't know yet," Garcia said gently, cutting in. "But these details—they're specific. We thought they might resonate with you."

I pressed my lips together, unsure how to respond.

These weren't random decisions John made on a whim. Nothing ever was with him. He'd always been methodical, precise in the way he handled people, his career, every detail of his life.

Lilah's expression hardened, her eyes narrowing slightly as she shifted on her feet. "After I heard about the tattoo, I feared this would be the case," she said. "He's fixated on you, for some reason."

"He knew everything about me. He knew my likes, my fears, the things that made me feel safe. And now he's going to use that against me, isn't he?" My voice sounded foreign.

Agent Roberts leaned forward, the wrinkles in his face deepening. "This could be his way of trying to communicate with you, or maybe it's a form of psychological manipulation. Either way, it's clear that you are central to whatever plan he has."

The room felt smaller, suffocating almost. John was someone I'd trusted, someone I'd loved. And now, all of that—every vulnerable part of me—was being weaponized against me in the worst possible way. My stomach dropped, the tea I barely touched churning in my stomach.

Dorian's hand swept gently against my thigh, so slight, so subtle that no one else would have noticed. But it was enough of something to hold onto.

"Anything unusual, any increase in aggression in the months leading up to this?" Agent Garcia asked.

I drew in a steadying inhale. "He used to ask me to come with him on business trips, but I couldn't just drop everything. At first, he was fine with it, but over time, he started getting upset, trying to guilt me into going. It didn't feel right, but I didn't think much of it until… Ugh, why is he dragging me into this?"

Garcia's face softened, but her eyes remained intent, unwavering.

"Does he know you were planning to move to Woodstone?" Lilah asked.

"No," I replied. "I didn't decide to move until after."

"Good," she said, her tone firm. "Stay vigilant. Always be aware of your surroundings. It seems like his recent victims have been further away, which is good. He might not know you're here."

"We'll make sure she's safe," Dorian said. His gaze moved to Colt, seeking reassurance.

"That's how family works," Colt replied.

For a moment, tears pricked the back of my eyes. This town—these people—they were becoming a haven I never thought I'd find outside the city.

SEVENTEEN

Dorian - August

I'M STILL FINE - THE RED CLAY STRAYS

As we stood in the doorway, I couldn't tear my eyes away from her. She carried herself with such strength despite all that surrounded her.

The agents questioned Noah for over an hour, dissecting her relationship with John like surgeons, peeling back layers she'd spent so long trying to seal. She'd agreed to the questioning, wanting him locked up, but watching her relive those memories unsettled something in me. Every time she spoke about it, I felt like I was selfishly unraveling right alongside her.

"Thank you for your time," Lilah said as she turned toward the others. Her voice carried a polite detachment, though there was something softer in the way she looked at Noah.

"Detective Dodge," Colt said to Lilah, his voice curt as he nodded.

"Detective James." Her jaw tightened, but she held his gaze for a moment before turning on her heels to follow the agents out.

"I'm headed out, too," he said, giving Noah a brief but meaningful nod. "Take care."

His footsteps faded into silence, leaving us alone in the doorway. Noah stood still beside me, arms crossed and gaze far away.

I turned and took the opportunity to observe her, trying to understand how she managed to hold it all together. She was so good at hiding it—like she could push everything down and not let it affect her relationships with the people she cared about. She was always so present for Gracie, Dotty, even me. But I'd seen the cracks before. I'd been there when she couldn't hold it together—like months ago in the hospital, even when we barely knew each other. And later, when she let the weight of it all show for a moment before locking it away again.

But seeing her like this, distant and lost in thought, I realized just how much she was carrying and how much she did alone.

And I hated it.

I wanted to reach for her, to take some of the weight off her shoulders. But I wasn't sure if she'd let me or if I'd be able to let her go once I did.

A bird's call snapped her out of her trance. She dropped her arms, but her eyes stayed fixed on the horizon. Her posture was rigid, but then, in a subtle move, her pinky brushed against mine. And that slight touch was both a question and an answer, an unspoken plea that neither of us was ready to address.

"You okay?"

She didn't answer right away. Instead, she rotated the rings on her fingers, lost in some thought.

"Sometimes," she said finally, her voice so quiet it almost didn't reach me, "I wonder if I'll ever escape this. If it'll ever really be behind me."

"You will."

"I let him into my life, into my home." Her voice cracked, her words trembling. "I didn't see it. I didn't see him for what he really was."

"It's not your fault," I said. My hand moved instinctively, brushing a stray curl from her face. Her skin was warm against my fingertips.

She flinched slightly, but didn't move away.

"Noah, you can't punish yourself for what he did," I said gently. "He fooled everyone, not just you."

For a second, I thought she might believe me. Her lips parted as if she wanted to say something but couldn't find the words.

It was impossible not to notice the way her mouth moved, the subtle twitch of her lips, the way she drew in a breath like she was steadying herself. I felt myself leaning closer without realizing it, drawn to her in a way that defied logic.

"You can't keep blaming yourself," I said, my voice firmer now. Reaching out, I linked her fingers through mine and squeezed gently. "You're the victim here, Noah."

Her lips quivered as she shook her head. "No, I'm *not*," she said, pulling her hand from mine. "The victims are the women he murdered. The ones who lost their lives. Their families—the mothers, children, husbands, wives. They suffered. Not me." Her words came faster now, tinged with anger and guilt. "I was barely a step away from being complicit."

"He was a master manipulator. He built lies so perfectly crafted you never had a chance to see through them. This isn't your fault. None of it is."

Her breath hitched. "But what if you're wrong? What if I missed something? What if—"

"Noah, stop." I cut her off, spinning her gently to face

me and tilting her chin up so her eyes met mine. "He's the monster, not you."

She stared at me for a long moment and then nodded. But the fear in her eyes didn't fade. It was still there, lurking beneath the surface, a constant reminder of the hell she'd been through.

"I don't understand this. I don't understand why he did this or how he did this or if I could have stopped it. I don't understand how a boy I met at fifteen, charming and smart, liked me, then decided to grow into a man who is capable of all this." Her arms flung out to her sides, but I let my thumb trace idle circles along her cheek.

"You know, someone really smart once told me, *you're allowed to be angry, to be confused, and to not know how to process it*. It's okay not to have it all figured out right now."

"I just... feel like I'm too broken to fix now," she whispered.

"You're not broken. You're stronger than you think, Noah. Stronger than anyone I've ever known."

Her gaze dropped briefly to my mouth, and at first, I thought I might have imagined it when she met my eyes again.

I could see the way her jaw tightened, like she was fighting with herself. But then it happened again, lingering this time. Her eyes darted back up to meet mine, wide and uncertain, but she didn't pull away.

Instead, she bit her bottom lip—just a small, nervous tug—and my chest tightened.

And fuck, I wanted to kiss her.

To kiss her and tell her it would all be okay. That somehow, I'd make sure she came out of this safe, and he ended up behind bars where he belonged.

But we were playing with fire, both of us.

I could see it in her eyes—not only fear of John, but

fear of this, of us. And she wasn't the only one who was scared. That fear twisted in me too, an ache I couldn't ignore. I was terrified of what would happen if I gave in, if I let myself feel everything I'd been trying so hard to bury.

I couldn't risk it.

I needed to be her support, her protection, not someone who confused her more than she already was.

I dropped my hands, clenching my fists to give them something to do before I pulled her back to me and found out just what it'd feel like to give in.

"We can't," I said. "Not right now." I pulled back, my chest tight.

Her face fell.

"Shit, Noah. It's not that I don't want to. *Fuck*, I want to kiss you every second of every damn day. I think of nothing except your lips all day, every day. But you've had a hell of a day, and I don't want this kiss to be one more thing you'll have to question later. I should go."

I wanted her to kiss me, to really want me. But I wanted her to when it wasn't about him, or today, or any of this mess.

"Yeah… You're right," she whispered.

Her eyes followed me, that same uncertainty lingering there. For a second, I thought she might say something, maybe even stop me.

But she didn't.

And so, I stepped back again.

Because if I didn't put distance between us, I was afraid there would be no going back.

I walked away, each step dragging me further from the porch and her. I turned for one last look to see she hadn't moved, her eyes fixed on me. This felt wrong, leaving her like this. But staying would only make it worse.

"Take care, Noah," I muttered, barely loud enough for her to hear, and opened my truck door.

And with that, I was gone. But I knew damn well that I wasn't leaving her behind. Not really. Because no matter how far I went, how hard I tried to run, she was always there. Haunting my thoughts. Plaguing my dreams.

EIGHTEEN

Noah - August

FEELS LIKE - GRACIE ABRAMS

GRACIE'S FINGERS MOVED SLOWLY ALONG THE LINES OF THE book, her lips forming each word with careful precision. Her brows knitted together, her focus unshakable, even when a particularly tough word gave her pause. We'd met several times over the last few weeks, and she was improving with each session.

"That was a tricky one," I said, offering an encouraging smile as she finally made it through the sentence. "But you nailed it."

Her face lit up, and a shy but proud smile lifted at the corners of her mouth. "Thanks, Noah." She hesitated, the tip of her finger tapping the edge of the page. "You know, I think I learn more from you than I do from my teacher. Or even from Daddy."

A genuine laugh escaped me. "Oh, really? Why's that?"

She tilted her head, considering her answer like it was a math problem she wanted to solve. "You make it... easier and fun. I can understand it better when you explain it."

My heart squeezed. "Well, you're working so hard. I'm so proud of how far you've come already."

Her cheeks flushed, and she looked down at the book, a bashful grin playing on her lips.

Moments like these were why I became a teacher—the small victories, the moments when a child's confidence grew word by word, step by step. That helped me study and learn and research everything I could to find new ways, tactics, and strategies to help my students. I wanted to be the teacher they needed. The one who they would remember when they were thirty years old, thinking fondly back to their childhood.

"Can we read another one?" she asked, her enthusiasm bubbling over. I nodded.

"Of course. Let's pick a good one."

As we continued, I noticed how much more at ease she seemed. It wasn't just about getting through the pages anymore—she was actually enjoying herself. There was something about that change that made me proud of this little girl I'd only recently met.

Eventually, Gracie set the book down and met my gaze with a serious expression.

"Do you think I'll ever be as good at reading as the other kids?" Her voice was small and uncertain, and the question tugged at my heart.

"Everyone learns in their own time. What matters is that you're getting better every day."

I leaned forward slightly. "Remember that drawing you made for me last week? It was amazing—better than what I could have done."

A small smile formed on her face. "Yeah, I do love drawing."

"And that's your special talent," I continued. "Some kids are great at reading, others are great at math, and you—you're fantastic at art. Everyone has something that makes them unique. Just because reading might be a bit harder right now doesn't mean you're any less smart or talented than anyone else."

She paused, her eyes thoughtful as she processed that. Finally, she nodded, a smile spreading across her face. "I guess I never thought of it like that. Thanks, Noah." Then, without warning, she hugged me.

After a few more stories, I glanced at the clock, smiling when I realized we'd already gone over our scheduled time. "Well… we are all done for today. You did amazing," I said, gathering all our materials from the evening.

She surprised me with another quick hug. "See you next week?"

"Of course," I replied.

I turned to leave, but as I stepped toward the door, I noticed Dorian sitting at his small dining table, looking up from something in his hands.

"Got a minute?" he asked, his tone casual but with an edge.

"Sure."

We hadn't talked much over the past few weeks—just a few messages about Gracie, making sure the tutoring sessions were set. After he admitted he wanted to kiss me—and how much I wanted it too, despite knowing it was a bad idea—I was more than okay with the distance.

Gracie burst into the room. "Hi, Daddy! Can I watch a movie now that I'm all done with my reading?"

"Of course. Remote's on the coffee table, G," Dorian answered, not even looking up.

"Bye, Noah!"

She dashed out, already halfway into the other room before I could respond.

"What's up?" I asked, taking a seat in the chair across from him.

His concern always brought out a certain intensity in his

eyes. "How's she doing?" he asked, nodding toward Gracie, who was sitting close by, now watching a movie but still out of earshot.

"She's progressing every session," I replied, as I watched her. "Honestly, she's really smart. I think she just might learn a little differently than what most consider the conventional way."

Dorian's brow furrowed, his dark eyes locking with mine in a way. "What do you mean?"

His tone wasn't defensive, just curious, like he was trying to piece it together. He always wanted the best for Gracie. It was one of the things I admired most about him—his quiet but unwavering commitment to the people he loved.

"Well," I started, shifting slightly in my seat, our knees brushing lightly under the table, the small contact sending a jolt up my leg. "Some kids don't respond as well to the traditional phonics-first method of learning to read—you know, where they sound out every letter and try to blend them. Gracie seems to rely more on patterns and whole words. She's more visual. She remembers how words look as a whole, kind of like she's memorizing pictures instead of sounding things out one letter at a time."

I paused, trying to explain it in a way that wouldn't feel too teacher-like.

"It's like… some people learn best by listening, some by doing. Gracie? She seems to connect with things she can visualize. So instead of drilling her on the alphabet, I've been using more visual aids—pictures with words, context clues, and repeating those visuals until it clicks. It's not about breaking down every word but seeing the word and understanding its meaning in one glance."

Dorian nodded slowly. His gaze moved to Gracie before shifting back to me. "So, she just learns a little differently?"

"Exactly," I said. "She's just as capable as any other kid, but her brain works differently in a way that the classroom may not cater to. Once we figure out her rhythm, she'll take off. We just need to teach her in a way that makes sense to her, not force her into a box that doesn't fit."

"Okay, got it." He cleared his throat, but worry was still etched into his features.

"You're a good dad. You're doing all the right things by letting her learn at her own pace," I said.

His eyes met mine, an unspoken understanding passing between us before he shifted back to his usual composed self. "Thanks. That… it means a lot."

"Only speaking the truth," I said, standing from the table. "I'm going to head out."

He smiled, his stupid dimple popping out and making my heart do a little pitter-patter. "Have a good night. Thank you… for everything."

"Of course," I said, shutting the door behind me and taking in the quiet of the night.

Dorian and Gracie had this way of making everything feel effortless, like it all just fit together perfectly. It was in the little things—Gracie's bright smile when she looked at her dad, the way he always made her his priority, no matter what else was happening. The unspoken understanding between them, the ease in which they moved through life together. It was love in its purest form—steady, unwavering, and completely natural.

That warmth lingered as I slid into the car, settling deep in my chest as I turned the key. The engine rumbled to life, but my mind stayed with them—the quiet bond they shared, the kind of love that didn't need words. It stayed with me, even as I drove away.

NINETEEN

Dorian - August

INVISIBLE STRING - TAYLOR SWIFT

The bell above the wooden door creaked as I stepped into The Pine Ridge Lodge, and nostalgia washed over me. The rustic charm was exactly how I remembered it—log beams overhead, a crackling stone fireplace in the corner.

The walls were filled with framed pictures of locals, each one adding to The Lodge's sense of history. It felt like stepping back in time.

I glanced around, nodding at a couple of familiar faces tucked into the corner booths. Woodstone had always been a place where everyone knew everyone, and The Pine Ridge Lodge was one of the places at the heart of it all.

Friday nights here were about as lively as it got—families gathering after football games, locals grabbing dinner after a long day, the kind of crowd that felt like home.

Every now and then, my dad would forego cooking, and we'd get takeout for Sunday family dinner instead. With school starting soon, it seemed like the perfect time to do so.

"You ever think about how long this place has been

here?" Sawyer asked, glancing around as we approached the counter.

Colt shook his head. "No."

I let out a laugh. "Look, Sawyer." I pointed to his picture on display. "You need to update this. That thing's got to be over ten years old."

He shifted his gaze to the picture. "Yup, that was my rookie year in the NFL. Damn, I miss those days."

"What, when you weren't old as fuck?" Colt said, deadpan.

"No, back when I had good knees," Sawyer shot back.

"Tough getting old, huh?" I smirked.

Sawyer gave me a knowing look. "You're right behind me, brother."

"Yeah, but I'm not getting tackled for a living, so I'll be alright," I replied.

Colt stifled a grin, glancing at Sawyer. "Once you hit mid-thirties, it's all downhill, regardless."

We reached the counter, where Mary Whitmore, one of the owners, greeted us with a wide smile. "Your order's almost ready, boys," she said, her tone warm and familiar.

"How's your mare holding up?" I asked, thinking back to the last time I'd been at their farm to see she was recovering nicely.

"She's doing great. Thanks for askin'," she said, smiling up at me.

"Glad to hear it."

"Oh, the golden boy vet, are ya? Hey, Mary, did you know my team is predicted to go to the Super Bowl this year?" Sawyer smiled, teasingly taking over the moment.

"I'll be watching. Although I did see that sack in the last game. Isn't it your job as a lineman to protect your quarterback?" she teased him right back, putting him in his place.

"I wasn't on my game that day. Give me some slack. It's still preseason."

"Super Bowl winners don't get slack," she replied, the corners of her mouth lifting.

Colt let out a low laugh. "She's got you there."

She handed over two brown paper bags filled to the brim with food. "Tell your dad I said hello, and if you ever need help with that little girl of yours, don't hesitate to ask."

"Thanks, Mary," I said as Sawyer accepted the bags.

We headed to the truck, and I slid into the passenger seat.

"Let's get home before Gracie convinces Dad to have ice cream for dinner."

Colt started the engine, and we headed back toward the ranch. The lights from The Lodge faded into the distance as we drove along the winding country road.

Stepping into the ranch house always hits me in the gut. Some of my fondest memories lived in every corner of this place. Sleepovers in the living room with Trent and Dotty, the three of us fighting over couch space, whispering and laughing until we finally passed out. Nights spent with my brothers, glued to video games until our eyes burned, laughing so hard our stomachs hurt.

And my mom—her voice echoing from the kitchen as she made pancakes every Sunday, Dad's old records spinning in the background.

It was all still here, lingering in the walls, reminding me of the life we once had. A life that changed overnight when she passed. Yet somehow this house managed to mold itself into something new over the years.

The ranch house would always embody her—more than anyone of us could. Even though I'd spent more time in it without her than with her, she was still woven into every piece of it. The ranch was a reflection of her love.

But there were other memories here too—faint, fleeting ones of Hallie.

She'd been part of this space, but not quite like my mom had. I was in my early twenties when Gracie came along, and it all happened so fast—Hallie's high-risk pregnancy, the whirlwind of trying to figure out how to be a dad while still feeling like a kid myself, then losing Hallie so quickly during Gracie's birth.

She gave me Gracie, and for that, I'd be forever grateful. But if I was being honest, I was never in love with Hallie the way people might expect. We weren't destined to be soulmates, bound together by some grand love story. She was sweet, kind, and would have been a great mother, but what we had was more… circumstance than fate.

Losing Hallie stung, but my world didn't shatter. It shifted. It reorganized itself around Gracie.

Initially, I didn't know how to feel, but I knew I had to care for my daughter.

There was a part of me that once imagined a life with a wife, our kids growing up together, telling stories about how disgustingly in love their parents were.

But Gracie was the one thing I never knew I needed. I was handed this fragile, perfect little girl, and in that moment, she filled every gap.

Now, I didn't want more than my quiet life with her. I didn't get attached in relationships because I didn't need to. I didn't want to.

At least, until recently.

But the hardest part wasn't the grief. It was knowing that my daughter would grow up without a mother, just like I did.

Hallie's loss was part of our story, and I always made sure Gracie knew about her mom. We'd talk about how much Hallie loved her, though the meaning of those words only really started to click for her recently.

When she started school, she noticed other kids had moms and dads, while she only had me. But we've made it work. Gracie has her village, a small army of people in her corner, even if she doesn't have a mom.

The ranch house wasn't filled with memories of Hallie the way it was with my mother, but sometimes, I could still hear her in Gracie's laughter echoing down the halls. Or catch a glimpse of her in Gracie's bright, expressive eyes—so much like Hallie's—as she climbed onto a step stool to carefully place the star on top of the Christmas tree.

I let out a slow breath, pushing those thoughts aside. Because no matter how much changed over the years, this place, and the people in it, were still my home.

Dad was setting out all the takeout food like it was any other dinner, but the house felt fuller tonight—maybe because Sawyer was home for the week or because Noah was here.

Sawyer was already at the head of the table, his arm loosely draped around Gracie, who was practically climbing into his lap.

The girl loved her uncles.

Colt sat to the right of him, leaned back in his chair, looking entirely too smug as he watched Sawyer try to wrangle her. I stood and watched the whole scene unfold, taking in how many people loved my daughter.

"Dang, he comes back, and you forget all about me, huh, G?" I said, crossing my arms.

Sawyer grinned like the cocky jerk he was. "She's more interested in my stories than your dad jokes. Right, Gracie?"

Gracie giggled, looking up at Sawyer with wide eyes. "Daddy, did you know Uncle Sawyer's the fastest runner in the whole world?"

Colt let out a low laugh from across the table. "Fast? Didn't you trip up the steps outside walking in?"

Sawyer shot him a glare. "That has nothing to do with speed, brother."

"Yeah, you're just clumsy and slow," Dotty cut in, smirking as she took a seat next to Noah.

Noah laughed beside her, nudging Dotty. "I was expecting a peaceful dinner again tonight, but this is already exceeding my expectations in the best way."

I couldn't help but smirk at that, moving to grab the pitcher of iced tea from the counter.

"You know, your mom used to always call the four of you the chaos crew," my dad chimed in.

"Can I be the new chaos crew?" Gracie asked.

"Well, there is only one of you, but I do think you cause enough chaos for four kids." I chuckled.

Gracie wiggled in Sawyer's lap and then turned her attention to Noah. "Noah, is Uncle Sawyer faster than Daddy?"

Noah's smile grew as she looked at me. There was something about the way her eyes lingered, weighing her next words, but she quickly turned her attention back to Gracie.

"Well, your daddy's got the brains. Uncle Sawyer has the… speed."

I couldn't help the grin that spread across my face. "Brains," I echoed. "Glad someone around here appreciates intelligence."

Colt, ever the smartass, muttered, "Someone has to. The rest of you are rather questionable."

Gracie's head swung back toward Dotty. "What about Aunt Dotty?"

Dotty didn't miss a beat, puffing her chest out in mock pride. "Oh, I've got the whole package. Brains, speed, and charm."

Trent looked at his fiancée, the dumb fuck, too smitten for his own good. "I'd agree with that," he said.

Sawyer let out a loud laugh, tossing a crumpled napkin in her direction.

"Charm? Says the girl who put gum in some kid's hair in elementary school."

Dotty rolled her eyes, grabbing the napkin and tossing it back. "That was warranted."

"Sure," Colt added, chuckling.

Noah leaned forward, resting her elbows on the table, grinning.

Gracie glanced up at me, her face full of innocent curiosity. "Daddy, would you put gum in someone's hair?"

I laughed, shaking my head. "No, I leave that to your Aunt Dotty. That's her specialty. Like she said, she's the whole package," I said sarcastically. Dotty shot me a look that was half amused, half defensive, and I couldn't help but smirk.

"Finally, some respect," Dotty said, bowing dramatically, reaching for a bread roll.

My dad, who'd been watching all of us from his spot at the end of the table, finally spoke up. "If you're all done bickering like children, we should eat before the food gets cold."

"Don't have to tell me twice," Sawyer said, already reaching for takeout containers.

The conversation moved on as we all started to eat.

Gracie, still sitting close to Sawyer, began talking about lessons with Noah, her new drawings, and everything that was currently occupying her six-year-old world.

She beamed up at Noah every time she chimed in with encouragement, like her approval was the most important thing in the room.

"So, Sawyer," Dotty said, leaning back in her chair. "Any big games coming up?"

Sawyer groaned dramatically. "Yeah, preseason's started, so we are getting back into the swing of things."

"Uncle Sawyer, can I come to one of your games?"

Sawyer grinned. "Of course, kiddo. But..." he paused, giving me an apologetic look. "What if I could do you one better?"

"What do you mean?" she asked.

"You know, I know some really important people who happened to give me tickets to Ellie Miles's tour."

Here we fucking go.

"And if it's okay with your dad, we can all go. It's right after Dotty's wedding."

I groaned.

"Wait, what about me? I thought I was getting married too?" Trent teased.

Noah, sitting quietly beside Dotty, smiled through most of the conversation, occasionally glancing my way.

I could sense her gaze on me, but I didn't meet it. Not yet.

Instead, I focused on Gracie, still perched in Sawyer's lap, firing off questions about the concert.

Gracie turned to Noah, tugging at her sleeve. "Noah, will you come see Ellie Miles with us?"

Noah smiled, though there was hesitation there. "Oh, I don't know about that, Gracie. I bet your uncle only got enough tickets for your family."

Sawyer's grin stretched wide, smug as ever. "Actually, I have a whole suite. Perks of the job."

Gracie's eyes lit up. "See! You and Aunt Dotty can come, and we can have so much fun!" she squealed.

Dotty laughed. "You know I'm not missing it," she said, a playful smile on her lips.

"Where's the concert?" I asked.

"San Francisco. Vista Stadium," Sawyer replied, clearly pleased with himself.

The last thing I wanted was to travel, stay in a foreign city, and go to a pop concert.

But I'd do it for G.

Trent gave him a suspicious look. "Why do you look so damn happy about this?"

Across the table, Colt didn't miss a beat. "Because he's got a crush on Ellie Miles."

Sawyer flushed red, running a hand over his buzzed head. "I do not."

"Oh shit, you totally do." Dotty burst out laughing.

"She's just really cool, okay?" Sawyer shot back defensively. "She donates to good causes, she's great with her fans, and she's got a solid vibe. That's it. Leave me alone."

Gracie leaned forward and started singing, "Sawyer and Ellie, sittin' in a tree, K-I-X-X-I-N-P!"

We all erupted in laughter as my dad shook his head. "That's not how you spell kissing, G."

Gracie huffed, crossing her arms. "You know I'm not very good at spelling! I'm working on it. Right, Noah?"

Noah looked at my daughter with so much love, my heart threatened to bottom out. "You are, and you are doing so well, G."

Well, I wanted to stay away from this girl, but then she went and called my girl by her nickname.

Fuck.

"We can all drive and make a fun weekend out of it," Sawyer said, grinning.

"You can count me out," Colt replied, not even looking up from his plate.

"Me too," my dad and Trent said in unison.

"You couldn't pay me to go to that shit," Colt added.

"Colton!" my dad scolded, though the corner of his mouth twitched.

Sawyer tossed a crumpled napkin at him this time, which sent Gracie and Noah into a fit of giggles.

The noise, the laughter, the teasing—it all swirled around the table.

I glanced at Noah again, catching her smile. And this time, I held her gaze.

She fit here so effortlessly, like she'd always been part of this. And maybe that was what scared me the most.

TWENTY

Noah - August

RUMOR - LEE BRICE

I STALLED FOR A MOMENT BEFORE STEPPING INTO OUTLAW'S Bar, where my first Friday teachers' night out was already in full swing.

The atmosphere in the bar was full of laughter and the occasional clink of glasses. It had that familiar buzz of a small-town bar, where everyone knew everyone.

Earlier in the week, I'd run into Miss Lane while setting up my classroom again. We'd talked for a while about teaching and life in Woodstone Falls, and by the end of the conversation, she'd convinced me to come join her.

Now, standing at the entrance, I wasn't entirely sure what I'd gotten myself into. But I'd promised her I'd make an effort. So, here I was.

As my eyes adjusted to the dim lighting, I scanned the room and quickly spotted a table with a group of people toward the back of the bar. They claimed a table beneath a buzzing neon sign that cast a blue hue over their heads. Their laughter stood out in the otherwise subdued atmosphere, giving the place a coziness that contrasted with its rustic, cowboy-bar charm.

Miss Lane spotted me and waved enthusiastically. She gestured to an empty chair beside her, and I grabbed a water from the bar and made my way over.

"So glad you could join us," she greeted, her tone friendly and welcoming.

"Wouldn't miss it. Thanks for inviting me…" I said as I slid into the seat. The chair let out a faint creak beneath me, blending with the low hum of chatter.

"You can call me Lana, please," she said with a smile.

I thought back to my old school in Seattle, where everyone clung to their titles—even outside the classroom. But this wasn't Seattle. Woodstone had a much more relaxed pace, a reminder of just how different life was in this small town.

"Noah, this is Chad, Mr. Thompson. He teaches kinder," Lana said, gesturing toward a tall man with glasses who looked like he hadn't had a full night's sleep in weeks.

"Great to meet you, Noah," he said with a nod.

She quickly introduced me to the others at the table. Mrs. Rodriguez, the no-nonsense third-grade teacher with kind eyes, and Brooks, who taught second grade and had an enthusiastic energy that instantly made me feel welcome.

"I'm basically the unofficial tour guide of Woodstone Falls," Brooks said. "Need to know where to get the best coffee, or where to hide during your free period? I've got you covered."

Lana chuckled. "Don't mind Brooks. They like to tease."

She then gestured to a man with thinning sandy hair that was combed back neatly. His glasses caught the low light of the bar as he glanced up, offering a polite but reserved smile.

"And that's Mr. Harris," Lana added.

"It's nice to meet you. We're glad to have you on board," he said.

Something about him made me uneasy, though I couldn't quite put my finger on why.

After the brief introductions, Chad cleared his throat. "How have you been settling in?"

"Good, good," I replied. "Everyone's been really welcoming."

"A change from city life, huh?" Mrs. Rodriguez said with a wink.

I nodded. "Yeah, definitely different, but I like it. Needed the slower pace."

Mr. Harris leaned in slightly, his eyes lingering. "A fresh start can be good," he said smoothly, something about him making the hairs on my neck stand up.

I hated how I would overthink the simplest of interactions lately. But that was my reality after John. He made me question everything: myself, other people, even the most basic conversations.

I forced a smile. "It's definitely a nice change of pace for me," I replied lightly, steering the conversation away from whatever he was hinting at.

Brooks smiled casually. "Woodstone definitely has its charm," they added, brushing a strand of their short hair out of their face with a light laugh.

After a while, the others headed to the bar to order more drinks. I decided to stay behind with Lana, not trusting myself with alcohol around new colleagues.

I still felt like the new kid trying to find my place. I was trying to navigate my way through this new small-town life as a single, almost thirty-year-old woman recovering from not only a failed relationship, but the ultimate failed relationship.

Lana was easy to talk to though, making me glad I'd

come tonight.

I turned slightly, and my breath caught when I saw him.

Dorian stood at the entrance of the bar, Colt beside him. His tall frame was unmistakable, even in the crowded space. His eyes locked onto mine immediately, like I was the only person in the room.

Lana continued talking about the small-town quirks of Woodstone, but despite my best efforts, my attention kept drifting.

I noticed her gaze move past me, following the spot where my eyes kept moving to, and she paused mid-sentence. A knowing smile tugged at the corners of her lips.

"Dotty is your friend, right?" she asked.

"Yeah, she's my best friend. That's why I moved here," I said, hoping my voice stayed firm despite the rush of thoughts in my head.

Lana's smile deepened as she raised an eyebrow. "So, you know her brother, Dorian?"

"Yeah, we're…just friends," I replied, keeping my tone casual.

"Friends?" she said, the word dripping with playful doubt. She glanced over her shoulder, then turned back to me with a knowing grin. "Because from where I'm sitting, it looks like he's staring at you like he's seeing something more than just a friend."

I could feel the heat creeping up my cheeks, betraying me. "It's not like that."

Lana leaned back in her chair. "Noah, I might not know you well yet, but I know that look. Trust me, that's not how a guy looks at just a friend. That look says he's ready to jump your bones and then propose."

I nearly choked on my sip of water, coughing as I wiped my mouth.

I couldn't help but glance back at Dorian, who was now making his way through the bar.

"I'm not really in a good place right now to get into a relationship," I said, trying to keep my voice steady.

"I mean, you could always do something… uncomplicated."

"What do you mean?" I asked.

She crossed her arms. "You know… friends with benefits. No strings. Casual. Just fun. Not exactly a new concept."

The words made my mind spin. I stared at her for a moment, trying to process what she was suggesting.

But she had a point. I could… let go for once, without overthinking it.

Maybe Dorian didn't have to be complicated.

Maybe he could be… fun.

I caught sight of him heading toward our table, his gaze fixed firmly on me.

"I don't know… I don't think it's like that with us." The lie slipped off my tongue. I forced a smile. "I think he's just protective, that's all."

She gave me a knowing look, one that said she wasn't buying it, but thankfully, she didn't push any further. "If you say so," she said.

Before I could respond, Dorian reached us.

"Noah," he greeted, his gaze glancing briefly to Lana before moving back to me.

To my mouth.

Well, so much for trying to convince her otherwise.

"Dorian," I replied, my voice more breathless than I'd intended. "Out for a drink with Colt?"

"Yeah. Trent is wedding planning with Dotty, but my dad texted me, wanting to spend time with Gracie, so I thought I'd swing by since it's the weekend."

"Makes sense," I said, and his gaze lingered on me.

His tongue brushed over his lower lip as he studied me, and I almost combusted right there.

"Well, I just wanted to say hello." He nodded toward the bar, where Colt was talking with the bartender. "I'll let you two get back to it."

"See ya," I said as he turned away.

Once he was out of earshot, Lana shoved my shoulder. "Yeah… That was not"—she looked back to where Dorian now stood across the bar and made little air quotes—"just friends."

"Oh, shut it." I chuckled.

TWENTY-ONE

Dorian - August

PLAY WITH FIRE (FEAT. YACHT MONEY) - SAM
TINNESZ

I FOLLOWED HER.

Like the dumb fuck I was.

I knew she would be at Outlaw's—Dotty had let it slip earlier when I spoke to her. So, I roped my brother into coming along, just to keep things from looking too obvious.

My dad had been asking for a night with Gracie anyway, so I figured what better time than when the girl that I couldn't stop thinking about was going out?

I spotted her the second I walked in. She was sitting at a table across the bar, one leg crossed over the other, the hem of her skirt riding up, making me wonder what was underneath. She shifted slightly, adjusting her posture, and I couldn't help but say hi before settling at the bar.

I knew almost everyone in Woodstone well, but when it came to the teachers, I only knew their names and faces. And that made it harder to shake the unease gnawing at me about letting my girl wander off without anyone she knew around.

Fuck. She was not my girl.

She couldn't be mine, no matter how much I wanted her to be. It was ridiculous to even entertain the thought.

Because if I let myself care about Noah, I'd be asking for trouble, especially with John still out there.

The thought of us together was like standing on unstable ground, and while the urge to protect her pulled at me, the fear of what might happen kept me at arm's length.

Somehow, Noah managed to get under my skin in a way I couldn't quite comprehend. It was infuriating—this magnetic draw I felt toward her, this unshakable desire to protect her, even if it meant distancing myself, like I had every time she came over to tutor Gracie lately.

But here I was, sitting at the bar with my grumpy as fuck brother, who couldn't hold a conversation for shit, while I spied on my sister's best friend.

"So, how's everything?" I asked Colt.

"Fine," he replied, his eyes not meeting mine.

I nodded, not sure how to keep the conversation going. "Alright."

He let out a long sigh. "Did you really ask me to go out to eye fuck Dotty's best friend all night?" he asked.

I groaned, letting my head fall back and downed the rest of my beer. I looked over at him. His hair was pulled back in a man bun, despite how much we all teased him to just cut it.

"Is it that obvious?" I groaned.

"Yup." He took another sip of his whiskey, clearly enjoying my discomfort.

"Great." I pinched the bridge of my nose, trying to shake off the frustration. "I'm going to take a piss. I'll be back."

I needed a moment to clear my head. I moved through the crowd, dodging a couple of rowdy patrons and weaving between tables. The room was alive with conversation, the clinking of glasses, and the occasional bursts of laughter. The low lights, combined with the haze of smoke from the patio, made the atmosphere feel suffocating.

As I turned the corner into the narrow hallway, I nearly collided with someone. I instinctively stumbled back, mumbling a quick apology before my eyes finally adjusted and landed on her.

Noah.

She stood there, freshly out of the restroom, her head tilted downward as she adjusted her hair, sweeping a loose curl behind her ear. She glowed under the amber light overhead.

She blinked up at me, surprise flickering in her eyes. For a second, we just stood there, locked in place. My heart stuttered.

Then the corners of her mouth lifted into a small smile. "Hey."

"Hey," I replied, the words scraping against the tightness in my throat.

I took a step closer, narrowing the distance between us as my resolve began to fall the longer I was in her presence. The closer I got, the more impossible it was to stay away.

"How's your night?" I asked.

Every hair on my body stood on end. I was close enough now to see the way her pulse fluttered at the side of her neck, close enough to reach out and touch her if I wanted to—if I dared to.

The tension that had simmered for the last several months threatened to boil over.

"It's… good," she replied.

She didn't back away, didn't move a muscle. I wasn't sure if she was frozen in place or if she was waiting, just like I was.

"Good, huh?" I asked.

My hand moved to hover over her throat, the heat from her body searing through the space between us. She sucked in a breath, and I watched her pretty lips. So damn tempting.

My fingers skimmed her side, a barely-there touch that still sparked between us like a live wire. Her breath hitched again, and she leaned into me, making my fingers press a little deeper. My other hand finally made contact, gently holding her throat. I let my fingers rest against her, feeling the rapid pulse beneath my touch.

"Noah…" I whispered, her name a plea on my lips.

She gazed up at me, her eyes searching mine for something—maybe the same answers I was looking for. Her hand reached out, hesitating before she rested it lightly over my pounding heart. Her touch sent a jolt through me, and I could feel my restraint slipping away, inch by fucking inch.

Colt was right.

This was obvious.

How she affected me was so damn obvious.

My pulse thundered, each beat reverberating in my ears. Her exhales mingled with mine, brushing against my lips as I leaned in, my nose grazing hers. I could feel the silkiness of her skin, the sweet scent of her filling my senses. My eyes closed for a moment, savoring the closeness.

When I opened them again, I found hers locked on mine, searching, wanting, but also holding back.

"I can't do anything serious right now," she whispered.

"Yeah, me either," I agreed, though the words felt hollow.

She hesitated, her eyes flicking down to my lips before meeting mine again. "My life's a mess."

"And I don't get attached to anyone," I said, as my hand slid up her side.

She bit her lip. "Yeah, and I dated a man who was murdering people."

"Right… and I'm a single dad. My focus is on G," I said, my gaze dropping to her mouth.

"And I'm her teacher," she said, gripping the fabric of my shirt.

"And I'm your best friend's brother," I replied, my thumb skimming back and forth.

"Yeah, we shouldn't do this," she said, her voice faltering, though her eyes never left mine.

"Definitely not," I said, my grip tightening just a fraction at her throat.

Her chest rose and fell rapidly, matching my own. Her lips were so close now, just a breath away.

"I'm scared," she admitted.

"Terrified," I breathed, backing her into the wall. The way she looked up at me, full of surprise and need, made me lose it. "Fuck it."

And then, without another word, my lips were on hers.

The kiss was fire, the kind of flame that ignites in a spark but quickly spreads, consuming everything in its path. The need that had been building between us for months, finally roaring out of control.

This fucking girl.

It was everything I'd ever wanted, all at once. I knew her lips would drive me mad but tasting them had tenfold the reaction on my body.

She was a perfect mix of sharp and sweet, like a damn summer peach. I wanted to taste her forever.

Her kiss ruined me. It felt so right, and I knew that no other lips would ever compare.

I needed her *everywhere*.

My hands slid down her back and hoisted her up. She wrapped her legs around my waist, her hands locking behind my head. I grabbed her wrists with one hand, pinning them above her head.

I allowed myself to get lost in her, in the feel of her, the taste of her. All the fear and doubt melted away as we gave in to what we both knew was inevitable.

And I fucking loved it.

Every brush of her lips, every touch of her hands, sent electricity coursing through my veins, making it impossible to think, impossible to care about anything other than this moment.

Anything other than *her*.

TWENTY-TWO

Dorian - August

TOO SWEET - HOZIER

SETTLING BACK INTO MY SEAT AT THE BAR, I SHOT A BRIEF LOOK at Colt, doing my best to hide what just happened. As if kissing my sister's best friend—my daughter's teacher— wasn't still replaying in my mind.

I invited her to meet me at my truck later, and at the time, it didn't seem as reckless as it should have. For months, I'd convinced myself that getting attached was a mistake—no matter how much I wanted to.

But now?

Pretending it hadn't happened wasn't possible.

A slow sip of my beer gave me something to focus on, but it didn't stop my thoughts from racing.

"Have fun making out with Noah?" he asked.

I choked on my bitter liquid and started coughing.

"I'll take that as a yes," he replied. He slapped cash down on the bar, enough for both of our drinks. "Now that you have done what you came for, I'm out. I have an early shift tomorrow."

"Always a pleasure, brother," I replied.

While I had a reputation for being a bit grumpy, Colt

took it to an entirely different level. I kept things short and to the point, but I was never intentionally rude. Colt didn't give a single fuck what others thought of him the way I did.

He softened for two people, though. Dotty and Gracie. Everyone else, including me, was lucky to get more than a grunt.

I added a bill to the bar, nodding to Colt as he left, then stepped outside.

I glanced over to where the group of teachers moved to a pool table and decided it'd be best to wait for Noah by my truck. My thoughts were a mess, and I could use a minute to sort myself out.

I knew I wasn't getting anywhere with Colt, and talking to Dotty was off the table. So, I dialed the only person who might actually get what I was dealing with.

Sawyer answered on the second ring. "Hey, what's up?"

"You got a minute?" I asked, leaning back against the wall outside the bar, staring at the stars.

"Yeah, just finished up a training session," he said. Sawyer was out in San Francisco living the dream, making a name for himself as one of the best linemen in the NFL.

"I've got a… situation," I said, trying to get my thoughts in order.

"Let me guess. You're into the new teacher?"

"How the fuck does everyone know about that?" I asked, half laughing.

"Well, one—I heard you guys were caught almost kissing a while ago. Two, Colt texted me just now."

"Great…" I muttered, running a hand over my face.

"Listen, man. I know you've been through a lot, but you deserve something good. Just… be careful, okay? Dotty's gonna kill you if you mess up."

"You're probably right about that," I said, a small smile tugging at my lips.

"You do deserve good things, and that girl? She's good," Sawyer said, the words sounding more serious now.

"She is," I agreed, the words slipping out before I could stop them.

"So, what's the holdup?" Sawyer asked, his tone now curious.

"Honestly? I don't know," I admitted. "I think I'm… scared."

"Shit, man."

"Yeah… I just… I've never wanted to pursue anything with anyone. All these fucking women in town, and I've never wanted a single one of them. Then she just prances her merry fucking way into my life, turning it upside down and… I want to know her."

"Oh damn," Sawyer laughed, low and surprised.

"Tell me about it," I muttered.

"Good luck with that."

"Thanks for the help, asshole," I said, shaking my head.

"Whatever you do, don't fuck it up."

"Noted," I said, ending the call.

My sister protected those she loved fiercely. Apparently, Dotty's best friend came before her twin brother, and I couldn't really blame her for it.

Noah was always kind, always smiling, and her presence could make the weight of the world feel a little less heavy. But that wasn't all there was to her. Beneath the surface, she carried a silent kind of pain. The aftermath of what John had done to her was still there, something she wore like a shield. It made her stronger—more resilient than anyone gave her credit for. She still found a way to care, to put others first, even when she was hurting.

It was no wonder Dotty adored her. She'd been there when no one else could break through her walls, offering a kind of support I couldn't match. I couldn't blame Dotty for choosing her every time.

She deserved to be protected.

But to Dotty, I was just the single dad who kept everyone at arm's length.

While I still wasn't entirely sure of what I was doing, kissing Noah and asking her to meet me at the end of the night, I knew that I wanted her.

Every time I looked at her, I told myself I couldn't care about her more than I already did.

But every day I proved myself wrong.

TWENTY-THREE

Dorian - August

HEAVEN - JULIA MICHAELS

GRAVEL CRUNCHED BENEATH MY BOOTS AS I MADE MY WAY across the lot toward my truck. But I stopped mid-step when I saw Noah leaning against it, arms crossed, her gaze fixed on the ground.

I hadn't known what to expect when I asked her to meet me, but seeing her there, waiting, made me glad I did. Whatever this was between us, I couldn't keep pretending I didn't feel it. I couldn't keep pretending it wasn't real.

"I didn't realize you'd left," I said, stepping closer. "I figured you were still inside, playing pool."

Her brown eyes met mine, and for a moment, everything else faded.

"Yeah, I slipped out a minute ago," she said.

"How was your night?" I asked, stepping closer.

"Uh, good... It was... good," she replied, though her gaze held something back.

I moved in, closing the space, standing just over her where she leaned against the truck.

"Good, huh?" I echoed from earlier. Without thinking,

my hands moved to her hips, fingers curling into the waistband of her skirt.

A small gasp escaped her as I tugged her forward, away from the truck.

With a flick of my wrist, I dropped the tailgate, the thud echoing through the stillness of the lot. Our gaze locked on each other as my hands slid back to her hips with slow, deliberate precision. Her muscles trembled under my grasp as I lifted her onto the tailgate, her small frame light in my arms. Her legs separated just enough for me to step between them. I closed the distance until we shared the same breath.

Hesitation and desire glimmered behind her irises, but she didn't pull back. She was navigating this moment just like I was, trying to figure out what came next after that kiss in the bar. I leaned in, close enough that the heat of her exhale brushed against my skin.

Every instinct in me screamed to close the gap, to kiss her again.

I savored it—the way she leaned into me, waiting for me.

"Hey," I murmured.

Her golden-brown skin melted against my hands as I tightened my grip on her.

"Hi," she whispered back.

She bit her lip, her eyes searching mine, and I could see the same battle raging within her that continued to tear through me.

One kiss could go down as a mistake.

Two couldn't.

I dipped my head, the softness of her skin brushing against mine as I came closer. The scent of her was intoxicating, and every second near her pulled me in deeper.

"What if we did… something casual?" she said, her nose lazily grazing mine.

"Casual?" I repeated.

"Yeah, no big feelings, just… me and you," she murmured, as she rested her head on my shoulder.

Her body pressed against mine felt good, natural.

Like maybe this could work.

"I don't have much to offer right now. I just know that I want you," she whispered against me. Her words were muffled, but clear enough to knock the air out of me.

I tilted her chin up, making her meet my eyes. "I think I can do that," I said, and the words felt like a release.

Close, but not too close. No expectations, no pressure, no risk of getting hurt.

She smiled, and fuck, I wanted to bottle that smile up and save it for a rainy day.

"Yeah?" she asked.

This was the solution. A way to have her without crossing the line. Keep things light, simple. The truth was, I'd been fighting what this was between us for so long that maybe going casual was the only way I wouldn't completely lose myself in her. Because the minute I let myself fall for her—for real—it'd be game over.

But this? This I could manage. At least, that's what I told myself.

"Yeah," I murmured, letting my knuckles brush lightly across her cheekbone before leaning in and capturing her lips again.

She whimpered, and the sound made something deep inside me tighten.

Her lips were soft and warm. I cupped the nape of her neck, drawing her closer. She let out a breathy sigh, her mouth parting just enough for me to take my chance, teasing my way in. The moment her tongue met mine, a low groan rumbled from me—the taste making my head spin.

She felt perfect, too perfect.

Her skirt bunched higher on her thighs as I pressed forward, the heat of her body radiating through my jeans. It was maddening, feeling her this close. I wanted more, but I savored the moment.

"We should stop," she murmured between kisses, her words half-hearted.

"Why?" I asked, not letting her pull away, my lips finding hers again.

"Someone might see us," she said against my lips, though there was a teasing smile in her words.

God, I could drown in her kisses and never come up for air.

I moved back just enough to study her. Her throat moved as she swallowed, eyes fluttering shut for a second. The low light only made her even more irresistible. The parking lot was dark, with only a few streetlights in the distance illuminating the space around us.

We were tucked away at the far end of the lot, hidden in the shadows. I glanced around and gestured to the empty lot. "I think we're safe."

She rolled her eyes, and I chuckled. My gaze dropped to her lips again, still swollen from my kisses. Even in the darkness, those damn lips drove me as wild as they did in broad daylight.

"What?" she asked.

"I like you," I admitted, the words spilling from me before I could stop them.

Her smile faded into a flat line. "No feelings, remember?"

I stepped back, running a hand through my hair, trying desperately to recover. "Yeah, sorry... No feelings..."

I leaned in and captured her lips once more.

I had to. I was sinking, and the only way to survive was to lose myself in her completely. Her kiss was heated, intoxicating—stirring something primal inside of me.

As her mouth moved against mine, every brush of her lips had my body reacting. My jeans grew tighter by the second. I pulled back to catch my breath, watching her eyes flutter open, dazed and heavy with the same want that coursed through me.

"So, what does casual mean exactly then?" I asked, arching a brow.

"I thought you were smart." She chuckled, her eyes lighting up. "It means no feelings… yes sex."

"Well, in that case," I murmured. The gravel dug into my knees as I knelt before the tailgate. "Now that I've tasted your mouth, all I can think about is what your pretty pussy tastes like. Be a good girl and lean back for me," I said, bunching up her skirt around her hips, exposing the soft brown skin of her thighs.

I trailed my hand slowly up her stomach, over the curve of her torso, and pressed down gently. She watched me intently as she slowly lowered to the bed of the truck.

"There's my girl." My hand moved down her body to hover above her exposed panties. I hooked my fingers into the thin bands biting into her hips, pushing the fabric down her legs. Her decadent skin brushing against my hands sent my heart racing as I tossed her underwear into my pocket. Our eyes locked in a heated gaze as I moved before her.

My hand trailed down her stomach. I slipped a finger into her core, and I felt for the first time how this wasn't one-sided. Her arousal coated my fingers. A groan rumbled from within me as I relished the effect I had on her.

"You are dripping. Is this all for me?" I asked.

A small, breathy sound escaped her. Slowly, my head

dipped between her thighs. My tongue flicked across my lips before meeting her center. At the first taste, I almost lost my mind. She was everything I needed and more.

I pressed a second finger inside her, working in sync with my mouth.

Every sweep of my tongue and pull of my lips consumed her, savoring her as if she were the last thing I'd ever taste. I pressed my arm down, holding her in place as I dove deeper.

"Stay still, peach," I murmured.

"Peach?" she gasped out as I continued to move.

I nodded, unwilling to speak.

"I… I don't usually…" she panted, her hand pressing my head away for a moment. Her eyes connected nervously with mine as I sat up.

I pulled away, waiting for her to continue.

"I haven't done"—she waved her arm around to where my head still sat between her pretty thighs—"this before… I don't know if I can come like this."

Oh, hell yeah. I loved being the first one to have her like this.

I rose to meet her face to face, her eyes trained on me as I steeled my gaze.

My hand gripped her face to bring her close, the other rubbing the soft flesh of her exposed thighs. "Baby, I'm going to make you come like this at least once before we leave this parking lot."

"But—I," she started but I cut her off with my fingers, pressing them back into her and relishing in the way she gripped them.

Her head fell back, letting out the sexiest moan I had ever heard. I knew she'd make intoxicating sounds when I got her like this.

But she was even outperforming my dreams.

I knelt back down and added my tongue to her clit, swirling around.

She coated my lips, my tongue, and my chin as I found a rhythm. Savoring her reaction to my touch, so responsive.

I could barely see her in the dark of the night, but damn, did she look so good spread out on my tailgate, skirt bunched up, with my head between her thighs.

The sounds pouring from her pitched higher as she approached the edge, her body fidgeting as she got closer and closer.

She tried to push herself up, but her arms trembled, barely able to hold her weight.

"Be a good girl and stay still," I said, and she moaned in response. "You like that? When I call you my good girl?" My hand scaled her body, pressing the middle of her chest down against the truck bed.

The way her pussy felt on my tongue sent my blood roaring through my body. I snaked my hand down her stomach, enjoying the way her skin reacted under my fingers, as my own need built as I devoured her.

Soon, I was trailing my hands down her thighs, her knees, her shins. As they dropped at her ankle, my fingers found my belt, unbuckling it to release some pressure.

I continued licking, sucking, and paying close attention to how her body reacted to me.

"Dorian…" she panted.

I felt her release building by the way her pussy was clenching my fingers. I pressed my tongue to her clit, moving in circles while my fingers curved inside her, and she let out a little whimper.

"Fuck," she moaned.

"Come for me. Be a good girl and come for me."

Her release barreled through her body. "I'm coming… fuck, Dorian, I'm coming," she panted desperately.

Her body folded, and her legs attempted to close around my head. I pushed them open but lessened my intensity to match everything she needed and concentrated on the way she was pulsing.

The moment slowed, and I watched my fingers as they gently pulled out of her. I pressed soft kisses to the delicate skin of her inner thighs before looking up.

"You coming on my tongue with my name coming out of that pretty mouth might be one of the best things to ever happen to me."

She sat up, my body following her. My knees ached from kneeling in the gravel, and I'd feel it tomorrow. But I liked that thought—knowing the pain was from making her come apart for me.

Wiping my mouth with the back of my hand, I grinned. "Do you have any idea how much I needed that?"

"You?" she asked. "You needed that?"

"I did. I already want it again," I mused. "But we should probably go somewhere more private for what I have planned next."

Her eyes heated for a moment before softening.

Something shifted. The heat between us transformed into something else—something tender. She glanced down at my hands resting on her thighs. I quickly pulled down her skirt, covering her.

"What is it?" I asked gently.

She hesitated, not meeting my gaze.

"Thank you..." Her voice trailed off. "I... I always thought something was wrong with me. But now... I'm thinking maybe I wasn't the problem."

I tipped her chin up, forcing her to look at me. "You were never the problem," I echoed.

Her eyes searched mine, and then she nodded.

I leaned in and kissed her again, soft and slow this time.

This kiss wasn't like the others. It wasn't fueled by urgency or desire.

It was sweet, delicate—just like her.

And I melted into it. I melted into her.

All the reasons why we shouldn't do this, why this could end badly, screamed in the back of my mind.

But for once, I didn't listen.

A bigger man might hold back. A better man probably would. But all I could do was hold her tighter and kiss her deeper.

I knew that I might be scared shitless doing it, but I was willing to forcibly silence that noise in my head that screamed this would end badly.

TWENTY-FOUR

Noah - August

WIND UP MISSIN' YOU - TUCKER WETMORE

My mind was already replaying what had just happened —me propped up on my elbows, looking down at him on his knees.

It was ecstasy. Static sparking through my veins, setting a wildfire in my soul. His touch was unlike anything I'd ever experienced. The coolness of the truck bed beneath me contrasted with the heat building inside, as he kept pushing me higher.

Dorian now stood between my legs, his eyes full of desire. But before he could say or do anything, the sharp sound of footsteps on the uneven ground interrupted us.

A flash of light streaked across us, and Dorian moved instantly. His hand pressed my legs together as he moved in front of me, blocking me from view.

"Woodstone County Police," someone called out, the words firm but not harsh. A tall figure approached; their features mostly hidden in the dim light.

Dorian stood his ground, his shoulders loose as though this were an ordinary encounter. "Oh hey, Henry," he said, calm and unhurried.

"Dorian?" Henry stopped a few feet away. His mouth opened, then shut, before he raised an eyebrow. "What the hell is—" His head tilted slightly as he glanced down, his gaze snagging on Dorian's pocket—where my underwear peeked out, half hanging over the edge.

Well, that's just great.

Dorian cleared this throat. "Busy night at the bar," he said, his tone giving away nothing.

Henry let out a short exhale through his nose, the corner of his mouth twitching upward in something between disbelief and amusement.

"Right. Busy. And I'm guessing you didn't think to pick somewhere less obvious?"

I shifted behind Dorian, every inch of me burning under Henry's scrutiny. "We're sorry, sir," I muttered.

Henry's head turned toward me, his brows knitting together for a moment before he let out a resigned sigh.

Henry's hands landed on his hips, and he rocked back on his heels. "Look, I'm not writing you up for anything, but maybe take it somewhere more… private. If it were anyone else patrolling…" He let the sentence hang, shaking his head.

Dorian tilted his head slightly, one hand moving to rub the back of his neck. "Noted," he replied, his tone casual, almost too casual. "Thanks, Henry."

Henry waved a hand dismissively, but his eyes narrowed slightly. "Yeah, yeah. It's the least I could do. Just… keep it professional, Doctor James."

I bit down on my lip and nodded again, unable to trust my voice.

Henry gave Dorian one last look, then turned sharply on his heel. "Have a good night," he called over his shoulder, his tone clipped but not unkind.

"You too, Officer Reynolds."

Reynolds?

We waited until his footsteps faded completely, the silence wrapping around us once more.

"Well," Dorian said finally, glancing back at me, a faint smirk tugging at his lips.

"Wait… was that…" I started.

"Chris's brother?" Dorian turned back to face me. "Yeah. Good guy. Feels awful about everything. He's been friends with Trent for a while, but we get along too."

I swallowed, processing how his brother was the one responsible for Trent being shot and taking Dotty months ago. "I hope he's doing okay… considering."

It couldn't be easy finding out your brother was responsible for something that horrific, then losing him in the process.

"Yeah, from what Trent said, he's holding up." Dorian brushed a curl from my face, his fingers lingering in my hair. I couldn't meet his eyes, suddenly self-conscious.

"What's that look?" he asked, his brow furrowing.

"It's just… I've never really liked my hair."

"I do," he said, tugging at a curl gently, and admiring the way it sprung back to life.

My brow furrowed. "You do?"

"Yeah," he said, his voice lowering, sending a spark through me. "It's part of you, and every part of you is beautiful."

A smile tugged at the corner of my mouth. "You're relentless."

"With you?" He leaned closer, his smile teasing. "Absolutely."

Before I could respond, his mouth found mine again, slow and tentative, like he was gauging where my head was at. And honestly, I wasn't entirely sure of that myself.

But I knew one thing—I wasn't ready to stop. His tongue gently teased mine, rekindling the fire between us.

He moved back a fraction. "Come back to my place?" he murmured against my lips. "Gracie's with my dad."

I hesitated, still rattled by everything that had unfolded. "I don't know… I have to let Walker out."

My body was ready, but my mind wasn't sure it was all lined up just yet.

"We can pick him up on the way or go to your house," he said. "Watch a movie, have a drink. We don't have to do anything. I'm not ready to let you go yet," he promised, crossing his heart in an exaggerated motion.

I couldn't help but chuckle. "One drink."

The drive to Dorian's house was quiet as I followed him. He'd come with me to my place to grab Walker, making sure he wouldn't be left alone too long. Now, we were headed to his house, the evening ahead of us.

But as I drove, that stupid truck bed stared at me. The scene flashing in my mind, one that would forever be engraved in my memory. Someday I'd be ninety years old, telling my adult grandchildren about how, when I was young and wild, I once had my pussy eaten by a handsome vet on a tailgate back in the twenties. Maybe using slightly more appropriate language.

But really, the silence was welcomed.

We'd said everything that needed to be said for the moment, letting us just be. Finally.

My thoughts kept spinning, my heart doing weird flips in my chest. Kissing Dorian felt so right—and that scared me as much as it excited me.

It felt like a betrayal, though I knew it wasn't. I moved on without closure from John, and that nagging sensation wouldn't let go. Months later, he still found a way to cast a shadow over my decisions, making everything harder than it should've been.

By the time I cut the engine, Dorian was already at my door, yanking it open before I even had a chance to unbuckle my seatbelt.

"Antsy, are ya?" I teased, raising an eyebrow.

I reached for my bag, but before I could grab it, he leaned down, his face inches from mine.

For a moment, I just watched him, letting myself take in the way his dark hair fell over his forehead, that lopsided smile of his, the way his T-shirt clung to his strong frame, outlining every inch of power beneath.

"You just going to sit there and stare?" he teased. "Or should we go inside so I can make you a drink?"

I laughed, trying to ignore the way my body reacted to the closeness of his. "It's hard to move when you're practically on top of me."

He reached over me, and with a single motion, the seatbelt retracted, the click breaking the silence. His gaze stayed locked on mine as he stepped back and extended his hand. I placed my hand in his, and he guided me out of the car and into the house.

Inside, he flicked on the light, filling the space with an inviting glow. His home carried an unspoken sense of ease, a place that felt safe, as though nothing bad could reach us here.

He strode into the kitchen and opened a cabinet, revealing an assortment of liquor bottles.

"Pick your poison," he said, his tone light, though something unspoken lingered beneath it.

I leaned against the counter, grinning. "Tequila."

He glanced over his shoulder with a smirk. "You've been spending too much time with my sister."

"What can I say? She has good taste."

"Margarita?" he asked, grabbing a bottle.

"Now you're speaking my language."

He quickly made two drinks, handing me mine with a faint clink of ice against the glass. His eyes followed the slow sweep of my tongue as I licked a trace of salt from the rim.

The corner of his mouth twitched like he was fighting back a comment, but he turned away, heading toward the couch.

I followed, settling in beside him as he grabbed the remote. He scrolled through the options, his movements unhurried, until a familiar title popped up—the show we watched together back in Seattle, back when life was simpler.

He glanced at me, a silent question in his expression. I nodded, and he hit play, the opening theme sparking a bittersweet pang of nostalgia for that weekend.

"Still hate him?" I teased as one of the more controversial characters appeared, his smug grin lighting up the screen.

"Hate is a strong word," Dorian replied, settling deeper into the cushions. "But yeah, he's the worst."

I raised an eyebrow. "This from the guy who yelled at the TV every time he made a bad decision?"

"That was constructive criticism," he shot back, the faintest smirk tugging at his lips.

"Oh, sure," I said, feigning seriousness. "Because shouting *Just jump off the cliff already* is totally helpful."

"It would've been faster, and less painful for the rest of us."

We laughed, the sound mingling with the dialogue on

the screen, but there was an undercurrent now, something unspoken weaving through the ease of our connection. It wasn't the show, or the teasing, but the way we fit so naturally into each other's lives.

In the middle of the episode, Dorian's hand brushed mine. The touch was light, hesitant. I didn't pull away. Instead, I looked over at him, my heart seemingly thudding louder than the dialogue on the TV.

"You know," he started, "I've tried to stay away from you." He shook his head and continued. "I mean, when we met, you were still with…"

"John," I said. "You don't have to be afraid to say it."

His jaw tensed. "Just the fucking sound of his name out of your mouth pisses me off," he growled.

The words hit me square in the chest. The TV faded into the background.

Dorian leaned closer, his breath ghosting over my cheek. "Noah… This feels…"

It felt right—terrifyingly, overwhelmingly right.

"Don't say it," I muttered.

Saying it aloud made it real, and I wasn't ready for that.

I wasn't ready to admit how deeply I wanted this.

But then his fingers brushed my cheek, and all my doubts began to dissolve.

"Okay," he said.

But there was something about Dorian that pulled me in —the way he made me feel seen in a world that often felt dark and suffocating.

I leaned closer, the fear and thrill of the moment blurring together. His hand threaded through my curls, his touch so purposeful that it quieted the chaos in my mind.

"Noah," he said, his gaze dropping to my lips. A silent question lingered in his eyes, waiting for me to answer.

I teetered on the edge, torn between the urge to give in and the fear of what that would mean.

This wasn't a heated moment, fueled by desire. This was raw and real and everything we'd just agreed to stay away from.

What if this was another mistake?

But when his lips hovered closer and his brown eyes locked onto mine, it made it hard to breathe.

My heart screamed that I wanted him—needed him—more than I ever wanted anything before.

So instead of giving into the fear, I leaned in, closing the space between us. His face tilted down, and his hand slipped to the nape of my neck, threading through my hair with a certainty that sent a shiver down my spine.

His other hand found my waist, pulling me closer in a way that left no room for hesitation. I fisted the fabric of his shirt, needing something to hold on to as everything else fell away.

When his lips finally met mine, the first touch was unhurried, almost reverent. He kissed me as if he had all the time in the world, testing the waters, as if memorizing the shape of my lips against his.

I couldn't stop the way my body responded, leaning into him as if drawn by some invisible string. My hand slid upward, grazing his jawline, feeling the roughness of his stubble beneath my fingertips. His lips pressed harder, coaxing mine to part, and I let him in, unable to resist.

His tongue swept against mine, slow and deliberate, igniting a heat that spread through me like wildfire. I matched his pace, my hand drifting to the back of his neck, fingers tangling in his hair. He groaned into my mouth, the sound vibrating between us and sending my pulse racing.

It was a dance—his movements confident, almost possessive, while mine searched, explored, and gave back as much as I took. He tilted his head slightly, his fingers tightening just enough to keep me anchored in the moment. A moan rose in my throat, spilling into his mouth.

This kiss.

This damn kiss.

It was the kiss I'd only dreamed about, the kind I'd convinced myself didn't exist outside the pages of a book or the screen of a sappy drama. It consumed me, leaving nothing untouched, pulling me closer until nothing else mattered.

Then suddenly, there was a loud knock on the door, followed by it flying open, slamming against the wall with a thud.

TWENTY-FIVE

Noah - August

SAFE & SOUND - TAYLOR SWIFT, THE CIVIL WARS

"Dorian," Colt's voice cut through the room, urgent and breathless, shattering the fragile moment like a pane of glass.

I jerked back, but Dorian held my neck, not letting me retreat.

Colt didn't even register the scene he'd walked in on as he held up his phone and then finally looked at us. Walker stirred for a moment, then settled back down.

"Figured you'd be here," he said to me.

"Why the fuck are you barging into my house late at night, you jackass?" Dorian exhaled and released me, standing and stepping toward Colt. My skin still burned where he had touched me, my heart pounding as if it hadn't caught up to reality yet.

Colt paused, giving me a sympathetic glance. "It's John…"

My stomach dropped, a sour taste rising in my throat as every nerve in my body snapped to attention. I pushed myself to my feet.

"What?" Dorian's tone was sharp, the heat in his gaze replaced with a cold, hard edge as he focused on Colt.

Colt stepped closer, handing his phone to Dorian. I leaned over to catch a glimpse of the screen. I stared at the headline, my stomach twisting tighter with every word. The headline flashed in bold letters.

Another Marketplace Murderer Victim Found in Arizona.

My chest constricted as I scanned the article. Beside me, Dorian's posture went rigid, his eyes narrowing on the screen.

The heat of the moment evaporated, replaced by something much colder.

"How the hell is he still doing this?" Dorian's tone was laced with frustration.

"He's always one step ahead," Colt replied, running a hand over his hair that was tied back. The calm, composed exterior he usually wore was cracking. "Lilah called me before the news broke."

My mind raced as I handed the phone back to Colt. "There's something new with this victim," he said, pausing and glancing at me.

"What is it?" I asked as unease crawled up my spine.

Dorian cleared his throat. Colt turned to him, then nodded. "First the earrings, then the nails... now it's rings."

"Two of them?" I asked.

"Yeah. Two rings." Colt looked down at my hand, where the two rings I always wore caught what little light there was, their shine stark in the dim room.

Four. Three. Two.

"It's a countdown," I said.

"Seems that way," Colt replied.

Dorian blinked rapidly, as if trying to put the pieces together. "A countdown?"

Dorian turned toward me, his eyes gentle, sorrowful. "Four earrings, three fingernails, two rings," I said.

"Exactly," Colt added.

My stomach churned, and bile rose in my throat, though I fought to swallow it down. Dorian's arm wrapped around my waist, his touch comforting. I let myself melt into him, drawing on his unfaltering stability.

"A countdown to what, though?" Dorian asked.

"I don't know. Lilah can only get so much information and of that, she only gives me pieces." He sighed. "I just… I needed you to know. You need to be careful."

I knew my relationship with John had been unraveling before he even disappeared. We were growing apart, but I hadn't expected this to be the reason why.

I had, at the very least, believed he was a good person. And despite all the hours I'd spent trying to make sense of it, I still couldn't reconcile the man I knew with the monster he turned out to be.

Colt's voice snapped me back to the present. "You okay?" he asked me. I blinked, forcing myself to stand straighter.

"I'm fine," I lied.

I wasn't fine, not even close, but I couldn't fall apart.

"This is more than taunting. He's trying to break her," Dorian said.

I turned to him, my throat tight. He wasn't wrong. John wasn't playing games anymore. He was pushing me closer to the edge with every murder, every clue left behind.

I still couldn't understand my role in all of this. After years of taking lives without hesitation, why has he suddenly shifted his focus to me? What was it about me that had him making this personal now, when it never had been before?

My hands were shaking. "Thanks, Colt," I managed.

"Please be careful," Colt warned.

"I'll make sure she's safe," Dorian cut him off. His hand slipped from my waist, but the heat of his touch lingered.

"Get some rest," Colt said, softer now. He gave a small dip of his head before walking to the door. "Goodnight," he called out before stepping outside.

I paced back and forth, the floor creaking under each step, before I ended up in the kitchen, my heart hammering in my ears.

Dorian followed me, pulling me into his arms. "I got you." His words washed over me, and I leaned into him, letting him carry the burden for just a second.

This was my fight, even if I didn't want it to be, but leaning on Dorian, letting him see how this affected me, made it a little more bearable.

"You don't have to do this alone," he said softly. "I know you think you do, but you don't."

"I want to believe that... But I don't know how to trust anyone," I admitted. "How could I after everything?"

I could see the impact of my words hit him for a moment before he regained his composure.

"You don't have to trust me. You can be wary all you want, but I will be here proving you wrong every step of the way," he said.

"You don't understand," I said, taking a step back, my hands clenched at my sides. The heat in my chest spread to my face.

"You're right, I don't understand. I will never understand what it's like for you, what you've gone through, but that doesn't mean I can't be here for you."

"And do what? What is this?" I motioned between us. "We have both made it abundantly clear that we can't jump into something. So what? What are we? Fuck buddies?

Only there for each other when one of us is falling apart?" My voice wavered.

Casual was what we agreed on, but it felt like we were brushing aside something deeper. We both knew it was more, but neither of us was willing to admit anything more.

In one effortless motion, he lifted me, gently setting me on the counter.

"You want a fuck buddy? You got it, peach, but I'm also your friend. I'm always here for you. The good, the bad, all of it."

Without thinking, I leaned in, my lips finding his. He seemed surprised at first, taking a beat before responding. When he did, it was slow and tender. He tasted like tequila and mint.

I wanted to stay lost in his kisses forever, to be drunk on him, consumed by the feeling of his mouth on mine.

His lips brushed mine again, gentle and patient, like he was asking for permission. I parted mine slightly in response, feeling the press of his tongue against my lips. It wasn't forceful, just an invitation, and I met it.

Gods, I knew he'd be a good kisser.

He had that sexy, broody, nerdy thing going on, but even his kisses were devastating, as if he could fix even the most broken parts of me.

I had never been kissed like this—so intense, so all-consuming. It was as if every answer to every question was somehow contained in this moment, in the way his lips moved against mine.

It wasn't urgent or desperate. It was perfect. His kiss was a quiet reassurance, not the fiery, reckless kind, but the kind that made you feel safe, even in the midst of uncertainty.

I hadn't expected it to feel this way—calm, yet

somehow still full of everything I hadn't known I needed. He moved back, a playful smirk tugging at the corner of his mouth.

"Let's go back to watching the show," he said, nodding toward the couch, though I could still feel the heat of his lips on mine.

I nodded. "Yeah… that sounds… good," I said, slipping off the counter and taking his hand as we walked over to the couch. Dorian grabbed the remote, pressing play.

It was the kind of noise that let us just be. We sat close, his arm naturally draping over the back of the couch. I nestled into him, my head resting on his shoulder, feeling the rise and fall of his breathing.

We didn't say much—there wasn't a need to. There was something comforting about the silence between us, his body next to mine. My eyelids grew heavier with each passing minute. His hand found its way into my hair, gently threading through the strands, and the steady, soothing motion made it harder to stay awake.

"I like this," he mumbled, looking down at me with a soft smile.

"Hm?" I hummed.

"Being here with you," he whispered, his voice barely audible. He pressed a kiss to the top of my head.

"Me too."

I maybe liked it too much, because being with Dorian was natural. I didn't have to constantly analyze if what I was doing was wrong, or if he was upset and not speaking about it. I didn't have to stress about my day. For some reason, being around him made the noise go quiet in my head. I was able to let go and be present.

The only other person who ever made me feel like that was Dotty.

And maybe that was their twin superpower. Maybe they had this ability for everyone.

But I wanted it just to be for me.

TWENTY-SIX

Dorian - August

I FEEL LIKE I'M DROWNING - TWO FEET

A SMALL WHINE PULLED ME FROM THE HAZE OF SLEEP, SLOWLY dragging me back to reality. I groaned, reluctant to leave the dream I'd been in—Noah was curled up around me, her legs tangled with mine, her exhales brushing against me. I blinked, trying to shake off the fog, and realized Noah was still nestled in my arms.

My heart pounded a bit harder as I tugged her closer, savoring the sensation of her against me. For a moment, I just stayed there, listening to the sounds of her breaths. I took her in—her curls spread across my chest, the soft curve of her slightly parted lips, and all I could think about was kissing her again.

Another whine came, louder this time, snapping me out of the moment. I looked over to see Walker eyeing me. His claws tapped against the floor as he pranced around.

"Alright, alright," I said. "Let's get you outside," I whispered, hoping to not wake Noah.

She stirred slightly as I moved her from me, careful not to wake her as I stood. The TV droned on, the show we hadn't paid attention to still playing. I definitely didn't plan to fall asleep with her on the couch, but I was not mad at that outcome.

Stretching, I headed to the back door, my muscles stiff from a night spent on the couch. The door slid open with a small whoosh, and Walker shot outside.

I rubbed the back of my neck, glancing at Noah sprawled out on the couch, completely at ease. My chest squeezed, and the corners of my mouth curved up.

Fuck, I like this girl.

Nope. No, I don't. I don't.

This is casual.

In the kitchen, I filled the coffeepot with water and switched it on. The drip of brewing coffee filled the space as I leaned against the counter. I went to the door, letting Walker back in as he jogged in happily. Soon, my thoughts began to spiral. Pressing my palms into the cool surface of the counter, I replayed last night over and over.

Every damn detail was etched into my head, refusing to leave. The way she moved. The sounds she made. The way her narrowed eyes burned with desire as she looked at me. And how fucking perfect she was.

Nope.

Casual, I reminded myself again.

Casual.

Before I could reel myself back, smooth arms wrapped around my waist. I hadn't even heard her wake. Her head rested against my back, her hands slipping under my shirt, her palms were like fire against my skin as she gave a gentle squeeze.

She didn't speak, and neither did I. I let myself sink into her touch, a fleeting moment I wished could stretch longer, but the pull to face her was impossible to resist.

I flipped around, taking in how stunning she was, even after just waking up.

She was still rumpled from our night on the couch, her eyelids heavy, her cheeks faintly flushed. Beautiful. Too damn beautiful.

"Morning," she murmured.

I couldn't help but grin. "I'd say it's a good morning." I threw her a wink.

She smirked, her lip caught between her teeth. "Yeah, I guess so," she replied.

That smile undid me, and I leaned down, giving in to the restraint I couldn't seem to hold on to when she was around.

There was a moment of hesitation—both of us caught between wanting this and questioning it. But then, slowly, we surrendered to the kiss. I reached up, my hand cradling the back of her head, my fingers threading through her hair.

My other hand slid down her backside, smoothing along the gentle curves of her body. Her body moved against mine, a silent answer to everything I wasn't saying aloud. She whimpered, a sound so undeniable.

There was no hesitation now, no second-guessing what this was anymore.

It was her. It was now.

And it was impossible to stop.

My hand slid lower, gripping her ass, firm under my palms. She moved against me, her hips bucking, and I pulled her up, her legs wrapping instinctively around my waist.

She rocked against my cock, her small frame held tight to me. A moan escaped me before I could stop it.

"Take me to your bed," she said, brushing my lips.

I paused, pressing my forehead to hers. My eyes searched hers, wondering if she really wanted this.

"Now," she demanded. But just then, Walker let out a

whine. "Walker, bed," she added firmly. With a reluctant huff, he retreated.

I shook my head, my tongue darting across my bottom teeth.

Adjusting my grip, I moved quickly, hooking her legs securely into my arms.

She laughed, caught by surprise. "What are you doing?"

"Exactly what you told me to," I replied, already moving, her laughter following us down the hall. "Before I fuck you in my kitchen, peach."

I walked across the house, her chuckling in my arms. I kicked my door open, grateful my daughter was still with my dad so I could have Noah exactly how I wanted her.

Under me, on top of me, I didn't give a fuck, but in my bed, moaning my name.

I laid her on the bed and crawled over her.

"Take off your clothes. Now," she said, surprising me.

"That's the last order I'm taking from you," I said as I removed my shirt, tossing it to the floor.

She blushed and nodded.

After removing my sweatpants and boxers, I crawled over her body. She stared at me, unblinking.

"Dorian…"

"Let me make you feel good," I said, peppering kisses up her body.

I grabbed the seam of her skirt, that same one I pulled up her body last night as I devoured her sweet cunt. My hands trailed up under her shirt.

She gasped. "Fuck, Dorian. Please, I need you."

Shit, how could I possibly deny her?

Lifting her shirt over her head, her arms got stuck in the sleeves. She tried to get them loose, but I grabbed her wrists, holding them there.

"Leave it," I said, but tilted my head in a question, making sure I wasn't pushing her too far.

She nodded and I smirked.

I moved my hands, stroking my cock that was aching for her. I reached for a condom from my nightstand, grateful I kept some stashed, even though I'd never needed them until now.

Tearing open the package, I rolled it over myself, glancing down at her as she licked her lips.

"Patience, baby girl." I leaned down, then slowly pushed my fingers inside her and groaned. "You always this wet for me?"

She nodded and I replaced my fingers with the head of my cock, running it through her center, gliding it back and forth.

Her eyes rolled back in her head. "You like that? You like feeling my cock rub against your pussy…" I said, stroking it down again. "Like that, peach?"

"Stop teasing," she gasped as I inserted just my tip into her. Her hips bucked up, daring me.

"Tell me how much you want me, peach. Tell me how badly you need my cock."

"Please, Dorian. Fuck, I… I need you so bad."

I took the opportunity and plunged in.

Oh fuck.

She gripped me so perfectly, and I bit back a groan. I couldn't let it end too soon. Every inch of her pulled me in deeper, and the way she moved, so naturally in sync with me, threatened to unravel my control. Her hands slid along my back, nails raking deeper with each thrust, pushing me to the edge of losing myself. I could feel her everywhere— tight and hot, pulling at my sanity.

I looked down, watching the way our bodies collided, her movements driving me higher, faster. The sight of it, the way she fit with me, how she responded, had me nearly losing it.

I slowed, moving back just enough to savor the pressure, needing to stretch this out. I wanted the moment to last, wanted to make every second count.

She followed my lead, her eyes locking with mine, and I knew she felt it too—the urgency to draw this out, to let the tension build until we couldn't hold back anymore.

But there was a knock on the door. Her eyes went wide. *Shit.*

"Baby, you have to come for me. Now." She nodded, and our movements came faster, moving in and out with a pace that could only be described as primal.

She moaned. "I'm… almost there. Fuck, Dorian. I'm going to come."

"Come for me, baby. Let me feel you come all over my cock."

She met my gaze, gasping, her walls gripping me tighter.

I continued ramming into her, my own release building.

She tensed, her eyes fluttering shut.

"That's it, baby. Be a good fucking girl and come for me." Another knock. "Now."

She obeyed, her back arching off the bed. Her whimpers and moans, combined with her pussy clenching me, sent me over the edge.

"Fuck, Noah… I'm coming."

I spilled into her, trying to hold myself up so I didn't crush her tiny frame. Our breaths were wild, coming out in fast pants.

And then another fucking knock.

I jumped into motion.

"I'm sorry, peach. I gotta get the door." I said, throwing on my pants and shirt before leaning in for one last kiss.

"Bathroom is right there." I pointed to the master bath. "Take your time."

"Uh…" she panted, trying to catch her breath. "Thanks." She nodded.

I ran out of the room, quickly trying to compose myself and think of spiders, bad sushi, or even singing the fucking national anthem in my head to try to push away what had just happened.

And how much I liked it.

Fuck, no. Spiders. Creepy crawly spiders crawling on my nuts.

"Alright, alright, I'm coming," I muttered, opening the door.

There, on the porch, stood Gracie and my dad, looking a little too awake for this early in the morning.

Gracie's face lit up the second she saw me. "Daddy!" They walked inside, and Walker's ears perked up at the sound of her voice before he greeted her with a flurry of excited kisses.

"Did you get a dog without me, Daddy?"

"No, that's Walker, Noah's dog."

She laughed as Walker peppered her with kisses.

I couldn't help but smile, crouching down to her level. "Hey, munchkin. What are you doing here so early?"

Dad stood behind her, scanning the living room, arms crossed. His expression was both amusement and knowing. "We tried calling. Guess you were a little… preoccupied," he said, looking out to where Noah's car was.

I rubbed a hand over my face. "Yeah, something like that."

Before I could say anything else, Noah walked out, somehow looking completely composed, but she still had a flush to her cheeks, the only evidence of what had unfolded.

Good.

"Daddy, why is Noah here?"

"Uh, hi, Gracie. David." She nodded.

"Who is David?" Gracie asked, her lips pulling into a thin line. "Isn't your name Dorian, Daddy?"

"David is Papa's name," I replied.

"No, his name is Papa," she argued with a small frown.

"Yes, but his real name is David. David James. Just like you're Gracie James and I'm Dorian James."

"Oh, like Aunt Dotty is Dotty James? And Noah is Noah James, right?"

My dad's gaze moved between the three of us before he let out a howling laugh.

"No, Gracie. Her name is Noah Reid, remember?" I choked out.

"Oh, that's right. Miss Noah Reid. I remember now."

"Noah James would be a good name though, huh, G?" my dad said.

Groaning, I muttered, "Dad," scolding him.

Noah walked over to where we all stood near the entryway.

"Hi, Gracie," she said, trying to figure out how to manage this delicately. "Your dad and I were just hanging out last night, watching a movie, and I fell asleep."

"You had a sleepover without me! No fair. Daddy, I need a sleepover." She stomped her foot and crossed her arms.

David chuckled, quickly disguised it with a cough after my stare.

"You have a sleepover with your aunt coming up, remember?"

Her arms fell back to her sides. "I forgot! Miss Noah Reid James, can you come?"

And then it was my turn to laugh.

"I think we can arrange that," Noah said.

"You don't have to," I said.

"I know. I want to."

"On that note, I'm heading to the ranch. Give me a hug, G." Gracie leaned over to hug my dad's knee before he picked her up with a groan. "Girl, I'm not sure I can do that for much longer," he said, before giving her a kiss on her forehead.

She chuckled in response. "Love you, Papa."

"Love you too, sweet girl."

"I'll catch you two later," he said, giving me a wink on his way out the door.

"Hey, Daddy, do you think Noah can stay for breakfast with us? It's pancake day."

"I'm sure she has things to do, Gracie girl." I couldn't tell if she wanted to say no, but I wanted to give her an easy way out. My eyes narrowed gently at her.

"You know, I'm actually free and would love to have pancakes with you," Noah replied.

"Gracie, go put your things away, and I'll meet you in the kitchen in a minute."

Gracie darted away, smiling.

I led Noah through the house, away from Gracie's room. I stopped at the end of the hallway, resting my back on the wall.

"You don't have to stay just because she asked," I said.

"Dorian, I want to be here. If I didn't, I would have left already."

"Okay…" I replied.

"Okay."

I expected Noah to back out, to make some excuse and leave. Instead, she smiled like she belonged here—like this was normal, like this was home. And for a second, I let myself pretend it was. I stepped closer, invading her space, grabbing her chin and lifting it.

"What are you doing?" she whispered.

My response was my mouth meeting hers. The kiss was unfortunately quick, and she stole all the air from my lungs as she pulled away.

"You look pretty all the time, but something about you first thing in the morning, waking up in my house, made it hard to resist you for another second. Especially if I have to go out there and dance around you in my kitchen for the next hour with my daughter playing chaperone."

"Daddy!" a shout came from the other room. "Are you coming?"

"Yes, G."

As she moved away, my heart pounded against my ribs. I wanted more. I craved it—but pushed that thought aside.

Just casual.

TWENTY-SEVEN

Noah - August

PHOTOGRAPH - ED SHEERAN

THE SMELL OF COFFEE FILLED THE KITCHEN AS I WATCHED Gracie pull a chair over to the counter, her eyes wide with excitement.

Dorian grabbed a mixing bowl from one of the lower cabinets.

"Alright, G. You ready to show Noah how we do pancakes in the James household?" Dorian asked, ruffling her hair.

Gracie beamed, her cheeks still pink from the morning chill outside. "I'm ready, Daddy! Noah, do you know how to make pancakes?"

I chuckled, tying an apron around my waist. "I think I can manage, but you might need to teach me your secret tricks."

She hopped off her chair, grabbing a whisk with the seriousness of a chef. "Okay! First, we need our ingredients. Daddy, you are the only tall one here. Can you reach everything?"

Dorian reached into the pantry, pulling out a few containers and setting them on the counter.

"Flour, eggs, milk, and a little magic," he said, glancing at me with a wink.

Walker whined from where he was instructed to stay outside of the barrier of the kitchen. I grabbed a treat from my bag, and he retreated to his bed with a small sigh.

Gracie was already busy cracking eggs into the bowl, a bit of shell falling in. I stepped closer, leaning over her shoulder.

"Oops, looks like we have a little extra crunch in there. Let's scoop it out."

Gracie giggled as I fished out the shell, her small hand brushing against mine. "I'm not the best egg-cracker yet, but I'm getting better."

"You're doing great," I reassured her. "Besides, pancakes with a bit of a crunch might be a new invention."

Dorian chuckled from across the counter. "I'm not sure I'm ready for that kind of innovation."

As Gracie continued to mix, flour puffed into the air, coating the counter and splattering a bit onto her face. She gasped and giggled, wiping her cheek with the back of her hand, leaving a trail of white powder.

"Oops!" she exclaimed, her giggles contagious. I couldn't resist leaning over and tapping her on the nose with a bit of flour.

"Now you really look like a chef," I said.

Gracie let out a loud laugh, but before I could react, Gracie grabbed a handful of batter and tossed it at me.

"Now you do too!" A playful gasp escaped me as the flour hit my apron.

"Oh, it's on now!"

Before I knew it, Dorian joined in, flicking a bit of powder in my direction.

It was almost surreal, like a scene unfolding on a movie screen. So simple, yet so real. I let my fears and doubts fade into the background, allowing myself to savor the time with two people I had come to care for more than I ever expected.

I watched Gracie, who was laughing so hard she held her side, flour in her hair, on her clothes, everywhere.

I shook my head with a grin. "I thought we were making pancakes, not a mess."

"We can do both," Dorian said, stepping behind me and wrapping his arms around Gracie's waist, lifting her up into the air. "But maybe we should focus on breakfast before we end up covered in it."

Gracie squealed in delight as Dorian spun her around and set her back down in front of the bowl.

"Okay, okay! No more food fights. Let's finish so we can eat. I'm hungry." Dorian said.

The three of us got back to work, stirring the batter and pouring it onto the griddle.

As the first pancake started to bubble, Gracie leaned over toward me. "Can you help me flip it?"

"Of course," I said, picking up the spatula. I handed it to Gracie and helped guide her hand as she flipped the pancake over, revealing the perfectly golden side.

"You did it!"

Gracie's face lit up with pride. "We're the best pancake team ever."

"Agreed," I said, smiling at her as the smell of cooking batter filled the air.

"Um, excuse me. What about me?" Dorian said.

Gracie giggled. "I don't think I've ever had this much fun making breakfast."

I glanced at Dorian, who was looking at his daughter with all the warmth in the world. There was no doubt this man, who seemed closed off to others, would burn the world down for his little girl.

And that fact had my insides tingling.

After a few more pancakes, we all sat at the table, a stack of golden goodness in front of us. Gracie, still grinning, doused hers with syrup and started cutting them into tiny, uneven pieces.

"Noah, what's your favorite kind of pancake?" she asked between bites.

"Hmm," I said, thinking. "I'm a fan of blueberry pancakes. How about you?"

"I like chocolate chip pancakes the best. Daddy makes them sometimes when it's a special day."

"Chocolate chip pancakes sound amazing. Maybe next time, we can make those together."

Gracie's eyes lit up at the idea. "Can we? Please, Daddy?"

Dorian gave me a look, his lips twitching into a smile. "Sounds like we've got another pancake date on our hands."

"Yay!" Gracie cheered.

"And maybe Noah can come to more breakfasts with us?" Warmth spread through me at her words. I glanced at Dorian, unsure how to respond, but his gaze softened as he nodded.

"Maybe she can," he said, low and thoughtful. The moment was simple, but it meant more than I could put into words. As we finished breakfast, I realized how much I'd come to care about this little family—and how that terrified me more than anything.

I listened intently as Gracie nailed the passage she'd been working so hard to master over the last few weeks. She finished and looked up at me with a smile on her face, clearly revealing how proud she was of herself.

And that made my heart want to burst.

This sweet, creative girl worked so incredibly hard to get to where she's at now.

"You did it, Gracie. That was flawless!"

"I did it, I did it! Wait… what does flawless mean?"

I chuckled. "It means it was perfect," I explained.

"I was perfect!" She beamed.

"Daddy!" she called into the other room where Dorian sat on the couch, laptop open and glasses on. "I did it! I was flawless!"

He looked up and smiled. "I knew you could do it, G," he said, lifting his glasses up to his forehead.

In that moment, it was more than a lesson. Watching her eyes light up as she mastered something she had been working so hard toward, I realized how much I cared about her progress.

"You okay, Noah?" Gracie asked.

"Yeah." I smiled at her. "But I do think we are done for tonight. We'll pick up next week," I said, tapping her little nose.

She let out a giggle that released all the dopamine in my body.

Gracie had been a big part of my adjustment to Woodstone Falls, whether she knew it or not. Tutoring her turned out to be one of the most rewarding things I'd done all summer.

What started as a way to keep myself busy—something to focus on besides the tangled mess of John's investigation —became the highlight of my days. Our tutoring sessions over the last couple of months became more than just work.

They became moments where we shared stories, laughed about silly things, and slowly built something that felt almost like a friendship. As much as you could build a friendship with a six-year-old.

It wasn't just about school for her—or for me. It was about being present, about having someone who listened and cared and wasn't wrapped up in the chaos surrounding them.

It started with little things.

She'd ask me to stay a few minutes longer after a session to watch her draw, showing me these incredible sketches of animals.

Then it became more, telling me about her friends, or the latest Ellie Miles drama.

Which apparently was that Ellie had broken up with her longtime boyfriend and was about to go on tour—which Gracie was very excited to attend.

I was too, honestly.

Woodstone Falls had a way of slowing things down, giving me space to breathe—something I hadn't known I needed until I got here. Being able to take the time to settle in over the summer made me realize just how much I needed this move.

This town was so full of life. The community offered something that was unmatched, making it hard to miss my time in the city. Back in Seattle, life had been a blur, fast and relentless, with my relationship with John always teetering on the edge of disaster, even if I wasn't ready to admit it.

But after spending time with someone who made me feel like I belonged here, I realized maybe I did belong here.

Not only for Gracie, but for the entire town. I loved feeling like I belonged after years in the city. I contemplated leaving many times, but for a while, I stayed for Dotty. And then for John. And then… because I didn't want to run.

But coming to Woodstone wasn't running. It was freeing.

Even if the noise of John's investigation echoed in my brain. The chaos ever swirling in the background. Knowing John was still out there, continuing to harm innocents, loomed like a storm I couldn't quite escape. There were days where it felt like the world might collapse under everything I didn't know.

But somehow, this town, with its quiet streets and friendly faces, pulled me out of it. I was enjoying my new routine—tutoring Gracie, taking long walks through town, catching up with Dotty in the evenings, preparing for the school year. I found purpose in the peace.

And as much as the investigation into John's life continued to swirl around me, for now, I had something solid to hold on to—this new life in a small town that had become a safe haven.

Not to mention Dorian.

Who was also a big perk of Woodstone.

Especially as he sat there, with his glasses and disheveled hair, looking unintentionally sexy as hell.

Something told me he could read my thoughts from across the room as I stood, meeting his heated gaze.

We hadn't spoken much over the past week since… well, since that night.

The kiss. The little tailgate escapade. The way he took me back to his house afterward. All of that.

We were both so busy, with him working long hours at the clinic and me getting ready for the school year. Last we spoke, we agreed it would be casual, but the way he made me feel, the way he looked at me, felt anything but.

But he said he didn't get attached. And I wasn't ready for anything serious.

"Gracie," Dorian said, his dark brown eyes not leaving mine. "Go get ready for bed. I'll be there in a few."

On cue, she let out a yawn. "Okay, Daddy." She turned toward the hallway and into the bathroom.

His steps were commanding and purposeful toward me. Once he reached me, he grabbed my elbow, pulling me over to the other side of the living room, out of direct view from the hallway where Gracie had retreated. Once we were around the corner, I chuckled.

"Dorian, what are you doin—" And his lips were on mine.

My body relaxed, letting go of everything that had been building since his lips last met mine. He pressed me against the doorframe, trapping me between his body and the wall.

He pulled back to whisper into my mouth. "This fucking hair."

Kiss.

"These fucking lips."

Kiss.

"And this tight ass," he said, lifting me up so the doorframe dug into my back. I relished the slight sting as his mouth devoured mine. He slid his tongue against mine in teasing strokes that left me whimpering, needing more. Needing him.

"I've waited all damn week for this. For you," he said.

"Me too," I admitted.

He tasted like mint and everything I knew I should stay away from but everything I wanted. His hand moved to wrap around my waist, his fingers imprinting into my skin, and all I could think was *more*.

I needed more.

I bucked my hips slightly, waiting for his response.

"Peach," he moaned. "You're killing me."

"Shush," I scolded him, not wanting his lips to leave mine ever again.

My hand slid around his neck, fingers threading

through the wavy strands of his dark hair. His kiss was urgent, as if he were heading off to war, rather than to his daughter brushing her teeth in the other room. The thought should've sobered me, but it didn't. All I could focus on was wanting more.

We were a tangled mess of desire and need when Gracie's voice rung out in the distance. Dorian groaned and put me down on my feet just before Gracie came barreling around the corner. I was still trying to get back my bearings when she appeared.

Dorian's glasses fell from where they were resting on his head to the floor, and Gracie looked back and forth between the two of us.

"Daddy..." Gracie's brow furrowed as she planted one hand on her hip. "Were you kissing Miss Reid?"

I nearly choked on a laugh, not just at the seriousness in her tone but also because she'd gone full formal and called me Miss Reid, as if stepping in to protect me while scolding him.

Dorian, wiping his mouth with impeccable timing, shook his head. "I was not."

"Uh-huh..." She narrowed her eyes at him before turning to me. "Noah, was my daddy kissing you?"

I exchanged a quick glance with Dorian, still struggling to recover. "Nope, we were just... uh..." I fumbled for something believable. "Playing a game to see who could stand closest to the door without touching it. Your dad lost." I pointed my thumb in his direction.

"Oh, whatever, I definitely won."

"You did not!"

Gracie crossed her arms, scrutinizing me. "Are you sure that is what you were doing?"

"Absolutely. He's awful at it. Big head and all. Gets in the way."

After a beat, she shrugged and smiled, somehow buying my ridiculous excuse.

"Okay. Let's go, Daddy. I'm tired."

"Yes, ma'am." Dorian gave me a look of gratitude as Gracie marched down the hallway, leaving him no choice but to follow.

As he passed me, he leaned in close, sending a wave of heat flooding through me. His voice was low as his breath brushed against my skin. "Meet me on the porch in a few?"

I swallowed, nodding slightly, biting my lip.

Dorian's gaze never left mine as he pulled back, his eyes dark and heated, holding my attention until the very last possible moment when he finally looked away.

I took a breath and walked out, the crisp evening air greeting me. The soft sound of crickets filled the air as I sat on the porch of his home. A gentle breeze rustled the leaves, and for the first time in a long while, I felt at peace.

And then my mom called.

TWENTY-EIGHT

Noah - August

CALL YOUR MOM - NOAH KAHAN

"Hey, Mom," I said, answering the phone.

Our texts were few and far between lately. With settling into Woodstone and the mess surrounding John, it was hard to find balance.

"Hi, Noah. I wanted to check in—how are you doing?" There was a warmth in her tone that caught me off guard.

"I'm good, thanks. Been settling in and getting to know the town a bit more."

"It sounds like you're liking it, though, right?"

"Yeah, I really am. I feel... at peace here." It was odd finding comfort amid the chaos that still lingered in my life, but I had.

"Well, I'm glad you're doing well." There was a soft rustling on the other end of the line before Mom's voice returned, quieter now. "You know... you may not always understand why we do things but just know your dad and I always mean the best for you. Even though you didn't choose a path I would've picked for you, I'm proud of you."

Her words took me by surprise, their weight landing heavier than I expected.

"Thanks…" I said softly. "That… means a lot."

"It's true, honey. Don't ever forget it."

"Thanks, Mom," I said, unsure of how to process her unexpected support. "How are you and Dad?"

"Oh, the usual. Your dad and I are busy with work."

"Hi, Noah!" my dad's voice popped in. "Your mom's trying to talk me into a hot yoga class, but I told her I live in Seattle for a reason. I'm not a fan of triple-digit temps," he chuckled, his signature laugh making me smile.

"Yeah, that doesn't sound like your thing."

"Definitely not." He paused before asking, "Have you heard any news? About John?"

"Not much," I said, not wanting to divulge or rehash anything if I didn't have to.

He sighed into the phone. "If you need anything, Noah, we're here. We love you."

"I know, Dad. Thank you. I love you guys too."

We talked for a while longer, exchanging small updates about my new life in Woodstone. They asked about the town, and we shared a few stories, but the tension surrounding John was always lurking beneath the surface.

"Well, we'll let you go, dear. I'm glad I got to talk to you and hope you have a good rest of your night."

"Night, love you guys," I said, hanging up the phone as the old screen door creaked open behind me.

I turned in my seat, and there was Dorian, stepping through the doorway, his footsteps soft on the old wooden boards. His dark hair was more tousled than usual, and his glasses sat perched on his nose.

"Who could stand closest to the door, huh?" he teased, his lopsided smirk tugging at the corners of his mouth.

I groaned and let my head fall into my hands, leaning forward in the chair.

Dorian crossed the small porch, dragging the chair across from me closer, the scrape of wood against wood filling the night.

He sat down, his knees brushing against mine in a small movement that sent my heart skittering.

Without hesitation, he reached for my wrists, pulling my hands free from where they were hiding my face. The gesture forced my gaze to meet his, and the intensity in his eyes made my breath catch.

There was something raw in the way he looked at me. His eyes tired from a long day, his hair in messy waves that caught the light. For a moment, he looked more vulnerable than I'd ever seen him. The glasses perched on his nose only added to his charm, somehow making him look both disheveled and composed—like someone who'd seen too much of the world, yet still managed to hold something back.

He was simply beautiful.

"You know," I began, trying to lighten the tension building between us. "I kind of like the glasses. You've nailed the hot nerd vibe."

His laugh was low, a rumble that sent shivers across my skin. "Ran out of contacts," he said, shaking his head. "I never let that happen, but my mind's been a little… distracted lately." His eyes softened as he said it, and for a fleeting moment, I let myself believe I was the reason. "Forgot to order more, so I'm stuck with the glasses until next week."

"Well, feel free to wear them around me anytime." I giggled, the sound light and carefree despite the tension coiled between us.

He leaned forward, his eyes locking with mine, and for a brief second, his gaze dropped to my lips.

My patience faltered, and before I could think better of it, I closed the gap. His lips met mine in a hesitant brush, soft and tentative at first. But when I parted my lips, allowing his tongue to meet mine, the kiss deepened into something more.

Something that made me feel alive.

A low groan escaped him, his hands skating across my thighs, gripping my hips, and moving me onto his lap. I giggled against his mouth as I settled onto him.

His breath mingled with mine, and he chuckled, the sound vibrating through me. "Peach," he murmured against my lips, "you gotta stop."

"No," I whispered, refusing to let the moment slip away.

But he pulled back, his eyes full of something that made my stomach drop. Admiration. Warmth. Fear.

"We gotta talk about this," he said.

I slid off his lap, back into my chair. The distance between us was necessary, a barrier to keep my emotions in check.

"Let's talk, then," I said, wiping my mouth with the back of my hand.

He reached for my hand, his fingers intertwining with mine like he needed the contact to stay grounded. I didn't move away. The heat of his skin centered me.

"We didn't really have a full conversation. I know we said casual, but for me, that means there's no one else. Only you."

"Of course," I replied.

I didn't want anyone else. Only him.

"I'd be lying if I said I wasn't scared, Noah," he admitted. "But I like you. I like being with you, kissing you. I like hearing about your day. I like listening to the witty things you say, and I especially like watching you come apart." His voice dropped, rough and raw, and my heart raced. "I'm not really sure what the fuck that means, but I don't bring anyone around Gracie, but you're already in her life. I don't know how to navigate this, but for now, like you said, let's keep it casual."

I could see the conflict written all over his face—the way his brows furrowed, the way his lips tightened. He was looking for answers, desperate for them, and I wasn't sure I had any to give.

"Casual." I paused. He was searching my features as if they had the answers he so desperately needed. His smile was slow, but when it came, it lit up his entire face. I continued. "Everything feels so heavy lately. I could use something simple."

His eyes caught mine in the glow of the porch lights. "You don't have to do this alone, you know," he said, low and steady.

"I know," I whispered, but the truth was, I didn't know how to let anyone else in anymore.

Not after everything that happened. He reached out, his fingers brushing against mine. The touch was gentle, almost hesitant, as he started tracing the lines of my hands.

"You don't always have to be strong. Not with me. I know this isn't anything"—he paused, seemingly trying to come up with the right words—"isn't anything serious, but I'm still here for you."

I swallowed hard, and the tightness in my chest loosened, if only for a moment. There was something about the way he looked at me, the way his presence calmed the storm inside.

"Maybe I don't know how to be anything else," I admitted.

Dorian's hand continued to trace circles around my wrist.

"Then let me help you figure it out."

For a second, I let myself lean into him, just enough to feel the solid warmth of him. But even in that closeness, there was tension—a pull between us that was both inevitable and terrifying.

I bit my lip, a smile tugging at the corners of my own mouth. "I should get home. Dotty and I need to get ready for the sleepover tomorrow."

"Oh, right. I'll drop Gracie off around six at the cabin? She has a birthday party in the afternoon."

"Sounds good. I'm sure Dotty will send Trent over here by then. No boys allowed," I teased, standing up. He followed suit, towering over me.

"Goodnight, Dor," I said, leaning up to give him a small kiss before turning to leave.

He laughed. "Dor, huh?"

"Yeah, since you're *so* good at standing so close to doors."

His laugh echoed through the quiet night as I walked down the porch steps. "Goodnight, peach."

When I knocked on the cabin door, Dotty's muffled voice came from the other side. "Did you really knock? Walk in, Noah."

I stepped inside, slipping my shoes off.

"I missed you." I walked over and wrapped her in a hug, letting her presence wash over me.

"Ugh, I missed you too." I stepped back and put my bag down. "Where's Trent?"

"He's out running errands. I told him to get lost so we could have some time. You know, I thought we'd see each other more now that you're back in town, but work and the wedding have me all over the place."

"You know I'm your maid of honor. I'm happy to help."

"I know. I think I have everything ready. Trent insisted on it being the shortest engagement known to man, so I've been rushing to get everything done."

"Well, I'm here if you need anything." I knew Dotty liked control and routine, so I let her run the show, but always made sure she knew I was there to help.

"Always." Her smile was so big and genuine that, for a moment, I felt a twinge of jealousy.

Her happiness was infectious, yet it was almost overwhelming. I loved that for her but couldn't help feeling a pang of longing for the same in my life. I wasn't ready for happy.

Dotty's expression shifted, her gaze keen as she noticed the subtle change in my demeanor.

"What's going on with you?"

"Nothing," I lied, hoping to deflect her curiosity.

"Where were you before you got here?" Her hand found her hip, striking a pose that reminded me how much Gracie was her mini-me.

I hesitated, the words stuck in my throat.

"I was tutoring G."

"Oh," she said, her eyebrows raising with interest. "So you saw Dorian?"

I sighed, the blush creeping up my cheeks. "Yeah, considering he's her father, I saw him."

"So, is what Colt said true, then? You are hooking up with my brother?" she asked, her voice a mix of excitement and disgust.

"Jesus, I thought Colt was the quiet one," I said, pinching the bridge of my nose.

"You totally are! I can see it all over your face."

"Maybe…" I mumbled, the heat in my cheeks intensifying.

"Noah Dane Reid!" she mock-scolded, laughter dancing in her eyes.

I stayed silent, and Dotty smirked, leaning closer.

"Spare me the details."

"Happily," I replied, grinning despite myself, but then I noticed Dotty's smile falter.

"I'm happy for you. Just… worried," she said, her tone shifting to something more serious.

"Dotty," I said, grabbing her hand. "I'm literally going to hold your hand while I say this. I love you. You're my person. I know you're worried, but let it be."

She squeezed my hand. "Okay. I trust you." Dotty sighed deeply, her shoulders dropping as she leaned back against the couch, pulling her legs up beneath her in a cozy, almost childlike way.

"I just… you're my best friend."

"Well, that's good because you definitely aren't getting rid of me anytime soon."

"Let's talk about the sleepover with Gracie tomorrow. Any fun ideas?" she asked.

I could see the familiar spark in her eyes, the one that emerged whenever she talked about her favorite people.

"Cupcakes?" I suggested, my face lighting up. "Gracie loves baking, and we could let her go wild with the frosting and sprinkles."

Dotty's face brightened. "Cupcakes sound perfect! And we could do some arts and crafts. Gracie's been obsessed with making friendship bracelets lately. We should get a kit and make some together for the Ellie Miles concert."

I grinned, picturing the colorful mess we'd be making. "That sounds awesome. She'll love it."

"Definitely," Dotty agreed, her smile widening. "Seems like you guys have been getting along well in your tutoring sessions?"

"Yeah, she's great. Spending time with her always puts me in a good mood."

Dotty looked at me with a fondness that only comes from years of friendship. "She adores you, you know. I can see how much she lights up when you're around."

My heart warmed. "I love spending time with her, so I think tomorrow's going to be fun."

Dotty reached for her phone, her fingers moving swiftly as she began to text Trent. "I'll have Trent pick up everything we need—arts and crafts, extra frosting, sprinkles. We'll make it a super fun girls' night."

The rest of the evening unfolded in the comfortable, familiar rhythm the two of us always shared effortlessly. After a while, Trent showed up, bringing enough supplies for a thousand sleepovers, before slipping into the other room to give Dotty and me space to enjoy our time together.

At some point, we migrated to the kitchen, diving into preparations for the sleepover. Dotty poured us each a glass of wine as we baked far too many cupcakes.

"Okay, I think we've got enough sugar here to keep G bouncing off the walls all night," Dotty teased, holding up a jar of neon-colored sprinkles.

"Good. We'll just send her home to Dorian with a sugar hangover the next day."

Dotty grinned, clinking her wine glass against mine. "That's the plan."

When we finally settled on the couch, the smell of fresh popcorn filling the room, we turned on an old rom-com. I nestled into the side of the couch, tucking my legs beneath me, while Dotty sprawled out, one arm draped over the armrest.

It felt oddly familiar to all the years we spent living together, and I relished in the reminiscing.

We didn't talk much as the movie played. Instead, we shared a few laughs, some wine, and the comfortable companionship that had seen us through years of changes. There was no need for words—the silence between us was comfortable, filled with the kind of ease that comes from knowing someone inside and out.

Dotty was my person for so long. My rock.

And while our lives had changed, I knew at the end of the day, she would go to bat for me every day of the week.

By the time the credits rolled, Dotty was dozing off, her head resting on a throw pillow, her wine glass half-empty on the coffee table.

I smiled, pulling the blanket up over her shoulders. This was why I loved her. She would drop everything for me and was fiercely protective of the ones she loved. She was always there for me, no matter what life threw at us. I quietly gathered my things, not wanting to wake her.

As I slipped on my shoes and headed for the door, I paused for a moment, glancing back at Dotty. My heart swelled with gratitude for her, for this friendship that weathered so much. I'd always known that no matter where life took us, we'd always have this—our unbreakable bond.

The sound of a door clicking open and footsteps padding across the hardwood broke the silence. Trent appeared in the doorway.

He glanced at Dotty, her face peaceful in sleep. The look he gave her was full of love and devotion, the kind of love that ran so deep it almost felt sacred.

Then he turned to me, his easy smile still lingering as he spoke. "Headed out?"

"Yeah," I replied, tucking a strand of hair behind my ear.

Trent and I had developed a friendship over time, one that wasn't just because he was Dotty's fiancé. He was a good guy and truly fit into the James family effortlessly. I knew how much he adored her—he loved her in the once-in-a-lifetime kind of way that made me believe in forever, despite everything they'd been through in their past.

I turned to grab my jacket and keys from the entryway table when Trent's voice stopped me. "Noah."

I turned back, raising my brows.

"Yeah?" He took a step forward, his expression hardening, though his gaze remained gentle.

"Dorian's my brother," he said, carrying a protective edge, though there was no hostility behind it. He glanced back at Dotty once more, then continued. "And Dotty's the love of my life. I know she's worried about you getting hurt in this more than him, but..." He hesitated, searching for the right words, but his gaze was filled with empathy. "I see the way he looks at you. The way he acts around you. I've known Dorian my whole life, and while I didn't know Gracie's mom well, I can tell you that he never looked at her the way he looks at you."

I swallowed hard as I processed what he was saying. Trent wasn't the type to interfere or push, but his words hit a nerve I hadn't fully acknowledged myself.

"Just..." He sighed, running a hand through his hair, his tone careful, like he didn't want to overwhelm me but needed me to hear this. "Be gentle with him, okay? I'm not sure where your head is at, but I have a pretty good feeling about where his is, even if he won't admit it."

I nodded, not trusting myself to speak right away.

Dorian was… complicated. I wasn't ready for complicated, not with everything else that was happening.

"I'll do my best," I finally whispered. It was the only promise I could make right now, unsure of anything more. Trent gave me a small, understanding smile before glancing back at Dotty.

"That's all I'm asking."

I glimpsed back at my best friend, now curled up on the couch, completely unaware of the conversation happening around her. She was the kind of person who gave everything to the people she loved, and I knew if she could, she'd try to solve everything for me too.

But this, me and Dorian, that was something I'd have to figure out on my own.

"Goodnight, Trent," I said, my hand on the doorknob.

"Night, Noah," he replied softly, as if sensing the storm of thoughts I was walking out into.

With one last look back at the warmth of the cabin, I slipped out the door.

TWENTY-NINE

Noah - August

SATURN - SLEEPING AT LAST

THERE WAS A FAINT CREAK OF FOOTSTEPS ON THE PORCH, followed by a small knock.

Dotty arched an eyebrow, her lips curling into a bemused grin. "Come in!" she called.

The door creaked open, revealing Dorian and Gracie. His shoulders were slumped, lips pressed into a thin line, and a shadow of worry clouded his brown eyes. Gracie clung to his shirt, peeking out from behind him.

He stepped aside, gently guiding Gracie into the room ahead of him.

Gracie stayed close to him. Her usual energy was missing, replaced by a muted stillness that felt out of place for her.

I caught his eye and mouthed, "Bad day?"

His jaw tightened briefly before he nodded once, his movements slower than usual. The tension in his shoulders was unmistakable.

Dotty rose from the couch, crossing the room with a calm, reassuring presence. She crouched in front of Gracie. "Hey, sweet girl. How was the party?"

Gracie shrugged, her fingers playing with the frayed edge of her bear's ear. Her focus stayed downward, avoiding Dotty's eyes.

Dorian reached out, his fingers grazing her hair before dropping his hand to his side. "It wasn't the best day," he said, his words careful. "But we all have bad days sometimes," he said, looking at Gracie.

"G," Dotty said, smiling gently, "want to come with me and get your room set up for tonight?"

"Okay," Gracie replied.

Dotty and Gracie disappeared down the hallway, leaving Dorian and me alone in the living room.

"What's going on?" I asked.

He raked his hands through his hair. "She was so excited this morning. I'm not sure what happened to make her go quiet since the birthday party. She won't talk about it."

I could hear the frustration in his tone, each word dipped in worry. His eyes were tired—the kind of exhaustion that came from not just lack of sleep, but the helplessness of a father who couldn't reach his daughter.

"We have lots of fun plans, so hopefully that will cheer her up," I replied, and he pulled me into an unfortunately quick hug.

Gracie and Dotty appeared, and I stumbled back quickly. Dotty's eyes locked onto mine, but then she glanced at Gracie.

"Hey, G. What do you think? Cupcakes or a movie first?" I asked, trying to coax something out of her.

"Cupcakes, I guess..." Her words were barely audible.

"Good choice," I said, offering a smile.

Dorian wrapped Gracie in a brief hug before heading out, looking back a few times before the door shut behind him. I watched him go, a strange mix of relief and longing tangling in my chest.

For the next hour, we stayed in the kitchen. The sweet smell of vanilla frosting filled the air as Gracie sat at the counter, her small hands carefully adding dollops of frosting to each cupcake. Sprinkles—vibrant pinks, yellows, and blues—scattered across the counter, some sticking to her fingers as she worked. The frosting smeared in delicate, uneven layers, and a few stray sprinkles spilled off the cupcakes. Gracie's brow furrowed in concentration, but there was something distant in her expression, like her mind wasn't fully here, lost somewhere I couldn't quite place.

Dotty filled the silence with stories from her own childhood, her laughter light and infectious as she joked about things that happened years ago. She even mimicked her younger self, crossing her eyes for a moment to make us laugh. But Gracie didn't seem to notice. She stayed quiet, her shoulders slumped, and her gaze fixed on the cupcakes in front of her as though they held all her thoughts. The more Dotty tried to coax her out of it, the more withdrawn Gracie became, her silence louder than anything Dotty said.

After we'd decorated the last of the cupcakes, the kitchen heavy with the sweetness of frosting and the crumbs from our own indulgence, Dotty looked between Gracie and me. She stood with her hands on her hips, her brow raised in thought.

"All that sugar… we should probably have something real to eat. How does pizza sound?" Dotty asked, trying to keep the energy light.

Gracie barely reacted. Her shoulders gave a small, almost imperceptible shrug, still lost in whatever thoughts she was keeping to herself.

"Pizza sounds perfect," I said. "Want me to order?"

"No, I'll go pick it up. Delivery would take forever at this hour."

"Sounds good. We'll be here," I replied.

Dotty hesitated for a moment, her expression gentle as she looked at Gracie. "You sure you'll be okay?"

"We'll be fine," I said. "Go get the pizza. Maybe a little extra cheese will help."

Dotty didn't seem fully convinced, but after grabbing her keys from the counter, she gave us a small wave.

"Alright, I'll be back soon." The door clicked shut behind her. The oven's hum and the ticking clock was the only sounds filling the silence.

Gracie sat at the kitchen table, her legs dangling off the chair, swinging back and forth absentmindedly. She hadn't said much all night, only answering in one-word responses, and my heart ached knowing what was weighing so heavily on her.

With Dotty gone, I decided to try again, hoping that the quiet would give Gracie the space she needed to open up.

"You know, Gracie," I began, crouching down so I was at her eye level, "if you ever want to talk about anything, I'm always here to listen."

She shifted uncomfortably, her little fingers fidgeting with the hem of her shirt. "Okay…"

I waited patiently. Gracie's eyes peered up to meet mine, full of hesitation. "But… will you tell my Aunt Dotty or my dad?" she asked, her voice small, but loaded with concern.

"That depends," I replied. "If it's about keeping you safe, I might have to tell your dad, but if it's something else, my lips are sealed."

I made an exaggerated motion of zipping my lips, locking them, and throwing away the key. That earned me a tiny smile from her, but it quickly faded.

She hesitated, staring down at her shoes. "My…" I

waited, giving her time to gather her thoughts. Her voice wavered as she spoke again. "My friend Candace… she wasn't very nice to me today."

A cold knot formed in my stomach when I saw the expression on Gracie's face. Her eyes were red-rimmed.

I gently cupped her chin and lifted her face so she would meet my eyes. Her focus faltered, as though she wasn't sure if she was ready to look at me, but I could see the silent plea in her expression.

"What did she say?"

She sniffled. "She said I'm not smart." Her bottom lip turned down. "And that it's weird that I don't have a mommy." Each word came out as if it hurt to say it.

A sharp, aching pain stabbed through my heart, and I wanted to grab her, hold her tight, and never let go. But instead, I stayed there, frozen, my heart breaking into a thousand pieces.

"No one should ever say that to you," I said, my throat tight. My breathing felt shallow.

Gracie let out a shaky exhale, her shoulders slumping, defeated. "I'm not good at anything," she mumbled. "And I don't have a mommy like all the other kids. It's just Daddy… I love him, but sometimes I wish I had a mommy too."

"Oh, Gracie." I sucked in a shaky breath, fighting back the pinch at the bridge of my nose. "None of that is true," I whispered urgently. "Hey, listen to me." I brushed a tear off her cheek. "You're amazing at drawing, remember? That's something special. You're so creative and kind, and you've got a heart that makes everyone around you want to be better." My own tears started to well. "You don't need to be like anyone else. You're perfect just as you are."

But it didn't seem to reach her. She didn't respond, only

stared at the floor as if she didn't believe me. The silence was suffocating, and the ache in my chest deepened.

"I'm sorry, Noah," she said suddenly, her words so soft it almost broke me. "I don't want to make you sad too."

I blinked, surprised.

"No, Gracie, no," I said urgently, taking her hands in mine. "You're not making me sad. I just… I just hate that anyone made you feel like this."

Gracie pulled back, her face still trembling with emotion. "But she's right. I'm not good at reading… and… and"—she let out a small hiccup—"everyone else has a mommy but me." Her eyes met mine, searching my face for any sign of reassurance. "If I don't have a mommy, does that mean no one will love me like that?" Her words cracked as they left her lips, and it felt like my heart splintered in a dozen places.

I swallowed hard, trying to keep my composure, but the lump in my throat made it hard to speak. "You have so many people who love you. Your daddy loves you more than anything. You have your Aunt Dotty, all your uncles, and your papa. And you have me too, G. We all love you, and that's what matters."

She wiped her eyes with the back of her hand, and I could see the confusion and uncertainty still clouding her face.

"Do you…" She paused, twisting a strand of her blonde hair before looking back to me. "Do you think you could maybe be my mommy? I know my Aunt Dotty can't be my mommy and she has Uncle Trent now, but I think if I asked my daddy really nice, maybe he would be okay with it?"

I thought my heart couldn't possibly fracture anymore, but I was wrong. The question hit me harder than any blow I could've imagined. It was as if the floor shifted beneath my feet, and I was no longer standing on solid ground. I wanted to say yes, to wrap her in my arms and tell her I'd be everything she needed, but the truth felt heavier than I could carry.

My breath caught in my throat as I stared at her, my heart shattering. She was so innocent, so full of hope, and the thought of letting her down felt unbearable.

"Oh, sweet girl," I said, gently cupping her cheek, my thumb brushing away another tear that slipped down through her lashes. "That's such a big, important thing to ask." I swallowed hard. "I would be the luckiest person in the world if I could, but being your mommy... it's not something we can decide like that."

My heart felt like it had been ripped from me as her face fell, her bottom lip quivering again. I quickly added, "But hey, look at me." I tipped her chin up gently. "I'm always here for you, okay?" I paused, my own tears falling down my cheek. "If you ever want someone to talk, I'm always here for you."

"But... I don't want you to go away," she said. She was just a child who didn't understand the complexities of love or loss but felt them all the same. "I want you here. Always. Like... like when you're around, it feels like everything's better."

I pressed my lips together, trying to hold back the tears, but it was impossible. They spilled over, unbidden, and I let them fall.

"I'm not going anywhere, Gracie," I promised. "This town and the people in it"—I tapped her little button nose—"have convinced me to stay."

She looked up at me again, her expression filled with longing, and I realized how much pain she was carrying. How much she placed on her tiny shoulders.

"Do you like my daddy, though?"

I froze. The question took me by surprise, the raw, innocent hope in her words making my chest ache even more.

I didn't know how to answer. How could I tell her that it wasn't that simple? There was no doubt I cared about Dorian, but I didn't want to give her any false hope.

Instead, I squeezed her hand. "I care about your dad a lot," I said, my voice cracking. "I don't know what the future holds. But what I do know is that I'm here for you, no matter what."

Her face softened, but I could see the sadness still lingering in her features. Yet, for the first time in our conversation, there was the tiniest bit of relief in her expression.

"Do you think maybe one day… you could marry my daddy?" she asked, looking down again, her shoulders slumping. "That way you could be my mommy?"

"Family isn't just about the people who love us, Gracie. It's not always about titles or names. It's about showing up for each other, being there when it matters. No matter what, you'll always have people who love you, including me."

Gracie nodded slightly, her expression still sad but lighter now, and I hoped that meant she was beginning to accept the love that was around her.

And though I couldn't give her the answers she wanted, the only thing I could offer her was my presence, my love. And hope that was enough.

She sniffled again, but this time it wasn't full of the heartbreak from earlier. Her small hand reached up to pat my cheek as if trying to comfort me too. We stayed like that for a few more moments, just the two of us, until I felt her relax against me, her breathing evening out as the weight of her little world seemed to ease a bit. Finally, Gracie gave me a small, tentative smile, her eyes still red but showing a spark of something more hopeful.

I found myself thinking about what she said, about what it meant for her to feel like I could be part of her family. And as much as my heart ached at the impossibility of what she wanted, a small, undeniable part of me wished I could let go of my fears and explore the possibility of something more with Dorian. Even if we'd agreed to keep things casual, every moment with him felt anything but casual.

But for now, I simply held her, my heart full and breaking all at once, and whispered, "I'll always be here for you, Gracie. Always."

Just then, Dotty returned with the pizza, the aroma filling the room as she set it down on the table. Gracie's face was a little brighter, the corners of her mouth lifting as she saw the pizza.

Her earlier tension started to melt away. She bounced back to life as Dotty placed the boxes on the table, and we eagerly dug into our dinner, laughing and sharing bites between conversations.

The evening unfolded comfortably, a mix of light-hearted chatter and quiet moments. We ate and made bracelets—Gracie beaming as she picked out the beads, her hands steady as she worked on her creation. It was the perfect sleepover in the warm space of the living room.

Walker padded over to nudge Gracie's hand, earning a giggle as she gave him a quick pat before he flopped down at her feet.

Eventually, we settled into sleeping bags on the floor in front of the TV, the soft glow of the screen casting gentle shadows across the room. Gracie fell asleep first, clutching her stuffed bear, and soon Dotty's quiet snores joined the mix, the comfort of the moment lulling me into sleep as well.

THIRTY

Noah - August

LAMENT - INVADABLE HARMONY

THE ROOM FELT COLD, THOUGH I DIDN'T REMEMBER TURNING the TV off. The blankets around me were gone. Walker wasn't at my feet, and Dotty and Gracie were nowhere in sight.

"Dotty?" I called.

No response.

The kitchen light was on, a dim glow spilling into the living room. I rubbed my arms against the chill and stood. Soft scrapes echoed through the quiet house as my feet carried me toward the kitchen.

"Gracie? Dotty? Walker?"

There was nothing but overwhelming silence, the kind that made my heart rate pick up. Something was wrong. I could feel it in the pit of my stomach.

As I stepped into the kitchen, something felt off. The back door was ajar, just enough for the faintest breeze to slip through, brushing the curtains in a lazy sway. The air felt cold. Too cold. I stepped closer, the floor creaking under my weight.

"Hello?" My voice was louder now, edged with panic.

A faint sound came from outside—a low, almost imperceptible rustle. My breath hitched as I approached the door, every instinct screaming at me to stop, to turn around and run.

It felt like my legs were sinking into the floor, as if the earth itself was holding me in space. But despite my uncertainty, my feet stepped closer.

Each step was a battle, my body begging me to listen, but my mind driven by some irrational, rabid curiosity.

The backyard was shrouded in darkness, the tall grass swaying gently in the wind. The faint silhouette of the tree line loomed in the distance, stark against the moonlit sky.

And then I saw it. A shadow, barely more than a ripple in the darkness. It lingered just beyond the edge of the light from inside, moving slowly, methodically—like it was watching me.

The shadow stopped, and for a moment, I thought it might have been my imagination. Then it stepped forward, the light catching just enough to reveal his face.

"John?" My heart seized in my chest.

Like a pillar of fear, John stood there, his hands sheathed in his pockets, his head tilted slightly, as if amused by my panic.

"Four," he said. His voice was smooth, deceptively calm.

He took a step forward. I stumbled inside, my legs trembling, my back hitting against the counter. My hand fumbled for something—anything—to defend myself, but all I found was the cold, empty surface.

"How? How did you find me?" I asked, shaking my head.

He advanced, his steps unhurried.

"Three," he murmured, his voice dropping to a chilling tone.

The air felt heavy, oppressive, and it was getting harder to breathe. I couldn't move, couldn't think, as he stepped toward me once again.

"Two," he hissed, his body only a few feet from mine.

The room tilted. Shadows stretched and deepened, swallowing me whole. My body locked up, every nerve screaming at me to run, but I couldn't move as he closed the final step between us.

He leaned down, his exhale brushing my ear. His voice was low and deliberate as he whispered, "One."

I bolted upright with a gasp, my chest heaving, my body drenched in sweat. The room spun as I tried to make sense of my surroundings while the ghost of his breath still was burning on my ear.

It took a moment for everything to register—the soft glow of the TV, the blanket half-draped over me, Dotty and Gracie fast asleep on the sleeping bags beside me, Walker laying at our feet. Gracie's little hand rested against her cheek, her curls spilling over the pillow, and Dotty's sleeping breaths filled the room.

It was just a dream.

But it didn't feel like one.

My hands trembled as I pushed the blanket off and stood, the room suddenly too warm, too stifling. I stumbled into the kitchen, gripping the counter for support as I tried to steady my breathing.

I reached for my phone. Before I could comprehend what I was doing, I scrolled to Dorian's name with shaking fingers. I hesitated for a moment before hitting call.

He answered almost immediately, despite it being the middle of the night.

"Noah?" His voice was groggy and confused.

"I…" My voice cracked, and I swallowed hard, willing myself to speak.

"What's wrong?" he asked.

"I don't know. I… had a bad dream," I blurted out, still trying to catch my breath. "It was him, Dorian. It felt so real. He was counting down, and he was there. I swear he was, I could feel him right there and it was like I couldn't move, I couldn't breathe, and I just—I just wanted to hear your voice."

"I'm on my way," he said without hesitation.

"No, you don't have to do that."

"I'm already walking out the door. I'll be there in a few."

"Okay," I replied, clutching the phone to my chest as the line went dead.

Five minutes felt like an eternity, but when the knock finally came, I almost ran to the door.

Dorian stood there, his dark eyes scanning me. He didn't say anything, just pulled me into his arms, holding me tight.

"It's okay," he murmured, his hand running soothingly down my back. "I'm here now."

The sound of his voice, the steady warmth of his embrace, broke something inside me, and I let the tears fall.

"Thank you," I whispered against his chest, my voice muffled but full of relief.

"Always."

He led me to the couch, sitting beside me as I attempted to push the dream away, but failed. His hand never left mine, his fingers brushing gentle circles atop my skin.

"I got you, peach. I've got you," he said softly.

I nodded, my breathing finally evening out.

"Can I stay? I'll just tell G I missed her." His gaze searched mine.

"Okay, but I have to sleep down there," I said, pointing to my spot between Dotty and Gracie.

"Fine." He teased. "If you have to."

I wedged my way down to the floor as he settled onto the couch, pulling a blanket over himself. My attention stayed locked on him—the steadiness of his presence easing the tension that had gripped me.

His hand dropped, brushing against my temple, the touch tender as his fingers slowly moved back and forth.

I leaned into his touch, sinking into the calmness of the moment. It was the same feeling he had brought out in me since the very beginning.

My eyes grew heavy, my heart settling into a steady rhythm. Just as sleep began to claim me, I heard a small creak of the couch—and then the faintest pressure, a soft, lingering brush of his lips against my head.

THIRTY-ONE

Dorian - September

CHERRY WINE - HOZIER

SCHOOL WAS IN FULL SWING, AND GRACIE WAS ALREADY thriving in Noah—Miss Reid's—class. I wasn't entirely sure what happened a couple of weeks ago when she was so upset after the birthday party, but she came home the day after the sleepover with her usual bright smile.

When I asked Dotty about it, she didn't have much information either—only that Noah had a conversation with her that seemed to make a difference. Seeing my usually cheerful daughter so down had been gut-wrenching. I would have ripped my heart out and given it to her if it would have worked.

But when we woke up the next morning, I was grateful I had come over—seeing them in much better moods made everything feel a little brighter, especially after seeing Noah so shaken up too.

The last couple of weeks had been filled with long hours at work and the start of a new school year. Noah and I were navigating this casual arrangement, or whatever we were calling it, without any labels, just trying to live in the moment.

Somehow, she effortlessly became part of my life, weaving herself into my day-to-day, slipping into the smallest cracks of my routine.

I'd catch myself thinking about her in the middle of a long workday. I'd hope it was a day she'd come over for Gracie's tutoring, or if not, a day I could hopefully convince her to sneak over after Gracie was in bed, so I could pretend she was mine, even if it was only for a few hours. There was something about her that cut through the noise in my mind.

I always thought I would be single forever. It was complicated enough for Gracie without a mom. The last thing I wanted was to open myself up to Noah completely, only to have her leave us one day, unwillingly or not.

And that scared the hell out of me.

But the more time I spent with her, the more that agreement was a flimsy excuse. Deep down, we both knew that *casual* was a facade.

I sighed, grabbing my coffee from my desk and took the last sip. It was now cold from sitting untouched for hours. The day was a blur of appointments and tasks, but in the back of my mind, all I could think about was Noah. I had to face the truth. I wasn't just scared of losing her. I was scared of needing her.

I glanced at the clipboard on my desk, the lists and notes blurring together. With a groan, I pushed back my chair, ready to escape and finish the day. As I reached for the door, my phone buzzed on the desk behind me. The name on the screen made my heart skip for a second.

NOAH

Hey, you free tonight?

It was simple, but something in the pit of my stomach

twisted. Casual, just like we'd agreed. And yet, I couldn't shake the feeling that there was more to it—more to us. I quickly typed a reply before I could overthink it.

ME

Yeah, what's up?

NOAH

Can I come over after Gracie's asleep?

ME

Of course. I'll text you when she's in bed.

NOAH

Sounds good. I've missed you.

The lingering buzz in my chest stayed with me as I stepped out of the office.

I glanced at the chart. "Mr. Pickles?" I announced, trying to keep my tone professional as I stepped into the waiting area.

From the corner of my eye, I spotted Mrs. Hargrove, one of the town regulars, shuffling forward with her ancient tabby cat in tow.

The cat was a legend around here—mostly because he hated everything. I'd been treating him for years, and no matter how often I saw him, he still looked at me like I was number one on his shit list.

"Well, if it isn't my favorite troublemaker," I said, nodding toward the cat. Mrs. Hargrove chuckled, her familiar smile creasing the corners of her eyes.

"I swear, I think he knows we're coming here before we even leave the house," she said, struggling to keep him from wriggling out of her arms. "He starts sulking the second I mention your name."

"Smart cat," I muttered under my breath, suppressing a

smirk. "Come on back. Let's see what's going on with him this time."

Mrs. Hargrove followed me into the exam room, setting the cat down on the table, where he immediately crouched low, his tail lashing. Mr. Pickles glared at me, clearly not pleased with the situation.

Me neither, buddy.

"How've you been?" I asked, more out of politeness than genuine curiosity. Mrs. Hargrove had a habit of talking at length once she got going, and I didn't have time to get lost in small-town gossip today. But she was a good client—loyal and always kind.

"Oh, you know, the usual. Arthritis is kicking up again, but that's what happens when you get old." She gave a light laugh. "How about you? How's that sweet little girl of yours?"

"All is well," I replied curtly.

She gave me a run down on her cat, who'd been vomiting a lot more often over the last month. I focused on examining him but could feel Mrs. Hargrove watching me.

But my mind started to drift back to Noah. It had been over a week since we'd spent time alone together, and the ache to be near her was eating me alive.

It was maddening.

Even when I had her, it wasn't enough. Her body tangled with mine, her nails dragging down my skin, her breath hot against my neck—it still didn't quiet the constant need for her. She was in my head all the time, a relentless ache I couldn't satisfy, no matter how many nights we spent together.

Fuck. Now is not the time to pop a boner in front of Mr. Pickles.

"Nothing too serious," I finally said, moving away from

Mr. Pickles. "A little upset stomach. I'll give you some meds for him, but he should be fine in a few days."

"Oh, thank heavens," Mrs. Hargrove sighed.

"Thank you, Dr. James. I don't know what we'd do without you." I offered a small nod.

"Just doing my job."

As I handed her the medication and walked her to the door, I couldn't help but think how easy it was with animals—they didn't ask for more than you were willing to give.

No complicated feelings, no expectations. With them, I knew exactly where I stood. But when it came to people, especially one person in particular, things weren't that simple.

Thankfully, Mr. Pickles was my last patient of the day, and I was able to spend some time catching up on paperwork and all the miscellaneous admin tasks that always seemed to pile up.

My phone buzzed on my desk, and Colt's name lit up the screen.

"Hey, man, what's up?" I answered, leaning back in my chair.

"Wanted to see if you and G wanted to go to The Lodge tonight with me," he said.

My eyebrows raised. "Did you just ask me out?"

"Not for you, jackass. Want to see my niece."

I chuckled, leaning forward again. "Right, of course." He didn't say anything, so I sighed. "Yeah, she'd love that."

"Meet you there?"

"Yup, I'm finishing up paperback and will be headed there in ten."

Colt grumbled an okay before hanging up, and I set the phone down, grinning.

THIRTY-TWO

Dorian - September

HEAR YOU ME - JIMMY EAT WORLD

THE LODGE WAS THE SAME AS EVER. WARM, NOISY, AND packed with locals. It wasn't fancy, but it was the kind of place everyone in Woodstone Falls came to for a decent burger and a break from their day. Gracie was already bouncing up and down as Colt and I followed the hostess to a booth near the back.

"She's excited," Colt commented dryly, watching Gracie practically vibrate in place.

"Food always does that to her," I replied, sliding into the booth, while Colt and Gracie sat across from me. Gracie started coloring on her kids' menu.

"I'm not like that!" Gracie protested, her little face scrunched up in mock offense. I shot her a teasing grin.

"You literally asked for snacks five minutes ago." Colt shook his head, smirking as he opened his menu.

"But I was hungry," she whined.

The door swung open, and a group of teachers strolled in. I recognized a few faces. Miss Lane walked in with a relaxed confidence, even as her eyes darted to Colt the moment they walked in.

"Great," Colt muttered under his breath, catching sight of his ex. "That's exactly what I needed tonight."

She caught our eyes and offered a polite, albeit strained, smile as she made her way toward us. Mr. Harris trailed behind her. I'd never got a good read on the guy and wasn't sure if I liked him or not.

But I didn't really like most people, so…

"Well, look who it is," she said as she approached, her tone chipper but tight. "Dorian." She nodded at us. "And Gracie!"

Gracie smiled up at her, shy but polite.

"Hi, Miss Lane."

Colt gave a curt nod, leaning back in his seat, clearly not thrilled by the sudden reunion. "Lana."

"Colt." She looked at him for a beat longer, her eyes moving away as Harris caught up. He glanced from me to Colt with a slow, deliberate gaze.

"Mr. Harris," I greeted, trying to sound casual.

"Dr. James." He nodded once, then turned to Colt, his eyes lingering a second too long. "Detective." He nodded.

"We're just here for dinner," Colt grunted, clearly not in the mood for small talk.

Lana shifted awkwardly, her smile not quite reaching her eyes as she glanced between us. "Well, don't let us interrupt. Just wanted to say hi."

"Right," Colt said, clearing his throat, visibly uncomfortable.

"Enjoy your night."

There was a beat of silence that stretched just a little too long before Lane gave a tight nod and tugged on Harris's sleeve.

"Come on, we should go grab our table."

"See you around," he finally said, a little too calmly as Lana dragged him away.

After the waitress came by and took our orders, Gracie look to me.

"Miss Lane and Noah are friends now. They eat lunch together sometimes," Gracie said, looking up at me innocently before returning her focus to coloring.

Colt groaned at her name.

I chuckled, trying to lighten the mood. "Come on, man. Don't tell me you're still sore over her."

Colt shot me a deadpan look. "She cheated on me with a guy who owns a beekeeping business. I don't exactly have fond memories."

I laughed, shaking my head. "Fair enough." I smirked at Colt's grumpy response. I leaned back in the booth, crossing my arms. "But are you ever gonna tell me what really happened with her?"

Colt grunted, clearly not thrilled about diving into that particular conversation. He stared hard at the menu, like it held the answers to life's mysteries. "Nothing to tell. She cheated. End of story."

I remember several years ago, Colt letting it slip that a girl had gotten under his skin, and ever since, he's never been the same. I wasn't sure if that girl was Lana or not, but whoever it was, I was curious about who had been able to crack through his exterior.

"Come on, man. It can't just be that simple."

He shifted uncomfortably, his fingers tightening around the edge of the menu before he set it down. "It's that simple. People don't change. They do what they're gonna do, and you move on." His jaw clenched.

Gracie glanced up at Colt with wide eyes. "Uncle Colt, why are you mad?"

The hard lines in his face eased as he turned to her. "I'm not mad, G. Just… talking."

Gracie gave him a little frown, clearly not buying it. "I

don't like it when you're mad. You look all scary and grumpy."

Colt let out a low chuckle and ruffled her hair. "I'm not scary, kiddo. I'm your favorite uncle, remember?"

Gracie giggled—her mood instantly brightened. "You're my favorite... today. And you're not scary to me. You're just like Dad. He can be grumpy sometimes too."

"Hey!" I protested but couldn't help smiling at the way Colt's entire demeanor shifted.

It was always like this with Gracie—he could be closed off with everyone else, but the second she entered the picture, his guard came down. She was one of the few people that could reach him, and I loved seeing that from my grumpy brother.

Gracie wriggled in her seat, her curiosity not satisfied. "But Uncle Colt, why did Miss Lane leave if she was your girlfriend? I thought girlfriends were supposed to stay."

I saw Colt hesitate, his gaze flicking to me for a second before landing back on Gracie. He cleared his throat.

"Well, sometimes people leave, G. Even when you don't want them to."

Gracie's brow furrowed, and her small face scrunched up in thought. "Like my mom?"

My heart sank and Colt sighed, running a hand through his hair. I started to speak, but Colt raised his hand gently, indicating he had it.

"Your mom didn't leave you because she wanted to. She loved you a whole lot, but..." He paused. "Sometimes people get really sick or hurt, and their bodies can't keep them here anymore."

Gracie blinked, her eyes wide and searching his face. "But why didn't the doctors make her better? Maybe she can come back?"

Colt swallowed hard. We'd had this conversation a

handful of times, but she was getting to an age where these questions were coming up more and more.

"They tried, kiddo. They did everything they could. Sometimes, even doctors can't fix things. Your mom's body was too tired, and she had to go."

Gracie was quiet for a moment, processing his words. "So, she didn't leave because she didn't love me?"

I spoke up, pushing down my emotions. "No, G," I said. "She loved you more than anything." My voice was hoarse, despite my efforts. "She didn't want to go. It wasn't her choice. I know if she could be here with you, she would."

Gracie gave him a small, sad smile, her eyes wet but bright. "I miss her."

I rubbed my chest in an attempt to dull the ache. Gracie had never even met her mother, so her statement was nothing short of devastating.

Colt gently pulled her into a hug, wrapping his arms around her. "I know you do, G. But you've got a lot of people who love you, okay? We're all here for you."

Gracie snuggled into him, her small arms wrapped around his neck. "You're the best, Uncle Colt. I don't think anyone's better than you." The corner of Colt's mouth twitched, a rare smile breaking through his broody exterior.

"Hey, what about me?" I teased, needing to lighten the mood.

Colt's eyes fluttered shut as he held my daughter. After a moment, he shifted in his seat, letting her go.

He picked up his water and took a long sip before turning back to me.

"So, no Lana," I said, watching his reaction carefully. I wasn't going to let him get off the hook just because of change in subject. "Anyone else you're interested in?" I teased.

His jaw clenched, his eyes darkening.

"No way… There *is* someone. Who?" I asked.

"Doesn't matter. She's not interested."

I raised an eyebrow, intrigued by his rare admission. "I thought girls were into the man bun, beards, tattoos and broody exteriors these days?"

He groaned. "I have… baggage." He gestured to Gracie, indicating he wasn't going to say anything in front of her.

But we both know without her, he was not nearly as open, so it was a lose-lose situation if I ever wanted to know what the hell went on in his head.

"You don't have baggage, Uncle Colt," she said with a small pout, clearly confused by the term. "Wait, what's baggage?"

Colt smiled faintly, shaking his head. "It's nothing, G."

Gracie seemed satisfied with that answer and went back to her menu, but I wasn't letting it go so easily. I studied Colt for a second, noting the tension still lingering in his shoulders.

"So, this woman you think would never be interested in you," I said, keeping my tone casual, "have you maybe asked her?"

He scoffed, shaking his head. "Trust me. She knows."

"Well," I said slowly, leaning back in my seat, "maybe you should give yourself more credit. Despite the whole grumpy thing, you're not as much of a jackass as you think."

Colt let out a dry laugh, shaking his head. "Yeah, thanks for that, Doc."

Gracie suddenly perked up, her eyes wide as the waitress approached with our food.

"Ooh, food's here!" she chirped, bouncing in her seat again. Colt helped make sure she didn't knock over her drink in her excitement.

"What about you? You're the one with googly eyes lately." He raised a brow at me.

I scoffed. "I don't know what you are talking about."

"Sure you don't."

"Not at all."

Gracie, who seemed too engrossed in her food to notice our conversation, suddenly perked up. "Uncle Colt, are you talking about Noah? I mean, Miss Reid? I think my daddy likes her too!"

I let out a groan as Colt burst into laughter. I quickly ignored the turn in conversation, unsure of how to respond.

The truth was, I didn't even know what Noah and I were, if we were anything at all.

But I wasn't ready to talk about that, especially to my brother.

THIRTY-THREE

Noah - September

BUTTERFLIES - ABE PARKER

Dorian stood in the kitchen, leaning against the counter with a relaxed smile that never failed to send butterflies fluttering in my stomach as I walked in.

"Hi," I said, taking in his casual attire—a T-shirt that hugged his shoulders just right and black joggers that managed to be loose but still cling perfectly to his muscular thighs.

He was effortlessly handsome, and my pace quickened as I walked into the kitchen. He grabbed a water from the fridge, our fingers brushing for a moment. It was the kind of touch that was electric.

I nodded in thanks. "Long day?"

"Yeah," he said, pushing off the counter and moving toward the living room. "You?"

"Same," I replied, trying to keep my tone light as I followed him into the cozy, dimly lit living room. "With the wedding planning, I've been on the phone constantly trying to get everything figured out."

He chuckled, a deep, rich sound that made me smile. "I take it she finally let you take something off her hands?"

"Yeah, I'm in charge of the cake and flowers," I said, moving to sit on the couch while he settled in next to me.

"I'm surprised she let you have that much."

"Me too," I said, shaking my head, laughing along with him. I shifted to fit into his side, and he wrapped his arm behind me, nuzzling me closer.

"So, what's it like being the maid of honor?" he asked, a playful glint in his eyes.

"No disasters yet."

His gaze lingered on me, and I felt my cheeks heat under his attention. "Dotty's lucky to have you," he said as he placed a kiss on the top of my head.

I smiled, turning to face him. "No need for flattery, Dr. James," I replied, nudging him with my foot.

"Just stating the obvious," Dorian said, a sinful glint in his eye. "But if you keep calling me doctor like that, you might make my dick hard."

I chuckled in response. "I might be okay with that."

His phone rang. He pulled it out of his pocket and looked at the screen.

"It's Colt," he said, glancing at his phone. I motioned for him to take it, feeling a knot tighten in my stomach. "Hey, man. What's up?" he answered, his voice casual, but I could already sense a shift in the air.

I couldn't make out the words on the other end, but Dorian's face fell, and my heart pounded in response. I moved nervously on the couch, my thoughts spiraling.

Is it John? What if it's bad news? What if it's about another victim? What if he's continuing to drag me into it? How do I play into this stupid game of his?

I hadn't been entirely able to shake the anxiety that had settled in my body ever since John vanished. I pushed it aside for the sake of trying to start over. A new chapter in a new town. A new job and new coworkers and new friends.

But he was still out there, a dark specter haunting my thoughts as I waited for the other shoe to drop.

"Not good. Where?" Dorian's brow furrowed, and I leaned in closer. The pause seemed like an eternity, stretching my anxiety thin. "Okay, thanks." His tone was clipped, and my palms grew clammy. "Yeah, sounds good. I'll let her know. Bye."

As he hung up, Dorian ran a hand through his hair, his shoulders tense.

I straightened up on the couch. "What is it?"

"Another victim," he said.

The words seemed to echo in the silence. I felt the world tilt beneath me, a pit of dread forming in my stomach, and a bitter taste surged in the back of my throat. The intensity in his eyes eased as he looked at me. He opened his arms and motioned for me to join him.

I moved to him, but all I could hear was the whooshing sound in my ears, drowning out everything else.

Each time there was another victim, I thought about her.

Was she a mom? A sister? An aunt? Someone's best friend?

I thought about her life, what she did for a living, how she spent her free time. Who would miss her.

All because someone vile and evil decided her life wasn't worth it. It disgusted me, thinking about how I let that very person into my life for years. I forced myself to take a deep breath.

"Where?" I asked.

He shook his head, but the concern etched onto his face didn't reassure me. "Not far from here. Northern California. They found her body this morning."

"What did he leave behind?" I asked, desperation creeping into my voice.

He hesitated but then ultimately spoke. "She had a scar."

"Just one?" I asked.

"Yeah…"

"Above her brow? Right here?" I said, touching the scar on my brow I rarely even thought of.

"Yes."

Bile rose in my throat at the thought of it all. "Thanks for letting me know," I said, trying to keep my composure.

"We will figure this out together," he said, nuzzling his chin in my hair.

"I think I should head home."

"Stay," he pleaded, tugging me closer, his body pressed against mine. "Just for a little while. I can throw something on, and we can sit and watch. I don't want you to be alone right now."

"Okay," I relented.

We nestled into each other, my head resting on his shoulder as he scrolled through the channels until he found something to watch, like we always did.

He was both comforting and dangerous, and I didn't know how much longer we could tiptoe around the truth.

For now, this was enough. I was content to be here with him, the world outside forgotten. I could almost convince myself that this was how it was meant to be—that we were two souls intertwined in this dance.

I closed my eyes for a moment, letting the warmth of the room wrap around me, and I silently hoped that this feeling would last just a little longer.

THIRTY-FOUR

Noah - October

BETTING ON US - MYLES SMITH

I ADJUSTED THE HEM OF DOTTY'S DRESS AND STEPPED BACK TO take it all in. The soft ivory gown hugged her figure, the intricate lace trailing elegantly to the floor. Her blonde waves of hair were loosely curled, framing her face in a way that highlighted the glow of her blue eyes. A subtle touch of makeup—the perfect hint of blush, rosy lips, and a shimmer around her eyes—enhanced her natural beauty without overwhelming it.

She was a vision of grace, but what stood out the most was the excitement in her expression, her emotions barely concealed beneath her radiant smile.

"You look beautiful, Dotty," I said, giving her a soft smile. "I don't think there will be a dry eye in the house."

Dotty smiled back, but there was something thoughtful in her expression. "Thanks, I'm feeling... everything right now. But I know it's right. Trent and I—it's always been more with him. I'm excited to call him my hot cowboy husband." She giggled then paused, letting her gaze drift toward the window where the guests were beginning to gather. "Enough about me. Tell me... how's it going with a certain brother of mine?"

I fumbled with the fabric of her veil, pretending to fix an imaginary crease. "It's—complicated."

Dotty raised a brow, a playful smirk tugging at her lips. "Oh, come on. I know you better than that. What's really going on? Is Dorian just someone to pass the time or... is it more?"

My pulse quickened at her question.

Was he just a distraction?

Or was there something more?

I glanced at Dotty, knowing I couldn't hide from her forever.

"I—I don't know," I muttered, though my voice betrayed me. It wasn't the truth, not really.

I knew.

And that sat heavily in my chest. Dotty wasn't one to let me off the hook.

She reached out, her hand gentle but firm on my arm. "Noah. You do know. I can see it. Not just with you, but him too." She sighed. "The last couple of weeks... I thought this was just you guys fucking around at first, but the more I see him around you, it's clearly more."

More.

I swallowed hard, feeling my defenses crack under her gaze. "It feels like... more." I admitted, the words slipping out reluctantly, like I'd been holding them in for too long.

Dotty's face softened, a knowing smile playing on her lips. She didn't say anything though, just nodded.

I exhaled, my heart pounding now that the truth was out there between us. "But it scares me, Dotty. Everything with John... it changed me. I'm not the same person I was before all that happened. And Dorian, he's been through so much. I don't want to be another complication in his life."

Dotty shook her head. "Noah, you're not a complication. You're part of his life already, and from where I'm standing, it seems like he wants you to be even more than that, though neither of you will admit it."

I forced myself to meet her eyes. "It just feels so… overwhelming. Like if I let myself fall for him, there's no going back. And I don't know if I can survive another heartbreak. How can I trust anyone? How can I trust *myself*?"

"Noah…" She paused, searching my eyes carefully. "I love you more than anything, and you know that. But with John… it was different, and deep down, you know that too. I don't doubt that you cared about him, maybe even loved him in your own way. But while you were together, it didn't really feel like you were together. You were probably with him because it's what your parents wanted, or it was more comfortable than leaving."

I let her words sink in. It wasn't easy to hear, but she wasn't wrong. Memories flashed through my mind—how John and had I drifted, the way our relationship felt more like two people coexisting rather than truly being together. I thought about all the times we barely spoke during our dinners, the awkward silences that stretched between us, the way we lived like two parallel lines, always close but never truly meeting. I ignored the signs, convincing myself that we were okay, that it was just the way things were.

But deep down, I always knew. And now, hearing it from her, it was like the truth I buried was finally surfacing, and there was no more pretending.

She continued. "He was always busy with work—and, apparently, other things," she added with a sad smile. "You were wrapped up in your own life. You spent time together occasionally, but it was always surface level. I could tell your feelings weren't as deep as they should have been for a real relationship. You used to push me to get out there and find my person, but Noah… deep down, every time we had those talks, you knew John wasn't yours. Neither of us said it out loud, and I wasn't exactly in a position to criticize when I was still hung up on Trent after a decade, but we both knew."

Dotty squeezed my hand, her eyes full of understanding. "I get it, but you can't spend your life running from what might hurt. You deserve the very best, and while I might argue that isn't my brother, I want you to do what is best for you. If Dorian is that person, you owe it to yourself to see where it goes."

A lump formed in my throat as everything crashed down on me. "It just feels so scary."

It was hard to let go of the fear. To trust myself, to trust someone else. I was afraid of everything after John wrecked my life. But here I was, letting the echoes of his threats and violence dictate my future, but I didn't want to anymore.

"That's because it is," Dotty said with a weak smile. "But scary doesn't mean bad. Sometimes the things that scare us the most are the things worth holding onto."

I nodded. "It feels like more," I whispered again, almost to myself. "Like he's already more than I ever expected."

Dotty grinned, her eyes sparkling with that playful, knowing look again. "Well then, that's something definitely worth fighting for."

We both fell quiet, her words lingering in the silence. My mind swirling around everything I hadn't quite admitted to myself until now. But as heavy as the day was, it wasn't about me—it was about Dotty. I took a breath, deciding to tuck all those feelings away.

"Okay, little miss cupid. Enough of that. How about we focus on getting you married?" I laughed, wiping at my eyes.

"If we must." Dotty chuckled, her excitement returning as she adjusted her veil.

I sighed. Maybe it was time to stop hiding from what I knew deep down. Maybe it was time to stop letting fear hold me back.

The wedding ceremony took place indoors, framed by a grand floor-to-ceiling window that perfectly showcased the snow-capped mountains beyond. The venue was breathtaking, with its high, timber-beamed ceilings and large stone fireplace, radiating rustic elegance.

It was perfectly Dotty and Trent.

My heart squeezed as they began exchanging their vows, every word filled with love, hope, and a sense of renewal. I swallowed hard, feeling the familiar sting in my eyes. I'd watched Dotty navigate heartbreak, loss, and the uncertainty of trusting again.

And yet, here she was—standing before the man who'd shown her that love could heal.

It felt surreal, like watching everything come full circle, standing at the altar with Dotty and Trent. As I glanced across the room, my gaze naturally found Dorian, standing next to Trent. He looked so composed, yet there was something in the way he stood.

My breath caught as he gave me a small wink from across the altar. My heart raced as a thousand thoughts rushed through my mind. All the moments we'd shared—the kisses, the stolen glances, the undeniable connection—they all seemed to culminate in this one look.

THIRTY-FIVE

Noah - October

WONDERING WHY - THE RED CLAY STRAYS

A SMILE TUGGED AT MY LIPS AS I TOOK IN THE SCENE FROM THE edge of the dance floor. The gentle hum of conversation, the love that filled the air—it was all part of this place, all part of Woodstone Falls.

And then there was me.

The people of Woodstone were kind, and extremely welcoming, but I didn't share the same history they did. I wasn't rooted in this town, its traditions, or the quiet rhythms of life that seemed to come so naturally to them. My ties here were fragile—delicate strings connected to Dotty, to her family, and maybe to this job that was supposed to be my fresh start.

I couldn't deny the effect this place had on me. It was more than the beauty of it, more than the simplicity of small-town life. Maybe it was because I wanted to belong here more than I'd admit.

I tried telling myself that there wasn't anything truly keeping me here. Nothing I couldn't walk away from if I wanted. But deep down, I knew that wasn't true. There was more tethering me here, whether I was ready to admit it or not.

A throat cleared next to me, and I looked over to see Sawyer holding out his hand. "Care to join me for a spin on the floor before someone else steals your attention?"

"Of course," I said.

I took Sawyer's hand, letting him lead me to the dance floor as the music picked up, a soft melody filling the space. He spun me around dramatically, earning a laugh from me, and then pulled me closer with a grin.

"So, are you excited for the concert coming up?" Sawyer said.

"I am." I paused as he moved me closer, his hand finding my waist gently. "I think it will be a good time. I can't wait to see Gracie's reaction most of all, though."

Sawyer was tall, handsome, and a damn NFL star, and I was almost disappointed I felt nothing while dancing with him.

Not a spark.

Not a tingle.

Not a damn thing.

I wanted to believe that everything I felt with Dorian was due to his stupidly handsome face and how he pulled off the perfect balance of handsome and nerdy. And not how his kisses made me feel like I was transporting between universes. I wanted to think it was only because he was just that good-looking and nothing more.

But Sawyer dancing with me only proved that I was full of shit. Unfortunately.

"It's going to be epic. I can't wait to see her perform live," he said.

My smile grew. "So, you really do have a crush on Ellie Miles then?"

Sawyer shrugged, unashamed. "What can I say? The

heart wants what it wants, and mine wants Ellie Miles belting it out live and in person."

I laughed, giving him a playful shove. "I never would've pegged you for a pop music guy. Do you have one of her albums stashed away in your truck?"

"Yup, I blast it. Full volume. Windows down," he said, my dress flowing around as he spun me around. "Nothing like driving down the highway with Ellie on repeat."

"Oh my God," I giggled, shaking my head. "You're ridiculous."

"Very true," he continued, unbothered by my teasing. "I'm happy G is into her music as much as I am."

"She definitely is," I teased, trying to imagine Sawyer and Gracie singing along at full volume.

"I didn't know you were so deep into the Ellie Miles fan club. Doesn't hurt she's pretty too, huh?"

"That she is." He smiled, pulling me a little closer, his brown eyes sparkling.

Before I could add anything more, a familiar voice interrupted.

"Mind if I cut in?" I looked up to see Dorian standing there, one hand casually tucked into his pocket, the other extended toward me.

His eyes locked on mine, and I could feel that familiar warmth crawling up my neck. Sawyer let out a dramatic sigh but stepped back with a grin.

"If you must," he replied.

Dorian rolled his eyes but smiled. Sawyer gave me a wink before walking off, leaving me standing there in front of Dorian.

There was something about the way he was looking at me that made my heart skip a beat.

"Shall we?" he asked, as he took my hand.

I nodded, feeling that flutter in my stomach as we began

to sway to the music, the world around us falling away for a moment.

"You alright?" he asked.

"Yeah, just… a lot on my mind."

He tilted his head. "Care to share with the class?" He smirked, his gaze dropping to my lips.

"Everything. Seattle. Woodstone. You."

The words felt heavy. His grip tightened at my waist, just enough for me to notice.

"Me?" His voice dropped even lower, sending a shiver through me. I finally glanced up, meeting his eyes, my pulse pounding.

"You."

Dorian's eyes darkened, and the air around us suddenly felt suffocating.

"Peach…"

I cut him off before he could say more. "This isn't easy."

He didn't respond, but the way his hand slid a little lower on my waist, fingers brushing the curve of my hip.

I could feel the electric current running between us, like something was about to snap.

He groaned, and I let my head fall to his chest. "It's *too* easy," he breathed.

My jaw tightened, and he took a step closer until our bodies were almost flush. "What do you mean?" I asked.

"Being with you, it's so easy just to be around you, to be myself with you. You make it hard to know what I want anymore."

"What do you want, Dorian?" I asked.

My heart lurched as his hand grazed the exposed skin of my lower back. He leaned down, his breath hot on the shell of my ear.

"I want you. Now," he whispered before pulling back to meet my gaze.

I couldn't hold in the small gasp that escaped me, his eyes never leaving mine.

"Noah…" But it wasn't a warning—it was a plea.

I answered it by closing the small gap between us, pressing my body against his.

His hand slid up my back, tugging me closer until there wasn't a single space between us as we swayed to the music. My heart raced, every nerve in my body on fire.

The song ended, but Dorian didn't let go. His hand stayed at my back, fingers pressing into the fabric of my dress. I could feel the heat between us. I didn't pull away, nor did I want to.

"We can't keep doing this," I said.

"We can't stop either," he muttered, his lips brushing my ear, sending a shock through me just before he nipped at my skin.

"Then why do I feel like we're playing with fire?" I asked.

He chuckled, the sound low and dangerous. "Because it feels really damn good to play with fire sometimes." I smirked, my heart racing with both fear and exhilaration. "Especially when the fire is you."

Before I could respond, he took my hand, tugging me through the crowd. His steps were urgent as he pulled me toward the bathroom.

THIRTY-SIX

Noah - October

SHAMELESS - CAMILA CABELLO

We slipped in, the door clicking shut behind us before he locked it. It was a fancy, overly clean bathroom, making me think this was hopefully more than just a sleazy hookup spot.

The cool tile wall he pressed me against eased the rapidly growing heat between us, as his hands left a burning sensation wherever they touched. The fervor of his exploration made it feel like he couldn't touch me fast enough.

"I can't stop fucking thinking about you," he murmured, pressing his body harder against mine. The pressure of him sent a ripple through my stomach as the tension grew higher.

A whirl of laughter sounded outside of the bathroom door and snapped me back to reality.

"Maybe we should stop," I breathed.

But the way his body felt against mine made me forget everything else. He leaned in teasingly, his lips brushing against mine, making my pulse skyrocket in ways I've only ever felt with him.

"Are you asking me to stop?"

I shook my head, a heated blush creeping across my cheeks. "No, but—" Before I could finish, his lips met mine, deep and hungry, unraveling all the tension we'd kept locked up.

This wasn't just teasing. This was need and desire and so much more.

My fingers clutched at the fine, silken strands of hair at the nape of his neck as the flames grew higher and my patience grew thin.

Dorian pulled back. "I fucking need you."

My teeth caught my lower lip as the corner of my mouth quirked in a small smirk, nodding in agreement.

His hands latched onto my hips. Slowly, his lips trailed from my jaw, down to my pulse point, then meeting my throat. The slowness and passion behind each kiss caused me to tremble against him.

My hands gripped at his shirt before gliding them down his chest. The hard ridges of his muscles contracting under my touch. I slipped further down, tracing the line between his abs, before hitting the cool metal of his belt. His hardened length pressed taut against his pants. Slowly, I slid down his zipper. I wrapped my hand around him, causing a groan to rumble through him. He hardened further at my touch, sending a surge of electricity through me, straight to my core.

His calloused hands grazed the soft skin of my arms, sending a shiver through me as they glided downward, pressing deeper into that space that ached for him. Each movement was careful, a mix of anticipation and need. My hands reached back, gripped the counter as his fingers brushed closer. My legs parted as an invitation for the rest of him.

"I've been thinking about you—about this—all fucking day," he said.

Slowly, his fingers made their way under my dress. His touch was lazy as he took his time, enjoying the way I melted into him. His finger hooked into my underwear, pulling it aside before his thumb pressed against my clit. My gasp rang through the bathroom at the feel of him. Another finger joined, pressing into me and causing my hands to bolt to his shoulders for strength.

"Is this all for me, peach?"

I nodded desperately as I looked to him for a moment of reprieve. He was ruggedly handsome—his perfectly fitted suit now unbuttoned, tie loosened, and an expression on his face that was nothing short of wild.

And I loved it. *I craved it.*

The intensity in his gaze, the way he made me feel like I was the only thing that mattered in that moment.

I took in the sensation of his fingers slipping in and out, my thoughts turned hazy, as a moan escaped me. Then, I moved, forcing him back.

"What are you doing?" he asked.

"I think it's my turn to have a little taste."

His eyes widened as he met my gaze with curiosity.

My hands trailed down his body again as I lowered myself down, my fingers digging into the back of his thighs, until my knees met the cool tile. His body tensed as the realization hit. His breath stuttered, and his pupils dilated as he watched me. Raw, unspoken understanding passed between us.

"Oh fuck."

I bit my lip in playful amusement. Our gazes locked.

Pulling out this dick, I grinned up at him then rolled my tongue around the tip, savoring the way his taste covered my tongue.

"Are you gonna take me in that pretty little throat?"

I responded by letting the head of him graze the roof of my mouth as he worked his way in. He tipped his head back as his hands shot to the front of my neck, his groans filling the small space. I watched the way he got lost in himself.

The same way he got lost in me.

"Good girl," he groaned, his hands tightening. Peering down at me breathlessly, he managed to speak. "Now, put those fingers into that pretty little pussy while you take my cock into your throat."

Excitement coursed through me at his words.

My heart pounded in my chest as I reached down to grab the flowing fabric of my dress, sliding it up until I felt the slickness on my fingers. I slowly started to circle around my clit, my moans escaping my mouth, vibrating on his cock. I forced myself to relax as I swallowed him back into my throat.

His eyes darkened, a low curse escaping his lips as he gripped my hair. "You feel so fucking good, peach."

I pulled back, gasping for air, a surge of confidence coursing through me. His gaze was locked on me with a desperate hunger. My hands wrapped around his length, taking long strokes as I glanced up at him, watching the way he unfolded for me.

He panted as he watched me, pressing his cock toward my mouth. My lips opened just enough to allow the head of him to slide through. A satisfied hum escaped me as I wrapped my tongue around it, his head tossing back again as his fingers in my hair gripped tighter.

"Shit, Noah. You're doing so fucking good. Go deeper, baby, you can take it."

The desire in his eyes drove my pulse higher, giving me

the willpower to press him even farther down. A groan echoed in the small bathroom as he hit the back of my throat.

"Fuck," he gritted through his teeth.

He pulled out of my mouth, gripping my hair to hold himself up. His chest rose and fell as he tried to gain his composure. The brown in his eyes shined as he moved his hand from my hair to graze against my cheek. A storm churned low in my belly.

"Stand up," he commanded. "As good as your mouth feels, I need to be inside you."

He reached behind him, retrieving his wallet and opening it to fish out a condom. His eyes met mine for a moment, before his thumb traced my swollen bottom lip. He took the opportunity to place the edge of the wrapper in my mouth.

"Open it," he said, placing it between my teeth. And once again, I obeyed, as if under his spell.

The foiled corner caught between my teeth, and with a gentle tip of my head, I ripped the edge away. He took the package from my mouth, his eyes never leaving mine as he expertly moved it over himself.

"There's my good girl. You listen so well, don't you, peach?"

He grabbed my waist, spinning me around before he pressed his palm into the middle of my back. He lifted the fabric of my dress before he lined himself up to my entrance. The feel of his head teasing me sent shivers through my entire body.

His stare connected with mine through the mirror, dark and intense, as if waiting for something. Slowly he pressed in, inch by torturous inch. My head tossed back as he stretched me, his gaze locking onto where he pressed in before my eyes rolled back at the sensation of him. My breath hitched and my eyes fluttered shut involuntarily.

He halted his progression as his hand wrapped around the back of my neck, and he leaned over my back. His other hand gripped my hip as he held himself there. "Eyes on me, peach," he murmured, his voice low, almost a growl.

I hesitated, feeling the pressure building. Slowly, I forced my eyes open, meeting his in the mirror. The intensity of it made everything feel heavier, like the world was suspended between us, waiting for him to move.

His eyes were dark, intense, watching me as he slid in, slow and deliberate, each inch of him filling me with a mix of pleasure and longing. It was as if he was savoring every moment, drawing it out to make sure I felt every bit of him.

The touch, the pressure, it was everything but still not enough. He peppered kisses against my shoulder as his hips started to move. Every inch of him brought me farther away from this planet and into a black abyss of mind-numbing pleasure. I hardly remembered I was bent over a bathroom counter. His thrusts picked up as his grip on my neck shifted to the front of my throat, forcing my head back to connect with his in a devouring kiss.

Deep and urgent, it stole my breath as his movements continued—never slowing, never hesitating. Each move of his body was rhythmic, purposeful, like he couldn't get enough. His hands gripped me tighter. He tasted like desire and desperation. Every brush of his lips sent sparks through me, making the world outside of us disappear.

His tongue intertwined with my own, full of desperate need. He started at my lips and then trailed down my throat, sending shivers through me. A breathy moan broke through the bathroom that I attempted to hold back. His hand tightened where it was wrapped around my neck with an intensity that made my pulse race.

His hand on my hip loosened to drift between my legs, rubbing into my clit as his thrusts turned frenzied, his control slipping the longer he stayed inside of me.

"Come for me, Noah. Come on my cock like the—" *Thrust.* "Good." *Thrust.* "Fucking." *Thrust.* "Girl." *Thrust.* "You are." He panted. "Look at you," he growled. His eyes were tracing our movements. "You look so perfect like this."

His words were the tipping point that sent me over the edge. My body shattered, tunnel vision creeping in, as a sound I couldn't control escaped my lips.

"Fuck… fuck. I'm going to come, baby," he said, letting his head fall to my shoulder, his breath coming in fast pants on my neck.

He let out a feral groan, leaning back enough to watch me as he found his release. His eyes stayed on mine, our exhales heavy and ragged as we both came down from the high.

"You look so good taking me here," he squeezed the tiniest fraction on my throat.

After the moment slowed and I caught my breath, I pushed off the counter and turned around, fixing the skirt of my dress. I peered up to meet his eyes. His thumb brushed the side of my jaw, back and forth. I leaned into him, my nose brushing against his, letting my eyes shut, savoring every touch. He gently threaded his fingers through my hair, lingering at the nape of my neck for a moment.

"So fucking beautiful. So fucking *mine.*"

My eyes snapped open as his words echoed in the charged silence, and something deeper began to stir.

I turned back around as the sharpness of reality cut through the haze. I swept my hands over my curls before tying it up.

This wasn't just about desire or the thrill of the moment anymore—it was more complicated than that. And I was done dancing around it now.

After a stretch of silence, I met his gaze over my shoulder.

"This is more. Isn't it?"

THIRTY-SEVEN

Noah - October

WINGS - BIRDY

My voice was steady, though my heart thudded in my chest. I turned around and reached out. My fingers lightly grazed his arm as I stood there, waiting. The air was full of uncertainty as my pulse quickened, but I held my breath, needing him to say something—anything.

Dorian blinked, his brows knitting together in confusion as he zipped up his pants.

"Isn't it?" I repeated.

His hand came up to my wrist, but the disbelief in his expression felt like a wall. I met his gaze, refusing to back down.

"Come again?" he asked, but I knew he heard me.

"I mean… I could if you wanted." I didn't let my hand fall from him. Instead, I let my fingers glide down to his hand, locking our hands together for a moment.

"Noah," he scolded. His thumb grazed mine, a tiny gesture despite the serious look on his face. But then he pulled his hand back, running it through his hair.

"*Isn't it?*" I pressed again, holding his gaze. I could see the muscle in his jaw tighten.

"It *can't* be," he said, more of a reflex than a reasoned response. His gaze moved away from mine.

"Why not?"

"*Because*," he muttered, his voice clipped, as if the word alone would be enough of an answer.

"Because why, Dorian?" I asked, frustration now bubbling to the surface.

He exhaled heavily and stared at the floor like it held the solution. "Because this isn't what we agreed to."

But we both knew those rules didn't mean anything anymore. I crossed my arms, needing somewhere to keep my hands other than on him.

"What do you think this is, then?" My words were sharp as I searched his face. "You think this is still some casual fling? You think this is just two friends with benefits, hooking up in the bathroom? When you tell me you can't stop thinking about me, you can't keep your eyes off me, and tell me that I'm *yours*? This seems like a lot more than a fucking hookup, Dor."

His gaze snapped back to mine, frustration flaring in his eyes. "Don't Dor me right now," he warned.

"Then tell me what this feels like to you," I demanded, stepping closer.

His shoulders tensed. "It feels complicated," he growled.

My pulse thundered in my ears as I shook my head, a bitter laugh escaping my lips. "Complicated?" I repeated, incredulously. "It's complicated because you *know* this is more."

I sighed, meeting his gaze with unflinching determination. He stepped toward me, his hands fisted at his sides.

"It *is* more," he finally admitted, harsh and clipped, but his eyes flashed with something raw, something he didn't want to acknowledge.

"Then what's the problem?" I shot back, louder now. "It's complicated now, but it's always been complicated. We just weren't willing to admit it."

I could feel the heat rising in my cheeks, the weight of everything I'd been holding back for so long crumbling on top of me.

"Tell me if I'm alone in this, Dorian, and I'll stop. Tell me this is one-sided, and I'll walk away right here, right now." My voice trembled, but I pushed forward, refusing to let him retreat.

"I can't, Noah," he said finally, his voice cracking. "And I can't tell you you're alone in thinking that this isn't more." He turned away from me, his shoulders slumped. "But I can't let it *be* more," he whispered, his back to me. The rawness of his words hit me hard, the fear in them cutting deep.

"Why?"

He turned back to face me, his eyes filled with a pain so deep it stole the air from my lungs.

"God, I want to, Noah. It'd be the easiest thing in the world. When you enter a room, I feel it before I even see you. My body knows you're there before my mind can catch up. It's like my soul recognizes yours, like we've been tethered in a way I can't even begin to understand. It's immediate. It's *desperate*. Every inch of space between us feels like universes, and I'd tear through every last one just to find you. Even if all I could do was watch from a distance, even if it meant I couldn't have you—could never touch you—I'd still find you.

"But that's the thing—I did touch you. I let myself kiss you, let myself taste you, let my hands feel the warmth of your skin and the way you fit against me, like we were always meant to be there. I let myself get to know you in ways I *never* should have. I convinced myself I could keep it casual, that I could pretend this was just physical, that it didn't mean anything more. But that was the dumbest fucking lie I've ever told myself, because you are *anything* but casual to me."

"How can you feel like that and still push me away?"

"Because every person I've cared about has had something terrible happen." He turned away from me, pacing. "My mom? Taken from me in a drunk driving hit-and-run —just gone in an instant. Hallie, the mother of my child? Died giving birth to Gracie. And then my sister returns to town for the first time in years, only to be kidnapped by a stalker who, by the way, killed my mom." He faced me again. "I can't allow this to be more because I can't stand the thought of losing *you*."

His words stung, leaving me breathless. I swallowed hard—my throat tight as I tried to make sense of the fear that had been driving him all along. He started pacing in the small space between us again.

"And with your crazy ex out there, obsessively carving your tattoo into his damn murder victims, it feels reckless to even consider it. So, I've let myself believe that casual is enough because it *has* to be enough. But it's not. It's never enough. I always want more from you, but I'm not willing to jeopardize your safety because of what I want."

The thrum of my pulse echoed in my ears.

"Do you even realize how messed up that is? How utterly illogical you sound?" The words tumbled out faster than I could control them. "You've been dealt a shit hand, and people you loved have died. It's awful and I can't imagine the pain it has caused you. But it doesn't mean every person you care about is going to meet the same fate."

Dorian stopped pacing and turned to face me again.

"If you're willing to sacrifice whatever this is"—I

gestured between us—"because of your delusional view-point, then so be it. I'll walk away. I'll leave you, and I'll leave this town if I have to."

My hands trembled at the thought, and I bit down on my lip to keep from spiraling. I wasn't ready to leave this town. To leave Dotty or Gracie.

But he didn't move. Didn't respond.

His eyes bored into mine, full of conflicted emotions. "What if I let you in and everything falls apart?" He tried to mask his words with anger, but his voice trembled at the edges.

"If you keep getting lost in the what ifs, you'll only end up regretting all the chances you didn't take."

I reached out, placing my hand on his chest, feeling the rapid thump of his heartbeat beneath my fingers.

"I'm scared too. John's still out there, taunting me, blaming me, killing because of *me*." My voice cracked. "The only things that have given me a reason to let go and finally hope for a future are you and Gracie. But don't think I'm not waiting for the worst—for him to sweep in and hurt one of you." I looked up into his eyes. "The possibility of it being undone is a small price to pay for something real."

Dorian's hand shot up, catching my wrist, his grip firm but not harsh. His eyes were dark, filled with emotion as he spoke. "If you think I'd let him anywhere near you or my daughter and wouldn't strangle him with my bare hands, you're wrong."

His grip tightened slightly, the anger in him barely contained, and I relished it. I relished him giving into the emotions and finally letting it out, rather than hiding it under numbness.

I was never threatened by him, never feared he would hurt me. I knew he wouldn't. I'd known all along.

"But you're already running away," I snapped, pulling

my hand from his grasp. I took a step back, needing distance from him, even though every fiber of me wanted to close the gap. "You're running away because you think it's easier than letting yourself care."

His shoulders sagged, and he ran a hand over his face, exhaustion creeping in. "It *is* easier," he admitted, his voice cracking just enough to betray him. "Because I can't lose you. I can't lose anyone else. I'm not just scared, Noah. I'm fucking *terrified*."

My throat tightened, and tears pricked at the corners of my eyes.

"Terrified." I agreed, letting the words from months ago echo between us.

Dorian's expression changed, the anger fading just slightly, replaced by something vulnerable. He studied me, his brow furrowed, as if he didn't know whether to pull me closer or push me away.

Just then, his phone buzzed in his pocket, breaking through the heavy silence. The sound was jarring, pushing us back to reality. The moment shattered, and we both froze.

My heart leaped into my throat, and I watched as Dorian glanced at his phone, then back at me. The intensity in his eyes made something twist inside me, a growing fear creeping into my thoughts.

What if he says something I can't handle? What if the next words out of his mouth are the ones that finally break me? What if he isn't willing to try?

The thought sent a wave of panic through me, my hands trembling at the possibility of needing to leave this place.

I couldn't bear to hear it.

I swallowed hard, my heart racing, the weight of his silence pressing down on me. The distance between us suddenly felt insurmountable—like a chasm that was growing wider with every second that passed.

The fear was suffocating, making it hard to breathe.

I couldn't wait for his response. I couldn't stand here and face the possibility of him telling me I wasn't enough, that this—whatever we had—wasn't worth the risk.

I had to get out.

"I can't do this right now," I finally managed to say, stepping back.

All I could think about was fleeing, putting space between us and the mess of emotions that had already undone everything I thought I knew.

"Noah, wait!" he called after me, but I was already gone.

THIRTY-EIGHT

Noah - October

HOLD ME WHILE YOU WAIT - LEWIS CAPALDI

As I walked back into the reception, the glow of fairy lights and the lingering scent of flowers enveloped me. The lively music and laughter echoed around me, but the room felt hollow. I pushed back the tears that wanted to fall and forced a smile at the guests who mingled, clinking their glasses together in celebration while my mind spiraled.

I wandered aimlessly, chatting with locals and trying to appear busy so no one I knew well would have the chance to ask what was wrong.

Dorian appeared relaxed. And it pissed me off how he could just pretend everything was okay. He was crouched down, sharing a joke with Gracie, who was giggling uncontrollably. The two of them were the picture of happiness.

The reception started to wind down, and guests began filtering out, offering hugs and goodbyes. I caught snippets of happy chatter, making my heart heavier.

As I prepared to leave, I headed toward the exit, hoping to catch Dotty one last time before the night ended, but she was busy dancing with Trent, so I sent her a quick text instead. All I could think about was escaping.

As I reached the doorway, I nearly collided with Colt, who was walking in with a serious expression.

"Hey, Noah." I could tell by the look on his face he had bad news.

What a day.

"Another one?" I asked, not wanting to hear the next words from his mouth.

"Yeah." He grabbed the back of his neck, his long hair pulled back in a bun, his tattoos peeking out from the sleeves of his suit. "I wasn't going to tell you or anything. Didn't want to ruin the night."

I felt my stomach drop. "This soon?"

He nodded, his brow furrowing deeper. "Yeah. I just found out. It's not good."

I straightened. "What did he leave behind?"

He hesitated, eyes lowering before returning to mine. "Nothing."

My stomach twisted, and I took a sharp breath. "What do you mean?"

His tone lowered, his expression tense. "Not even a butterfly."

"Zero?" I asked, disbelief swirling as John's countdown replayed in my mind.

"Yeah… I think so."

I forced myself to stay calm, but my mind raced as the full impact settled in. I only nodded in response.

The unease in his eyes clear even as he tried to hide it. "Are you leaving?" he asked, his tone cautious.

"Yeah, I'm going to head home."

He hesitated, his brow furrowing deeper. "Are you going alone?"

I felt his concern pressing down on me. "Yeah, I'll be fine. Promise."

It was clear he wasn't satisfied with that. "Can I drive

you?"

"Colt..." I met his eyes, trying to get him to understand. "I'm okay. I'll text you once I get there. I just really need to be alone right now."

He stood there for a moment, his lips tight as if searching for a way to argue. "You should have someone with you, Noah. This isn't safe."

I pulled out my phone, tapped on the location settings, and shared it with him for the next twenty-four hours.

"Here. Now you can see exactly where I am. I'm going straight home."

He glanced at the phone, his expression reluctant but resigned. "Fine," he said. "Just... be careful, okay?"

"I will," I promised, though I felt the knot of unease settle deeper in my stomach.

"Text me when you get there."

I nodded, then turned, fleeing out of the building as I hurried down the steps and into the parking lot. The echoes of laughter and the wedding fading out behind me.

I'd almost convinced myself that maybe, just maybe, Dorian would have wanted something real with me.

But after our conversation, my heart sank deeper. Sliding into my car, I pulled out my phone, only for the screen to flash once before going black. Dead.

Starting the engine, I took a few deep breaths, trying to calm my racing thoughts. As I drove, the dark road ahead was dimly lit by streetlights, but every mile was just a reminder of how heavy the last year of my life had been.

After a few miles, a jolt interrupted me, and the car lurched violently to one side. I wrestled the wheel, managing to pull over as the shredded rubber slapped against the asphalt.

Of course.

I pulled over to the side of the road and stepped out of

the car. As I approached the front passenger side, my heart sank at the obvious flat tire.

"Perfect timing," I groaned. It felt like the universe was conspiring against me.

I could probably change it myself with the help of a video, but in this dress, at night… with a dead phone. That wasn't going to happen.

Plus, I had no idea what else might be lurking in the dark and already hit my quota of shit hitting the fan today.

Rain started to come down, and I glanced around, searching for an alternative, or even just something to keep me going.

Woodstone was still somewhat foreign to me, and I didn't know the layout well enough to find help on foot in the dark.

But there was one house I was familiar with close by— Dorian's. The thought of going there sent my heart racing, a chaotic mix of longing and dread intertwining. I hesitated, wrestling with my thoughts as I trudged through the downpour.

Dorian was scared, and I'd seen that fear in his eyes before I ran out. He wanted to protect me, to shield me from the darkness he believed would follow if he let himself get closer.

That fear struck a chord. It reminded me of the warnings I'd heard my whole life—my parents always telling me I was too trusting, too caring, too much. And with John, those warnings became reality. He'd drawn me in with his charm, his smile hiding the monster beneath. The betrayal shattered something in me, cutting deeper than losing him ever could.

Rain fell on my cheeks as those memories surfaced again. I didn't want to let myself get close to Dorian. I convinced myself it was something fun and lighthearted, something I needed after everything with John.

As I approached his house, my steps slowed, doubt creeping in as I hovered just outside.

Should I really be here? What if he told me to leave? What if he didn't want to see me? What if he closed the door and turned away?

But the weight of my fear felt less important in that moment.

I needed to feel safe.

And he always made me feel safe.

We'd had a knack for sidestepping the hard conversations, finding solace in simply being there for each other when it mattered most. I would set everything else aside if I had to, just for tonight, and call a truce if it meant getting one more night.

With a shaky hand, I knocked on the door. I stood there, the chill of the rain seeping through my dress as my heart pounded in my ears.

When the door swung open, revealing Dorian, his expression shifted from surprise to concern, and I couldn't hold back the tears any longer. They spilled over, mingling with the raindrops, as I found myself searching his eyes for the reassurance I craved.

THIRTY-NINE

Dorian - October

I FOUND - AMBER RUN

I PACED THE SMALL LIVING ROOM. THE CONVERSATION WITH Noah kept replaying in my mind, each word she said ricocheting off the walls of my mind, refusing to let me forget.

I can't do this right now.

Her voice still echoed, laced with that quiet panic, her vulnerability on display in the tremble of her words. I could see it in her eyes—the worry, the careful way she'd tried to distance herself, pulling away before I had the chance to push her away first.

She put everything out there, faced the truth head-on, and I stepped back. I couldn't handle it. Instead, I fumbled.

I rubbed the back of my neck, trying to push the knots of frustration and fear from my mind.

I thought about how I'd failed to protect the people I loved. My mom, Hallie, Dotty, and all the promises I made to Gracie. I swore to keep her safe and from experiencing any more pain. And now… now I was facing the real possibility of losing someone else.

I needed to protect Noah. I needed to keep her safe from the danger surrounding her.

But was keeping her at arm's length the best way to do that? Was it enough to just keep her out of my heart, out of the danger I feared?

That pull.

It was like an invisible thread, winding its way around my chest, tightening with every glance, every laugh she shared. Every time her eyes met mine, it was as if the world shifted. There was an undeniable force drawing me to her, something I couldn't explain, something that felt like it had always been there, waiting for me to notice. And I was so damn tired of pretending I didn't feel it—tired of holding on to the fear that had kept me from reaching for what I wanted most.

She was right. I didn't want to be the guy who wasted his life hiding from what mattered, who let the fear of loss keep him from something real.

I couldn't keep letting fear rule my decisions, either.

I needed to be honest with myself. I needed to admit what I already knew—that I wanted her. Not in some fleeting, casual way, but fully. All in.

But even as that truth began to hit, another wave of doubt crept in. What if I was too late? What if I'd already fucked this up too badly?

I couldn't push her away again. Not after everything. I needed to hear her voice, to tell her I was ready, that I wanted more, that I was done running from what we both needed.

I grabbed my phone, my hands shaking as I clicked her number, but it went straight to voicemail.

I looked out the window. The rain was coming down hard, the sound of it pounding against the glass—a reflection of the turmoil inside my head.

I ran a hand through my hair, frustration clawing at me.

This wasn't how I wanted things to end. I needed to fix this, to let her know.

The knock on the door broke through my thoughts. My heart jumped.

I moved toward the door, every step heavy, my chest tight with anticipation. I pulled it open, and the sight of Noah standing there, soaked to the bone, took my breath away. Her tears glistened, shimmering in the dim porch light.

"Noah?" My voice cracked, unsure if it was the moment of relief or the final blow.

I stepped back, instinctively opening the door wider. She crossed the threshold as water pooled at her feet.

She was here.

And for the first time, I was ready to let her in.

"What's wrong?"

"I didn't know where else to go."

My chest squeezed as I took in her in. Her small frame was trembling.

"What happened?" I asked.

"Flat tire."

"Come on, let's get you dried off."

I led her into the living room, where the soft glow of the lamps illuminated the space, pushing aside the conversation we needed to have.

I disappeared into another room to grab an extra set of my clothes. They'd be huge on her, but it was better than what she had on. I returned, handing them to her.

"Here."

"Thanks," she muttered, meeting my eyes. "For this"—she held up the clothes—"and for letting me in. I wasn't sure if you'd tell me to leave."

"You can always come here," I replied, stepping closer.

"Can I though?"

"Of course," I said, my own heart pounding so loudly in my head it made it hard to speak.

I opened my mouth to tell her how deeply I felt for her, but the truth was messy.

"I don't know how to do this," I finally whispered, feeling the helplessness creep in.

Tears pricked at her eyes, and I could see the change in her expression—a mixture of understanding and frustration.

"Me either," she admitted.

"I tried to call you. Just a few minutes ago."

"My phone is dead."

"Oh."

"What were you going to say?" she asked hesitantly.

"That I'm done fighting this."

Her eyes went wide. "What?"

"I'm done, I'm done trying to fight this. I want you. I really fucking want you, and not in the I *only want to fuck you* kind of way. I mean I also do want to fuck you, but—" I paused, knowing my words were coming out faster than I could comprehend. "I've wanted this since you fell apart in my arms months ago at the hospital. Hell, even before that, if I'm being honest, but I don't want to risk you in the process. I don't want to risk dragging you into my chaos."

Her eyes widened slightly, and I could see the realization wash over her. "I *want* to be part of your chaos," she said, each word a challenge that struck deep within me. "I want to be here for you, but you have to let me in."

I pressed on, feeling a rush of emotion spilling out. "I don't want to run anymore. I've been running away from things that made me feel for far too long. I'm terrified of everything that's happened in the past, but I also don't want to let it have control over me anymore."

Noah was fighting this same battle, no doubt these same thoughts going on in her head, but she was the first to admit it, to dare to ask for more.

"Do you want this? You really want us?" I asked, desperately trying to keep my face composed while my mind whirled with possibilities.

Each word was a weight lifted off my shoulders, a chain breaking free. Her face lit up, her smile striking me right in the gut.

"Yes, I do." A small chuckle-sob escaped her lips, and I felt my heart soar. She placed her hand on my chest, and I fought to stay on my feet. "I'm scared of something happening, to me, to you or Gracie, but staying away from you isn't going to change that."

"Nothing is going to happen to us," I said confidently, for once believing it, letting go of all the worst-case scenarios that had kept me away from her. "I have too much to live for now."

The storm outside raged on as the one inside me quieted. The rain poured down outside, but I was focused on Noah.

Without thinking, I closed the distance between us, my hands finding her waist, pulling her closer. She let out a little gasp. I leaned in, capturing her lips with mine.

It was a small, tentative brush at first, a question, an invitation. When she responded, deepening the kiss, I felt the weight of our past lift, replaced by more. *So much more.*

I poured every ounce of my longing and promise into that kiss, vowing silently to protect her, to cherish this moment and every damn moment that followed that I was lucky enough to get with her.

Time stood still as the rain pounded against the windows, a symphony of chaos that somehow harmonized with our newfound clarity. Her body against mine centered me, and I could taste the salt of her tears mingling with the sweetness of her lips.

I would fight with everything I had to look beyond my past and make room for her.

Because in that moment, I knew I was kissing my future wife.

FORTY

Noah - October

WHEN I LOOK AT YOU - MILEY CYRUS

Dorian's fingers tightened in my hair, tipping my head back as he deepened the kiss, turning what was once a moment of vulnerability into something raw, something so much more.

I let the clothes slip from my hands, my fingers trailing over his body, eager to memorize every inch. Beneath his skin, I felt the hard, corded muscles tense under my touch as I traced the lines of his chest and abdomen.

Each movement I made sent a shiver through him, and I couldn't help but want to explore every inch, to touch every part of him, even those broken, shattered pieces he believed were too unworthy to be loved.

My hair was soaked from the rain, but the shiver that coursed through my body had nothing to do with the cold. He matched my desire, his hands moving up and down my body with purpose. He pushed us back until I was met with a hard surface. With my back up against the wall, I looked up and saw nothing but pure need in his eyes.

Slowly, he glided his fingers from my arms to my hands, interlocked our fingers, and brought them above my head.

"Are we playing another round of who can stand closest to the door without touching it?" I asked deviously.

He smirked. "It looks like I've won this round. But what's my prize?"

Stepping up on my tiptoes, I slowly ran my tongue up his neck and whispered, "Me."

His mouth was unleashed—hungry and urgent, and I could feel him harden against me.

"My bed," he growled between fevered kisses. "Now."

He slid his hands under my legs, lifting me effortlessly and wrapping them around his waist. Carrying me through the house, he pushed into his room, kicking the door shut behind us. Clothes disappeared in a blur—my soaked dress slopping to the floor with a thud.

His fingers traced my cheekbone with a surprising tenderness, but his mouth was devouring me as though he couldn't get enough. We were a tangle of limbs, our bodies moving in sync, both of us caught in the storm we'd created, the chaos only driving us deeper into each other.

He bent down, capturing my nipple between his mouth. A moan escaped me that I was unable and unwilling to hold back. Now that I had him, I wanted him, all of him, everywhere.

He moved us to the bed, setting me down gently.

"Noah," he started.

"Need you. Now," I whimpered against his lips, the words spilling out in a breathless string.

"Yes, ma'am."

He stood in the dim room, the only light spilling through the window in pale slivers. The moonlight touched the edges of his figure, illuminating the sharp lines of his jaw and the subtle flex of his muscles. The rest of him remained cloaked in darkness, a silhouette framed by the glow of the night.

"Off," I said, pointing to the last remainder of his clothes. His eyes darkened. "Now."

"Maybe I could get used to you taking charge." He ushered them down his muscular thighs and started stroking himself. "Now, it's your turn," he said, nodding to my panties that were still on. "Wait, I take that back." He leaned over me, peppering my legs with kissing as he worked his way up. "I want to do it."

He grabbed the lace, pulling it down gently, his heated gaze fixed on me. After he pulled them off, he stood at the edge of the bed again, watching.

"Please, Dorian."

He grinned. "Hmm. I like this. My name coming out of your mouth as you lie naked and needy in my bed."

He walked over to the nightstand, grabbing a condom and rolled it along himself. My mouth salivated simply looking at him. In one quick motion, he was hovering over me again, staring at me.

"Please," I repeated, my desire ready to swallow me whole.

And then he filled me, stretching me, every inch of him deep inside, leaving me breathless. The sensation was a mix of heat and fullness, a pressure that both burned and soothed at once. It was overwhelming, like nothing else existed but him, filling every space of me, claiming me in a way that left me dizzy, my body trembling beneath him.

"Oh fuck." My words came out in quick pants as we found our rhythm.

"Baby, you feel so good."

I bucked my hips up, causing a groan to slip from his mouth. He leaned into me, letting his head rest on my shoulder as he continued to move in the perfect motion as my release started building.

"Fuck, Noah. It's too good. You are too fucking good."

He gripped my hips, and my eyes fluttered shut, knowing it would leave marks—marks that claimed me, that made me *his*.

"Noah, eyes on me. I need to watch as you come undone for me."

My eyes snapped open at the command. The look on his face was unlike anything I'd ever seen before—completely consumed by desire, raw and unrestrained.

Our movements grew faster, and I relished it all.

I whimpered. "More, I need more, Dorian."

"Baby, I'm taking this all in. Don't rush me."

He lifted up slightly, placing his hand between us and finding my clit. He pushed down, moving in circles, and I was suddenly spiraling, my orgasm ripping through me. His mouth was back on mine, stealing my moans.

His groan filled the room, raw and deep, as his release tore through him. He collapsed onto me, his weight a welcome pressure. I wanted him close, no longer holding back, and I was relieved to finally have him completely, without reservation.

After a moment, he rolled over and we lay there, tangled in the sheets. Our bodies were slick with sweat, our heavy breathing the only sound filling the room.

The room still felt charged, both of us caught in the intensity of the moment, but there was comfort, too—an unspoken understanding.

Dorian's hand moved absentmindedly, tracing lazy patterns along my spine, his touch soothing. I shifted slightly, my gaze meeting his, and I could sense his walls finally fall.

It wasn't lust or desire or need anymore. There was something deeper.

His lips curved into that half-smile I'd come to know so

well, but there was a softness in it that made my heart flutter.

"What?" I whispered, still dazed from everything.

"You're right," he said, his tone almost hesitant, like he was working through something he'd been carrying for far too long.

I tilted my head, unsure of where this was going. "I know, but about what?" I teased.

He paused, his eyes dropping for a moment, gathering his thoughts. Then, with a small sigh, he began again, his words deliberate and heavy with meaning. "I got back home, put Gracie to bed, but when I sat down after, all I could think about was you. Everything you said, it kept replaying in my mind, and you were right. I don't want to look back on my life when I'm old, wishing I'd taken the risk. I don't want to lie there on my deathbed, thinking about the one that got away—the one with curly hair, striking eyes, and a heart of pure fucking gold. I don't want that. I want you. I want to take the risk."

My breath caught, a surge of emotion flooding through me as I watched him confront his fears. The raw vulnerability of it pulled something tight inside me.

He was offering me something I knew wasn't easy for him. "I want that too," I admitted.

He moved closer, his hand gently cupping my face, his thumb grazing across my cheek with a tenderness that made my heart ache. "I want to grow old with you. I want to go with you to Gracie's graduation, thinking to myself, damn, where did the time go? I want to make pancakes on weekends, get another dog, and do all those silly, mundane things that we always think are so small, but with you... they're never mundane. They're everything."

His words warmed me from the inside out.

This was it. This was the kind of love I never thought I

deserved, settling for so much less, and yet here it was—offered to me. The fear that once held me back faded.

And for the first time in a long time, I felt it. Hope.

Hope that I could be happy and loved and still have the life that seemed impossible the day I learned the truth about John.

I leaned in, my forehead resting against his, our breaths mingling in the space between us. "We have all the time in the world," I whispered, a sense of peace washing over me.

FORTY-ONE

Dorian - November

THIS LOVE (TAYLOR'S VERSION) - TAYLOR SWIFT

As I sat in the driver's seat, the familiar scent of Noah's shampoo invaded my senses, reminding me of everything from the last week. We agreed to do this, to see where this would go between the two of us.

Except I already knew.

I was a fucking idiot to pretend I didn't know it before. Every time she laughed, every time she looked at me like I was worth something—I felt it. And now, I was sure I'd never let her go.

I don't even know why I was such a dumbass denying it for so long. She was so clearly it for me.

I looked in the rearview mirror, taking in her dark curly hair, loose and falling over her shoulders. She looked so fucking pretty, her makeup all done up in glitters and sparkles for the concert. She wore some ridiculous fringy outfit, but I loved it.

I loved *her*.

I wasn't sure about coming to this concert. I'd hesitated, asking Noah if coming was a good idea with John's recent escalation, but Noah insisted it would be fine.

Dorian, it'll be fine. There are security guards everywhere, and it's a concert. John isn't ballsy enough to even find women in public, resorting to the internet to find his victims. I am done letting him control my life.

Her confidence settled some of my nerves, but the gnawing feeling in my gut lingered. I wanted to enjoy the night, but I also couldn't shake the fear entirely. But right now, I needed to push those thoughts aside and focus on Noah and Gracie.

The happiness that bubbled within me was strong enough to overshadow the worry, at least for now.

Gracie bounced eagerly in the backseat. "Are we there yet?"

"Gracie, the drive is a few hours, not a few minutes," I chuckled, catching her eager gaze in the rearview mirror. "You'll survive, I promise."

"But it's Ellie Miles!" she squealed, wide-eyed. "What if she sings all my favorite songs before we get there?"

Noah twisted in her seat, shooting her a playful grin. "We'll be there with plenty of time, G. Don't worry."

Sawyer, sitting in the passenger seat, leaned back, always ready to throw in his two cents. "I would never let you be late. I'd come running through the parking lot with you in a football hold if I had to get you there in time," he said with his signature goofy grin.

"Yeah, right. You'd probably trip over your own feet before you even made it to the door."

"You realize I'm a professional athlete, right?" he shot back, his grin widening. "I could have her there in record time."

"Sure," Noah added, her tone light and teasing, "because sprinting a hundred yards is totally the same as dodging Ellie Miles fans in a parking lot."

Sawyer crossed his arms, pretending to be offended. "You don't think I could handle a couple of screaming fans? I could bring my football gear and tackle anyone in our way!" His mock seriousness made Gracie giggle from the backseat.

"I wanna see you tackle someone!" Gracie shouted, her laughter filling the car.

Sawyer grinned at her. "Then you'll have to come to one of my games."

I glanced at Noah again in the rearview mirror, which I definitely didn't position perfectly so I could see her. I watched her for a moment and then focused back on the road.

"You guys ready for this?" I asked.

"I was ready a month ago!" Gracie piped up, brimming with excitement. "It's going to be a huge party!"

Sawyer turned around, a mischievous gleam in his eye. "You know what would really make this a party? Turning this car into a concert on wheels."

I groaned. "Do we have to? I'm about to listen to Ellie Miles for three hours—I don't need to start now."

"Come on, Dorian," Noah pleaded with a grin.

"Yeah, bro. Don't be a party pooper," Sawyer echoed, nudging me in the ribs.

"Fine," I sighed, giving in.

Sawyer grabbed my phone, changed my playlist, and cranked up the volume.

The unmistakable beat of Ellie Miles's latest hit filled the car. As the chorus kicked in, the infectious energy of the music washed over us. I caught a glimpse of Noah, her head bobbing to the rhythm, a smile dancing on her lips.

The music surged through me, and before I knew it, I was singing at the top of my lungs, caught up in the moment. Sawyer's grin was infectious as he threw himself into the performance, drumming the air to the beat.

Glancing back at Noah, I saw her laughing as she held her phone up to record. She was so carefree, her laughter a melody in itself. The sight made my heart swell.

Gracie chimed in from the backseat, her giggles interspersed with the lyrics as she tried to keep up with our off-key notes. The carefree vibe pulled us all in, and laughter erupted from the entire car as we tried to outdo each other with ridiculous dance moves in our seats. The song ended and the next one was a slower beat. I turned the volume down.

"You're going to ruin my grumpy small-town reputation if you try to post that video anywhere."

Sawyer shot me a teasing look. "Your reputation was toast the second you started dating Noah. Everyone knows it now."

Noah laughed. Their friendly relationship had already reached the point of being able to tease each other back and forth. I opened my mouth to fire back, but before I could, Gracie leaned forward in her seat, her face lighting up.

"Wait a second… Daddy is dating Noah?"

We all paused. I glanced at Sawyer, who gave me an *I'm sorry* look. While everyone else knew that Noah and I were now together, we'd been debating on how and when to tell Gracie. With all the questions she had about her mom lately, I knew I needed to approach the subject carefully.

Gracie beamed, her eyes wide with excitement. "Are you two going to hold hands at the concert?"

I glanced at Noah, feeling the heat rise in my cheeks. Her playful smirk told me she was enjoying this.

"Uh… maybe," I replied, trying to keep my words casual while my heart raced.

"Yes!" Gracie squealed, bouncing in her seat. "You have to! You can't be a couple and not hold hands!"

Laughter filled the car again. With Gracie and Sawyer's excitement in the air and Noah's presence, I hit the gas, ready for the concert—and whatever came next.

FORTY-TWO

Noah - November

LONG LIVE (TAYLOR'S VERSION) - TAYLOR SWIFT

WE MET UP WITH DOTTY AND TRENT, WHO DROVE SEPARATELY since they were leaving for their honeymoon the next day. The stadium stretched out before us, a sprawling sea of movement and color as we all watched from the suite. Ellie wasn't just performing, she commanded the entire space. Thanks to Sawyer's NFL connections, we had the perfect view—close enough to see her on stage but far enough to enjoy the moment without being overwhelmed by the crowd.

I'd always enjoyed her music, but something about seeing her live… it was different. Every lyric hit deeper, every melody resonated with something unspoken inside me. The way she moved, graceful but powerful, reminded me of all the times I'd gotten lost in music. It could carry you away from reality long enough to make you feel invincible, like you could accomplish anything.

And seeing Gracie light up, singing every word to every song was something special. She was having the time of her life, and I knew Sawyer would be getting serious uncle points for pulling this off for her.

Dorian stood at the back of the suite, arms crossed, watching the stage with that same intense expression he wore when he thought no one was looking. I caught his eye a few times, and he smiled.

Dotty sang along with Gracie to every word, while Trent stood beside them, attempting to join in but clearly guessing half the lyrics.

When Ellie played her acoustic set, the energy shifted. The lights dimmed, and the entire stadium seemed to hold its breath. Her voice was raw and haunting, filling the space as she sang about heartbreak, love, and everything in between. It was impossible not to get swept up in it. I found myself thinking about everything that had happened over the past few months—John, Dorian, Gracie—and how tangled up my life had become. It was a whirlwind of emotions, but despite all the heartache, I wouldn't change a damn thing.

But then, just like that, the moment was over, and the tempo kicked up again, fireworks bursting overhead as Ellie launched into her final song. The crowd roared, phones up in the air, trying to capture the magic on their screens, but I didn't even bother. Some things couldn't be recorded. They had to be felt.

As the last note rang out and Ellie bowed, the stadium exploded in applause, and I was grateful to be able to experience this with not only my best friend but with Gracie and Dorian too.

"Well, G. What did you think?" Sawyer asked, grinning widely at his niece.

"That was amazing!" She ran over to give him a hug so forcefully, I knew it would have knocked me on my feet, but Sawyer easily had a hundred pounds on me, maybe more, and he barely flinched. "I think this might be the best day ever!"

"I'm glad you had fun. You were a freaking rockstar yourself out there, singing along to every song," he said, ruffling her blonde locks.

"Daddy even said I could say the bad words during the songs this one time!"

We all laughed, letting the moment sink in.

"We better make our way down there if we are going to do the meet and greet with Ellie," Sawyer said.

"Meet and greet?" Dotty asked.

"Yeah, did I not mention that?" he said, smiling as if he knew that little bit of information would be a surprise. Gracie pretended to faint, letting the back of her hand on her forehead.

"Okay, I lied. This is definitely the best day ever."

FORTY-THREE

Dorian - November

RUNAWAY - RAMIN DJAWADI

THE ENERGY IN THE ROOM BUZZED AS WE MADE OUR WAY backstage. The concert was everything Gracie had hoped for. Ellie Miles had given one hell of a performance, and now, minutes from meeting her idol, Gracie was practically bouncing on her toes. Her wide eyes gleamed with excitement, and the contagious thrill of the moment was enough to make me smile.

The backstage area was bustling—every corner filled with quick-moving staff, security guards in dark uniforms, and fans in line still buzzing from the concert. The room was full of the sound of conversations and the low hum of background music coming from hidden speakers. Tall walls surrounded us, painted a sterile white that contrasted with the vibrant energy of the crowd.

"Do you think she'll like me?" Gracie whispered, nervously fidgeting with the hem of her Ellie Miles T-shirt she threw over her outfit.

Noah crouched beside her, offering a reassuring smile. "I think she'll love you."

I smiled at their interaction, but something in the air felt off. I glanced around the space, my eyes briefly locking on the security guards stationed at the far ends of the room. Their gazes constantly scanned the crowd, alert and calculating.

Sawyer showed his passes, and a staff member ushered us down a long hallway. After a quick security check, we entered the room where Ellie would be signing autographs and taking photos. The floor was lined with people eagerly waiting their turn to meet the woman they idolized.

Gracie's grip on my hand tightened as we turned the corner, her breath catching at the sight of the crowd. She was practically vibrating with excitement as we reached the front of the line. The staff signaled for us to approach.

The room itself was full of celebrity glamour and the humdrum of event logistics—glossy promotional posters of Ellie on the tables, with oversized banners behind her, swaying slightly with the air conditioning. Behind the tables, Ellie herself stood like a beacon.

"Next!" a voice rang out, and the six of us moved forward. The woman behind the counter waved a hand. "Three at the table at a time," she said, glancing at us. Then her gaze shifted to Trent and me. "You three," she said politely, gesturing to a spot beyond the tables, "if you could wait over there, please."

Ellie tossed her blonde hair behind her shoulders, greeting Gracie with a radiant smile as Trent, Sawyer, and I walked to where the woman had instructed.

Ellie's expression lit up at Gracie's beaming face. Gracie let out a small gasp, and I couldn't help but grin.

"Hi! What's your name?" Ellie asked, leaning forward with a warmth that instantly put Gracie at ease.

"G-Gracie!" she squeaked.

Ellie's smile widened. "Well, Gracie, it's so nice to meet you. I just love your outfit!"

She reached out to take Gracie's hand for a photo when another odd prickling sensation washed over me. Something still felt... off. I forced myself to shake it off, to focus on the moment.

"Hey, you have to wait in line until it's your turn," a security guard said, his hand hovering over his radio.

I turned to see what was causing the commotion, and my breath caught in my throat.

John.

He was standing next in line. His hair tucked under a low baseball cap, and he'd grown out his facial hair, but that walk, that presence... He was draped in all black, the edges of a VIP badge glinting as it swung from his neck. My heart slammed against my ribs, the world tilting for just a moment as I struggled to process if it could really be him.

"Fine, I'll wait."

A chill ran down my spine. My blood went cold. I fought the urge to react, to move, to act.

I couldn't be sure. Maybe it wasn't him. Maybe I was overthinking this, overwhelmed and paranoid.

He stood there, arguing with the security guard. I glanced at Noah, trying to gauge if she'd noticed, but she was focused on Gracie, her smile wide, her attention completely on her. Dotty stood next to them, her eyes fixed on Gracie and Ellie. Trent stood next to me, his demeanor alert but unaware, and Sawyer stood beside him.

I clicked my tongue, drawing their attention. Sawyer turned to me, his eyes narrowing as I subtly nodded toward John. Trent tracked the movement, the unspoken message passing between us. *Be ready.*

They both glanced over, their gazes scanning toward John.

I moved subtly to stand closer to Noah and Gracie, but a guard next to me held his arm out.

"You have to wait here," he said.

My fists curled at my sides, but I forced myself not to react, barely holding myself in check. I couldn't make a move without tipping him off.

"Gracie, Noah. Come here."

Both of them looked at me, confused. Neither moved.

"I'm fine, Daddy," Gracie said, her voice full of innocence.

Noah's brows knitted at my clipped tone, but she didn't press, her focus remaining on Gracie. My mind raced, adrenaline coursing through my veins as I tried to think of a plan in case this was the worst-case-scenario.

What's the best way to keep them safe? How can I get them out of here?

As I looked at Gracie, my stomach twisted. She was still starstruck, her eyes wide, completely unaware of the threat just a few feet away.

And then it happened.

John's eyes flicked to mine, a sharp recognition flashing across his face. In that moment, I knew. I wasn't imagining things.

He was here.

And this was the endgame.

I went to push past the guard, but he stood in front of me.

"Wait. Here," he said. "Or I'll have to escort you out."

Something dangerous passed through his expression as John ignored the security guard and took a step forward. I knew we were past the point of no return. He was here for something, someone.

And I had an idea who. *Noah.*

"We need to go." My heart hammered as I moved closer to Gracie and Noah, my protective instinct kicking into overdrive.

"What? No, not yet!" Gracie protested, her disappointment palpable.

But then his posture shifted, his body tensing as his eyes narrowed, locking onto Gracie. A cold, predatory gleam entered his gaze.

No. Not my daughter. My chest constricted. He wasn't after Noah. He was after Gracie.

"Now Gracie!"

I knew Gracie was just a kid to him—a weapon, an easy target. A way to punish Noah. To prove he still held the strings, even now.

His gaze lingered on Gracie, his movements calculated.

"*Hey!*" the guard shouted as Johns stepped forward. "I said you need to wait your turn."

I had to stop him. I couldn't let him hurt her. Not now. Not ever. John's hand shot into his jacket, and I saw the flash of metal.

Before I could even process it, a guard shouted, "Gun!"

The room erupted into chaos. Two guards pulled out guns, but most were unarmed. They moved quickly, one lunging for John's arm, trying to wrest the weapon away, while the other pulled a baton, aiming for his wrist.

Gasps rippled through the room, followed by a shrill scream. Chairs scraped against the floor as people scrambled to get out of the way.

I didn't know how he got a gun past security, but if anyone could do it, it was John. He was too smart, too determined.

And then a gunshot rang out.

The crowd ducked instinctively as the shot echoed through the room. One of the guards lunged toward John again, while the other shielded civilians, shouting for people to move.

"Get down!" the taller guard shouted.

People were moving, stumbling over each other in panic, while John moved closer to Gracie.

Someone tried to move in front of him, but John pointed the gun at them, an unsettling calm in his posture.

The command came. "Lockdown!" a guard shouted into their radio.

"Drop it!" someone commanded.

John's attention snapped back to me, his lips curling into a cruel smile. "I don't think so," he sneered. "Everyone but blondie and the girl, stand over there. Now."

"No," I growled, stepping closer to Gracie and Noah, the guard finally preoccupied and allowing me pass.

"You think I'm playing around?" John spat, then shot a guard in the leg, sending him crumpling to the ground.

A sickening gasp swept through the room.

"Gracie!" I shouted, as I lunged to grab her.

John's hand shot out, grabbing her by the arm and yanking her behind him. A cruel smile twisted his lips as he shifted her under his arm, keeping the gun aimed at anyone who dared move closer.

The sight slammed into me—a raw, gut-wrenching twist of agony that felt like my insides were being torn apart.

"No!" I shouted. But it was too late. Gracie was in his grip.

Then his other arm shot out, clamping around Ellie's wrist. She stumbled, and a gasp tore from her lips as her eyes locked onto the barrel of the gun.

Everything spiraled into chaos. People were shoving, panicking, running for the exits. Guards moved in but were too slow.

"Let them go!" Sawyer shouted, standing beside me, his eyes fierce, darting between John and Gracie.

John's grip on the gun tightened, his gaze cold. "Stay

back!" he snarled, his gaze moving between us, the barrel of the gun now aimed at Gracie's trembling form.

My life flashed before my eyes at the sight of my daughter held at gunpoint. It was like the world collapsed in on itself, everything shrinking down to the horrifying image of Gracie, *my Gracie*, in a murderer's grip.

"Move and she dies," he hissed.

Her wide eyes, filled with panic, locked onto mine, searching for reassurance I couldn't give. I only hoped that she didn't truly understand the severity of the situation.

I couldn't breathe. The gun now pressed against her temple, her small body shaking under his arm. All of it. It was as if someone had ripped my heart from my chest.

Every memory, every moment I'd shared with her, rushed through my mind in painful clarity. Her first steps, the way she used to reach for me with her tiny hands when she was scared. The bedtime stories, the laughter, the arguments over silly things like too many snacks. Every single thing I loved about her, everything I promised to protect, now teetering on the edge.

My fists clenched at my sides, powerless to do anything without risking her safety. I'd faced dangerous situations before, but nothing, *nothing*, prepared me for this kind of fear.

The kind that gripped on the deepest part of your soul and refused to let go. I wanted to rip him apart. I want to tear him apart limb by fucking limb for even thinking about fucking with my daughter.

I heard Trent's and Sawyer's voices cutting through the fog, but they didn't register.

All I could see was Gracie. My mind spiraled as I envisioned her life—graduating school, discovering her passions, living the kind of life Hallie never had the chance to see.

That my mom never had the chance to see.

And here she was, caught in this same nightmare.

John's fingers twitched, his elbow tightening around Gracie's torso. I caught his gaze again, that sick smirk playing on his lips.

My body tensed, every instinct telling me to act.

"I'll take her place," Noah's voice cut through the chaos.

"Noah, no!" Dotty yelled, raw with fear, trying to step forward. Trent grabbed hold of her, pulling her back behind him. Sawyer stepped forward, positioning himself in front of Dotty like a human shield.

The moment Noah's words sank in, something deep inside me ached and tangled with a surge of gratitude. She didn't flinch. She didn't waver. She stepped up without a second thought, willing to sacrifice herself for my daughter.

But she wasn't just offering herself up for Gracie—she was offering herself up for me and everyone that loved my daughter. She was willing to face whatever John had planned, knowing exactly what he had done to his victims. My stomach twisted at the thought. Noah wasn't just someone who cared about Gracie—she was willing to fight for her, to protect her, the same way I would.

The same way any parent would.

That thought brought both warmth and dread, tangled together in a way I couldn't comprehend.

Gracie's wide eyes were glued to mine, her body trembling against John's cruel hold as he whispered something in her ear. The cold metal of his gun continued to press against her temple, the sharp, silent threat hanging in the air like smoke. I wanted to tear him apart right then and there, but Gracie was too close, her small body caught in the grip of a monster. My heart clenched. I couldn't act yet.

"Here's what's going to happen," John said, the words dripping from his lips like poison. He swung the gun from Gracie's head to a nearby exit to the left, the cold barrel gleaming under the harsh overhead lights. "I'm going to take these two"—he gestured to Ellie and Gracie—"and walk through that door. Then you all can spend the next hour or so trying to find us."

"No!" Noah shouted, her face a mask of determination. She took a cautious step toward him, hands raised in surrender. Her gaze never left his. "Let her go. Please. Take me. Take me instead."

"No," John yelled. "You need to stay here and suffer."

"I can't get a good shot," the security guard called out from behind the counter. His voice was tense, his gun aimed at John, but his hands were shaking slightly. "Put the gun down now, and we can all walk away from this peacefully."

"I don't want *peace*." John chuckled, his eyes never leaving Noah as his smirk widened. "So, looks like you really have moved on then, huh?" His words turned cold, venomous. "Already forgot about me? I thought I meant more to you than that, Noah. You surely meant more than that to me."

Her hands were still raised, her movements slow but deliberate as she took another cautious step forward. "You don't want her, John. You want me. I'll come with you. Just let her go."

John's laughter reverberated through the small hallway, dark and mocking, sending a chill down my spine. "Look at you," he sneered, his eyes gleaming with twisted amusement. "How adorable," he hissed. "Stepping in to try to save his kid. Already probably whored yourself out, haven't you? Just like the worthless piece of trash you've always been."

I glanced at John, now scanning the guards across the

room. Seizing the moment while his attention was else-where, I mouthed to Noah, *Trust me.*

Noah froze at the taunt, her body turning to face me. "I'm going to keep her saf—"

I cut her off with a shake of my head. "Stop!" I shouted, fists clenched at my sides, burning with the urge to lash out. "You don't want either of them. Take me."

I had a much better chance of getting out of this unscathed than Noah—or especially Gracie—did. If he wanted to make Noah suffer, I'd have to find a way to use that to my advantage.

"Dorian," Noah warned, but I couldn't stop.

John's grip on Gracie tightened, his finger twitching near the trigger, while his other hand kept Ellie's arm locked in place.

His eyes darted to me, and I saw the flicker of uncer-tainty in them.

That crack? I was going to push through it.

Gracie's small body trembled, but she didn't make a sound. Her wide eyes were still trained on me, pleading with every silent breath. I took a step forward.

"Take me," I repeated, willing my voice to make it all believable. "Let me play this game with you." I paused, letting out a fake sigh, hoping it came across as genuine. "Look, man… I've only gotten close to her because I wanted to get to you. It's you I want to know, not *Noah*," I spat her name, making sure he could feel the contempt in it. "I want to understand how… how you do it… what it feels like. I want to learn from you."

I kept my eyes on him, hoping he'd buy it. My stomach twisted, but I kept my gaze fixed, unwilling to show the hesitation eating at me. This was about survival. For Gracie, for Noah.

"Dorian!" Noah shouted. It hit me—this was real. I

knew it was real, but then she played along. "How... how could you do this? How could you do this to me?"

"Let's hurt her," I said to John. "Let's hurt her together. Take me and put her through the pain of losing us both." I hated that my daughter was hearing this, but I know Noah would explain everything to her later. I know Gracie knew me and I just hoped she didn't fully understand.

His expression remained cold. "I don't need anyone on my side," he growled, his grip tightening on the gun. "My plan is already set... But"—he paused, his lips curling into a smile that didn't reach his eyes—"I must admit, I do like the idea of hurting her together. How do I know you're not lying?"

John's eyes narrowed, calculating, and for a brief moment, I could see the conflict flash in his expression. The tension in the air shifted, the seconds stretching out, my heart thundering in my chest. I took another step.

"You don't, but..." I let the words hang before I took a slow step closer. "But I think you know. You and me? We're the same. You can see that. I know you can, just like I could always see you, even when we first met."

John's grin widened at the exchange, clearly enjoying that. He paused for what seemed like an eternity then continued. "Okay, fine. You can come with me. I don't care about the girl anyways." He motioned to Gracie dismissively. "But I do need her," he said, gesturing to Ellie, who stood frozen in fear beside us.

Noah stepped toward him, her hands trembling, but her voice didn't waver. "John, please—don't do this."

John's grip on Gracie tightened, the gun now aimed at her temple, and he hissed, "Stay where you are!"

The room seemed to freeze, but my focus never left Gracie, never left her terrified eyes.

"Come here," he ordered, his tone sickly sweet. "Come here and I will let her go."

"Follow his instructions," the security guard said firmly, nodding in approval of the switch.

Gracie's body shook, but she didn't make a sound. "Daddy, I'm scared," she whispered, barely audible.

"You'll be okay," I whispered back. I wanted to say more. I needed to say more, but I had to keep this narrative alive.

The tension built, thick as the air around us, and John coaxed, "Just step closer, and we can make it easy."

But I didn't care about making it easy. I cared about getting her safe.

I stepped within his reach, and John's hand pushed Gracie aside as he pointed the gun directly at my temple, a sickening smile spreading across his face. She fled to Noah, sobbing.

And then, just like that, Gracie's safety was no longer the focus.

For a fleeting moment, my body relaxed, grateful that my daughter was finally safe.

Even if I was the one in jeopardy now.

He turned back to Noah, his lips curling into a cruel, twisted grin. "You really thought I wouldn't notice, huh?" he said, his voice dripping with disdain. "That I wouldn't find you hiding out in that pathetic little town? That I wouldn't see you cozying up to him?" He spat the words, venom in his eyes. "You refused to ever travel with me, couldn't even give me that time to help keep me in check, but then you move to that town for what? For him?"

Gracie clung to Noah, her tiny hands gripping her shirt. Noah wrapped her arms around her, holding her tightly as she whispered soothingly, "It's okay. I've got you." Her fragile frame trembled against Noah, and I could feel the desperation radiating from both of them.

John's grin widened, and then his gaze locked onto Ellie, who stood beside us. His eyes narrowed, calculating his next move. He raised the gun, the cold barrel pointed at Ellie, and gestured with a tilt of his head.

"Let's go," he said, his tone thick with malice. "You're coming with me. We're going to take a little trip through the tunnels."

As the words left his mouth, security yelled, "Stop right there, and drop your weapon now!"

Two guards, weapons raised, stood firm, waiting for the right moment to fire. The air was thick with tension, but John's laugh cut through the silence.

"Oh, shut up, will ya?" he sneered, and without hesitation, he fired. The first shot rang out, quick and brutal, striking one of the guards. The second shot followed almost instantly, silencing the second.

"Move, now! Both of you," John barked, the barrel of his gun shifting between Ellie and me as he shoved us forward.

Ellie's eyes widened with fear, her words trembling as she protested. "You can't do this!" But John's grip never faltered, his control absolute.

"Get moving," he ordered, his tone cold and final as he shoved us toward the entrance of the tunnel. "Or I swear, I'll make this a lot worse for everyone."

I felt a surge of helplessness and fury as Noah's voice rang out, filled with defiance. "You won't get away with this."

John turned to catch her gaze, the cruel glint in his eyes sending a chill through me. "That's exactly the point."

With that, he dragged us into the dark shadows of the tunnel, his gun always trained on us, and his grip tight on both Ellie and me as we were swallowed by the darkness.

FORTY-FOUR

Noah - November

NO TIME TO DIE - BILLIE EILISH

PANIC COURSED THROUGH ME AS I PACED THE ROOM, MY HEART pounding in time with the chaotic whispers of the unaware fans beyond the walls. Ellie's security team quickly sprang into action the moment John disappeared, calling in reinforcements from the police. Apparently, being a superstar doesn't guarantee a large armed security detail—only a couple were approved to be armed. Weapons were prohibited in the stadium, and the unarmed guards had to rely on their training and instincts.

We still didn't understand how John made it through security with a weapon, but he had.

My mind kept replaying the scene—Gracie held at gunpoint, the expression of terror in her wide eyes. She was finally safe, but she still looked fragile, now sitting in Dotty's lap. I could see the tremors in her small hands as she held onto Dotty.

I had held her for a minute, pulling her into my arms and shielding her from the horrors that had invaded our lives. Dotty eventually offered to take over, knowing I was trying to figure out what to do to get Dorian out of danger.

"We need to get her out of here," Dotty's voice brought me back to the present. "Trent and I can take her somewhere safe."

A knot twisted in my stomach at the thought of letting her go, but I knew I wouldn't leave without Dorian. "It's for her safety," she said, her tone firm yet understanding.

Trent stepped closer, placing a reassuring hand on my shoulder. "We got her. Dorian needs you here."

The thought of leaving her, even for a moment, felt like a betrayal, but I could see the determination in Dotty's eyes. She was right. Staying here could put Gracie in even more danger. With a heavy heart, I finally nodded.

"Just for now," Dotty promised, her expression softening.

"There's a room with a couch you can use for now, until the police arrive. They'll want to question everyone," a guard informed us.

Gracie looked up at me, her small face trembling, and my heart shattered a little more. "Noah, I want to stay with you."

I crouched beside her, brushing the hair from her face, my fingers shaking. "I know, G, but you'll be with Dotty and Trent. They will keep you safe. I'll come find you as soon as I can."

"What about Daddy?" she asked, her voice shaking. Her eyes glistened with tears, and I fought back my own as I forced a smile despite the ache in my chest.

"It's going to be okay. I promise."

I only hoped I could keep that promise.

"I love you, Noah," she sobbed.

"I love you too, G." My eyes stung and I hugged her tight.

Trent led Dotty and Gracie to the room. My stomach churned, but the urgency of the situation left no room to waste time. Mayhem swirled around us as people hurried around, voices rising in confusion. Sawyer stood next to me, his expression serious as he surveyed the chaotic room, the weight of the moment heavy on his shoulders.

"The tunnels can only lead to two exits, and John will likely be making his way through them," he said, cutting through the noise. "I know this layout—we can set up teams at the exits. It might be the best chance we have to catch him."

"What if something happens to them?" I asked, my voice tight with anxiety. The very thought twisted in my gut, a sharp reminder of how quickly everything could go wrong.

Sawyer met my gaze, determination igniting in his features like a flame. "We'll make sure that doesn't happen. We'll find him, Noah. We'll bring him back."

His confidence was a lifeline I desperately clung to. Sawyer was always the goofy, fun one until it was time to get down to business, then it was like a flip switched, and he was all go-mode.

We moved toward the security team that had already gathered, talking through a plan on their own.

"Look, I'm a lineman for San Francisco. I know the ins and outs of this stadium better than anyone. I can help lead the search in the tunnels," he said, his tone firm, earning nods of acknowledgment from the officers gathered around.

One of the security guards raised a brow, skepticism etched on his face. "This isn't a game, man. We need to prioritize the safety of everyone here. You could put your-self in danger. Most of the stadium is already cleared out, with only a few people left who are now on lockdown, but we still need to ensure their safety and get Ellie back."

Sawyer shook his head, his jaw clenched with determination. "We need to get my brother back too. *Dorian*. That's his name," he spat. "I'm not leaving without him. I'm an asset here, not a liability."

Their faces contemplated the situation. I pushed my anxiety down as the security team eyed me, trying to understand my place here.

"You're going to have to drag me out of here before I leave without him," I insisted, locking eyes with the lead guard. "I won't let him go in there alone," I said, each word laced with raw desperation.

The lead guard, Officer Ramirez, paused. "We can't let you both out there. Someone could get hurt."

I stepped forward. "I'm not asking for permission to go alone. I'm asking to help. I'm not staying here while Dorian's out there in danger. Let me help."

Sawyer's voice was stern. "We're both going."

"I can't put you both in danger," Officer Ramirez shot back, his tone sharp. "We have enough problems without risking more lives. Half my team is already busy tending to the wounded until we get backup." Gesturing to Sawyer, he said, "He's someone I can make an exception for, but you need to stay behind."

My heart pounded, frustration surging. "I'm trained in first aid. CPR, too. You're low on officers, and we both know you're going to need help. While you're handling the critical stuff, I can assist. Odds are, he is going to hurt one of them. We both know your team is going to prioritize Ellie, so let me help." I paused, noticing the doubt still in his eyes. "I know John better than anyone here, and I can talk him down."

Officer Ramirez looked at me, his jaw clenched. He glanced at Sawyer, who stood there with his arms crossed. Ramirez's eyes softened, but only for a moment, before his shoulders tensed again.

He contemplated it, rubbing his hand on his jaw. "Fine, but I'm not here to babysit anyone," he muttered. "The second I say it's too dangerous, you listen. No second chances. Got it?"

"Understood," I replied, the flicker of determination in my chest swelling into full resolve.

He gestured at Sawyer and me. "I'll take you two toward the north exit. Keep your eyes peeled. You three"—he pointed at some of the unarmed guards—"you come with us. Backup is on its way, but we need to get moving now. The rest of you, take the south exit. Stick together and be ready for anything. Stay sharp."

As the plan took shape, hope surged within me, battling against the panic that threatened to overwhelm me. With Sawyer at my side and a plan forming, I felt a renewed sense of purpose. We wouldn't let John extinguish the light in our lives without a fight.

FORTY-FIVE

Dorian - November

RESCUE - LAUREN DAIGLE

FEAR CLAWED THROUGH MY CHEST WITH EVERY LABORED breath as John forced Ellie and me deeper into the tunnels. The sharp tang of blood filled my mouth, a sting radiating from where my teeth tore into the inside of my mouth. Our footsteps echoed in the cavernous space, sharp and rhythmic. Ellie's gasps punctuated the silence each time John jabbed the gun into her back.

Once we were out of sight of any possible rescue, he shoved us to a stop and tied our hands behind our backs and took our phones. He still didn't fully trust me, and I couldn't blame him for that. Coarse rope bit into my skin, every tug sending jolts of pain up my arms and into my shoulders. Ellie walked beside me, her chin high despite the tremor in her frame. Brave, though, the slight shudder in her breath betrayed her fear.

John's gun swung between us like a pendulum, his focus shifting with each imagined threat. His eyes burned with something feral, something broken.

"You know, *Dorian,*" he spat, my name venomous from

his mouth, "your precious Noah could have stopped all this. It's all her fault."

"I'm not surprised. She fucks up everything, it seems," I snarled, continuing to play his game.

"She could've saved them all," he said, voice rising, fingers tightening around the grip of the gun. "If she had just come with me all those times. If she'd given me what I needed, none of this would've happened. They'd all still be alive. She was the only person to ever stop the noise in my head."

My mind reeled, trying to make sense of his warped logic.

"Tell me more," I demanded, anger masking the fear simmering beneath my skin. "What do you mean?"

"She was supposed to fix me! To help me hold it together. I tried to be what I needed to be, but I needed her. And every time she said no, every time she chose something else—she pushed me to this!"

I looked beside me to see Ellie's face fall, the realization hitting her of just how dire this situation really was. She still believed I was on his side.

Her voice cut through the growing tension, her tone low but sharp like steel. "So, it's her fault you're a monster?"

He swung the gun toward her. She flinched but didn't step back, her wide eyes locking onto him.

"Don't pretend you understand," John growled. "You're just some spoiled pop star who's never been denied anything in her life. Noah was different. She was supposed to save me. She did save me, at least at first."

"And the murders?" I pressed, trying to keep his focus on me. "I like that you did that to drag this out, to torture her. It really did a number on her, and the butterfly. Nice touch."

John's smile twisted into something grotesque, his tone

softening in a way that made my stomach turn. "She was supposed to be *my* butterfly—my transformation. Every life I took was a message to her, a reminder that she couldn't just move on. She was supposed to be loyal to *me*. That was the only way."

"You're insane," Ellie snapped. "You're both insane. This isn't about her. It's about you. This is no one's fault but your own."

His jaw ticked, and his expression faltered for a moment, anger flickering like a flame starved of oxygen. "It is her fault. Her and that damn family," he hissed.

Ellie drew a sharp inhale. "Please," she said firmly, even as her body trembled. "Just let me go."

He ignored her, shoving us forward again. My legs felt like lead as we trudged deeper into the labyrinth of tunnels. I fought to keep track of landmarks, a poster here, a door there, but the dim light and endless turns disoriented me as we continued to walk and walk and walk.

Then, without warning, Ellie made her move.

It happened so fast I almost didn't register it. She spun, her heel driving into John's shin, then she kneed him in the groin. He stumbled with a curse, the gun jerking upward.

I stood in front of John, buying Ellie time. "Run!" I yelled at her as she ran.

He groaned, hunching over. Then the barrel of the gun swung toward my head, stopping me cold.

"So, you aren't on my side," John snarled, low and venomous. "Move and I'll blow your brains out."

Ellie's footfalls faded, and John roared in frustration, firing after her.

Two shots rang out, loud and final, but he missed.

Then the third shot made her stumble, clutching her arm, but she didn't stop.

"Badass," I muttered under my breath.

John's attention snapped back to me. "I knew you were playing me. What the hell do I do with you now, traitor?" he muttered, his voice dripping with disdain.

"Well, you could let me go." I shrugged.

His lip curled. "Not a chance."

The shot came without warning.

White-hot pain exploded in my leg, and I hit the ground with a cry, blood already soaking through my jeans.

"Guess you're not going anywhere," he said, his tone almost conversational, before taking off after Ellie.

My thoughts raced through the pain—to Gracie. Noah. My family.

I laid there, breathing in shallow, jagged gasps. The pain coursed through my body like fire. Each heartbeat felt like an eternity, even though I knew it was beating too fast, but I couldn't seem to move.

The blood pooled from my leg, seeping onto the cold cement. The pain was sharp, but it was the terror that really clawed at me. I knew enough to recognize the signs—the bullet had likely hit an artery. I could feel the blood pumping, fast and heavy. If I didn't get help soon, I wouldn't make it.

This couldn't be it. *Not like this.*

Only minutes ago, I'd been panicking about Gracie's future while she was under John's grasp. Worrying that she'd miss out on so many things. Graduation, her first love, her career—hell, even her next art class.

But now, I feared *I* would be the one to miss those things.

Tears burned in the corners of my eyes, mixing with the sweat on my forehead, but I couldn't stop them.

Gracie.

I didn't want her to wake up tomorrow to her world shattered. No warning. No chance for me to hold her, to tell her how much I loved her, to remind her that she was enough.

I thought about her tiny hands holding onto my finger when she was a baby, her face lighting up when I'd praise her. She had this way of seeing beauty in the world that no one else could.

My chest heaved, each breath a struggle. The world felt so quiet, so still. The blood was pooling, but what hurt worse was the realization that I wasn't sure if I was going to make it out of here. If I was going to be there to walk her through life.

The thought of leaving her alone was suffocating.

And Noah. God, Noah.

I hadn't even told her how much she meant to me. We'd danced around each other, hesitant and afraid to take the leap, but when we finally did…

Fuck, I was selfish and needed more time with her. I wanted to see her smile when I walked into the room. I wanted to be the one who made her laugh after a bad day, to share mundane moments in the kitchen, or to argue over something silly before falling asleep in each other's arms.

But instead, she'd carry this with her, wondering if she could've stopped it. Wondering if she could've saved me.

The hollow ache in my chest grew deeper as I thought about my girls. They didn't deserve this.

I couldn't let this be the end.

My leg was going numb, and the world around me was starting to blur. Panic and pain wove together in a storm of confusion and grief. I wasn't done.

Not yet.

I yanked off my belt with shaking hands, pressing it above the wound. Pain exploded through me, but I gritted my teeth and tied it as tightly as I could. My head swam, and my vision blurred, but I didn't stop. The blood soaked my clothes, puddling beneath me, but I had to hold on.

Too much left unsaid. Too many dreams to live. Gracie deserved her father. Noah deserved the future I so desperately wanted to give her.

The darkness crept closer, but I forced myself to focus. I couldn't let it end like this. Not when there was still a chance to fix it.

Panic still surged, but then I noticed the phone a few feet away that must have been dropped in the scuffle. My body screamed at me to give up, but I couldn't. Not now. I had to fight.

I dragged myself across the cement, my fingers scraping against the dust and grime, the pain in my leg so intense I nearly blacked out.

When my hand finally closed around the phone, I fumbled with it, my hands slick with blood and sweat.

I dialed her number. My vision was fading, and my pulse was erratic, but *I couldn't give up.*

Noah's voice crackled through, desperate and frantic. "Hello?"

"Peach," I rasped.

"Dorian? Oh my God, where are you? What happened?"

"I've been shot. I…. can't move."

"Where are you?" she asked, her panic rising. "What do you see?"

I turned my head, my attention narrowing to only her voice—her words. I tried to focus, to make sense of what I saw, but everything was slipping through my fingers. I managed a halfhearted chuckle, a dry rasp that barely made it past my lips. "Sawyer… picture of Sawyer. Running."

There was a pause. A long, agonizing moment before

Sawyer spoke in the background. "I know where that is. We're coming."

And just like that, hope glimmered, fragile but *alive*.

But the pain was relentless. I didn't know how much longer I had. I could feel the darkness creeping in at the edges of my vision, pulling me closer.

"I'm... I'm bleeding out, baby," I slurred. Each inhale was ripping through me, and I couldn't fight the darkness closing in.

"Dorian, stay with me." Her voice cracked, trembling, as the sound of her frantic breaths filled the line. "Keep your eyes open. I'm coming. Do you hear me? We're coming." Her words were thick with panic and desperation, and it was the only thing keeping me from falling unconscious.

I wanted to tell her everything. To make it right. To promise that I'd be there, that I wasn't going anywhere. But my body was already betraying me. I couldn't even keep my eyes open anymore.

"Noah..." I could barely get her name out.

"Dorian, *no*." Her words were raw, desperate. "Stay with me. I need you. Gracie needs you." The pain in her voice tore through me like a thousand cuts, but I couldn't make myself breathe deeper.

I was fighting to stay awake. Every inch of my body screamed for sleep, for relief, but I couldn't give in. Not now. Not when her voice was still in my ear, begging, pleading for me to stay.

My chest felt like it was being crushed, my breaths shallow and ragged. But I had to make sure she knew.

"Tell G... I love her." The words scraped through my throat, barely above a whisper, but they were everything. They had to be everything.

"I'm not telling her anything. You're going to tell her

when you see her." Her voice was stronger now, but I could hear the tears—the deep, guttural sobs. "You hear me, Dor? You are going to tell her. You are going to tell her tomorrow and the next day and every fucking day until you enter the next life, but that day is *not* today. Hold on for me."

I wanted to fight to hold on. I wanted to be the man who kept her from feeling that fear, that devastation. But I was losing this fight.

"Take… care of her for me…" The words were barely escaping.

My body felt numb, like I was already slipping into another place.

"*No.* We are going to take care of her. You and me. You hear me? *We* are going to take care of her together! Keep your eyes open. Stay *with* me!"

She screamed now, loud and frantic. Every word a plea for me to fight. I felt her desperation in the pit of my stomach, but I couldn't hold on. I was already falling, already surrendering to the void, and no matter how hard I tried, I couldn't stop it.

I still didn't have the strength to respond. I let her voice wrap around me, curling through my mind like a tether, something soft and fragile, trying to keep me from drowning.

"We still need to finish that dumb show we started. It's almost Sunday, and you need to be there to help put way too many chocolate chips on Gracie's pancakes. We can get a dog and name him Stewart like you wanted. There's so much we still have to do. Please, Dorian…"

My heart sank with every word as she told me all the reasons why I couldn't leave, all the reasons I had to fight. But the darkness was too strong.

And then, as if she knew, she whispered, "Please, don't leave me. We're not done yet."

We're not done yet.

I barely managed to croak out the words, so weak, it didn't even sound like it wasn't mine anymore. "I love you."

"No, no, no. *No!*" Her scream was louder, more desperate than anything I had ever heard in my life.

And then there was nothing. No sound. No light. Only the cold, empty void.

FORTY-SIX

Noah - November

BREATHE ME - SIA

I raced down the dimly lit tunnel, Sawyer and Officer Ramirez at my side. Every echo of our hurried footsteps seemed to magnify the dread coiling around my chest. My mind kept replaying Dorian's voice, faint and breaking, warning me he was fading. I had to get to him. I couldn't lose him.

Tears still streamed down my face, but I pulled myself together, needing to find him and needing to find him now.

"How much farther?" I asked, the panic creeping up despite my best efforts to hold it back.

Sawyer's jaw tightened, his eyes scanning ahead. "We're close."

As we rounded the corner toward what I hoped was the exit, the dim light flickered and stretched into the next stretch of tunnel. A shadow moved ahead.

My heart lurched. "Did you see that?"

Sawyer nodded toward a door at the end of the corridor. "Yeah."

"Let's *go.*" My tone was strained, the need to get to Dorian growing unbearable. Every second counted.

We moved faster now, adrenaline pumping, but then I heard it—the faintest sound. Muffled voices, too close for comfort. My breath caught in my throat.

"That's John and Ellie," I whispered, my skin prickling.

Fuck.

We didn't have time for this.

I needed to get to Dorian. I had to find him. I needed to get to him now. He was fucking bleeding out and I couldn't get to him.

Sawyer motioned for silence, his hand coming up in front of me. "We're going to have to get through them. Stay behind me."

I nodded, my heartbeat hammering in my ears. The closer we got, the louder the voices grew. And then, just ahead, I saw them. John, leaning against the wall, Ellie standing just a few feet away, her eyes wide and terrified.

"Look what we have here," John said, oozing malice. He smirked at us, sizing us up like we were nothing more than prey.

I could feel Ellie's fear from where I stood, but she didn't move. She was frozen, holding her arm that was bleeding.

"Get back," Officer Ramirez ordered, his voice steely and calm, but with the unmistakable edge of command. He stepped forward, putting himself between us and John, his gun never wavering.

"Let her go, John. This ends now," Ramirez said.

John's eyes moved between us. "You think you can just come in here and stop me?" he sneered, raising the gun, eyes gleaming with something dangerous.

Ellie's body tensed, and my mind raced. I needed to get to Dorian—this couldn't keep going on.

He needed me.

He needed me *now*.

"Put the gun down," Ramirez said sharply. He moved closer to John. "You can walk out of here, or we'll make you. But Ellie's coming with us, no matter what."

My stomach churned. I couldn't think about this anymore—couldn't think about John or Ellie. All I could focus on was getting to Dorian.

John's smile faltered for a second, a moment of hesitation crossing his face as he kept his gun trained on Ellie, his eyes on his watch. It gave me a glimmer of hope. Maybe we could end this without anyone else getting hurt.

I was trembling with fury now. "End this now, John." My words faltered as John aimed the gun at Ellie's head, his finger resting lightly on the trigger.

I could feel the helplessness creeping up on me.

"Stop!" I shouted. "Let her go, John. Don't do this."

His eyes locked on mine, cold and dark, as if savoring every moment of my panic. "You think you can stop me?" he taunted. "You're all bark. No bite."

I couldn't back down. I couldn't let him have this victory.

But then I heard it—footsteps. Heavy, urgent footsteps echoing from deeper in the tunnel. A surge of hope shot through me, and I seized it.

"John!" Officer Ramirez shouted. "You're surrounded! This ends now!"

For a heartbeat, he faltered, his gaze darting around nervously. The sound of approaching officers only made him more erratic.

The security team rushed in then, overwhelming us with their numbers. "Get down!" Officer Ramirez shouted as they swarmed the area, and John, realizing his position, suddenly shifted the gun toward Ramirez.

And then something unexpected happened. John glanced at his wristwatch.

"Well, looks like it's finally time," he said. "You can have her now. I just needed her to make it to midnight. You definitely would use a lot more resources to get her back than you would anyone else, after all." He winked.

I froze. A sickening realization washed over me. John was waiting for something. Waiting for this moment.

Without warning, he shoved her away. Ellie stumbled forward, nearly falling, but Sawyer was there in an instant, his arms catching her before she could hit the ground.

"You're okay. I've got you," Sawyer said, pulling her close.

Ellie's wide, terrified eyes met his as she clung to him, her body trembling from the adrenaline. Sawyer held her tight, but his eyes never left John, who still had Ramirez at gunpoint.

This wasn't what I expected. There was no fight, no final showdown.

Except he didn't back down. His weapon was still in his grip, a threat.

The room held its breath. John's face twisted in fury as he pointed the gun at me. I went to run past him, to get to Dorian. I needed to find him.

"Don't move," he hissed, his voice trembling with an insane rage. "You can't get there in time. Don't even try."

I could barely hear anything through the blood rushing in my ears, but my focus was razor-sharp. I had to do something, anything.

"Hey!" Sawyer called out, his tone surprisingly calm. "Let's not do this, man. You don't need to go out like this."

John's attention snapped to Sawyer, confusion flashing across his face for a moment before his anger returned.

"What the hell do you know? You can't fix this." John spat.

Sawyer took another step forward, his hand gently

guiding Ellie behind him. "Yeah, I don't know if I can fix it," he said, his tone still level. "But I'm damn sure gonna try."

John's gun wavered slightly, his grip uncertain as he studied Sawyer. Sawyer's chest rose and fell as his focus locked on John—but there was something else in his eyes when he glanced briefly at Ellie.

"Ellie," Sawyer murmured, so low it was almost a whisper. His fingers brushed her arm. He turned his full attention to her, his gaze softening for just a heartbeat. "Trust me."

Before any of us could react, Sawyer reached for her, his hands framing her face. Then he kissed her.

Ellie froze for a split second, her eyes wide with shock. But as if pulled by some invisible thread, she leaned into him, her hands clutching his jacket. The room seemed to suspend in time.

John blinked, his grip on the gun loosening ever so slightly. "What the hell?" he muttered.

The lead agent seized the opportunity. "Now!" he barked, his voice slicing through silence.

Chaos erupted. The agents surged forward in a blur of motion, colliding with John and wresting the gun from his hand. He thrashed, shouting in rage, but the team was on him, forcing him to the ground. In seconds, they had him pinned, his wrists cuffed, and the weapon kicked out of reach.

I needed to get to Dorian.

Sawyer's grip tightened on Ellie as he looked over at me, his face set with grim determination. "Go straight down the tunnel. Find him, Noah."

My heart hammered in my chest, blood pounding in my ears. I started running.

Every beat was dragging me further from the moment I

could reach Dorian and make sure he was still breathing. I gasped, barely able to catch my breath as panic clawed at my throat.

"I'm coming with you." Officer Ramirez's voice came from behind me, sharp and commanding. His eyes locked onto mine, calculating as he caught up.

He turned, running backwards and yelled toward an officer standing nearby. "You, with me. We've got a GSW, and I need backup until the EMTs arrive."

He moved quickly, no questions asked, but all I could focus on was getting to Dorian.

My body continued forward, each step an eternity.

I'd never run like this in my life—faster than I ever thought possible—every step pushing me closer to him. He had to be okay.

I wouldn't accept any other possibility.

Officer Ramirez kept pace beside me, while the other officer trailed behind us.

Ramirez said something—probably an instruction—but it was drowned out by the roaring in my ears, my pulse deafening as my mind raced ahead, imagining what I would find.

The tunnel stretched out before me, endless and suffocating. My lungs burned. My throat was dry, as if the air was thick, too thick to swallow.

What if I'm too late?

No.

I couldn't think like that. I wouldn't.

Ramirez seemed to sense my spiraling panic, glancing at me as we sprinted down the dark corridor. "We're almost there," he said, but I could barely hear him over the chaotic pounding in my ears.

I nodded, my mind barely registering his words. All that mattered was Dorian. Nothing else.

Ahead, I spotted him.

My heart stopped. There was so much blood. It pooled around him, seeping into the ground. His leg… his leg. The belt he'd tied around it was barely holding, stained through with red.

My body moved before my mind could process it, and I was at Dorian's side in an instant, dropping to my knees beside him. The blood—his blood—was *everywhere.*

I knelt by Dorian's side. His breath—thank God—was there. Shallow, ragged, but still there. I checked his pulse and sighed in relief as I felt a small, steady rhythm. I closed my eyes briefly in relief, my heartbeat pounding in my ears.

Ramirez was already springing into action. He was on his phone, speaking in low tones to dispatch, updating them on Dorian's condition and requesting more backup. I barely registered their movements, my focus solely on Dorian.

"You're going to be okay. You hear me? Don't you dare give up on me, Dorian."

I reached for his face, hands trembling as I cupped his cheeks, my fingers slick with the blood that painted his skin.

"I love you too," I whispered, willing him to hear me. I brushed away his hair from his forehead.

His eyes fluttered open just enough to find mine. He didn't say anything, and then his eyes closed again.

"I love you too," I begged, my voice hoarse. "Stay with me, Dorian. *Please.*"

Before I could say more, I heard the shuffle of footsteps behind me.

An EMT crouched down by Dorian's leg. His hand hovered over Dorian's torn jeans, accessing the damage.

"Femoral artery is the main concern. He's losing a lot of blood." His voice was calm, focused.

I barely registered anything beyond the panic surging through me. "He's breathing," I said, my gaze locked on Dorian. "Pulse is weak, but steady. He... he opened his eyes, then closed them again."

Then Officer Ramirez was beside me, his face tight with concern. He leaned down, his hand brushing mine as he gave me a firm but gentle glance. "We need to move him, Noah."

I shook my head, unwilling to let go. My fingers tightened against Dorian's hand.

Officer Ramirez's voice softened. "I know, but he's losing too much blood. We need to get him stabilized."

A small team of EMTs arrived with a stretcher, their voices low but urgent. One of them knelt by Dorian's side, his gloved hands moving to assess his vitals. "Shallow pulse, breathing's labored. We need to transport him *now*," the EMT called out, already adjusting the oxygen mask that had been placed on Dorian's face.

Reluctantly, I released my hold on him, but only enough for them to slide the stretcher beneath him. My heart thudded painfully in my chest as they moved him, and I couldn't help but grab his hand.

His grip tightened for a moment, weak but unmistakable.

FORTY-SEVEN

Noah - November

WORK SONG - HOZIER

No matter where you went, hospitals always smelled the same. Like desperation, masked under layers of chemicals. As if it was trying to disguise the reality of what happened in these walls.

My fingers twitched against the edge of the waiting room chair, a restless movement I couldn't control. Across the room, someone's phone buzzed, the vibration cutting through the sterile silence, but I couldn't focus on anything beyond the thought of Dorian lying on an operating table.

I'd lost track of how long I'd been sitting in this waiting room. The clock on the wall was frozen in place, its second hand moving too slowly and too fast at the same time.

My mind wrestled with the chaos John left behind—the unanswered questions, the loose ends I still couldn't untangle. But that was a problem for another time. For now, I forced it aside.

Gracie was curled up in a chair a few feet away, her tiny frame swallowed up in one of Dotty's sweaters. She'd fallen asleep hours ago, her head resting on Trent's shoulder. Trent looked as exhausted as the rest of us, his face lined with worry, but he kept his arm securely around her.

Dotty sat nearby, her hands twisting together in her lap. She hadn't said much since we got here, but every now and then, she glanced at me, her lips pressing into a thin line like she wanted to say something but thought better of it. Sawyer was leaning against the wall, arms crossed, his jaw set tight as he stared at nothing.

Colt and David made the trip down the moment they heard. They stood further back, speaking in low tones, though I wasn't listening. The room was too loud from the sound of my own heartbeat.

Earlier, when the nurse came out to tell us Dorian was in surgery, everyone turned to me, their questions pressing down like a wave I wasn't ready to face. I'd barely managed to answer. Now, the silence felt unbearable.

I got up again, pacing the length of the room. The tile was cold under my feet, even through my shoes, and the lights overhead buzzed faintly. Every step seemed like my body was dragging, my muscles heavy with fear and exhaustion.

Gracie stirred, her head lifting slightly. Her eyes blinked open, big and glassy, and she glanced around before they landed on me. "Is Daddy gonna be okay?"

My throat tightened. I crouched in front of her. "The doctors are taking care of him right now, G. He's really strong, and they're doing everything they can to help him."

She nodded, but her bottom lip wobbled. "I'm scared."

I reached out, smoothing her hair back. "Me too," I admitted. "But we're here for him, okay? All of us." I motioned toward the others, who were doing their best to hold it together.

She sniffled and leaned back into Trent, who whispered something to her I couldn't make out.

Watching him, I remembered how Dotty had fallen apart when Trent was the one in that hospital bed, how I was just as broken that day and Dorian was the one to pull me through it.

But now it was he fighting for this life.

"The James family?"

The nurse's voice jolted me. I stood too quickly, nearly losing my balance. The entire room froze, everyone turning toward her.

"Dorian's out of surgery." Her words came in quick, clinical sentences. "The procedure went well. We were able to repair the damage. He's stable, but he's going to need time to recover. You can see him soon, but he'll still be under the effects of anesthesia."

I felt a rush of air leave my lungs, like I'd been holding it in this whole time. Around me, everyone seemed to exhale at once. Sawyer let out a relieved curse, and Dotty reached for Trent's arm.

"Would you like to see him?" she asked me.

"Oh no, I can't. Someone else should."

"Noah, go," David said. Everyone else nodded.

Gracie's small voice broke through the haze. "Can I see him too?" The nurse hesitated, glancing at me.

"I'll check on him, and as soon as he's awake, I'll let you know, okay?" I told her.

Her lip wobbled again, but she nodded. Trent gave me a small, encouraging nod, his hand resting on her shoulder.

The walk to Dorian's room seemed like the longest journey of my life. The nurse led me through the maze of hallways. The same speckled white tiles from before taunting me. My palms were damp, and I kept clenching and unclenching my fists, trying to shake off the tension that wouldn't leave me.

When she pushed open the door, I stopped in the doorway.

Dorian lay there, pale but breathing. Machines beeped softly, monitoring his vitals. His leg was propped up, wrapped in bandages, and an IV snaked from his arm. He looked so still, so unlike himself, that it made something in my heart twist painfully.

I stepped inside and sank into the chair next to his bed. For a long moment, I simply sat there, staring at him, trying to process the fact that he was here.

He was *alive*.

But the fear was still there. It sat there, a heavy knot in my stomach, refusing to let go.

"I'm so mad at you," I murmured, my voice barely steady. "You told me you loved me when I wasn't even there to say it back to your face. I'm so mad at you for doing this, but I'm so in love with you."

The room was silent except for the machines. I wanted to take his hand, to feel some kind of connection, but I was afraid of jostling him, of doing something wrong. So, I just sat there, waiting.

Waiting for him to wake up.

FORTY-EIGHT

Dorian - November

IRIS - GRACE DAVIES

MY BODY FELT HEAVY, MY LEG WAS THROBBING, AND THE PULL of sleep still tried to drag me under.

I blinked, trying to understand where I was. There was constant beeping as blurry shapes around me came slowly into focus.

Then I remembered. Everything.

John. The gun shot. The call. Noah.

Looking next to my bed, I saw Gracie curled up on a chair, tucked into Noah's lap. Her face was pressed against Noah's chest, her hair tangled, eyes puffy. Noah's head was tilted back against the chair, her mouth slightly open, her arms protectively wrapped around Gracie.

For a moment, I didn't move. I only watched them.

Gracie stirred as she stretched her arms. She opened her eyes, squinting at the harsh light, and then stopped. Her gaze locked on mine.

"Daddy?" Her voice cracked, and it hit me like a freight train. Her lip wobbled as realization set in, and tears filled her eyes. "Daddy!" she cried again, scrambling off Noah's lap.

Her sudden movement jolted Noah awake, her body tensing as her eyes shot open. She blinked, her gaze darting from Gracie to me. And then she froze.

Gracie was already climbing onto the edge of the bed, her little hands gripping mine like she was afraid I might disappear. She was sobbing now, hiccupping between gasps, her tears falling onto my hospital gown.

Noah's chair scraped back as she stood, her hands trembling as she pressed them to her mouth. Her eyes were wide, shining with relief.

"You're awake," she finally managed.

I nodded weakly, lifting my hand to touch Gracie's hair. "It's okay, Gracie. I'm alright," I murmured, my throat dry and scratchy.

Gracie buried her face against me, her sobs muffled, and I felt the tight band of fear finally loosen.

Noah moved closer, brushing a strand of my hair from my forehead reassuringly.

Gracie's cries began to quiet, her tiny hand clutching mine tightly. "Don't ever go away ever again, Daddy," she whispered.

"I won't," I promised. "I'm not going anywhere."

The door opened moments later, and a nurse walked in, followed by a doctor.

"Well, look who's awake," a voice said, warm and light, drawing my attention as the doctor stepped to my bedside. "How are you feeling, Dr. James?"

I groaned, the sound rough and dry. "Like my leg got run over by a truck."

I felt someone move, and I realized it was Noah reaching to hold Gracie's hand. The nurse adjusted the IV in my arm while the doctor checked my vitals.

"You're a lucky man," she said. "You lost a lot of blood. The bullet went clean through, but it nicked the artery, which made things worse. We managed to stop the bleeding, but it fractured your femur. We inserted a rod during surgery to stabilize it. You're going to need a lot of time to heal, and physical therapy will be crucial."

I tried moving, but pain shot through my leg, making me wince. "How long?"

"A few months, at least," the doctor replied. "Full mobility will depend on your commitment to physical therapy. For now, you can't put any weight on that leg for at least six weeks. After that, we'll reassess."

I let out a long breath and sank back into the pillow. "Great," I muttered. "So, no walking?"

"Not for a while," she said, her tone soft. "You'll be in a wheelchair at first, then progress to crutches. It'll take patience, but with the way things went, you're in good shape."

I let out a humorless laugh. "Patience, huh?"

"Yeah," she said. "It's going to be a bit of a process."

I glanced over at Gracie. She hadn't taken her eyes off me, still holding my hand like she was afraid to let go. I hated seeing that look on her face.

"Will Daddy be able to play with me again?" she asked, her voice small but full of hope.

The doctor smiled at her, kneeling slightly to meet her eyes. "Of course, sweetie. It's going to take some time, but he's a tough guy. He'll be back on his feet before you know it."

Gracie looked at me, her lip quivering. "You promise, Daddy?"

My hand squeezed hers. "I promise, kiddo."

She gave a little laugh, but it was shaky, like she was holding back tears.

"What happens next?" Noah asked.

"For now, we monitor him for any signs of infection or

complications," the doctor replied. "Once he's in the clear, we'll discharge him with a recovery plan and follow-up appointments. Physical therapy starts in a few weeks. But his main job right now is rest."

"Are you in pain?" she asked.

"Yeah," I admitted.

"We've got you on meds to keep it manageable, but I'll up your dose," the doctor said. "But we'll need to transition to lighter meds soon. We need to find the right balance so you can start moving when it's time."

I clenched my jaw, already hating the idea of being dependent on anyone. The nurse gave me a small, understanding smile. "You're healing. Let others take care of you for a while."

She glanced at Noah. "You've got a solid support system here. Lean on them."

"Any questions?" the doctor asked, her tone encouraging.

I shook my head, feeling the exhaustion catching up to me. "Not now."

"Alright," she said, nodding. "The nurse will be back shortly to check on you. Get some rest." She gave me one last smile before leaving with the nurse.

The door shut, and the room fell quiet. Gracie leaned closer to me, brushing her little hand across my arm. "You scared me, Daddy," she said.

My heart ached. I knew I'd scared her. Hell, I'd scared myself.

"I know, G. I'm sorry. But I'm here now."

Noah stayed close, hovering near the bed. Her eyes were on me, but she didn't say anything at first. I met her gaze and saw the tension in her face, the concern that never really seemed to leave her.

"You okay?" I asked, my voice still a little rough.

She blinked, clearly startled. "You're the one in the hospital bed."

"Still," I said, giving her the faintest smirk. "What… happened?"

Gracie looked from me to Noah, her eyes wide, curiosity lighting up her face.

Noah let out a weak laugh, shaking her head. "We'll talk about that later. Right now, you need to focus on getting better."

"You mean letting you two boss me around?" I said, feeling a small, painful grin tug at my lips even as I winced.

"Exactly," she said, her tone light but with an edge of affection. "Get used to it."

Gracie giggled, the sound of it making the heaviness of everything feel a little less suffocating.

For the first time since the chaos in the tunnel, I felt like I could breathe again.

The door creaked open, and I lifted my head, my neck stiff. My dad stepped inside, so quietly as if he was trying not to disturb the fragile peace of the room. He glanced at Gracie first, then at me, and his breath caught, something heavy in his exhale.

"It's damn good to see you, son," he muttered, and the words hit me in a way I wasn't ready for. I wanted to say something, but my throat felt tight, and nothing seemed enough.

"Let me take her back to the hotel. You need to rest, Dorian," he said, slowly walking toward Gracie, who was now curled up in Noah's lap. He picked her up, cradling her small body like a precious piece of glass.

His eyes met mine, and I could see the concern etched on his face, the worry that had been there for hours, days maybe.

I nodded slowly. "Thanks. I love you, Dad."

His expression softened, and he stepped closer, gently rocking Gracie in his arms. "I love you too, bud. Keep that one, will ya?" he replied, nodding toward Noah before walking out of the room.

I grinned. "I think I will."

Noah stirred, a small sound escaping her lips as she rubbed her eyes, still caught in the haze of sleep. She blinked a few times, then turned toward me, her movements slow and disoriented. The moment our eyes met, she let out a a sharp inhale, as if she momentarily forgot I was still here and was just now starting to process it all over again.

I let out a shaky breath. "Hey," I murmured.

Her lips parted, and for a second, she stared at me, as if checking to make sure I was real. She shook her head slowly, blinking hard, like she was trying to keep it together, still on the edge of disbelief.

"I thought you were gone," she whispered. "I thought we lost you." She stepped to the edge of the bed.

"You didn't. I'm here." I tried to reach for her, my hand trembling as I moved it closer, but she was already squeezing my fingers, like she was trying to ground herself in the moment.

"But we almost did." Her eyes glistened with unshed tears, but she swallowed and continued.

"I know, peach. I'm so sorry. I didn't mean any of that. Anything I said to him was all a ploy to get you and Gracie out of danger," I said.

"I know. I trust you."

She leaned down, moving a section of hair away from my brow. My eyes fluttered shut at her touch.

"For so long, it felt like John had taken everything from me—my safety, my choices, my peace. He stole the way I looked at the world, made me second-guess every good thing, every good person. And then, when I finally found someone who gave all of that back to me, he tried to take you too."

I let her words hang in the air for a moment, my heart tightening at the raw pain in her voice.

She exhaled, her gaze locking onto mine. "You told me you'd find me in every universe, even if it meant standing back and watching. But I wouldn't. I'd spend every lifetime searching for you, in every world, in every moment, but I would never stand by and watch. We were never meant to stand at the edges of each other's lives, Dorian. We were always meant to find each other."

Her voice quivered as she spoke, and her gaze, so intense and unwavering, burned into mine. She looked at me like I was the only thing in the world that mattered.

"And I refuse to accept a single universe where I don't get to spend every possible moment with you and Gracie. So you don't have to find me, Dorian. You already have."

She sat on the edge of the bed, placing her hand on my chest.

"I've spent so much time running from everything, from what I feel, from what we are," I began, my voice rough. "I told myself I could do it alone, that I could protect everyone, protect myself, by keeping my distance. But I was wrong. You've always been a part of me, even when I didn't know how to accept it." I took a deep breath, steadying myself as I looked into her eyes. "But I know now. You were never a choice. I was scared, afraid of what would happen if I let myself believe this—believe in us. But I can't keep pretending I don't need you."

I squeezed her hand that sat over my chest, trying to convey every ounce of emotion I was feeling, all the years of pain, fear, and longing.

"I need you in every way, in every part of my soul. I love you, Noah. I love you in a way I never thought I could. You're not just a part of my life—you're the one I was meant to find, the one I was meant to hold onto. There's no world, no universe, where I *don't* choose you."

Her eyes softened, and the words slipped out, almost like a release. "I love you."

I didn't think I could feel more vulnerable than I already did, but hearing those words from her—finally—was like a balm to all the raw places inside me. I held her gaze, my heart racing, and without thinking, I whispered back, "I think I've always loved you."

The moment hung between us, like we had both just stepped into a new reality where nothing could tear us apart. She leaned down then, brushing her lips softly against mine—a fleeting, gentle kiss that left a lingering warmth on my skin.

She pulled away. "There's still something we need to talk about," she said, her voice quieter now, guarded.

I sat up slightly, my brow furrowing. "Yeah… I know. Can you tell me what happened?"

Her eyes flickered to the side, as if she was carefully choosing her next words, weighing how much to reveal.

"Please," I added, my voice low but insistent. "I need to know."

She hesitated, her fingers grazing the edge of my hand. "John's in custody," she finally said, her words like stones sinking into still water. "He wanted to get caught."

The ground felt like it moved beneath me. "Why? Why would he do that?"

Noah stood, her posture tense, like she was trying to make sense of it all herself. She turned toward the window, her back to me. "I don't know," she whispered. "I just—I don't know. He's playing some kind of game, Dorian. I need to figure out why."

She was searching for answers, the same way I was. But there was something else. She needed closure, needed to understand the part she played in all of it.

"You want to go visit him?" I asked before I could stop myself.

She didn't answer right away, but I saw the way her body stiffened, the way her fingers curled into fists. "Yeah, I do."

I didn't like it. Not one bit. The idea of her facing him again—of her stepping into his world even for a second—made something cold and ugly twist in my gut. But I understood. She needed to know why, needed to face it head-on, even if I wanted to lock her away from him, away from all of it.

"When we were in the tunnels, before… before I got shot." I paused, trying to steady my breath, still shaky from the memory. "He said you were the reason he did all of this. That you could have stopped him."

Noah was silent for a long moment. I could see her eyes closing, as if the words were a blow she'd been expecting but hadn't fully prepared for. When she spoke, it was almost like she was talking to herself. "Yeah, I know…" Her voice faltered for a second. "Ellie told me."

I wanted to reach for her again, to pull her close, to shield her from all of it. But instead, I sat still, waiting for her to continue.

"Noah…" I started, my voice filled with the warning I wasn't sure how to say.

"I need to do this," she interrupted, shaking her head, determination set in her eyes. "I need answers."

I inhaled deeply, my jaw tightening, my heart heavy with the weight of it all. "Okay," I said finally, my voice thick with the words I didn't want to speak. "It's your choice. I'll support you. But you don't have to do this alone."

She squeezed my hand, her touch grounding me in a way I wasn't expecting. "I'm not doing this alone," she whispered, her words a promise. "Not anymore."

FORTY-NINE

Noah - December

THE SMALLEST MAN WHO EVER LIVED - TAYLOR
SWIFT

THE TOWERING CONCRETE PRISON LOOMED AHEAD, COLD AND
uninviting under the pale winter sky. It had been a couple
of weeks since everything came crashing down—weeks
filled with sleepless nights, healing wounds, and trying to
piece our lives back together.

I glanced at Dorian in the passenger seat as I pulled into
the lot and killed the engine. His leg was stretched out in
front of him, crutches resting awkwardly against the door.
The bulky brace encasing his thigh was a stark reminder of
just how close we'd come to losing everything.

"Are you sure you're up for this?" he asked.

"I have to do this," I said, gripping the steering wheel
tighter.

Dorian frowned, his hand reaching out to brush against
mine. "You don't have to do it alone."

I turned toward him, offering a small smile. "I know.
But right now, I need you to stay here."

"What? No, Noah, I can—"

"Dorian," I interrupted gently, my tone firm but affectionate. "Your leg. I'm not letting you hurt yourself walking in there when you don't have to. Stay here. I've got this."

He exhaled sharply, clearly not thrilled about the idea, but he didn't argue. "Fine. But if you're not out in thirty minutes, I'm coming in, crutches and all."

"Fine, you stubborn ass," I said, leaning over to press a kiss to his temple before sliding out of the car.

The cold air nipped at my face as I approached the looming prison entrance. My legs felt heavier with each step, the reality of what I was about to do pressing down on me.

Inside, the sterile halls echoed with the sharp clink of keys and distant murmurs. The lights buzzed faintly over-head, amplifying the tension that had been building since the moment we left Woodstone.

At the far end of the hallway stood my father, his back turned as if he were lost in thought.

"Dad?" I called out, my voice wavering between surprise and disbelief.

He turned slowly, his face lighting up in recognition. "Noah."

Before I could say another word, he closed the distance between us, pulling me into a tight embrace. I sank into the familiar comfort of his arms, but unease lingered at the edge of my thoughts.

"What are you doing here?" I asked, pulling back to meet his gaze. We have only exchanged a few calls and texts over the last couple of weeks.

Something I couldn't read crossed his face. "You said you were coming today. I wanted to be here when you did and see John too. Get some closure."

I nodded. For a moment, silence hung between us.

"Just be careful," he said, his tone dropping to a whisper. "I know you're strong, but John… he's not the person you knew anymore. I'll be here when you get out."

"Okay," I replied, the words barely audible over the sound of my own heartbeat as I prepared to confront the past and find my way toward a new future.

After going through a security checkpoint, I stepped into the visitation room, and a chill ran down my spine. The starkness of the surroundings, cold metal, harsh lighting, and the oppressive silence heightened my anxiety.

John sat behind the glass, his posture relaxed yet predatory, a sickly smile creeping across his face as he watched me approach. I felt my stomach twist at the sight of him— he looked almost too comfortable here, as if he belonged.

As if he didn't kill those women or put Gracie in danger. As if he didn't shoot multiple security guards, Ellie, and Dorian. The second our eyes locked, his lips curled into a smug grin, and my stomach churned.

"Hello, Noah," he said, dripping with false charm. I picked up the phone, forcing myself to speak.

"Cut the shit, John. I'm not here for pleasantries."

He chuckled, a low, mocking sound. "Feisty. What's the matter? You look a little shaken."

"Enough," I snapped. "You've hurt too many people. I'm here to understand why."

He leaned forward, his eyes narrowing with a predatory glint. "You want to know why? I thought you were smart. At least everything is going according to plan."

"What are you talking about?" I asked, confusion swirling in my mind. He chuckled, a sound that made my skin crawl.

"Well, guess there's no time like the present, so I'll get right to it." He chuckled. "You know how your dad had that—what was it—that shitty ex-wife? He was always complaining about her, wishing she'd get what she deserved in the divorce because she ended up taking him for half of what he was worth." He paused, letting the words hang in the air, and I could feel a sickening sense of dread creeping in.

"What does that have to do with any of this?" I pressed. He leaned in closer, a gleam of something dark in his eyes.

"It's a long story, Noah. I've been waiting to tell you, so shut up and listen." He paused, waiting for my response, but I said nothing. "I thought I'd do him a favor. I was young, still in college, and we"—he gestured to me—"weren't talking at the time. He wouldn't stop complaining about her, so I went over to her house to scare her a little. Just give her a piece of my mind, convince her to give back all the shit she got in the divorce... But things... escalated quickly."

My heart raced as I braced myself for what was coming. "What did you do?"

John's face twisted into a grimace of nostalgia. "She wouldn't listen to logic. She wouldn't understand how wrong she was. So, she may have accidentally fallen down the stairs." He smiled as if recalling a fond memory, and I felt bile rise in my throat.

"John..." I whispered. His name felt foreign, disgusting even, on my tongue.

For a moment, I caught a glimpse of something raw beneath his facade. "In my shock, I realized... hmm. I liked it," he admitted, a strange satisfaction creeping into his tone. "Seeing her dead made me happy. It reminded me of my mother. They were both so similar—both nurses, both in roles meant to care for others, yet unable to care for their own families."

I shook my head, disbelief washing over me.

"Well, wouldn't you know it. That was exactly ten years ago... just a few weeks ago, I'd gone to your dad, not knowing what to do. Rick told me what to do. I told him I didn't mean to kill her... even if I liked it, but he didn't need to know that. He didn't go to the police because, in the end, her being dead benefited him. He didn't want to be under a microscope being the bitter ex-husband, either. But then I kept thinking about it—about how I wanted to see someone else like them dead."

His gaze sharpened, and I knew he was savoring this moment. He held onto this, waiting for someone to listen. And as much as I didn't want to give him that, I needed to know. I needed to know how this all tied to me.

"He didn't see me as a threat, and I let him think that, but I needed to kill more. I needed to see them dead."

I felt the blood drain from my face as his words sank in. "That is insane."

"Yeah, maybe." He paused then continued his story. "So, then I became this—what do they call me?" He turned to the guard behind them, as if he would answer. "Oh yeah, the Marketplace Murderer." He let out a sinister chuckle. "It's easy to find them there, you know. They're always trying to sell their expensive shit online to make a dime. It was easy to lure them in." He looked up at the ceiling, pressing his hands together in a praying motion that made me sick.

"Thank the lord for social media. I found someone, watched them closely, and if they weren't taking care of their own family, I knew they were the one. They'd be so focused on pretending to care for others, but couldn't even give a damn about the people closest to them. I'd get them to meet with me, thinking they were getting off on selling some overpriced piece of shit, and then... well, you know the rest. I did that. Whenever you wouldn't go with me at least. Whenever you were there, I didn't need to. You kept me sane. For years, learning how to cover my tracks, making sure I was always strategic about where and how I did it.

"Then last year, my mother comes to me after years of pretending I didn't exist, and suddenly decides she needs my help. She's lost her job, her status, and all she can think to do is come crawling back, asking me to find her another rich husband," he said, a scoff escaping his mouth. His tone shifted, mocking her. *"I need you, John. I need your help finding someone for me,* she told me. After years of silence, she just expected me to fix everything for her. That's where it all went wrong." I stared at him, my heart racing as the pieces fell into place.

"What did you do?"

"I had to kill her, obviously," he said, his tone unnervingly casual, as if confessing to nothing more than an overdue chore. "It wasn't supposed to happen that way, though. I wasn't on my game. She surprised me, so it got messy. Sloppy, really. I forgot how damn organized she always was with her calendar, and my name was right there. Can you believe that? She had it right there in her schedule, bold as day. And me? I wasn't ready. No time to prepare. But you"—his gaze sharpened, the edge of frustration creeping in—"you had to ruin everything.

"I planned it all to happen in Woodstone, down to the last second. The countdown, the ten-year mark of my first kill—midnight. Not to kill you, but to make you suffer. It would've been poetic. But no, you had to run off to that stupid pop concert. Do you know how inconvenient that was? Do you have any idea what it's like to improvise in a stadium? Sneaking in a weapon isn't even the hard part— fake a maintenance uniform a week in advance, flash a badge, and you're golden. But still, it wasn't what I wanted. You threw a wrench into my plans, Noah. And now here we are."

I wanted to scream, to run away from this monster, but I was frozen in place, trapped by the horror of his revelations.

"You're telling me you killed your mother because she wanted money?"

"I killed her because she was awful. She shipped me off to some boarding school when I was just a kid, so she didn't have to deal with me. Whenever I came home, she was always too busy with work or her current husband to even notice I was there. Every summer, I'd come back to find a new dad. She never learned her fucking lesson, so I had to teach her."

The room went silent.

"So, I went to your dad again," he continued, his voice taking on a gleeful tone. "For the first time, I told him the situation—who I was, what I had done, assuming he would have my back, but he didn't. Instead of being grateful, he was upset and berated me."

I shook my head, disbelief mingling with anger. "I don't understand. My dad?"

"Yeah, your precious daddy," he sneered, his lips curling into a twisted grin. "So, I had to change my plan. I had to sacrifice myself," he replied, a chilling casualness in his tone. "I left you clues along the way, killing while I still could. It was all part of the game. I knew I had been caught and cornered, but I wanted to stall, to make your life as painful as possible. All leading to me here, confessing everything to make sure your dad pays, and you do too. The more madness I created, the more I drew your attention, the attention of the FBI. I wanted to extend this out as long as I could—make you suffer while I waited for your dad to come to his senses. He might think he's clever, but deep down, he was as complicit as I was. If I ended up in handcuffs, he would too. That was the beauty of it."

Tears blurred my vision as the weight of his words crashed down on me. "You're insane," I whispered, feeling hollow inside.

"This is your fault. It's your dad's fault. If I had never met you, none of this would have happened. If your dad hadn't covered up for me, I wouldn't have lived this life. If you had only gone with me, all of this could've been prevented. What better way to hurt you both than to take him down? The only person holding your little family together. You can't escape this."

"I can and I will. You turned my love into fear and my reality into a nightmare. But you don't get to dictate my future ever again."

I took a step closer to the glass, a rush of adrenaline flooding through me.

"You think you can drag my father into this mess, that you can place the blame for your actions on him? Whether he's at fault or not. I refuse to let your twisted fucking games dictate my life anymore. This isn't about you and your sick obsession and mommy issues. It's about my life, my choices, and the people I love. I won't allow you to destroy that anymore."

With every word, I felt the weight lift off my shoulders, a sense of clarity emerging from the chaos.

"I've fought too hard to reclaim my life and find happiness, and I won't let you tear it down. I control my story, my life. Not *you*."

I walked away from the visitation room, each step lighter than the last. I finally faced John, confronting the monster he had become—maybe the monster he always was, hidden behind the facade he put on.

Taking a moment to catch my breath, I leaned against the cool wall of the corridor, closing my eyes.

I stepped out into the lobby, the door closing behind me

with a heavy thud, and everything that just transpired settled in.

John was behind me now—locked away, both literally and in my mind. But as much as I wanted to believe this was the end, I couldn't shake the lingering unease that clung to me like a shadow.

Closure.

That's what I'd come here for.

I finally stood up to him, faced the monster who nearly destroyed me. I spoke the words I'd needed to say for so long, told him that he no longer controlled my life.

And yet, as I walked down the hall, my mind kept circling back to what he'd revealed. The dark secrets about my father, the things I never saw coming.

My dad.

The thought twisted in my chest, tighter than I expected. I spent my life looking up to him, trusting him.

While my relationship wasn't the best with my parents, it was always my mom I struggled to connect with, not him.

He was the one who was supposed to protect me, to shield me from the worst of the world. But apparently, he hadn't.

Instead, he'd been part of it, complicit from the very start of John's crimes. Not just a bystander, but someone who'd covered up a murder.

Someone who allowed this to happen, hoping it would all go away, hoping he could contain it. I wanted to be angry with him. I wanted to scream, to cry, to let out all the hurt and betrayal that was lodged deep in my heart.

But as much as I wanted to be angry with him, there was something else. Something more complicated. I couldn't deny the hurt, the betrayal.

Did my mom know? Or was this secret kept from her too?

He'd made terrible decisions, choices that changed the course of so many lives, including mine. But I refused to believe he was a monster.

Not like John.

Not the man that taught me to ride a bike, secretly supported my career when my mother hadn't, and helped heal my first broken heart when I was only thirteen, thinking it was the end of the world.

And that was the hardest part to understand.

I wanted to scream at him for what he'd done, for letting this spiral out of control.

But another part of me, the part that always saw him as my protector, couldn't quite let go of the fact that he hadn't done it out of malice.

He was afraid. Afraid of losing everything he had built, afraid of the scrutiny that would come with being tied to a murder.

I only hoped that in his mind, he thought he was containing the damage, holding it at bay, but even with that, it didn't make it right.

As I continued down the corridor, I tried to remind myself that this—this moment—was the closure I needed, even if it brought on more questions.

FIFTY

Noah - December

HURT - JOHNNY CASH

I FOUND HIM IN THE WAITING AREA JUST OUTSIDE THE visitation room, slumped in one of the hard plastic chairs. His face was drawn and pale, as if he'd been waiting for me, maybe even bracing himself for this moment.

He looked older than I remembered, more worn down, like the weight of the world had finally caught up with him. His hands were trembling slightly, his fingers flexing nervously as he stood when I approached. The look in his eyes was full of guilt and something deeper, something broken.

"Dad," I said, quieter than I'd intended.

He winced, like the sound of my voice physically hurt him. The space between us felt vast, each of us waiting for the other to break it open. But I didn't know how to start. How to ask the questions I needed answers to.

He ran a hand through his thinning hair, his gaze never quite meeting mine, as if he were searching for the right words in the cracks of the floor. "Noah, I'm so sorry," he said. "I should've told you. I should've told you everything." He knew John would tell me everything. And he let him.

I stared at him, waiting for him to continue, to make sense of the mess that John left behind. But there was nothing. No easy explanations, no comforting lies. Only the harsh reality of the truth John had finally dragged into the light.

"How could you have kept all of this from me?" The words came out before I could stop them, harsh and raw. Tears stung my eyes, but I didn't let them fall.

His shoulders sagged, a deep sigh escaping him. "When John came to me years ago… I didn't know what to do. He was a kid, Noah. A kid I thought had made a horrible mistake. I thought I could help him. Guide him. I thought I could make him better." For a moment, I saw the man I had once trusted so completely. "I never imagined… I never thought he would become what he did."

I swallowed the bitterness rising in my throat. "So, you covered it up. You let him get away with murder because you thought you could fix him?" The question came out as a whisper, but the sting of it hit me like a slap.

"No," he said quickly, shaking his head. "I didn't think it was right. I knew it wasn't, but at the time… John said it was a mistake, and I thought I was protecting you, protecting our family. I didn't cover anything up. I just… didn't report him. I thought if I kept him close, got him on the right path with my company, maybe he would be fine." He paused, his gaze moving down to the floor. "I was wrong. I see that now. I failed you."

I couldn't process it fast enough. My mind reeled, thoughts swirling like smoke. "And you let him… close to me? You let him be part of our lives after all of that? How could you?"

He flinched, the guilt in his eyes seeming to nearly

suffocate him. "I didn't know what he would become. He swore it was an accident. I believed him, Noah. I thought he was… I'm sorry. I thought he wanted help. But when he came to me about his mother's death… when I found out about the others…" His words broke off, and I could see the pain of that realization etched across his face.

I shook my head in disbelief, anger starting to claw its way up my throat. "And you still didn't go to the police?"

"No," he said, his voice raw. "When I knew—when I really understood what he had done—I went to the police. I've been working with the FBI, Noah. For months. Trying to help them track him down, find him before he killed anyone else. But I couldn't tell you. I couldn't tell anyone. Not until now. It was part of the investigation."

I stopped breathing for a moment, his confession hitting me like a ton of bricks. "You went to the police? After everything? After all this time?"

"Yes." He nodded, tears starting to well in his eyes. "The moment I knew, I couldn't… I couldn't let him keep going. I had to stop him. I didn't care what happened to me. I knew what I had done was wrong, letting him go free all these years. But I didn't know how else to fix it. I was willing to face whatever came, just to get him behind bars."

"But you're still here. Why aren't you in jail too?"

"Statute of limitations…" He swallowed. "It's three years for misprision of felony—failure to report a crime. I didn't hide evidence, I didn't lie, didn't cover up a body. It's been too long, Noah. They can't prosecute me for what happened. When I realized what John had become, I tried to turn myself in. I was ready to face whatever came to stop him. But now, there's nothing to be done. So, I offered to help the FBI track him down in any way I could."

I stared at him, a strange numbness creeping through

me. "So, you're not going to jail? You're not going to pay for what you did?"

He shook his head. "No, but that doesn't mean I'm free. I'll never be free of this. Of the guilt. I'll have to live with it for the rest of my life, knowing I put you in danger. Knowing I let him become who he is."

Tears threatened to fall again. "Dad, you didn't just let me down. You let everyone down. All those women. You let him become a monster." The words felt like poison as they left my mouth.

"I know," he whispered. "And I'll never forgive myself for that. I've been trying to make it right. Offering resources, helping however I can. But… I can't undo what's been done."

I stood there, frozen, trying to find the words that would make sense of everything. I swallowed the lump in my throat.

My dad made terrible choices—choices that affected my life in ways I didn't fully grasp until now. But in his own flawed way, he'd tried to make amends.

"I need some time… to process this," I whispered.

He nodded, tears welling in his own eyes. "I don't expect you to forgive me, Noah. I just… I want you to know that I'm sorry. I'm sorry that I ever put you in danger."

His words didn't feel like enough. I didn't know what to do with them. What to do with this shattered version of the man who was my father. But I knew I wasn't ready to forgive him yet.

But at least now I knew the truth. And for now, that was enough.

FIFTY-ONE

Dorian - December

CARRY YOU HOME - ALEX WARREN

The December wind rattled the windows, but the warmth inside the ranch house made it feel miles away. The smell of freshly baked bread filled the kitchen, blending with the sound of laughter and the occasional clang of a baking sheet. Gracie sat at the counter, her tongue poking out in concentration as she carefully piped pink icing onto a cookie.

"Don't forget the sprinkles," Noah said, sliding the container to her. She leaned against the counter, her apron tied neatly around her waist.

Gracie grinned and dumped a pile of rainbow sprinkles onto the cookie, sending a few flying onto the counter. "Daddy, look!"

I chuckled, as I wobbled by on my crutches. "It's perfect, G."

She beamed, holding up the cookie as though presenting a masterpiece. I leaned down, pressing a kiss to the top of her head. Across the counter, Noah's gaze lingered on us briefly, her lips curving into that soft smile.

No words were needed. Everything we had built, everything we had fought for, was written there in the way she looked at me.

She walked over to me, wiping her hands on a dish towel before tucking herself into my side. I slid my arm around her waist, pulling her closer and kissing her temple. She let out a soft sigh, her body relaxing into mine, her presence settling something deep inside me.

The front door creaked open, letting in a sharp burst of cold air. Colt walked in first, his broad frame silhouetted against the porch light. Behind him, Lilah stepped in hesitantly, her son Caleb clutching her hand.

I raised an eyebrow at Colt, and he leaned in as he shrugged out of his jacket.

"She's been going through a hard time," he murmured low enough that only I could hear. "Figured they could use the company. Dad already knows."

I nodded, glancing at Lilah's uncertain expression. Noah, of course, didn't miss a beat.

"Come on in!" she called out, her voice warm and welcoming. "Gracie's been decorating cookies—we've got plenty to share."

Caleb's eyes lit up at the mention of cookies, though he stayed close to Lilah's side. "Cookies? I love cookies. Cookies are yummy!" he said.

Gracie waved him over enthusiastically. "You can help me if you want!"

Lilah smiled gently, nudging Caleb forward. "Go ahead, buddy."

As Caleb joined Gracie at the counter, I caught Colt's gaze drifting toward Lilah. His usually guarded expression softened for a fraction of a second before he turned his attention back to the room.

Lilah stood near the doorway, her posture tense but her face relaxed as she watched Caleb pile frosting onto a cookie with all the grace of a bulldozer. "Thanks for having us," she said quietly.

"Always," I said, giving her a quick nod before turning my attention back to Noah.

I grabbed my phone from the counter and noticed a text from Dotty from earlier. I swiped it open and froze.

"What the hell?"

Noah glanced up. "What's wrong?"

I tilted the screen toward her, the bold headline glaring back at us.

NFL Star Sawyer James and Singer Ellie Miles: Officially Dating!

Noah blinked at the headline and then laughed. "Wait, what?"

"I have no idea," I said, gesturing toward the phone like it might explain itself.

"That man lives for drama," she said, shaking her head.

The front door opened again, and Dotty and Trent walked in, Dotty carrying a platter of brownies and Trent balancing two bottles of wine. Dotty arched a brow as she noticed Noah and me huddled over the phone. "Did you see my text?"

I held up the phone and nodded. "Just saw it."

"What text?" Dad asked as he walked into the room.

I tilted the phone so he could see the headline. His eyes went wide. "What the hell is going on?" he muttered.

Dotty threw her hands up in exasperation. "That's my question too."

Trent smirked. "That's one way to make an announcement."

Gracie bounced over, her hands covered in sprinkles. "What happened?"

"Uncle Sawyer has a new girlfriend, apparently," Noah explained.

Gracie's eyes went wide. "Is she nice? Does she like cookies?"

Noah smiled at her. "Well…"

Before she could go on, the front door opened again. This time, Sawyer strode in with Ellie by his side, his signature grin firmly in place. Ellie appeared both nervous and amused, her cheeks slightly flushed as she clung to Sawyer's arm.

Gracie gasped and ran toward them, her hands still sticky with sprinkles and frosting.

"Uncle Sawyer! You're dating Ellie Miles?"

"Surprise!" Sawyer announced, spreading his arms wide like a magician unveiling a trick.

Dotty gaped at him, a mix of disbelief and irritation flashing across her face. "Are you kidding me?"

Sawyer shrugged, completely unfazed. "What can I say? Go big or go home."

"I think you did both, buddy," Colt said.

THE END

Epilogue

I STOOD ON THE PORCH, WATCHING AS NOAH AND GRACIE giggled together in the yard. Their laughter filled my heart, a sound that felt like home.

That *was* home.

After everything we'd been through, this moment, this peaceful slice of life, was exactly what I needed. Noah looked radiant, her hair catching the light, her eyes sparkling with joy. It was surreal, seeing her like this, happy and free from everything she used to carry.

It seemed like just yesterday we were navigating the darkest corners of our lives, each day a struggle against shadows that felt impossible to escape. But today, the light seemed to pierce through those shadows, and for that, I was grateful.

Every second with my girls was something I cherished more than I could ever put into words.

"Daddy!" Gracie's tiny voice broke through my thoughts, her hands waving as she spun around. "Come play with us!"

I stepped onto the lawn, a smile tugging at my lips. "What are we playing today?"

"Tag!" Noah called out, her laughter infectious. "And you're it!"

Before I could process what she said, Noah took off running, her playful spirit igniting the evening air. Gracie followed close behind, her little legs pumping as she giggled, and without a second thought, I chased after them.

My heart soared as I took off, much slower than I used to be, but this moment still was pure bliss. For the first time in so long, life felt... easy. I tagged Gracie and scooped her up into my arms, her squeals of delight echoing through the yard. Her small body against mine sent a rush of gratitude through me. Gratitude for everything that led us here, even the hard moments, especially the hard moments.

"Okay, okay! I give up!" Gracie cried, collapsing into giggles as I pretended to struggle to hold her.

"No one gives up in tag!" I said, spinning her around playfully before setting her back on her feet.

Noah slowed to a stop, leaning over to catch her breath. Her face was lit up with sheer happiness, and I couldn't help but be in awe of her.

"You're a great dad, you know," she said softly, filled with sincerity. I felt a rush of warmth at her words.

"I'm just trying to keep up with you two," I replied, my eyes lingering on her.

She smiled, and in that moment, I saw the light of hope shining in her eyes, hope that hadn't always been there. She fought her demons fiercely, battled through pain and trauma, and I'd watched her transform over the last several months.

Therapy became a cornerstone for her, and even Gracie and me, a place where we unpacked all the hurt, the betrayals, and the baggage from our past. Watching her heal, day by day, was one of the bravest things I'd ever seen, and it wasn't just about John. She'd started to rebuild her relationship with her parents too. That process had been long and difficult, but I admired her strength and resilience.

I spent the last few months in physical therapy, regaining my strength slowly but surely. It wasn't easy, but I'd have no problem living with metal in my leg to be able to spend the rest of my life with my girls.

We had come a long way from the day I'd stood on her doorstep, secretly smitten with my sister's best friend.

And now, we were a family.

"Gracie, want to show your dad what you've been practicing?" Noah asked, a playful smile lighting up her face.

"Uh, duh!" Gracie's eyes sparkled with excitement. "Look, Daddy! I can do a flip now!"

"Let's see it!" I encouraged, grinning as I thought of the afternoons I'd peeked out the window to see Noah and Gracie practicing together in the yard, Noah patiently teaching her the right moves.

Gracie rushed to the grass, her little body twisting and turning as she attempted a flip. Her determination made me laugh but also filled me with an overwhelming sense of pride. Watching her grow and seeing how Noah stepped in to guide her—it was everything I'd convinced myself I could live without. A family filled with laughter, joy, and the simple pleasures that made life worth living. And it was mine.

After Gracie showcased her skills, we all collapsed onto the grass, breathless and happy. The sun dipped lower, painting the sky with hues of orange and pink. I wanted to hold on to this moment and remember it for years to come —when we were old and gray and Gracie was grown, and these simple moments were some of our happiest memories.

My heart had woven seamlessly into hers. As if every thread was carefully picked and placed. As heartbreaking as the journey was, it all beautifully came together in something that was uniquely us.

"Why are you looking at me like that?" she asked, her lips curling into a playful grin.

"Like what?" I asked, feigning innocence.

"Like you love me," she teased.

"Well… I kind of do."

"Kind of, huh?"

I reached over and pulled her close, wrapping my arms around her. "Maybe more than kind of," I said, pressing a kiss to her forehead. "I might be a little obsessed with you."

"He really, *really* likes you, Noah," Gracie said. "And so do I."

Her eyes shone with love, and a lump formed in my throat. I was so damn lucky to have her, to have both of them—my girls in a town that truly felt like home.

As the sun dipped below the horizon, I realized that despite everything we'd been through, there was a new beginning waiting for us. A chance to create memories, to heal from the past, and, most importantly, a chance to love each other without fear holding us back.

I glanced over at Noah, taking in her bare feet and the butterfly tattoo that still sat inked on her skin.

"You know, you could always get it removed," I suggested. "If it bothers you."

A long sigh escaped her lips. "For years, it meant something to me, only me. It was about me learning to gain my independence and freedom from my parents. Now, after everything that's happened, its meaning has only grown. It's a reminder of all I've endured and everything I've become."

A smile tugged at my lips as I took in the girl who

changed my life in ways I could never have imagined. That tattoo no longer represented his twisted vision of salvation. She emerged from the shadows he cast, and this mark on her skin reflected her triumph over the past. I was so damn proud of her.

I could only think about how I wanted her to be mine forever.

"Daddy, wait!" Gracie said, jumping up, a little ball of energy. "Can I show Noah the paper now? You said we had to wait for the perfect time, and this feels super perfect!"

Noah's brow furrowed, and I just nodded at G. She rushed inside and returned moments later with a piece of paper clutched in her hand, her eyes shining with excitement.

She turned to Noah with a big grin. "It's a note! A super special note I made. Well, Daddy said the words, but I wrote them all by myself. He didn't even have to help! But he's been making me wait *forever* to read it to you."

"Okay…" Noah said, eyeing us both.

Gracie handed her the paper, then took a seat beside her, her hands clasped together as she waited.

Noah unfolded the note, her brows knitting together.

"It says… Noah, will you marry my dad?"

The air seemed to still as she turned her gaze to me, her lips parted in shock.

I reached into my pocket, pulling out the small velvet box I'd been carrying for weeks. Opening it, I revealed a delicate band with a sparkling diamond that caught the light.

"Noah," I said, my voice steady despite the pounding of my heart, "you've brought laughter and light into places I thought would stay dark forever. You've given Gracie a friend, a mentor, and a mom. And me… you've given me hope again. Will you marry me?"

Noah's hand flew to her mouth. "Yes… yes, I'll marry you," she said, cutting me off with a knowing smile.

"You really want to marry me?" The words slipped out, as if I was surprised she'd actually say yes.

"No, I want to marry your brother," she teased, laughing as she shoved me playfully.

"Colt?"

"I think Sawyer's more my type, actually," she joked, her eyes twinkling.

"Is he single, though?" I asked, playing along.

"I don't think either of them are."

Gracie squealed with delight, throwing her arms around Noah. "Does this mean you'll be my mommy now?"

Noah hugged her tightly.

"Yeah, G. I think that's what it means," I said.

Gracie pulled back, her little face beaming with pride. "Can we have ice cream? This seems like a good time for ice cream," she said.

I laughed, feeling my heart swell. "Want to go to Scoops and celebrate?" I asked, glancing at the two of them.

"I'll never say no to ice cream," Noah replied with a grin.

We piled into the car and headed for the ice cream parlor. Listening to Noah and Gracie chat away, it seemed like they had always known each other. Like Noah was the missing piece to our puzzle all along.

The shadows of the past were receding, replaced by the warmth of hope, love, and the promise of a future I never thought I'd be lucky enough to have.

<h1 style="text-align:center">Acknowledgements</h1>

This book has been a journey, to say the least. There were so many moments in this process when it felt like I'd never reach the finish line—late nights, early mornings, and countless times when I thought I was in over my head. I considered giving up a thousand times, but I knew Dorian and Noah's story deserved to be told.

And I did it.

But I couldn't have done it alone.

There are so many people who got me through this process, and each of them deserves a spotlight.

To my husband—who constantly makes my dream his priority. Thank you for your endless support, unwavering confidence in me, and the sacrifices you make every single day. You give so much, and I hope you know how much I see and appreciate you. Despite being in the busiest season of life, you continue to show up for me and our babies in ways that go far beyond your line of duty. I get to write these stories because I have a prime example of love that I get to call mine.

To my mom—who I'd be lost without in every sense of the word. Thank you for believing in me every day. You would drop anything just to be there for me and my kids, and that alone speaks volumes about who you are. I'm convinced I will never live a day without you, because I cannot accept a world where you don't exist.

To my sisters, Mary and Kate—thank you not only for naming half these towns and characters but for always being the first to jump in and read. I love you both to the ends of the Earth.

To Aurora. We started out bonding over our striking similarities, but while those laid the foundation of our friendship, it's the way you've always pushed me—not just in my writing, but in embracing my authentic self—that has solidified it. Thank you. For the serious work you put into making this book the best it could be, and for being exactly who you are.

To Kiarah—who put her heart into making this book what it is. You spent countless hours helping me craft this story, and ensuring Noah's character as a biracial woman was represented authentically. I cannot thank you enough for your dedication, your insight, and most of all, your friendship.

To Rachel—my ultimate hype woman since day one. You are the light in the darkness, always giving me a reason to keep going. You make me smile when I'm down, hype me up when I feel like I'm not enough, and remind me just how special you are. I love you and cherish our friendship endlessly.

To Erika—for your unwavering friendship and loyalty. You always manage to lift my spirits on the heavy days and make me laugh when I need it most. Thank you for your constant encouragement and love. If I could bring a Wood-stone Falls man to life just for you, I would.

To the team at Books & Moods—who created a cover that fits Dorian and Noah's story so perfectly. Thank you for bringing this vision to life.

To Maddi at EJL Editing—I can't thank you enough for the time and energy you've spent with these characters. Your work helped shape this book into what it is, and I'm endlessly grateful.

To my beta readers—Cassi, Courtney, Morgan, and

Rachel—thank you for reading this story in its rawest form, through all the mess, errors, and inconsistencies, and still seeing the heart of Dorian and Noah's love. Your time, insight, and support have meant the world to me. This story wouldn't be what it is without you, and for that, I'm so grateful.

To Jess. Your insight and support, from the early drafts to the final touches, have been invaluable. Thank you for pushing this book forward and making my life easier with your marketing genius. I couldn't do this without you.

And, as always, to my readers—thank you. This book was fueled by your love for *Unbearable* and your excitement for more. My favorite moments of the day are when you all reach out to share your love for these silly stories I make up in my head—stories I one day decided to put on paper. This journey would be nothing without you.

Woodstone Falls has become more than just a fictional town—it's a home I return to every time I sit down to write. With each story, it has grown into a place filled with love, heartache, and everything in between, a place that feels as real to me as any I've ever known. There are still two more stories to tell—Sawyer's and Colt's—and I can't wait to share them with you. For now, I'm simply grateful to spend a little more time in Woodstone Falls.

Content Warnings

- Death of a Parent
- Serial killer
- Grief and Loss
- Maternal death in childbirth (discussed, but not shown on page)
- Descriptive open-door sex scenes (chapters 23, 26, 36 & 40)
- Violence on Page
- Captivity/kidnapping
- Gun Violence
- Vulgar language